what if you & me

RONI LOREN

Published by Sourcebooks Casablanca, an imprint of Sourcebooks
P.O. Box 4410, Naperville, Illinois 60567-4410
(630) 961-3900
sourcebooks.com

Library of Congress Cataloging-in-Publication Data

Names: Loren, Roni, author.
Title: What if you & me / Roni Loren.
Other titles: What if you and me
Description: Naperville, Illinois : Sourcebooks Casablanca, [2021] | Series: Say everything; 2 | Summary: "Horror author and true-crime podcaster Andi Lockley has spent so long researching real-life horror stories, she's practically forgotten what dating is. But when a detective moves next door and provides new fodder for her podcast-and a sense of safety she hasn't felt in a long time-she starts to wonder if it's time to retire her trust-no-man mentality."-- Provided by publisher.
Identifiers: LCCN 2021010442 (print) | LCCN 2021010443 (ebook)
Subjects: GSAFD: Love stories.
Classification: LCC PS3612.O764 W48 2021 (print) | LCC PS3612.O764 (ebook) | DDC 813/.6--dc23
LC record available at https://lccn.loc.gov/2021010442

Printed and bound in the United States of America.
VP 10 9 8 7 6 5 4 3 2 1

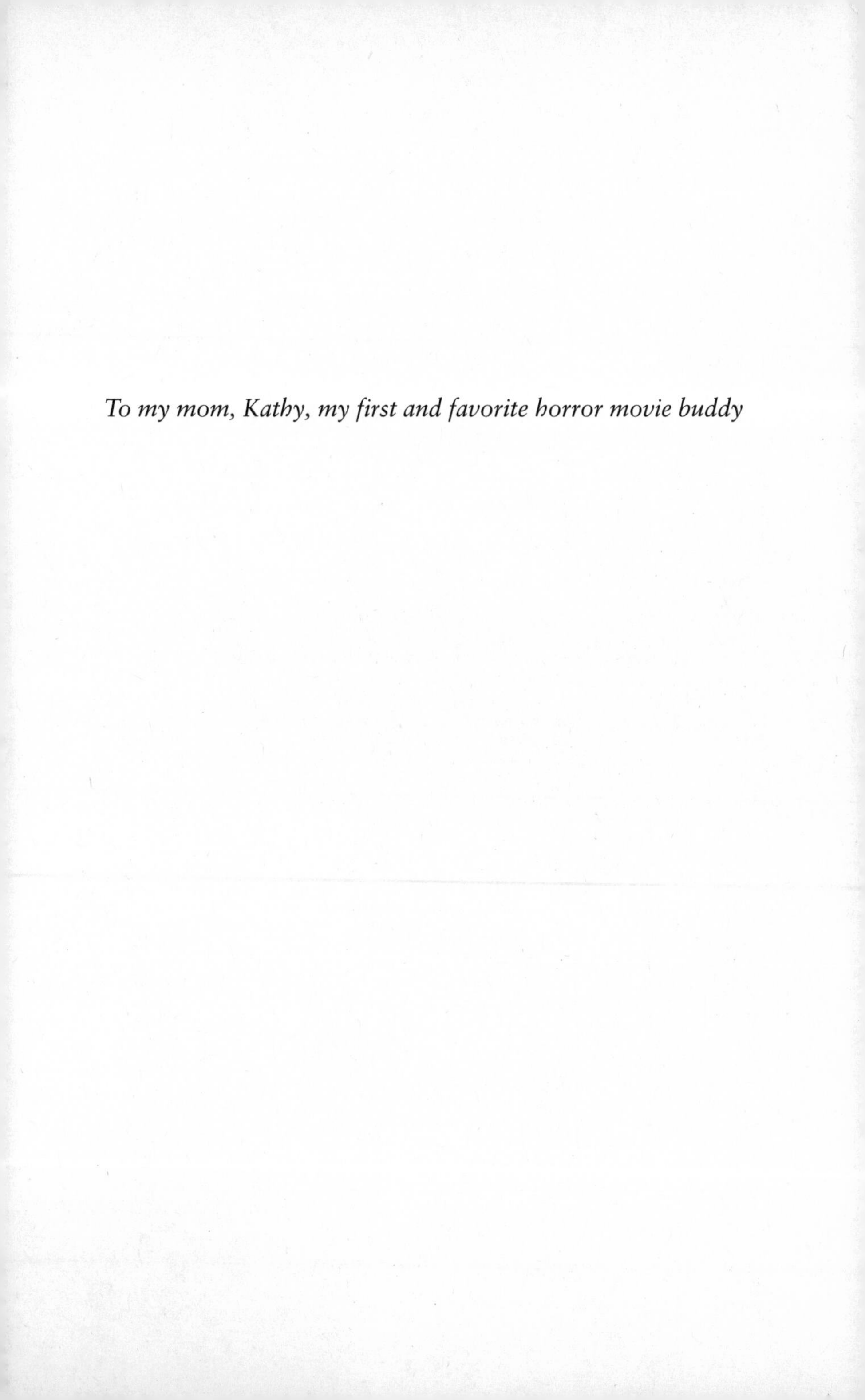

To my mom, Kathy, my first and favorite horror movie buddy

chapter **one**

ANDI LOCKLEY WAS HALFWAY CONVINCED HER NEW NEIGHBOR was a werewolf.

She'd never seen him outside since she'd moved into the duplex, and she'd only heard him moving around at night. The nocturnal wanderings might've made her lean toward vampire, but this guy made too much noise to be a vampire. *Thump. Thump. Thump.* His heavy steps paced back and forth as if he couldn't wait for the full moon and an opportunity to terrorize the villagers.

The old floorboards creaked again as neighbor dude made another round, and Andi tried to concentrate on the unfinished sentence on her laptop in front of her.

Blink. Blink. Blink.

That blinking cursor was a judgmental sonofabitch. She narrowed her eyes, trying to zero in on the words she'd written. *The scent of wet fur and death filled the small cabin, Collette's breath making clouds in the frosty air as she...*

As she what? Contemplated running? Took a nap? Knit a sweater? *Ugh.* Andi leaned back in her desk chair and rubbed the spot between her eyes where a headache was forming. How had the band-camp slasher story she was supposed to be writing morphed into some werewolf tale?

Thump, thump, bang!

She startled and turned her head, eyeing the pale-green wall that separated her from her neighbor. Her shelf of horror Funko Pops rattled with another bang, almost sending little Hannibal Lecter over the edge. She reached over and righted the doll.

This wasn't going to work. Maybe she needed to try writing while wearing her headphones, even though being unable to hear the noises around her tended to put her on edge. She usually only used headphones when she was editing the podcast. How many horror-movie scenes had she watched where some unsuspecting victim had headphones on or was listening to music too loudly while the deranged killer stalked around their house?

But she was running out of options. Nine to midnight was her magic writing time. She'd moved into this place because...well, mainly because the 1920s double-shotgun house was cheaper than her old apartment, but also because the cute office off the kitchen at the back of the house had seemed perfect for a horror writer. Creaky and cozy with a view of a tangled, overgrown garden in the back. She had loved it on sight, even though her parents would be horrified by the place and probably see it as one step up from living in a cardboard box. Anything that wasn't their sprawling mansion overlooking the golf course in Georgia looked like the slums to them.

Andi didn't need a mansion. This place was more than enough for now, but she hadn't anticipated such a noisy neighbor. At her old place, she'd shared a wall with Dolores, a septuagenarian who had gone to bed by nine and who had regularly brought her Tupperware containers full of delicious slow-cooked things like shrimp and crab gumbo and white beans and rice.

This guy seemed to be a creature of the night, and he'd never brought her so much as a bag of potato chips to welcome her to the neighborhood. Andi turned back to her computer, swept her bangs away from her eyes, and deleted the line about wet fur. No werewolves. That was not in the proposal she had sent to her literary agent.

She needed to stay on track. Despite the growing audience for her *What Can We Learn from This?* horror and true crime podcast, her advertising income was meager. The majority of her pay-the-bills money came from the minor success she'd found with a series of horror novels. But that series had wrapped up, the money from royalties was dwindling, and her publisher had decided they wanted out of the horror business, so no new contract. Now she needed to prove to her agent and other publishers that she wasn't a one-series-and-done author so she could get another book deal. She needed to send her agent a winner.

She focused on her screen again. *Deranged killers. Deranged killers. Must write a crazed summer-camp killer with a fresh twist.* Music started up next door.

She cocked her head.

"Oh sweet baby Jesus." The werewolf listened to country music. Would the torture never end?

She wanted to bang on the wall or storm next door and demand that he have some consideration for his neighbor. What if she'd been a normal person who was sleeping at this hour? She imagined the finger-wagging lecture she could give him about the importance of being an unselfish human, about realizing the world doesn't revolve around *you and your big feet*. But she knew there was no way she was going over there. She was a badass in her imagined scenario, but she'd covered enough true-crime documentaries on the podcast to know that no good would come of knocking on some stranger's door alone in the middle of the night. Scary news stories started like that.

And the last time anyone saw Andi Lockley, horror author and podcaster, was...

The music switched off. Small mercies.

She stared at the laptop screen again and then, with a huff, snapped her computer shut. The words weren't going to happen tonight. She might as well get something watched for the podcast instead and at least be able to check one item off her list. She pushed her chair back, the wheels rolling over the worn floorboards and making them creak. She stood and stretched, grabbed her cooling green tea, and headed toward the living room at the front of the house.

She'd left a lamp on, giving the room a warm glow, and she checked all the locks and windows before turning on the TV and shutting off the lights. Proper horror-movie watching required the dark. She grabbed the colorful afghan her former neighbor had made her when she'd moved. She'd told Andi, "This is for all those movies you watch. You can cover your eyes with it but still see the movie a little. And it's big enough to share with a date."

Andi smiled at the memory. Dolores had been very interested in Andi's love life—or lack thereof. She'd not so subtly work into their conversations things like *Have you met that nice blond boy down at the coffee shop? So tall and never charges me for extra whipped cream.* Or, *You know Mrs. Benoit's boy just graduated with a master's degree in English. I've always thought men who read are so much more interesting, don't you?* And she'd even tested the waters with *Mercy's granddaughter, Jess, just broke up with her lady friend. I think she's a movie buff like you.*

Andi appreciated her neighbor's effort and the sentiment behind it. Dolores would make a killer wingwoman, but Andi hadn't had the heart to tell her that the afghan didn't need to be big enough for two. She didn't bring guys home. Dates were reserved for public places only. Not that she dated much anyway. The minute she would imagine taking the next step with a guy, she would be seized by all the *what-ifs*, get that queasy feeling in her gut, and shut the whole thing down. Post-traumatic stress was hell on a love life. Her former therapist had assured her that it wouldn't always be this way, but Andi was beginning to wonder if the "post" part of post-traumatic would ever really arrive.

She curled under the blanket and scanned her streaming playlist, looking for something that would make for interesting fodder on the podcast. On *What Can We Learn from This?* she featured true-crime documentaries and horror films because much could be learned from both. Tonight, she needed a movie that could feed the creative part of her brain to help with her story, so she went through the slasher options, settling on one of her comfort watches. *Scream.*

She wouldn't have to take notes on this one or pause and analyze anything. She knew it mostly by heart, and she could use it on the podcast to talk about things like the overlap of comedy and horror, and how using the biggest name in the movie at the time—Drew Barrymore—in the opening scene was both a risk and a brilliant move. And for the "what can we learn from this" portion, there was a lot to talk about, including the ill-advised design of houses with walls of windows.

Andi sipped her tea and turned up the volume—because if her neighbor could blare country music, she could blast horror. She tensed as the portable phone rang on-screen again and again, a blond-bobbed Drew picking it up each time, her mood changing from flirty to terrified with each call. Lesson one, *Never engage with a prank phone call.* Lesson two, *Never leave a door unlocked.* Or in this case, every damn door in the house. *Damn, Drew.*

Andi didn't victim blame. That was her rule on the podcast and in life, but she shuddered at the thought of all those doors sitting unlocked at night. She quickly glanced at her front door, making sure the lock was in the horizontal position even though she never left it any other way.

Despite Andi knowing everything that would happen in the movie, her heartbeat picked up speed as Drew's character began screaming and crying. How many times could she watch a movie and hope that *this* time the person would escape and *not* get killed? It was one of the beauties of horror movies. There was often such a strong undercurrent of hope. Sometimes it was rewarded—the final girl escapes, the monster is defeated. Sometimes it wasn't. But the very presence of that beating heart of hope got her every time.

Drew upped her screaming game on-screen, and Andi's speakers vibrated with the shrillness of it. She reached for the remote, planning to turn it down a little. She didn't want to be a total dick. But before she could get her finger on the button, a thunderous boom echoed through the room.

She startled, a yelp escaping her, and nearly knocked over her tea. The loud sound repeated, and it took a second for her to realize it was coming from the door she'd just checked. *Boom! Boom! Boom!*

The afghan was clutched tight in her fist, and the movie still blasted, screams filling the living room. Her heartbeat thumped in her ears, and she stared at the door like it was going to splinter and the movie's Ghostface was going to walk right in and disembowel her with his knife.

Andi's logical brain registered this probably wasn't the case, but that part was a distant whisper at the moment. She couldn't move. She couldn't turn off the TV. She was frozen in place.

The thunderous knocking started again. "Fire department. Open up!"

The words *fire department* penetrated her fear fog. Fire. *Fire?* That didn't make any sense. Why the hell would the fire department be banging on her door in the middle of the night? Maybe something had happened in the neighborhood. Or maybe they had the wrong house.

Thinking it through helped a little. Finally, she was able to unfurl her fingers from the afghan and grab the remote to hit Pause. The silence that followed was almost as unsettling as the banging. The pounding on the door started again with an added threat to break down the door if no one responded. That got her moving. She hurried to her feet, headed to the door, and peered through the peephole. All she could see was a T-shirt clad shoulder as the man apparently leaned over to try to see through her front window.

A T-shirt, not a firefighter's uniform. She cleared her throat and called out, "How do I know you're a firefighter?"

Whoever it was stepped back and pointed to an NOFD insignia on his T-shirt, just visible in the peephole's view. "Hill Dawson," the man called out. "Your neighbor. Everything okay in there?"

Her *neighbor*? She reached for the pepper spray she kept in the drawer of her small entryway table, turned the latch on the lock, and opened the door, ready to spray if needed. Underneath the porch light, the outline of a man came into view. A very tall, broad-shouldered man. *The werewolf.* Complete with dark messy hair, a trimmed beard, and a scowl. He was equal parts gorgeous and intimidating—not unlike a real wolf—and her body tensed as though it couldn't decide whether she should run like hell or rush forward and volunteer to play villager.

His brown eyes met hers, his searching look sending hot awareness through her, but then his gaze scanned downward. Only then did she remember she was standing there braless in a thin tank top and a pair of Wonder Woman pajama pants with a very formidable stranger on her doorstep. That snapped her out of her ridiculous staring. Who cared that he was attractive? He could still be there to hurt her. She crossed her arms over her chest and tipped up her chin, trying to look tough. "What's going on?"

"So, you're okay?" he asked, brows knit, his voice a deep

rumble. His gaze flicked to the pink canister of mace still clutched in her fist. "I heard screaming. A lot of it."

"Screaming?" She frowned.

He shifted, and her attention jumped to his right hand, the one hanging loosely at his side. The one holding *a baseball bat*. She stiffened, her mouth going dry and her mind racing past suspicion and into worst-case-scenario territory. What if he wasn't a firefighter? What if he wasn't her neighbor? What if he was there to rob/rape/murder/dismember her and wear her head as a hat?

She uncrossed her arms, her finger poised on the trigger of the pepper spray. She was suddenly much less concerned about her lack of bra and much more concerned that she'd be caught off guard and attacked.

The man frowned, his gaze tracking her weapon before looking at her again. "There was yelling and screaming. I could hear it through the wall. I thought you were in trouble."

She narrowed her eyes. "How do I know you're really a firefighter? Anybody could get a T-shirt."

He tried to peek past her into the house and then lowered his voice. "Ma'am, if you're in trouble, if there's someone in there you're scared of, just step outside and I can help."

"Someone inside?" She closed her eyes and shook her head. "I'm alone. It was a movie."

Her brain screamed at her as the words slipped out. *I'm alone? Have you learned* nothing? *Don't tell the stranger you're alone in the house!* She should fire herself from her own podcast.

"I mean," she went on. "I'm not in trouble. The screaming was a movie. I was watching a horror movie."

The stiff hold of his shoulders relaxed, and his gaze met hers again, disbelief there. "*A movie?* It sounded like you were getting murdered over here."

"Just Drew Barrymore. Not me." She shifted on her feet. "Maybe I had it a little too loud."

He made a frustrated sound in the back of his throat, and she realized her imagination hadn't been far off earlier. This guy could be cast in a movie as lead werewolf. Scruffy and muscular in his navy-blue T-shirt and gray sweats. He was one full moon away from howling and ripping off that well-fitting shirt.

"*A little too loud?*" he asked, repeating her words. "It's midnight. The screams were damn near vibrating my walls."

That made her spine straighten and a flash of indignation rush through her. "Yes, it *is* midnight. And *someone* thought blaring songs about tractors was appropriate at this hour. I had to turn up my TV to drown you out." She nodded at his weapon. "Do you make it a habit to scare the shit out of new neighbors by brandishing a baseball bat on their doorstep?"

He glanced down at his bat as if just remembering he had it, like it was a normal extension of his arm. He leaned over and set it against a planter out of her reach, then lifted a brow her way. "Says the lady with the pink pepper spray."

"Hey, you're at my door, man. I didn't bang on yours." She wasn't going to put down her weapon. *No, thank you.*

He sighed, a long-suffering sound, and rubbed his forehead. "Okay, so you're not getting murdered or the hell beat out of you."

"I am not."

"That's good." He nodded, almost to himself, and ran a hand over the back of his head.

"Agreed. I consider it a good day if I haven't been murdered."

He stared at her for a moment as if at a loss for what to say to that, and she was momentarily struck by how well his beard suited his tense jawline, by how long his eyelashes were, how his brown eyes had flecks of green in them.

"I'm sorry if I scared you," he said finally. "But maybe not so loud on the movies. I'm trained to respond to screams."

Somehow the words *trained to respond to screams* sounded dirty to her ear, and heat bloomed in her cheeks. *God.* What was with her tonight? She cleared her throat. "Right. And maybe not so loud with the tractor music?"

His mouth hitched up at one corner, a lazy tilt of a smile. "I played no songs about tractors. There was no farm equipment referenced at all."

She crossed her arms again and gave him a knowing look. "What about mommas, trains, trucks, prison, or gettin' drunk?"

A low chuckle escaped him, and he coughed, as if trying to cover it. "Touché. No promises there."

"Fair enough. So, you're the neighbor," she said, trying to disregard the warm honey sound of his laugh. There was no way she needed to entertain any *Hey, how you doin'* feelings about the dude who lived next door. She couldn't even think of the box of nightmares *that* would open up.

He straightened a little, and his serious face returned. "Yeah. Hill Dawson. Sorry I haven't introduced myself before this. I've been...busy with things."

"I'm Andrea—Andi," she said, keeping one arm crossed over her chest and putting out her other to shake his hand. "Writer. Podcaster. Watcher of loud horror movies."

He took her hand, his grip big and warm around hers, and gave her a businesslike shake. "Nice to meet you."

"Yes, at midnight. In our pajamas. Exactly how I planned it." Well, *her* pajamas. He had tennis shoes on, so he probably hadn't been in bed.

She almost missed it, the quick flick of his gaze back to her outfit, but he seemed to catch himself and not let the look linger. He dropped the handshake. "It won't happen again."

She let out a breath and dropped the prickly attitude. This wasn't who she was. Being scared and caught off guard had brought out her sharp edges. "Look, I appreciate you coming over to make sure everything's okay. I guess we both need to be aware of how thin the walls are."

"Yeah, I didn't realize that until tonight either. Your side has been pretty quiet since you moved in. I'm glad you weren't being murdered."

She smiled. "Me too."

He nodded. "Well, good night, Andi."

"'Night, neighbor."

He grabbed the bat, setting it against his shoulder with the practiced ease of someone who'd played the game, and then tipped his head toward the pepper spray clutched in her left hand. "Also, that's decent if you're trying to deter a dog from attacking you, but you should look into the pepper gel for real protection. That's what my cop friends suggest. It won't blow back on you and is stronger."

"Oh." She looked down at the pink tube.

"And sorry to use the fire department thing. I didn't mean to scare you. I figured that'd be the quickest way to get you to open the door."

She sniffed. "It worked."

He shrugged. "It usually does."

"Next time, you can just say it's Hill, so I don't think I'm about to die of a gas leak."

His lips curved slightly, but there was a glimmer of sadness there—or wistfulness—before he turned back toward his side of the porch. "G'night."

"'Night."

Andi leaned against her doorway, maybe enjoying the view of his backside in a pair of sweats more than she should. He walked a little stiffly, like he had a knee bothering him or something, and headed back into his house without a backward glance.

She slipped back inside, locked her door, and leaned against it, her heart still beating fast—from the earlier scare, but also maybe from something else. She didn't want to examine that too closely. In her darkened living room, the paused movie was the only light. Drew Barrymore was frozen in place, lying on the ground with Ghostface above her. Andi scanned the room—the single indentation on the couch, the afghan for two, the cold cup of tea. All were waiting for her to return.

But a weird urge to go back outside and knock on Hill's door, invite him to watch the movie with her, came over her. Maybe he had trouble sleeping like she did. Maybe he liked scary movies, too.

The line from *Scream* drifted through her head. *"Do you like scary movies?"*

She could ask him. To be neighborly. To be friendly. To finally have a guy over.

But as quickly as the thought hit her, she tamped it down. He was a stranger. Yes, he seemed nice and was supposedly a firefighter with good intentions. But she'd learned not to trust her gut on things like that. Her instincts in that area were notoriously untrustworthy. Lots of people were good at *appearing* to be nice. Some people knew how to wield "nice" as the ultimate weapon.

Old memories leached into her brain. Whispered compliments from a boy she'd yearned for, one she thought she could trust. Gentle kisses. Locked doors. Fingers sliding a strap down a shoulder. *Promise you won't tell anyone. You're the only one I trust.*

She shook her head and squeezed her eyes shut. *No. Stop.*

She took a few deep breaths, pushing the images back into the vault she tried to keep them locked in. After a moment, she rubbed the goose bumps from her arms and swallowed past the sick feeling that welled up anytime she let thoughts of Evan Henry Longdale sneak into her mind.

No way was she inviting the new neighbor over. *Hello, mental trigger, how are you?*

As she plopped back down on the couch, she tried to shake off the memories her run-in with Hill had stirred, but after a few more minutes of the movie, she realized she wasn't paying attention to the screen. Movie night was officially a wash.

She clicked off the television, knowing the only way to get her mind off the old looping track it was now on was to take a sleeping pill and go to bed.

She washed her face, brushed her teeth, and focused on her nightly routine to block out her anxious thoughts. But as she was finishing up, she heard the shower turn on next door. The bad memories that were pushing at the walls of her mind were suddenly replaced by images of the man who'd been standing on her doorstep. Hill was on the other side of the wall, *right there.* She glanced at the wall separating them, listening to the sounds and imagining what was on the other side. Hill taking off his T-shirt, revealing what she suspected was a very well-built body. Hill sliding those loose sweats down his hips, revealing…

Not cool. Stop. No mentally undressing the guy. Nope.

But her inner protests were no use. She could hear him groan with appreciation, like the hot water had been a relief. Hill was taking a shower. On the other side of that thin wall, only a few feet away, he was naked and wet. Water droplets on bare skin were involved.

Thinking of anything else was suddenly impossible. Her starved libido was now fully in charge, popping popcorn for this new dirty movie.

She quickly finished up in the bathroom, trying to get away from the source of the images, but by the time she'd slipped under the covers of her bed, her skin was hot all over. The mental movie of Hill was there and not going away. And though fantasizing about the neighbor was a terrible idea, visions of him in the shower were a helluva lot better than the horrid memories that had taken over earlier. Maybe there was no harm in her little fantasy reel after all. There was nothing safer than fantasy. It was what had gotten her through all these years without a physical relationship.

It's not like her new neighbor would ever know.

The dirty thoughts were safely locked in her brain, and whenever she ran into him again, she would just have to employ her poker face. She had a good one. *No, of course I've never pictured you naked.*

She closed her eyes and listened to the water run, letting her imagination take over from there.

She forgot to take that sleeping pill.

chapter **two**

Hill Dawson groaned as he let the water run over him, feeling like an idiot for nearly busting down his new tenant's door over a damn movie. He'd been doing his nightly exercises, hoping they'd tire him out enough to actually get some sleep, when he'd heard the screaming. His instincts had kicked in, and he hadn't even considered that the noise was something innocuous—like a neighbor playing her scary movie too loudly.

All he could think of was the petite redhead, whom he'd only gotten a few glimpses of over the past few weeks, getting attacked. He'd imagined her trying to fight off an intruder or a violent boyfriend, losing the battle. So he'd rushed over like it was the old days, ready to bust down a door and save the day. He'd almost *hoped* that there would be a day to save. *Something* to give him that old rush of feeling like a hero to someone—even if only for a few minutes. Which was fucking bent. But anything to penetrate the numbness would've been welcome.

Instead, he'd ended up scaring the hell out of his new tenant—though she didn't know he was the landlord—and lying to her about his firefighter status. He'd conveniently left out the *former* part of that title. *Great job, asshole.* Nothing like starting off a meet and greet with a lie.

But he'd wanted to calm her, to make her feel like he could help. When Andi had first opened the door, pink pepper spray in hand, she'd been trying to look tough—chin jutted out, blue eyes glinting in the porch light—but he'd seen the fear underneath that thin layer of bravado. Her body had been trembling and her face pale. She'd looked so...vulnerable.

Seeing her like that had hit him square in the gut. He'd wanted to pull her to him and *hug* her. What the hell had that been about? He didn't hug strangers.

The urge had been weird and completely inappropriate. There was a difference between wanting to protect a citizen from danger and what he'd felt in that moment. That urge had been anything but professional.

Luckily, his training had gone on autopilot when he'd seen her pepper spray—the training that said to speak to her in a calm voice, to be professional, to assure her he was there to help—and he'd kept his hands and hugs to himself. *Thank God.*

He'd never gotten an up close look at Andi before tonight, and he hadn't realized how young she was. Or how beautiful. Big blue eyes with smudged black liner, a little silver ring in her nose, and a body that would've seemed boyish if not for the small, pert breasts he'd forced himself to look away from when he'd realized she was only wearing a thin tank top and the shadows of what was beneath could be seen in the porch light.

He had no business looking at her that way or allowing the surge of heat that had moved through him. At thirty-one, he probably looked like an old man to her for one, and two, he didn't do that anymore. No flirting. No charming his way into a fun hookup. Those days were long past him. He wasn't anyone's good time. He was a goddamned charity case at best, a pity fuck at worst. He'd learned that the hard way when one of his buddies had tried to set him up on a date after his accident and the breakup with his former fiancée. The woman had let it slip on the date that she was doing it as a favor to his friend. He wasn't interested in repeating that particular lesson in humiliation.

Not that someone like Andi would've been interested anyway. She looked like the type who dated skateboarders or vegans with full-sleeve tattoos or drummers in punk bands. Not disabled firefighters who'd been put out to pasture.

Hill grabbed the metal bar attached to the shower wall and eased down onto the bench he'd installed. He dipped his head and let the water run over him, his eyes stinging with the shampoo. Tomorrow, he'd go back to keeping to himself. He and Andi now had an agreement not to disturb each other. Perfect.

He didn't need a chatty neighbor, especially one that made him think about things he shouldn't, made him crave things he couldn't have. He'd let himself slip a little tonight, getting caught up for a moment and joking with her when she'd made a clever reference to a David Allan Coe song his aunt used to love. But he couldn't open up that kind of door with someone like Andi, even in a neighborly way.

He'd bought this duplex for the quiet, to start fresh somewhere, and to get a little rental income to add to his firefighter pension while he figured out what the hell he was supposed to do with the rest of his life. He didn't want to be friends with his tenant. That was why he had a management company handle the rental logistics. He wanted to be anonymous in this new place, left alone. Andi looked like the type who would organize the neighborhood watch and throw block parties. *No, thanks.*

He lifted his head, wiped the water from his face, and took a deep breath, feeling better now that he'd come up with a plan of action and had shaken off the weird feelings the conversation with Andi had left him with. Nothing had changed. He didn't need to worry about it. He met his neighbor. No big deal.

But as he settled down into bed that night, instead of being plagued by nightmares of fiery buildings collapsing around him like usual, he was plagued by dreams of fiery redheads.

He woke up in a sweat and didn't sleep for the rest of the night.

....

Andi weaved her way through the first floor of WorkAround, the coworking space where she spent her weekdays, feeling the ripple of energy from all those clicking keyboards. She adored the bottom floor of the building with its tall windows lining the back wall, the exposed red brick and ductwork, and the soaring ceilings. But what she loved more was that this floor was where the hot desks were located—desks that people could rent for a few hours or days. That meant a regularly rotating mix of interesting people, which was like candy for her extroverted self. On any given day, she could chat with a musician, an actor, a book blogger, a journalist, a day trader, a visual artist. The list went on and on.

People were endlessly fascinating to her, and though she knew the stereotype of a writer was someone alone in an attic room, her writer brain needed people. How was she supposed to come up with interesting characters if she never met any interesting people? So each morning, she made a point to stop by a few of the hot desks and make small talk—"desk" really meaning "any solid flat surface you can place a laptop on" because the floor was dotted with blue, yellow, and gray couches, cafe tables, and boxy chairs. But today she breezed past most of them with only a few waves or smiles of acknowledgment toward people she already knew. She had pastries to deliver.

She headed to the stairwell next to the in-house coffee bar and made her way up to the second floor, where she rented space.

She passed the podcasting and video rooms, cruised past her own office, and then knocked on a door at the end of the hall.

"Come in," her friend Hollyn called out.

Andi opened the door and slipped inside, the library quiet of Hollyn's office a stark contrast to the flurry on the first floor. She set a narrow black canister and a grease-stained bag from the bakery on her friend's desk and plopped in a chair. "Mornin', rock star. I come bearing gifts."

Hollyn glanced over from the entertainment article she was working on, her nose wrinkling a few times in a facial tic that Andi had gotten so used to, she barely noticed anymore. "Ooh, presents." Hollyn examined the offerings on the desk and tucked her lion's mane of curly blond hair behind her ears. "Well, I can guess what's in the bag. I can smell a cinnamon roll from a hundred yards away. But what's this?"

Hollyn picked up the black canister and turned it over in her hand.

"Gel pepper spray. A firefighter friend of mine says it's the best, better than the normal stuff because it doesn't blow back in your face." Andi opened the bag and pulled out one of the cinnamon rolls she'd picked up from Levee Baking Co. on her way in this morning. One of the bonuses of renting an office at WorkAround, besides being able to have actual coworkers in a job where she normally would be stuck alone, was that she had NOLA's endless supply of restaurants at her fingertips when she was craving something yummy. "I thought you should have one, too. You know, you can protect you and Jasper if you two are ever attacked."

Hollyn laughed. "You don't trust Jasper to be the action hero?"

Andi smirked at the thought of Hollyn's adorable improv-actor fiancé attempting any sort of violence. The guy would lay down his life for Hollyn, no doubt, but Andi couldn't picture him in a fight. "He would probably be able to talk a criminal out of robbing you guys."

Hollyn set the canister next to her bag, which she'd left on the back corner of her desk. "I wouldn't put it past him, but I'll keep this in my purse in case negotiations don't work out. Thank you."

"Of course."

Hollyn pulled her cinnamon roll out of the bag and grabbed two napkins from her desk drawer, handing one to Andi. "I didn't know you had a firefighter friend."

Andi spread the napkin on her lap and unrolled a piece of the cinnamon roll. "He's my new neighbor. I met him unexpectedly over the weekend."

Hollyn licked a glob of frosting from her fingertip and grimaced, but Andi knew the grimace was her friend's Tourette's acting up and not her opinion of the pastry.

"I love that you meet someone once and you call them a friend," Hollyn said. "There's like a ten-step application process and a gauntlet to make it through to get that designation from me."

Andi grinned as she swallowed her bite of dough. "Ha. Well, I feel honored to have been accepted into your circle of the chosen few. I have my own tests. Neighbor dude has only passed the preliminary quiz. I'm not inviting him over for grilled cheese or anything. But his pepper-spray advice was solid. I googled."

Hollyn watched her for a moment, chewing, her eye twitching a little. "Does he live alone?"

Andi shrugged. "I assume so. He wasn't wearing a ring." She frowned. When had she even noticed that? Her subconscious must've been taking notes. "Plus, I've only heard his big feet traipsing around over there."

"Big feet. Interesting." Hollyn's gaze took on a mischievous look. "Young guy? Old guy?"

Andi thought back to the other night. She'd been so freaked out to see anyone on her doorstep at that hour, and then taken aback by her body's reaction to Hill, that she hadn't thought about what his age might be. "Not old. Older than us but like, I don't know, late twenties, early thirties? He had that old-soul look like he'd seen some stuff. But that's not surprising if he's a firefighter."

Hollyn's brow lifted. "Old soul, huh? Is he cute?"

Andi scrunched her nose, the question catching her off guard, and she forced another bite of cinnamon roll down. Was he cute? *Cute* was not a word she'd use for him. There was nothing "cute" about that serious face, those wide shoulders, and that deep voice. Sexy, yes. Hot, for sure. Her fantasy from the other night flashed through her mind, and warmth rushed to her cheeks. She cleared her throat. "I guess. If you like the big, bearded, dark, and broody type."

"Please God, don't let that be her type," said a voice from the doorway.

Andi turned, finding Hollyn's fiancé, Jasper, leaning against the doorjamb with an amused look on his face.

He stepped inside, adjusted his dark-rimmed glasses, and then spread his arms, Hulk-style, trying to widen his lean frame. "But if it is, I can be beefcake."

Hollyn bit her lip, smiling adoringly at her guy. "What you are is exactly my type."

"Goofy improv actor?" he confirmed and walked over to peck Hollyn on the lips.

"Obviously."

"Sweet. I'm your man." He turned to Andi after stealing a piece of Hollyn's cinnamon roll and popping it in his mouth. "So, who are we talking about? What's the word? Give me all the details."

"Andi's new neighbor is apparently a hot firefighter," Hollyn said, tone playful.

Andi groaned. "I said no such thing."

"Uh-huh," Hollyn said.

"Fine," Andi admitted. "He's not...difficult to look at."

Jasper propped a hip on the corner of Hollyn's desk and grinned. "Uh-oh, Andi *finally* likes a boy. Fitz is going to be so bereft when I tell him. He's harboring a mad crush."

Andi gave him an *oh-please* look. Fitz McLane owned an investment firm that took up most of the fourth floor of WorkAround, and he was a nice enough guy, but he also could sell ice to an Eskimo. "Fitz acts like he has a crush on every woman in the building. He likes to be adored. And I don't 'like a boy.' Neighbor dude is definitely a man. And I never said I was into him. I'm just objectively saying that he is a nice-looking human." She pointed at them, narrowing her eyes. "Don't do that thing."

"What thing?" Hollyn asked, setting her chin in her hand and obviously enjoying the teasing way too much.

"That thing that people do once they're a couple and want everyone else to suddenly couple up," she said. "You become like gossipy grandmothers playing matchmaker."

Hollyn shook her head and held up her own wagging finger. "Oh, no you don't, Lockley. You were like my own personal cheering squad, trying to get things to work out with me and Jas. You don't get to pull that couple card on us."

Andi put her hand to her chest. "Me? I was simply seeing two people who obviously needed to be together and encouraging that. That was being a good friend. But you don't even know this guy. *I* don't even know this guy. He could be a crappy human. He could be married and not wearing a ring. He listens to country music, so we're already starting off at a deficit."

"Country?" Jasper cringed. "Yeah, sounds like a lost cause. I'll tell Fitz his crush is safe."

Hollyn offered the rest of her cinnamon roll to Jasper and

cleaned her fingers on her napkin. "Look, I won't be that person. You're a grown woman who can make her own choices on who she's interested in or not. But at the very least, it can't hurt to get to know your neighbor a little, right?"

Andi frowned, that old tight feeling filling her chest. Just because someone was a neighbor didn't mean they were someone worth knowing, someone worth trusting. But she didn't want to go there with her friends. They didn't know about her past. Didn't know that the story of her first crush involved a guy currently sitting in a maximum-security prison. These friends knew her in the After—as the quirky horror writer, as the weird girl who finds comfort in the macabre, as the woman who wants to run background checks on all her friends' dates but rarely goes on a date herself. She didn't want them to know what had gotten her here.

"Sure. I mean, maybe I'll need to borrow a cup of sugar one day," Andi said noncommittally.

Jasper's lips hitched at one corner. "Is that what the kids are calling it?"

Andi snorted and tossed her balled-up napkin at Jasper as she stood. "See if I bring you people pastry and weaponry again."

"Ooh, there's weaponry?" Jasper asked, turning to Hollyn.

Hollyn lifted her hand with an apologetic smile. "Fine. I'll drop it. Maybe we *are* doing that couple thing. Gross."

"No worries. I know it's coming from a place of love, but really, it's nothing. It was just a meet-the-neighbor." She nodded toward the computer. "I'll let you get back to your article."

"Thanks again for the presents. What's on your agenda today?" Hollyn asked.

"Oh, you know, the usual. I have to write a chapter of my book and then..." Andi stretched her neck from side to side like she was getting ready to enter a boxing match. "I have to put together a podcast episode covering this documentary about a guy who kidnapped and murdered three women. He hunted them at shopping malls in the eighties."

Jasper's eyes widened behind his glasses. "Fuck."

"Yeah," Andi said. "It's a grim case, but at least he was caught. I wanted to cover it because there's a lot to be learned from it. If nothing else, it will remind women that we have to check our back seats before we get into our cars. And not to trust some random guy appearing to be helpful at the mall."

"You realize you make what we do for a living look like utter bullshit when you say stuff like that," Jasper said. "You're like a crusader. You need a cape or something."

"Nah," Andi said, picking up her laptop bag. "We need people to make us laugh, too. If all we thought about all day was how sick and cruel people can be, we'd never get out of bed in the morning. I'd be in a bunker dug into my backyard." She smiled at her two friends. "We need people to entertain us. To make movies, to write books, to sing songs. It's all important. And it's not like I'm doing any real public service. I'm not investigating unsolved cases or helping catch the bad guys like some podcasters are. Not my skill set. I write scary books, and I tell people about real-life scary stories. I'm not fixing anything."

"I don't know if that's true," Hollyn said. "You're telling people what the victims would if they could. I know I'm a lot more careful after listening to your show."

"She keeps me safe," Jasper confirmed, setting his chin on Hollyn's shoulder.

Hollyn rolled her eyes.

"You keep each other safe, all right?" Andi wiggled her fingers in a little wave. "See y'all later." She looked back and forth between the two of them. "And I'll shut the door. Enjoy borrowing a cup of sugar."

They were laughing when Andi clicked the door shut. And though she doubted they were going to get it on at the office, it made her grin to see her friends so happy. She didn't believe coupledom was in the cards for her, but for some, it really was a beautiful thing to behold.

chapter **three**

THE ANCIENT OAK TREES LOOKED LIKE GIANT SEA MONSTERS rising from the earth in the early morning twilight, the curly Spanish moss swaying from their branches like seaweed, as Hill turned a corner on one of the jogging paths in City Park. He liked jogging very early in the morning, sometimes before the sun's rays had even peeked over the horizon, because the paths in the park were less crowded and the humidity and heat weren't overwhelming yet.

Plus, it gave him a reason not to have to lie in bed for hours staring at the ceiling as the sun came up. Even though it'd been almost two years since the fire that had taken the lower part of his leg, he still rarely managed more than four hours' sleep a night. Falling asleep took forever, and then when he did, he was often jolted awake from nightmares.

A tree branch broke in the distance as a squirrel leapt from it, and the instant bolt of adrenaline at the sound of snapping wood had him losing his breath. God, how he hated that sound. Wood splintering, giving way, plummeting to the ground in a rain of fire. That sound and those images fucking haunted him.

He closed his eyes, inhaled a deep breath, pushing down the memories trying to surface, and then refocused on keeping his strides even. *Right. Left. Right. Left.* He'd worked hard to finally get used to the C-shaped jogging prosthesis he used for runs. Being able to get outside and exercise were vital. Of all the suggestions the fire department's psychologist had given to him, that had been the most helpful. Hill had always leaned on hard workouts to channel whatever he was going through at the time into physical exertion, and now he needed it more than ever.

He didn't know how to do this new life—the one where he wasn't at the station daily doing his job, the one where he didn't have two working legs, the one where his ex-fiancée woke up every morning next to someone else.

But he knew how to run.

Until his heart was pounding and his T-shirt was soaked and he was too exhausted to think much of anything.

He jogged around another bend in the path, taking the long way, the morning light beginning to change the color of the sky and a woodpecker starting up a rapid rhythm in a tree off to his right. This was the only version of peace he was going to get today, so he wanted to enjoy the last few minutes. Once he got home, he had to set up a few doctor's appointments and then meet up with his friend Ramsey for lunch to talk "strategy," his friend's new favorite topic. The lunch should be something to look forward to, but lately Ramsey had turned into the teacher in that old Twisted Sister music video, constantly asking what Hill was going to do with his life. As if Hill were some fresh-out-of-college kid who had unlimited options.

He'd already made that tough decision in his life. He'd become a firefighter. It'd been the perfect job for him. He liked being on his toes, not knowing what the day would hold, being able to help and protect people in a very tangible way. Now that was gone. *Poof. Game over.* Like he'd lost a life in a video game and now he was starting back at the beginning, only this time with his original superpowers taken away and no chance of getting them back.

He didn't want to play that game. That game sucked.

The parking lot came into view in the distance, the end of his run in sight. He slowed his pace, preparing to cool down. The morning crowd was trickling in—the white-haired power walkers, a few college students, and parents pushing strollers. A lady in bright-pink leggings was headed toward him, a little boy who looked like her in tow. Hill shifted more to the right side to give them room as he passed them. The little boy noticed Hill as he got closer, and his eyes went wide. He pointed at Hill's running-blade prosthesis. "Mommy, it's a robot!"

The mother blanched, sending Hill an embarrassed look. "Flynn, that's not nice. He's not a—"

But the little boy had broken free from his mother's handhold and was rushing toward Hill. "Robot!"

"Flynn!"

The boy stopped in front of him, and Hill slowed to a halt, breathing hard.

The mother was right on the kid's tail, and she grabbed his hand quickly again. "Oh my God, I'm so sorry. He doesn't know any better and—"

Hill forced a practiced smile. "It's okay." He looked to the little boy who was openly staring at Hill's prosthesis, a look of amazement on his face. The sheer innocence of it softened some of Hill's edginess over being stared at. He appreciated that kids didn't play the polite games adults did. He remembered his little cousin, Jessa, at that age. Five-year-olds were honest as fuck. He lifted his knee, flexing the prosthesis so the boy could see how it worked. "I'm only part robot. We're a secret society, though, so don't tell anyone else you saw one of us."

"Wow," the little boy said. "Cool."

The mother gave Hill an apologetic smile. "Thanks. Again, I'm sorry."

Hill waved her off. "It's fine. Enjoy your day."

She tugged Flynn's arm and got him walking again. The boy gave Hill a little wave and finally went with his mother. Hill walked the rest of the way back to the car, draining his water bottle in the process, suddenly feeling exhausted down to his bones.

By the time he pulled up to his house, he wanted a shower so badly, he could almost feel the water hitting his skin. But the path to get into his little yellow duplex was blocked. There was an open bag of soil on the front lawn, a line of pink and purple flowers in containers on the sidewalk, and a redhead on her knees in the barren front garden. *Great.* So much for a stealth entrance.

At the sound of his tires on the driveway, Andi stood from her spot in the grass and turned his way. She'd piled all of that bright hair on top of her head in some sort of spiky bun. Her knees were covered in dirt, and she was sporting what looked to be a pair of black Doc Martens even though she was dressed in a T-shirt and cut-off jean shorts.

The look shouldn't do it for him.

She put one garden-glove-covered hand to her hip and waved at him like they were old friends. His mouth went dry and a flood of heat went straight to his dick. *Fuck.*

His two-year-long dry spell was making him react like a horny teenager. He took a breath and lifted a hand to return the wave. He took his time gathering his things, forcing his libido back in check before he climbed out of the car. He didn't feel like having a conversation with his neighbor. He'd successfully avoided her for the two weeks since their late-night meeting. But there was no way to avoid it now. Pulling the car back out would be a little obvious. Plus, he was sweaty and disgusting, which insured a brief conversation and a valid excuse for needing to hurry inside.

With another bracing breath, he pushed the car door open and climbed out.

"Hey there," Andi said, crossing the small lawn and heading toward him.

"Hey." Hill caught the moment Andi noticed his prosthesis for the first time. Her walk stuttered for a moment, a little freeze of movement, and her attention darted downward, then back up, then down again. But to her credit, she recovered quickly and offered him a bright smile as she stopped in front of him. "I was beginning to wonder if you'd moved out."

"What?" he asked, momentarily distracted by the sheen of sweat clinging to her skin, the way she smelled like grass and flowers.

She smirked. "You've been so good at being quiet, and I haven't seen you out, so if not for your car, I would've thought you were gone."

"Oh," he said, snapping back to attention. "Yeah. Still here. I haven't heard any screams coming from your side either."

She blinked.

As soon as the words were out of his mouth, he realized how bad they sounded. "I mean—not that I'm listening."

"I wanted to thank you for the tip about the pepper spray," she said quickly, saving him. "I got canisters for me and my friend."

Her cheeks had already been flushed from working in the sun, but he noticed the pink had spread to her neck. *Way to make the neighbor uncomfortable, jackass.* "Oh, good. That's good."

There was an awkward silence.

"So..." they both said at the same time.

He nodded for her to go first, but she waved him off. "No, go ahead."

"I was going to say, so you're gardening?"

She glanced over her shoulder at her work in progress, then back to him. "Yeah, I have no idea what I'm doing, but I've seen a lot of the neighbors planting flowers for spring, and I thought our place could use a little color. Plus, my brain is locked in the dank basement of writer's block, so I figured some fresh air would be good."

Our place. A little color. She had no idea how much color she was bringing to this faded house.

"I tried to only buy things the lady at the garden center said were hard to kill," she added. "We'll see. I once murdered a cactus, so I'm pretty dangerous."

He couldn't help but laugh as he looked down at the tiny woman in her ass-kicking boots. The laugh felt rusty in his throat. "Yes, you look quite lethal."

She put her hands to her hips, playfully affronted. "Hey, I'm small but mighty, man. I've got some badass pepper spray, I'll have you know."

He gave her a wry smile. "And write horror novels. I'm sure you murder fictional people regularly."

"Damn straight."

"What name do you write under?" He wasn't sure what his mouth was doing. He was supposed to be saying he needed to get inside, shower, and get to an appointment. Not make small talk. Not ask her about her life.

"A. L. Kohl," she said. "The horror genre likes an androgynous name. Some men think ladies can't write scary shit apparently."

He frowned. "That's stupid. Women see more horror than anyone."

She tilted her head, blue eyes narrowing a bit like she couldn't quite figure him out. "Yeah. We do. I guess you've seen a lot as a firefighter."

The words brought him back from the small-talk field trip he'd been on. "Yeah, about that. I think I gave you the wrong impression that night. I *was* a firefighter. I'm not active duty anymore." He shifted onto his good leg, wishing he didn't have to have this conversation. "For obvious reasons. I was only using it that night to get the door open as soon as possible."

"Oh." She nodded. "Right."

He cleared his throat. "Well, I better go in and shower before I wilt your flowers over there with my after-run glow. Good luck with the project."

She glanced down his body as if just noticing he was damp with sweat. Her eyes flicked once more to his mechanical leg, but then she was focused back on his face. She squinted. "Do you want me to do yours, too?"

"What?" he asked.

"Your garden." She cocked her head toward his side of the duplex. "I have enough flowers to go around. I don't mind spreading them out on both sides. You could avoid having to get down in the dirt."

She was trying to be kind. He had no doubt of that, but the offer hit him in a dark, knee-jerk place. "I'm capable of planting my own garden. I ran three miles this morning. I can plant a flower."

"I—" She pressed her lips together. "I didn't mean it that way. I just… I'm out here already. I'm already filthy. I have what I need. It wouldn't be that much more work, and then the house could look colorful on both sides."

He shook his head, taking a step back. "No, they're your flowers. I don't need any. The shrubs are fine."

The bright openness that had been on Andi's face during their entire conversation shut down. A little frown line had appeared between her brows. "Okay. No problem."

He stared at her for a moment and took a breath, reeling himself in. "Sorry. Thanks for the offer. I…I don't need flowers."

She crossed her arms over her chest and nodded. "Got it."

He jutted a thumb toward the house. "I've got to go."

"Sure. See ya."

He turned his back to her and headed toward the house, hating that he had to take the few steps over the uneven ground that led to the porch slowly. Hating that his pretty neighbor already saw him as a guy who needed her pity. As charity, not a man.

....

Andi watched as Hill made his way into the house, his prosthesis giving him an unusual but determined gait. She'd been shocked to see it when he'd gotten out of the car. She'd made sure not to stare, but then she'd stuck her proverbial foot in her mouth anyway. She'd offended him. *Way to go, Ms. Helpful.*

And things had been going so well. They'd had actual conversation. He'd looked embarrassed about his lie. Normally, lying would be an instant you're-dead-to-me offense, but the look of sadness that had crossed his face when he'd said he *was* a firefighter had hit her right in the gut. He hadn't lied as a manipulation. He'd lied because he wished it were true. She'd wanted to ask more. She'd wanted to know his story. But they weren't friends yet and that wasn't her place.

Now they may never be.

She'd said the wrong thing. Now it would be weird between her and Hill unless she fixed it. She pulled off her gardening gloves and stared at his door as he shut it behind him, an idea coming to her.

Hmm. Maybe.

chapter **four**

HILL PUT A POT OF COFFEE ON TO BREW AND THEN WENT TO the laundry room in search of a clean T-shirt. His body was sapped from his run, the strength workout he'd done when he'd gotten home, and the hot shower, which would normally help clear his mind, but he kept replaying the interaction with Andi. He'd handled it all wrong.

Logically, he knew Andi had only been trying to be nice by offering to plant flowers for him, but the simple gesture had reminded him of what other people saw now when they looked at him—someone who needed *help*. Someone to feel sorry for. While he'd been tamping down attraction to his pretty neighbor, she'd been thinking of ways she could volunteer to his charitable cause. His stomach turned.

You're not the man you used to be.

His ex's barbed words were like aggravating song lyrics he couldn't get out of his head, the chorus playing over and over.

He rummaged through the dryer for a shirt, but before he could grab one, his doorbell rang. He frowned, knowing that this time of day usually meant someone selling something. A knock followed, the visitor impatient. He huffed out a breath, shut the dryer door, and stomped toward the front of the house, ready to tell whoever it was that the *No Soliciting* sign on the porch wasn't a suggestion but a directive.

However, when he opened the door, he found Andi standing there, no longer covered in dirt and now holding a platter of something. She had a smile pasted on her face, but her eyes went wide at the sight of him. Only then did he remember that he hadn't pulled on a shirt yet.

"I, uh..." she said, her gaze sliding downward to the spot where a burn scar from the accident slashed across the side of his abdomen. He wanted to cover the scar tissue with his hands. "If this is a bad time..."

"Hey. Sorry. I was getting out of the shower. Give me a sec." He jerked a thumb toward the back of the house. "I'll grab a shirt."

Her gaze jumped back to his and she nodded. "Yeah, no problem."

He turned and took a few steps toward the laundry room, but when he glanced back, he saw that Andi was still standing on the porch like some reluctant Girl Scout. He waved her in. "You can come in. I'll be right out."

A quick flash of something went over her expression. Fear? Wariness? Whatever it was, he didn't like it.

"I don't want to interrupt whatever you were doing," she said quickly.

"You're fine. Just give me a sec."

She glanced around and then nodded, taking a step inside but still looking unsure. "Okay."

He left her there and hustled to the laundry room. Once he'd pulled on a shirt, he took a breath, trying to shake off his foul mood, and headed back to the living room. He needed to undo how rude he'd been to Andi.

Andi had perched on the edge of a chair in his living room, her eyes on the cookbooks he'd left strewn over the couch. She'd left his front door ajar. Clearly, she wasn't planning on staying very long.

He ran a hand through his still-damp hair. She was probably here to tell him he'd acted like a jackass. She wouldn't be wrong. He cleared his throat, bringing her attention upward and over to him. She gave him a tight smile and tucked her hair behind her ear. "Hey."

"Hi." He walked over and grabbed the books he had spread out on the couch and stacked them onto the coffee table. "Sorry. I wasn't expecting company."

"That's how my desk looks when I'm writing," she said, peeking toward the stack. "You like to cook?"

He rubbed his palms on his jeans, the back of his neck heating. His therapist had suggested Hill get back to cooking, even though he wouldn't be doing it for a firehouse anymore, but all he'd managed lately was flipping through cookbooks and then ordering takeout. Why bother cooking anything elaborate if he had no one to cook for anymore? "It's something I mess around with. I was the designated chef for my crew at the firehouse."

"That's cool. I have zero ability in the kitchen if it doesn't come in a box or can. I once went to a cooking-and-cocktails class with some friends for a girls' night out. I set a kitchen towel on fire before we even got started, and I think the grilled fish I attempted is still stuck to that pan to this day. I tried to convince the teacher that catfish jerky would be the next big thing."

Hill smiled. "I'm sure it wasn't that bad."

"Oh, it was bad. I had to pay an extra fee for damages and then didn't have anything to eat." She smirked. "I was really good at the cocktails though—drinking them, at least."

He huffed a quiet laugh.

"Sorry. I'm rambling. I have a tendency to do that. I'm sure you're wondering why I'm here." She offered the covered platter she'd been holding in her lap. "Now you're going to be scared after that story, but I wanted to bring you these. They're brownies."

His brows lifted, and he reached out to take the dish from her, the scent of chocolate wafting his way and the dish warming his hands. "You baked brownies?"

She shrugged. "They're from a quick boxed mix that I can't mess up, so don't worry. No fish-jerky mishaps."

"I've never met a brownie I didn't like," he said, "but you didn't have to do that."

"I kind of did." She dipped her head, her bangs falling into her eyes before she looked up again. "I said the wrong thing. We're going to be neighbors, and I feel like we've gotten off on the wrong foot." A look of horror flashed across her face. "I mean—"

He didn't get why her expression had turned to one of horror, and then it registered. She'd said *wrong foot* to a guy with a prosthesis. He stared at her for a second and then a snort-laugh escaped him. "Did you really just say that?"

She put a hand over her eyes and groaned. "Oh my God, I'm the worst. I feel like every time I talk to you, I do or say the wrong thing. I almost maced you the first night. Then I insult you this morning. Now this."

He smiled, endeared by her obvious embarrassment. "You didn't almost mace me. You never would've gotten that canister lifted before I had your arm pinned behind your back."

Her head snapped up, her eyes wide, and she glanced toward the open door.

The spark of fear on her face caught him off guard, and he automatically set the brownies aside and lifted his palms. "Whoa, I didn't mean I *would* do that. I'm only saying, I used to teach self-defense at the community center, and my training would've kicked in if you'd aimed a weapon at me."

"Right." She nodded, her hands clasped in her lap. "Sorry. You know I write horror. My mind goes to dark places first. It's a career hazard."

He frowned. "No, I get it. That's smart. It never hurts to be aware."

She scoffed. "I don't know if that's entirely true. Anything done to the extreme, even being aware, can backfire."

Something in the way she said it made him want to ask more questions. There was a story there, and part of him wanted to prod, but he also sensed she'd shut down if he did. Like she said, he was still a stranger. "And you didn't need to bring me brownies. I'm the one who should be bringing you a peace offering. I'm sorry I snapped at you. You were trying to be nice. I was an asshole. So I definitely don't deserve baked goods."

"I shouldn't have assumed you couldn't do your own gardening," she said, her blue eyes meeting his. "I don't like when people assume things about me."

He sighed and glanced out the front window toward the yard. "Honestly, your assumption wasn't far off. It *would* be a pain in the ass to get on the ground and garden, but I'm not looking for help."

She rolled her lips together and nodded. "Got it."

"I'm not giving the brownies back, though." He put his hand on the platter. "They're mine now, and you can't have them."

She laughed, and the sound ran straight down his spine, warming his bones. "No worries. I made some for myself, too." She glanced at his cookbooks again. "So, if you aren't with the fire department anymore, do you do a different job now?"

The question instantly splashed cold water on his mood. The thought of telling this sexy, vibrant woman that he was retired and on a disability pension and couldn't seem to get himself to do anything useful made his stomach turn. He'd grown up with a dad who'd sat at home, zoned out on pills or booze, who claimed a shoulder injury prevented him from working even though it hadn't prevented him from taking swings at his mom on a regular basis.

Hill knew his own injury had been very real, and the disability pension necessary, but at thirty-one, he hadn't planned on that being the end of his working life. He couldn't be a firefighter, but he was capable of other things—theoretically. But he'd made no headway on making something new happen. The fact that he was still without a job or a purpose two years in because of this fucking depression was his worst nightmare coming home to roost. He missed the pride of being able to tell someone he was a firefighter. He missed feeling like he was doing some good in the world. He missed cooking for his crew and feeling useful. But in this moment, what he missed most was the way women used to look at him like he was a possibility.

He shifted on the couch. "I own a couple of properties that I rent out, so I spend some time taking care of that." Part truth. He did own a few properties with his aunt and uncle, the people who'd raised him, but they had a management company handle the logistics. So it was income but not an actual job. "And a friend of mine thought I should try to write a cookbook, but I think knowing how to cook and writing about cooking are two different skill sets. So I'm kind of in the exploratory career phase again."

Andi nodded, a pensive look on her face. "That sounds both exciting and terrifying."

He scoffed. "Exciting?"

She shrugged. "Maybe that's not the right word, but figuring out what you want to do when you grow up is kind of two-sided, right? Terrifying because—holy crap, grown-up life choices. But on the other hand, you get to choose again, like a redo. Poof, new path." She moved her hands like she was casting a spell. "I work at this coworking space a few blocks from here—WorkAround—and it's full of people figuring out what they want to do with their lives on their own terms. Lots of them have tried a number of jobs or businesses and haven't quite landed on the One yet, but that's okay. Maybe there isn't a One. Maybe there's a Two or a Three. Or maybe we're meant to do a series of things in life."

"You believe that?"

"I think so. I mean, I love being a writer and I love podcasting right now, but who's to say that in ten years I'll still love it? Maybe I'll want to do something completely different then." She sniffed. "My parents think the whole concept is complete bullshit—very millennial/Gen Z of me, you know? Why can't I go and get a nine-to-five and a steady paycheck? And I get where they're coming from, but they don't see what I see at WorkAround. You can feel the energy of the place when you walk around. It's like we're all running our little life experiments. How cool is that?"

She was rambling again, but he found himself leaning in. "You do sound exceptionally millennial."

She grinned, looking not at all offended. "At the risk of sounding like an old hippie, life's too short, man."

"It definitely is." A shudder went through him at that. He was exceptionally aware of how quickly life could be snuffed out. When that roof beam had come down on him in a fiery blaze, he'd thought his ticket had been pulled. He probably should be all *Let's take life by the horns* now that he had gotten a second chance, but he couldn't access that kind of enthusiasm. His enthusiasm well was bone dry. He wished he could just plug into Andi and channel one percent of that kind of energy for himself.

"Well," she said, breaking him from his train of thought, "if you ever want to get some inspiration, I can give you a tour of WorkAround and introduce you to some people. Sometimes it helps hearing what other people are doing to spark some ideas in your own brain. I got the podcasting idea that way. And it's not that far from here. Plus, they have a chef vlogger there. He may be able to brainstorm with you about the cookbook thing. There's also a kitchen on-site that people rent out to do food photography or cooking videos or to host cooking classes. You might find that interesting."

The invitation caught him off guard. "Wow, that sounds like an alien planet compared to the firehouse."

She laughed. "It can be sometimes. There's definitely a variety of characters there. But seriously, I could show you around."

He didn't know what the point would be. He'd never been the entrepreneurial type. After what he'd been through with his dad, he'd never considered anything but the most stable of careers. "Thanks. Maybe one day."

She glanced at the clock on his side table, and he followed her gaze. *Damn.* He needed to be heading out for his lunch with Ramsey, but talking to Andi was like getting a taste of a drug. How long had it been since he'd had a conversation with someone who wasn't focused on his injury or mental state? Who wasn't calling or stopping by to check on how he was doing?

"It's getting late," she said, slapping her knees and standing up. "I better get going. I know you probably have things to do, and my book isn't going to write itself. It's lazy that way."

He let out a breath, already mourning the loss of her company, and stood to follow her to the door. "Yeah, I have to head out to meet a friend. But thanks again for the brownies. You really didn't need to go through that kind of trouble."

She stopped at the door and turned to face him. "Not a problem. I enjoyed making them. My friends tell me my love language is baked goods."

His eyebrows lifted.

She cringed. "And...that sounded weird." She laughed self-consciously. "I just mean that I communicate in baked goods—usually purchased, not baked. I promise I'm not hitting on you."

The words were playful, but they hit him like shrapnel, cutting in multiple places. Of course she wasn't hitting on him. Of course this wasn't flirting. Of course she was inviting him to tour WorkAround to be helpful, not to ask him out. She was being *nice*. Everyone was being *so fucking nice* to him these days. He forced a smile. "I knew what you meant."

She wiggled her fingers in a wave and stepped out onto the porch. "See you on the lawn sometime, neighbor. And let me know if you decide you want that tour."

"Thanks. Will do." He shut the door behind her and then pressed his forehead to the doorjamb, deflated. "Fucking pathetic, man."

He was so out of practice with women that he didn't even know how to distinguish a neighbor offering a favor from interest anymore. The old version of Hill would've flirted his ass off with Andi. He would've turned on the charm and had her laughing and would've gotten her to go out to dinner with him tonight—or better yet, let him cook for her. He would've taken her to his bed and shown her all the fun ways he could make her feel good.

Now he was left with none of the finesse and all of the wanting.

He needed to steer clear of his neighbor. He was trying to find ways to get out of this mental hole, not make it worse by reminding himself what he couldn't have.

....

"She baked you brownies?" Ramsey said between shoveling french fries into his mouth. "Dude, that was a clear opening to ask her out."

Hill dumped more spicy salsa on his plate of nachos and shook his head at his friend. He and Ramsey had a standing lunch date each week since it was weird visiting the fire station with Josh, the scumbag who'd slept with his fiancée, still working there. "It was not an opening. They were guilt brownies. She felt like she'd insulted me about my leg, and she's too nice to let something like that go. If you'd met her, you'd realize there's no chance this was an attempt at flirting with me."

"Why not?" Ramsey asked, dumping more ketchup on his plate. "She married or something?"

"That's not what I mean." Hill grabbed his phone off the table. He wiped it on his jeans where the sweat from his beer had gotten his screen wet, and then typed Andi's pen name into the search. Her author website came up, and he turned the phone toward Ramsey. "This is her."

Ramsey wiped the salt off his fingers and took Hill's phone, bringing it close to his face. "Whoa. Hot."

"Yeah. And young. And definitely not in the market for some washed-up firefighter who spends most of his time in doctors' offices and therapy appointments."

Ramsey scrolled, his gaze still on the screen, the light of the phone illuminating the faint freckles that redheaded Ramsey denied he had. A probie firefighter had once called Ramsey "Freckles" and had ended up on solo toilet-scrubbing duty at the station for a month. "Shit, she writes horror novels. That's kind of awesome—or concerning. I mean, she probably knows a hundred ways to kill a man. But she's also at a higher probability for being kinky."

Hill groaned. "That is one hundred percent a bullshit assumption." He forced his mind not to go there, not to picture Andi in all kinds of fun, naked situations. "All it means is that she likes scary books."

Ramsey set Hill's phone down and lifted his hands in surrender. "Okay, got it, man. But I don't see why you didn't ask her out. I mean, the worst that could happen is she says no."

"No, the worst that could happen is she has zero interest and I put her in a completely awkward position with a guy she has to live next door to. Or she could laugh—that'd be fun." He shoved a chip in his mouth, chewing with more aggression than necessary.

"She wouldn't laugh," Ramsey said, going back to his fries. "And awkwardness never killed anyone. At least you'd be putting yourself out there. That's better than this hermit routine you've got going on."

Hill put more chips in his mouth, choosing not to honor the hermit comment with a response. He couldn't deny his hermit state, but he also couldn't justify venturing back into the dating world. Everyone came with a little baggage, but he had so much right now, he'd have to rent off-site storage to house all of it. No woman deserved that in her life.

"All I'm saying," Ramsey said after taking a long swig of iced tea, "is that you need to look at the law of inertia."

"Inertia," Hill said flatly. "We're having a physics discussion now?"

"Yes. I'm not saying you should go out in search of the love of your life. Or even go out and search for your next long-term career—though I'm sticking by my cookbook suggestion. All that stuff is really big, heavy shit. You don't need more heavy stuff right now. But you also can't keep doing what you're doing because of inertia." He took an ice cube out of his glass and set it on the table between them. "An object at rest will stay at rest unless acted upon by a force." He pointed at the ice cube. "You are the object at rest. Your ass is going to sit there, unmoving, and let the rest of your life melt away."

Hill gave him a droll look.

"Unless." Ramsey flicked his finger, sending the cube sailing across the table and into Hill's lap. "Some force acts upon it—like me."

Hill brushed the ice cube onto the floor. "You're a force all right. Newton's fourth law—the law of pains in the ass."

Ramsey smirked. "I will gladly be a pain in the ass if it means getting you out of this dark, depressing place you're in. You need to get into motion, just a little bit, and then it will be easier to keep moving. Like asking your hot neighbor out would've put things in motion, even if she said no. It would've been easier the next time to ask someone else."

Hill let out a breath, feeling exhausted all of a sudden.

"Look, I can't say I've been there," Ramsey went on. "I don't know what you're going through, but I've had times in my life when I've felt stuck. If you stop moving, you get more stuck, more hopeless. So even if moving forward is the last thing you feel like you have the energy to do, you have to force yourself sometimes—even if it's little things. It's like working out. No one wants to do it, but the more you do it, the easier it is. Then it starts feeling good. Then you're running miles and can't remember why you used to hate working out."

Hill pushed his plate aside. "Right."

"And believe me, remembering how great it is to get laid is a way quicker trajectory than learning how to love working out." Ramsey picked up his burger with a flash of a grin. "Once you get past that first time, you're going to wonder why you waited so long to get back out there."

Hill's neck muscles tightened. He had not forgotten how great sex was or even just making out on the couch, but imagining doing those things now—with this new body and all its scars—made dread wash through him. After his accident, Christina had stopped sleeping with him. At first he'd thought it was because she was afraid she'd hurt him, but once he'd found out about Josh, he'd figured out the truth. She wasn't attracted to him anymore and was getting what she needed from someone else.

"I don't think I'm ready for the dating scene yet, but I hear what you're saying," Hill said, knowing his friend's heart was in the right place. "Maybe I can find some way to get moving on the finding-a-new-career thing. Andi offered to give me a tour of the coworking space where she has an office. She said meeting people who are doing all kinds of different things can be inspiring. And there's a test kitchen there that food vloggers use."

Ramsey paused midbite and lowered his burger. "What the fuck? You let me get halfway through lunch without telling me that part? She wants to show you around where she works? Help you figure out what you want to be when you grow up? You dumbass, you totally should've asked her out. You've got zero game. No, not even zero—negative points would have to be given."

Hill leaned back in his chair and flipped his friend off. Ramsey was a pain in the ass, but Hill loved that he still treated him like he had before the accident. Other people had become more careful around him, like he was so fragile he'd break. Ramsey still regularly insulted him. It was the best. "Fuck you."

"Yeah, yeah," Ramsey said, unperturbed. "But at least now you have a second chance to get this shit right. Tell her you'll take that tour and then ask her out for coffee after or something."

"And if she only sees me as the disabled firefighter she wants to help out because she's a charitable person?"

He shrugged. "Then at least you know what's what. And hey, she could become your hot friend and then *I* can ask her out. Because"—he picked up Hill's phone again and turned Andi's headshot his way—"hell yes."

Hill grabbed his phone out of Ramsey's hand. "Stay away from my neighbor. Our walls are thin, and I can't handle that kind of trauma."

Ramsey chuckled and went back to his food.

They moved on to a different conversation, but Hill couldn't get the previous one out of his head. Andi had absolutely not been flirting with him, but he found himself fantasizing about that being the case. That she'd come over because she was interested. That she'd invited him on a tour because she wanted to spend more time with him.

But as quickly as he let the thoughts spool, they started to unravel. He was deluding himself, and if he let those thoughts go in that direction, he'd end up embarrassing himself. He knew he needed to take baby steps, and Ramsey was probably right. He should have a hookup at some point to get past that initial fear and dread of sleeping with someone. But doing that with Andi would be a terrible idea, even if she was interested. Beyond the fact that she was his neighbor and tenant, a hookup was supposed to be a temporary, fleeting thing. Lighthearted. Low stakes.

Nothing about Andi said low stakes.

She seemed like the kind of woman who would make a guy want to push in all his chips. Bet the house.

He couldn't afford to risk that much again. He'd already lost it all.

Andi Lockley was off-limits.

chapter **five**

*"*E*VERY WOMAN KNOWS WHAT IT'S LIKE TO CONTEMPLATE murder. Not as the perpetrator—though some ex-bosses and ex-boyfriends can definitely inspire a fleeting thought—but her own murder. The loud guy trying to sell you something in the street. The man two aisles away in the grocery store who's watching you instead of inspecting the quality of the tangerines that are on sale. The random grammatically challenged dude on Instagram who thinks your pics with your dog 'r real sexxy.'*

"We're all familiar with that sick pang of warning in our guts, the tensing of muscles in our legs, our bodies readying themselves to bolt, or even just that vague sense of unease." Andi paused the recording to edit out a place where she'd coughed. She hit Play again. "*Listeners, that feeling is your personal oh-shit detector. Listen to it. Be best friends with it. Trust it like you trust your hairdresser. Don't let anyone tell you it's silly, that you're overreacting, that you're being ridiculous.*

"I think Janice Walters trusted her oh-shit detector about her new coworker. She brought up concerns about Cliff Bastrop to her boss, that she had a bad feeling about the new guy. Her concerns were dismissed. Where was the proof? He was a nice guy. He was helpful. He always had a compliment for every woman in the

office. No one but Janice seemed to question why he was so ready to help, to go out of his way for the ladies in the office, until one night when she was the last one out the building and Bastrop was waiting there to help her carry things to her car. Before she could decline, he grabbed her, the file box she'd been carrying hit the ground, and no one ever saw Janice alive again."

Andi inhaled deeply, trying not to imagine the scene and to focus on the podcast recording. She knew getting Janice's story out there was important, knew her listeners needed to hear the message the story held, but she also didn't want to have a complete freak-out the next time she had to leave WorkAround at night. Covering these cases and managing her anxiety was a fine line to walk every day.

Horror and true crime gave her an outlet to process her anxiety in a safe way. After what she'd been through as a teenager, she'd worried that she was demented for finding solace in this stuff, but her therapist had explained that it wasn't uncommon. She'd given Andi a stack of research articles to show her she wasn't alone. Andi had learned that the majority of true-crime enthusiasts were women. And horror movies and fiction were as popular with women as they were with men. Her therapist had said watching horror or studying true crime could act almost like exposure therapy, women looking their biggest fears straight in the face and coming up with mental plans for how they could keep themselves safe.

For instance, with Janice's story, Andi wanted her listeners to hear that trusting the this-guy-makes-me-uncomfortable feeling wasn't only valid, it could be lifesaving. And not to let others dismiss their instincts.

It was one of the main reasons Andi had started the podcast. She wanted to shine light on things that often remained in the dark otherwise. Scary stories gave people fuel to protect themselves.

Those stories gave them proof that their fears or bad feelings or instincts weren't "overreacting" or "being silly." There was power in knowing that. In not letting society gaslight you into thinking you were being paranoid if you carried mace or sent a photo of the guy you were going home with to a friend or didn't accept a drink that you didn't see poured. Knowledge truly was power.

Which was why it annoyed Andi so much when she got podcast reviews from the haters. She had loads of five-star reviews, but of course, her eyes always went straight to the ones and twos when she checked them. Tonight, she'd had:

> **LollyVR4:** People who listen to this shit and exploit these crimes are sick in the head.
>
> **BroWhoa62:** This show is called What Can We Learn from This? I've learned not to listen. She makes it sound like every guy in the world is a psychopath.
>
> **Mayh3m:** This chick probably watches true-crime shows and horror movies instead of porn to get off. I'll tie you up, baby.

The last one she was able to flag and get removed. But the reviews had also inspired her to open a bottle of wine for her evening podcast shift. She huffed, getting frustrated all over again, and pulled off her headphones. She clicked on a file and inserted an audio clip from the documentary on Janice Walters's murder.

Footsteps sounded on the other side of her wall and she frowned. The werewolf was prowling around again. Always heard, never seen. An image of Hill answering the door shirtless rushed back into her mind. Her tongue had nearly rolled out of her head like a cartoon character when she'd been greeted with that view. The man was built like a fucking gladiator. One who'd been through war. Next to the line of dark hair that had disappeared into his waistband, he'd had a swath of skin that was raised and pink with an almost melted texture. Burn scars.

The sight of him had made her blush, but it'd also made her heart hurt. This man had survived a horror. In that moment, that fear she always had around new men had softened some at the edges. She'd wanted to know more about him. She'd gone inside with him despite all the warnings that had automatically run through her head.

No one knows I'm here.

He's a stranger.

He's big and strong and could overpower me.

Being a victim of something doesn't mean he's not a bad guy.

Freddy Krueger had burn scars.

But the worries had been unfounded. He hadn't murdered her. In fact, he'd been nice and quietly funny, and she'd thought they'd made headway with the possibility of becoming friends. But she'd been wrong. It'd been almost two weeks since she'd brought those brownies over, and the handful of times she'd seen him outside, he'd given her a quick wave and then headed inside without a word. Dismissed.

He clearly didn't want to be friends.

Which was his prerogative but also kind of sucked. She didn't want awkwardness with the neighbor. But more than that, she was frustrated that she'd read the situation so wrong. That day at his house, she'd felt like they'd made a connection. He was clearly going through some stuff. She'd pieced together that his disability had taken him out of a career he loved, and she'd wanted to help. She didn't know what it was like to have that kind of physical loss, but she remembered what it was like not knowing what she wanted to do with her life.

However, once again, her instincts had been wrong. There'd

be no connection. He didn't want her help. He'd probably thought she was meddling.

Message received: the hot werewolf didn't want her around.

She sipped her wine and tried to shake off thoughts of Hill and refocus on her work. She needed to finish editing the episode tonight if she was going to post it on schedule tomorrow. She didn't have time to obsess about the neighbor anymore. She put her headphones back on.

"Janice was reported missing the following Monday when she didn't show up for work..."

Two hours and one too many glasses of wine later, Andi was done. She put aside her laptop, pulled off her headphones, and yawned, wondering if she should just sleep there on the couch. Getting ready for bed suddenly seemed like too much work. Her limbs felt heavy and her thoughts fuzzy.

Maybe not so much wine next time.

She swung her legs to the floor, checking to see if she was head-spinning drunk or only a little buzzed. The room didn't tilt, so that was a good sign. She rubbed her face, preparing to get up, but a thump from the back of the house made her pause. She lowered her hands from her face and turned her head toward the kitchen, listening. Was Hill still up and moving around? It was past midnight.

He seemed to be a night owl so probably so. But when she heard a creak, one that sounded distinctly like her back screen door, goose bumps prickled her arms. That sound hadn't come from Hill's side. He didn't have a screen door. Her body went stiff and cold, her ears straining.

She half expected her phone to ring with a voice on the other end asking her if she liked scary movies. The creak came again, and she inhaled a shaky breath. Okay. The latch on the screen door had probably come undone. It was windy outside. The door was probably flapping in the wind. *You're fine. The main door is locked tight.*

She reached for her phone, which she usually kept on the coffee table, but it wasn't there. Her heartbeat picked up speed. Where had she put it? She'd had it when she'd sat down to edit the episode. She'd gotten up to use the bathroom once and had gotten a refill on wine twice. She must've brought her phone into the kitchen.

Dammit.

How had she lost track of her phone? But she wasn't going to follow up that mistake with a second one. She definitely wasn't calling out "Who's there?" or going outside to investigate a weird sound. She hadn't watched hundreds of horror movies without learning *something*. Still, she needed to know what the noise was, but she wasn't going to look without some protection.

She swallowed past the dryness in her throat, and as quietly as she could, she rose to her feet, her knee making a soft popping sound. She swayed a little, the wine still coursing through her system, but the fear had sobered her thoughts. She glanced toward the kitchen again and then quickly but quietly hurried toward the front door in her bare feet. She'd left her purse on the table by the door when she'd come home, and she grabbed it like a lifeline. She rummaged around, and when her fingers closed around the gel pepper spray she'd bought at Hill's suggestion, a jolt of relief went through her.

She pulled out the canister and peeked through the peephole of the front door. Her porch was well lit and empty, but the darkness on the street beyond revealed nothing. She didn't want to walk outside at midnight, not knowing if someone was prowling around her place.

She turned away from the front door and listened. She didn't hear the creak anymore, but she was filled with the sense that the silence was not empty. It had weight. Like the air had changed. She slid the safety latch on the pepper spray, putting her finger on the trigger, and took a few steps toward the kitchen.

This wasn't the first time she'd been home alone and thought she heard a noise in the house. This was just the first time at this place. She'd learned to live with her hyperaware senses and overactive imagination. But this was the first time she didn't have her phone to call someone to stay on the line while she checked things out. Every other time, whatever sound she'd heard had been nothing. It would surely be the same now, but she wasn't going to take any chances. She held the pepper spray at-the-ready.

She placed her footsteps carefully, watching for a floorboard that she'd learned squeaked loudly. If she could get a peek at the kitchen and verify the main door was still safely closed and locked, she could end this. She got close to the entrance of the kitchen and took a deep breath. Steeling herself, she shifted to peek around the corner into the kitchen.

She almost didn't register what she saw, the image so preposterous for a woman who regularly checked that everything was locked up tight.

The back door was *wide open.*

Panic flooded her, electric fear zapping through her muscles like lightning, and a scream ripped out of her. She took off running in the other direction, shouting "Help!" the whole way. Her bare feet slapped against the floor, and she couldn't get a sense of whether anyone was behind her or not as she bolted toward the front door. Her fingers fumbled the dead bolt, and she started to cry, but finally the lock turned, and she flew out the front door like the house was on fire.

She had no idea if anyone was outside, and she didn't have her car keys, so she did the only thing she could think of. She rushed to Hill's door and banged on it with the sides of her fists, shouting for him to open it. Her throat hurt, her body was trembling all over, and her heart was going to pound out of her chest. *Please God, please. Come on, come on, come on.* "Hill!"

When she was about to give up and run to another neighbor, the door swung open. Hill took in the sight of her, confusion on his face, and she launched herself at him. He made an *oof* sound as she barreled into him and she slammed the door behind her. "Lock it!"

He put an arm around her, steadying them both. "*The hell.* What's wrong?"

"Someone's in my house," she panted, tears she hadn't known she'd been crying now streaming down her face. "Call the police."

His body stiffened against her. "Shit."

He let her go and shifted into action. Before she could process what was happening, he'd locked the door behind her, grabbed his cell, and called 911 to put in a report. He handed her the phone. "Stay on the line with them."

"What?" she asked, voice shaking. "Where are you going?"

The 911 operator was chattering in her ear for Andi to stay on the line, but she couldn't respond.

Hill left her for a moment, disappeared into a hallway, and then came out with his trusty baseball bat. "I'm going to check things out."

He moved to walk past her, but she reached out and snagged his T-shirt. "No!"

He frowned. "Andi..."

She couldn't let him out of her sight. Every survival instinct she possessed screamed at her to keep him right there with her. "What if they come over here while you're there? What if they have a gun? What if there's more than one person?" The questions rushed out of her without pause. "Please don't leave. *Please, Hill.* Stay until the police come. I can't—"

His determined expression softened at her frantic words. He set the bat down, then reached out, took the phone from her, and put his arm around her shoulders, giving her a little squeeze. "Shh. Okay. Take a breath. You're going to be okay. You're safe here. I won't leave you if you don't want me to." He put the phone to his ear to talk to the operator. "We'll be here waiting for the police. I have the neighbor here on my side of the duplex, safe. Please advise them that the problem is in Unit A. We are hunkered down in Unit B. I'll leave you on speakerphone, but I need to talk to her and help her calm down."

Hill set the phone on the arm of the couch. Andi was shaking all over, but the steady warmth of his arm around her helped a little. "I can't catch my breath."

"You're having a panic attack," he said, voice calm and soothing. "Here, come sit on the couch with me while we wait. My guess is whoever was in your place is long gone after all that screaming."

He kept his arm around her as they sat down, and she kept the pepper spray clutched tight in her hand, half expecting her intruder to bust through this door, too. "*You heard me?* Why didn't you come?"

He squeezed her arm. "Andi, I'm so sorry. I heard the screaming, but I thought it was one of your movies again."

"Jesus," she said, every part of her trembling now.

A distant police siren wailed, and Hill rubbed his palm up and down her chilled arm. "Try to take a few deep breaths. You're okay now. I won't let anything happen to you."

"I'm okay?" she repeated almost to herself, unsure.

"You're okay," he said. "I've got you."

The sound of his reassuring voice undid her, the reality of what she'd seen sinking in for real. *Someone had been in her house.* With her, while she sat there under headphones, oblivious. So many bad things could've happened. She leaned into Hill, pressing her face into his shoulder, letting the tears overtake her. The terror she'd felt when she'd seen that door wide open had been a sensation she'd experienced in her worst nightmares.

Hill made quiet, soothing sounds, letting her make a mess of his white T-shirt, and murmured gentle words to her, obviously used to being the calming presence in chaotic situations. "You're all right."

The man was a stranger. One she couldn't get a good read on, but in that moment, he felt like safety and comfort, like exactly the thing she needed right now. She let her pepper spray drop and wrapped her arms around his neck.

chapter **six**

HILL TENSED WHEN ANDI LOOPED HER ARMS AROUND HIS neck and pressed her face into his shoulder, her choking sobs putting little cracks in the armor he usually maintained when victims were upset. It did no one any good in a bad situation if the person there to help got emotionally swept up as well. But Andi's entire body was trembling against him, and he wanted to scoop her up, hold her, and assure her that he wasn't going to let anything happen to her, that she was safe with him.

But he had a feeling that when her panic eased, she was going to quickly remember who she was clinging to. He wasn't going to make this even weirder for her by giving in to that urge to hold her. He put a hand on her back and tried to calm her as best he could.

He could hear the sirens blaring out front, and he informed the 911 operator that the cops were here and ended the call. The siren turned off, blue and red lights flashing through the front window. Hill listened as the officers walked up the porch steps, the wood creaking, and then as they called out to anyone who was inside Andi's half. He could hear them as they inspected the other side of the duplex, knowing they wouldn't find anyone. If someone had broken in, they were long gone by now unless they were the dumbest criminal who ever lived. When the knock on his door finally came, Andi startled and lifted her head, her cheeks tear-streaked and eyes puffy.

He brushed her hair away from her face. "It's okay. It's the police. I'm going to get that."

Her gaze darted toward the front door. "How do you know it's them?"

"I heard them search the other side. Plus, I'll probably recognize them. I know most of the cops in this precinct. Stay right here, okay?"

She didn't look ready to let him go, but finally, she released him. She shifted to the corner of the couch and pulled her knees up to her chest, hugging them to her. Only then did he notice that all she was wearing was an oversize T-shirt and boy-short panties. He glanced at the door and then back to her. "Down the hall, in my bedroom, there's a basket of clean laundry next to the bed. You can borrow some shorts if you want."

She glanced down as if just noticing her state of undress for herself, and she hurriedly put her feet to the floor, clearly self-conscious. "Oh, yeah, thanks."

He gave her a second to head toward the bedroom, and then he went to the door. He checked the peephole, recognizing the face on the other side.

Of course. *Fucking hell.*

He took a fortifying breath and pulled open the door, schooling his face into one of mild impassivity. Officer Christina Morton was standing there, not a blond hair out of place in her tight braid, and her partner, Ben Brody, was by her side. Christina scanned Hill quickly with the cool detachment of an officer checking for injuries. If anyone had been watching, they never would've suspected he and Christina had been engaged once upon a time. That he used to unfurl that braid with rough fingers when they'd fall into bed. That she used to see him as irresistible.

"You all right, Dawson?" she asked, tone like a surgical knife—pointed, precise.

He wanted to reply, *In the grand scheme of things? No, not even a little bit.* But no way would he ever let Christina know he was living anything but his best life.

"Yeah. Everyone's fine. Neighbor ran over here, said her back door was open and she knows she locked it. She thought someone was inside," he said, matching Christina's businesslike tone. "I would've gone over and checked it out, but she was pretty upset and didn't feel safe being left alone."

"Understandable," Brody said in that genial way Brody said everything. If he were cast in a police drama, he'd always land the role of Good Cop.

Hill cocked his head toward Andi's side of the house. "Did y'all find anything over there?"

"No, the place is clear. Didn't see any damage or anything," Ben reported. "Can we come in?"

Hill took a step back and opened the door wide to let them inside. Christina's gaze scanned the room, no doubt critiquing Hill's sparse decorating style, which mostly involved buying nothing extra because it would only be extra shit to clean. When they'd lived together, she'd always been in charge of how their place looked, and she'd never met a farm-inspired tchotchke she didn't like. He'd lived in a place full of cows and chickens staring at him from every available surface. It'd nearly made him a vegetarian. Her gaze moved back to him. "Where's the neighbor?"

"I—"

But before Hill could get the words out, Brody's head turned as he caught sight of Andi coming out of Hill's bedroom. He gave her a warm smile. "Hello, ma'am, you okay?"

Hill turned. Andi's eyes were still swollen, but she'd dried her face, and she was now wearing a pair of his athletic shorts cinched up tight. Andi hugged her elbows and nodded. "I'm freaked out but all right."

"Why don't you sit down and tell us what happened?" Christina said in her calming cop voice.

They all settled into the living room, Andi taking the spot next to Hill on the couch, and Christina and Ben taking the chairs opposite. Andi tucked her hands between her knees, and he suspected she was trying to hide the fact that she was still trembling. Without thinking, he reached out and gave her knee a squeeze. "It's okay."

Christina cleared her throat, and he quickly moved his hand away.

Andi licked her lips. "Um, I was in my living room working—editing a podcast. I'd been doing that for at least an hour. I had headphones on, and when I took them off, I thought I heard something."

"What did you hear?" Brody asked, his notebook out.

Andi frowned, a little wrinkle appearing between her brows as she looked down, obviously replaying the incident in her head. "A thump at first. Not super loud but enough to get my attention. Then creaking. I thought my screen door had come unlatched and was blowing in the wind. My phone was in the kitchen, so I grabbed my pepper spray and went to the back of the house. I figured I was overreacting, but when I peeked in, I saw that my back door was wide open. I ran out the front of the house and banged on Hill's door since I didn't have my phone, and I know he stays up late."

Christina glanced Hill's way, then back to Andi. "Did you see anyone in your kitchen?"

Andi shook her head and then met Christina's gaze. "No, but I could feel someone there, if that makes sense."

Christina's brows rose. "Feel someone there?"

Andi rubbed her palms on her knees. "I don't know. I know that seems weird, but that feeling of someone else being there. A presence. Maybe I smelled an unfamiliar scent or felt the air shift. Something my subconscious picked up. It was a...sense of not being alone."

"A presence?" Christina asked, her mouth lifting at one corner. "Maybe this old place is haunted."

Andi pressed her lips together, obviously not appreciating Chris's little joke. "I doubt a ghost can unlock a door."

Hill noticed that Andi the horror writer didn't outright deny the possibility of ghosts being real, but he was happy to see that little spark of feistiness back. An irritated Andi was better than a terrified one.

"Okay," Christina said, letting her smirk drop. "Are you sure the back door was locked?"

"Absolutely," Andi said without hesitation. "I never leave any doors or windows unlocked. I'm really careful about that."

"Never?" Christina asked, skepticism in her voice. "It's easy to forget sometimes."

"She's a horror writer and researches true crime," Hill said, cutting Chris off. "She knows to lock her doors."

Christina's attention slid to him, giving him a discerning look. "So you two know each other well?"

He held the eye contact, playing poker. "Well enough."

"Hill's right," Andi said, not catching the tension in the exchange. "Some people may forget to lock their doors. I don't. My friends would tell you that I don't err on the side of caution. I err on the side of paranoid. That door was locked. It's my habit to check them at night, especially when I know I'm going to be under headphones."

"Right. Well. There was no sign of forced entry," Christina said. "Lock was intact. No splintered wood or marks on the frame. Maybe someone used a key."

"Do you have a friend or boyfriend who has an extra key?" Brody asked, hooking his ankle over his knee and leaning back. "Or anyone who'd have access to one of your extras that they could've swiped?"

Andi rubbed her forehead beneath the curtain of her bangs, looking exhausted. "No. I haven't lived there long. I have the only key."

"What about the landlord?" Brody asked.

Hill shifted on the couch. "I'm the landlord. I didn't unlock her door."

Andi's head snapped his way, a flash of shock there.

"Someone could have jimmied the lock without showing signs of force," Hill said. "These locks are pretty old. I was already planning on getting them replaced."

"Possible." Brody jotted down something in his notebook. "Or maybe the door didn't latch all the way and the wind knocked it open. We'd like to have Miss..."

"Lockley," Andi supplied.

"We'd like to have Miss Lockley do a walk-through with us, make sure nothing is missing," Brody said.

Andi tensed. "Are you sure you checked everywhere?"

"Of course." Christina smiled empathetically, suddenly looking like the woman Hill used to love. "We secured it before coming over here. You're safe to go back."

Andi took a shaky breath. "Okay. I can do a walk-through. Can you come with us, Hill?"

The plea in her eyes did something to him. God, he wanted to take that fear out of her. Andi was one of those people painted in bright colors. Bright-red hair. Big blue eyes. Thick black eyeliner. Bright bold lipstick. Brash attitude. Seeing her scared and pale seemed like a crime against sunshine or something. "Sure. We'll all go. We won't leave you alone until you feel safe."

She rolled her lips together and nodded.

He stood and put his hand out to help her up. She took it, but when he went to release her, she held on tight, sending a silent message. He squeezed her hand and kept hold of her. *I've got you.*

The exchange didn't go unnoticed by his ex.

Part of him wanted to make a show of it. Put his arm around Andi like, *Yes, this bright, beautiful woman is with me*—even if it was a lie. But he knew Christina wouldn't be jealous anyway. She was happily involved with Josh Matterhorn, the guy she'd left him for. The fellow firefighter who'd pulled Hill out of a burning building the night he'd lost his leg. The guy who used to be one of his closest friends.

The ghost of his old life rolled through Hill, and he had to breathe through the pain it stirred up. His relationship with Christina was dead. His relationship with Josh was dead. His leg was gone. His career was gone. The man he used to be didn't exist anymore.

He could see that reality every time Christina looked at him. The man she'd wanted to marry had died in that accident. All that was left now was the echo of who he used to be. A cheap imitation with missing parts.

Andi squeezed his hand, bringing him back to the moment, and he sent her a silent thank-you.

They all made their way over to the neighboring side, and Andi went room by room, staying close to Hill. She was supposed to be checking for missing items, but he could tell she was more focused on checking every closet and every nook where a person could hide.

Christina had pointed out Andi's big stack of horror DVDs and her shelves of scary novels and true-crime books. "Not into the lighthearted, Ms. Lockley?"

"Horror's my job," Andi had said, a little bite to the words.

When they made it back to the kitchen, Andi let out an audible breath. "I don't see anything missing. Maybe I scared them off before they could get anything."

"Or maybe you just spooked yourself," Christina said in an offhanded tone. "It happens. I know when I watch scary stuff, I hear noises that aren't there."

"Chris—" Hill started to call her out on the patronizing tone, but Andi got there first.

"I know what I heard," Andi said, tone polite but sharp. "I know what I felt. And I didn't imagine my door being open."

Brody nodded and jotted a few more notes. "If someone did get in, they probably didn't have long. Your phone's right there by the fridge. That would've been an easy grab. Your purse was out front. You either scared them off or the door wasn't latched correctly."

"Or someone was breaking in to do something worse than theft," Andi said grimly. "I'm a woman living alone."

The thought of some creep sneaking around Andi's place made Hill's fingers clench into fists. "I'll have the locks changed and get an extra dead bolt installed in the morning."

Brody snapped his notebook shut. "Yeah. An extra dead bolt is never a bad idea—maybe an alarm, too." He put his hand out to Andi. "Ms. Lockley, you let us know if you find anything missing or see anything suspicious."

"I will. Thank you," Andi said, her face drawn and tired as she shook Brody's hand and then Christina's. "I appreciate y'all checking everything out."

"Of course," Christina said.

Brody smiled a genial smile. "The good news is you have Dawson living next door." He clapped Hill on the shoulder. "So even though it doesn't feel that way right now, you're probably in the safest house on the block. He can be a grumpy dude, but I'd trust this guy to have my back any day."

Hill snorted.

Andi's gaze slid Hill's way. "Yeah, I was lucky to have him here tonight."

"I was glad to help," he said, meaning it. "Anytime."

Christina and Brody said their goodbyes, and Hill walked them out, stepping outside on the porch with them for a moment, closing the door behind himself. Brody glanced out at the darkened street. "We did have a break-in not too far from here last month, about four blocks over. Took a laptop and an Xbox. If there was someone here tonight, my guess is it's something like that. Probably thought no one was home and could make a quick grab."

"I'm going to get an alarm installed," Hill said.

Christina crossed her arms. "I don't know. If someone were here to steal, they would've taken the phone at least. Your neighbor seems like a sweet enough girl, but I think she freaked herself out. All that horror shit will make you jumpy." She cocked a brow. "Or maybe she just wanted to knock on your door in the middle of the night. She looks like she could be a bit of a drama queen—you know, with the hair and the nose ring and all."

Hill scoffed. "A drama queen?"

Christina had always been particularly tough on women who showed a lot of emotion. She'd been raised with brothers and thought an ironclad poker face was next to godliness. Andi's unedited, messy reactions wouldn't compute for her.

Christina shrugged. "She seems like someone who would enjoy being the center of attention. The whole damsel-in-distress routine, you know?"

Hill's jaw clenched. "Andi thought someone had *broken into her house*. I think she has the right to be dramatic over that. She didn't leave her door unlocked. She's the careful type. She was legitimately terrified."

Brody ran a hand over the back of his neck. "Yeah, the lady

looks scared. Go talk to her and reassure her she's safe. And if anything turns up missing, tell her to give us a call."

"Will do." Hill shook Brody's hand. "Thanks for coming out."

"Anytime."

Christina nodded instead of offering a handshake. Fine by him.

When Hill went back inside, Andi was standing in the middle of her living room, arms hugged to her chest, looking around like she was in a foreign place.

He ran a hand over the back of his head. "You okay?"

Andi turned to him, posture tight, guarded. "That female officer thought I was imagining things." Her chin tipped up. "I'm not. This isn't me creating scary stories. That door was locked. Someone who was not me opened it."

He sighed. "I know. I believe you."

Her shoulders drooped like her puppet strings had been cut. "You do?"

"Yeah. I know that feeling of someone being there even when you can't see them yet. I'm sure Christina does, too. Cops rely on all those senses and instincts in dangerous situations." He glanced back at the closed front door. "Don't worry too much about her. It wasn't about you. She was in a bad mood because I was here."

Andi lifted her brows. "Why's that? She have something against firefighters?"

"Just one." He double-checked that the door was locked, giving it a tug to make sure the lock caught, before turning back to her. "We used to be engaged."

Her lips parted. "Oh. Wow. Awkward."

"Can be." He shifted his weight off his prosthesis, his knee aching. "Do you need anything? I'll call a locksmith in the morning, and I'll get an alarm put in as soon as I can get someone out here."

She leaned against the back of the couch. "Why didn't you tell me you owned the place?"

He shrugged. "I use a management company for the rental properties I own. I didn't want you to feel like you had to be on your toes around me or something because I'm the landlord."

She twisted the string of the athletic shorts she'd borrowed. "Thanks for helping me tonight. I'm not sure what I would've done if you hadn't opened your door."

"You can always knock on my door," he said, shoving his hands in the pockets of his sweats and stepping closer. "Honestly."

Her mouth ticked up at the corner. "Even though you've been avoiding me since I barged in on you with brownies?"

He frowned. "I haven't been avoiding you."

She tilted her head, a wry look on her face.

He let out a breath. "Okay, maybe I have a little. It's not about you. I'm just..."

"Not a social butterfly. I get it. You won't be the first or the last to avoid my chatter. I can be hell on introverts." She gave a little smile. "But I'm willing to forgive you for this avoidance because you opened the door and were my hero tonight."

He shook his head. "Not a hero. Only a neighbor. You would've done the same for me, I'm sure."

"Oh, of course." She laughed and put up her fists like she was ready to box. "I'd totes protect my giant werewolf neighbor from the bad guys. They'd cower in terror at the mere sight of me."

Something tense released in his shoulders. It was hard to stay serious when Andi was shadowboxing in his oversize shorts. "Your *werewolf* neighbor?"

A little color came back into her cheeks as she put her arms down, and a flash of guilt crossed her face. "You know. Bearded, stomps around late at night, hides from humans."

He groaned and rubbed the spot between his eyes. "You're going to murder me in a book, aren't you?"

"Ha. No, you're safe," she said. "As long as you promise not to attack me when the full moon comes around. Or any moon phase for that matter."

Hill nodded. "Deal."

They stared at each other for a few quiet seconds, and he cleared his throat. "Uh, do you need anything before I head out? I'm sure you're ready to get to sleep."

She glanced at the front door, and the light in her eyes dimmed again, as if remembering why he was there in the first place. "I don't think I'll be able to sleep—possibly for the rest of my life now. But you're relieved of your duties. Thank you again."

He caught the waver in her voice, the anxiety there. She was putting on a brave face, but she was clearly still petrified. "I could stay."

The words came out before he could evaluate them and declare them certifiably insane. *I could stay? What the hell?*

Abort. Abort. Abort.

chapter **seven**

ANDI BLINKED AT HILL'S OFFER. "WHAT?"

Hill scratched his beard, looking altogether uncomfortable. "I mean, if you're scared to stay alone, I could sleep on the couch. Maybe you could get some rest that way."

Sleep on her couch? The neighbor she barely knew? *Oh, hell no.* She shook her head automatically. Guys didn't sleep over. Period. End of sentence. "I couldn't ask you to do that."

"You don't have to ask," he said with a shrug. "I'm offering. It's only a few hours 'til morning anyway."

Her gaze swept over him. The man was just so *big*. And intimidating. Even in sweats and a T-shirt, he looked like some comic superhero—or villain. Complete with bionic leg.

Sexy as fuck. But also scary as hell.

She didn't *know* him. And even though her gut was saying *good guy*, she'd learned her gut was far from reliable when it came to men. Her gut had almost gotten her killed. She hated that she could just as easily imagine Hill kissing her breathless as she could imagine him putting his hands around her throat and choking the life out of her. Her imagination was her best asset and her worst enemy sometimes.

When she was quiet too long, he lifted his palms. "I won't be offended if you say no. I'm fine either way. If you'd rather, I can give you my number, and you can call if you feel scared or want me to check on anything."

She rubbed her arms, trying to chase away the chill bumps. The thought of being alone sent a rush of fresh nerves through her. Honesty fell past her lips. "I'm legitimately freaked out to be alone right now, and the thought of having someone here sounds great, but it's kind of my policy not to let guys sleep over."

"Oh." He blinked. "Like ever?"

She made a slightly pained sound in the back of her throat. *Yes, like ever. Like ever ever. Like I haven't slept next to a Y chromosome since I was a teenager—and that chromosome was attached to a sociopath.* She forced a wan smile. "Paranoid, remember? I'm not so good with trusting men not to murder me in my sleep."

He stared at her for a moment, processing that. "Wow, Andi, that's—"

"Yeah, I know," she said, cutting him off. "I'm morbid. It's one of my most charming qualities." She met his eyes again, hoping the sarcasm in her voice would undo her TMI confession. "But maybe you could stay for a beer or something? Just for a few minutes until I calm down a little more and we're sure the murderer-rapist who possibly wants to wear my skin as a coat isn't coming back?"

He considered her. She sensed he wanted to ask more questions, but to his credit, he simply nodded. "Sure. A beer would be great."

She let out an audible breath, the amount of relief she felt surprising her. "Awesome. Thanks. Be right back."

Andi returned, finding Hill in her well-worn recliner, and handed him a bottle of Ghost in the Machine beer. "That's my good stuff. Only break it out for special company."

"I'm honored." He took it from her and tipped it back, his throat bobbing as he swallowed. He lowered it and smiled her way. "Oh, that's really good."

"Right?" She took a spot on the couch across from him and

sipped her beer, tucking her legs beneath her. She caught him staring at her feet. She looked down at her toes and then back to him. "What?"

"Uh." A little color came into his cheeks. "What?"

"You were staring at my feet."

He winced. "Sorry. The dark-blue toenail polish caught my eye. I have a bad habit of gathering details about people and coming up with my own story about who they are. It was a game I used to play in my head as a kid after reading a book about an FBI profiler."

"Writers do that, too." She looked down at her toes and wiggled them. "So you think blue nail polish says something about me?"

"Maybe."

She pointed the neck of her beer at him. "Do tell."

He gave her a wouldn't-you-like-to-know look. "Nah, people don't like to be FBI profiled."

She shook her head and smiled. "Oh no. You're on the hook now. What conclusions have you drawn about me? I'll give you a free pass to say what you want."

"There are no free passes in life." He gave her a pointed look as he took a pull from the beer. "That's a trap."

"Oh, come on." She flicked her hand in a bring-it-on motion. "I promise I'm not that sensitive. I write books and do a public podcast. I've had people on the internet post that I'm a hack, that I exploit crime victims, that I'm the reason women shouldn't write horror. Tonight, a reviewer offered to tie me up because I must get off on true crime, and I guess he was up for victimizing me."

His eyebrows scrunched together in annoyance. "The fuck?"

"Yeah, being a woman on the internet is fun. But the point is, you're not going to offend me. Give me your profile."

He stared at her for a moment and then set his beer aside. "All right. On the outside, you seem like a woman who'd be too cool for the room. Nose ring. Bright hair. Quirky toenail polish. Horror novelist. Like the girl in high school who only listened to bootlegged indie rock and who set trends with her retro clothes from Goodwill."

She took a long draw off her beer, amused by how he viewed her.

"The kind who would never date Mr. Popularity or Mr. Student Council President or Mr. Guy Next Door because they were so *not alternative*. Only poets and skateboarders for you."

She lowered her bottle, frowning.

"But you have no visible tattoos. No permanent marker of your alternativeness. And you have this down-home, welcoming, bake-you-brownies warmth about you. So, my guess is this look is something you use to weed people out. You want most people to categorize you quickly and dismiss you, because then you only have to pay attention to the people who see past the surface. Those are the people you think are worth your time. You have lots of friends but few who get your total trust. My guess is that in high school, you weren't too cool for the room, you were the nice girl everyone could count on. The friend people took for granted."

She stared at him. Floored.

He took a gulp of his beer, watching her the whole time, and then gave her a faint smile. "You're about to tell me I'm wrong and I can go to hell, aren't you? That you spent high school touring with a punk band, writing their songs, and dating the lead singer. That you really are too cool for the room."

Andi set down her beer, still processing all he'd said. "You got all that from blue toenail polish?"

"Not solely the polish," he said without elaborating. "Did I get anything right?"

She swallowed past the wave of vulnerability his assessment had brought on and tried for a light tone. "That's some goddamned spooky magic shit, Hill." She shook her head. "You got everything right except the tattoo. I have one. Just not visible."

"Oh."

He glanced down her body, a quick jaunt, but not quick enough for her not to notice. She found she didn't really mind him wondering where her ink was.

"That's a pretty amazing skill," she said finally. "Also, creepy."

He chuckled under his breath, a warm, sexy sound that changed his whole demeanor. "See. Told you."

She let herself take in the view for a moment. The sight of her handsome neighbor relaxing in her living room and shooting the shit soothed something inside her. The muscles that had tightened during the break-in finally loosened. She was glad she'd asked Hill to stay. Even though they were only neighbors, she let herself imagine that he wasn't here because of a scary night. That they'd gone on a fun date, had some drinks, seen a movie, and now they were hanging out and getting to know each other. Something normal. Something light.

The simple act of having a date over was so fraught for her. Something other people did without thinking, with an ease they took for granted. She wanted to pretend for a little while that she was capable of it.

"So," she said, picking up her beer and wanting to keep the distracting conversation going. As long as they were talking, the fantasy could remain and the demons from earlier tonight would stay away, outside in the dark. "Now that I feel totally exposed, I get to poke at you."

He glanced up, a line appearing between his brows. "I don't remember agreeing to that kind of deal."

"You did. Fine print in the contract. Should've gotten your lawyer to read through it first before you FBI profiled me." She tapped her fingernails along the side of her beer bottle, contemplating how best to torture him. "So. How long ago were you engaged to Officer French Braid?"

He coughed, choking on his beer a little. "Officer French Braid? God, she'd *hate* that nickname."

"Oh well," Andi said with a shrug. "How long?"

"Uh, right up until the point I found out she was screwing my best friend." He instantly winced. Like he hadn't meant to answer so honestly.

Andi's expression soured, her beer paused halfway to her mouth. "Ouch. That sucks."

He cleared his throat, clearly ready to pull the eject cord on this conversation. "Yeah. Wasn't great. But it's been about a year."

She shook her head in sympathy. "Sorry you had to see her tonight."

He shrugged. "It's fine. It's not that fraught. We're different people than we were back when we were together, so it's almost like we're strangers now."

Andi pulled her afghan from the back of the couch and draped it over her legs. "What'd she say about me when y'all went outside?"

He glanced toward the front door and then back to her. "How'd you know she said anything?"

Andi barely resisted rolling her eyes. That cop had disliked Andi in an instant. "Had a hunch."

"Now who's profiling," he said, a teasing note in his voice.

"Tell me I'm wrong."

"Can't. She said she thought you were a sweet girl but a drama queen."

Andi snorted, nearly inhaling her beer. "A sweet girl? Like I'm a five-year-old with pigtails?" She shook her head. "I know who I won't be calling to check on my case. She must think we're hooking up or something."

His forehead wrinkled. "What?"

"Just a vibe I got. She had no reason to dislike me that quickly. I barely talked to the woman. So it must be some residual territorial stuff."

"Huh." He looked pensive and then the corners of his mouth twitched up a little bit.

She shifted on the couch, the change in expression intriguing her. "What's that look about?"

"I don't know." He met her gaze. "I'd like to say I'm sorry if I gave her the wrong impression, but I'm kind of not."

A little tremor of pleasure went through her. "No?"

"Nope. I know it's petty as hell, but on the breakup score sheet, she's landed all the points so far. Having her think I've moved on with someone like you and her being annoyed about it? I'll take the point."

Andi narrowed her eyes. "Someone like me?"

His gaze skipped away and he cleared his throat. "Yeah. You know, someone smart and interesting. Obviously beautiful."

Her stomach dipped. "Oh."

Obviously beautiful? She'd never had anyone call her that. Like beautiful was a fact and not up for debate.

He cringed. "Sorry. I'm making it weird. I'm not hitting on you. All I'm saying is...you're great fake-girlfriend material."

The statement was so unexpected from someone like Hill that a laugh bubbled out of her. "Fake-girlfriend material? Someone's been watching too many rom-coms."

He smiled. "That's probably true. When I was recovering from my injury, my friends forced all the happy-ending movies on me. I wasn't allowed to watch anything dark, so there were a lot of rom-coms thrown at me. My friends were into the forced cheer."

"Ugh, that sounds like a nightmare." She took a slow sip of her beer, trying to settle herself after being called obviously beautiful by the werewolf. *Be cool, Andi.* "If I want comfort, I'm going straight to all the dark and scary stuff. That makes real life seem better because no matter what's happening in my life, at least a psycho with razor fingers isn't trying to kill me in my sleep and a demon's not trying to steal my soul."

"Is that why you're into what you're into?" he asked. "You find it comforting?"

She gave a little shrug. "It's partly comfort. Partly entertainment. It also helps me feel prepared."

"Prepared?" he asked. "What do you mean?"

She broke eye contact, focusing somewhere over his right shoulder. They'd had some honest conversation tonight, but she definitely didn't want to open up that chapter in her past. He'd predicted she was the nice girl in high school. What was closer to the truth was that she'd been the girl desperate for everyone to like her. So desperate she'd ignored what had been right in front of her face. "Most people want to ignore the dark stuff. Pretend it's not there. Imagine that human nature is inherently good. Close their eyes. *If I don't see it, then it can't hurt me.* But it *is* there—horror, crime, truly evil people—and once I realized that, I refused to ever look away again. If something bad is going to get me, I at least want to see it coming and have a chance—and a big-ass can of pepper spray."

He frowned. "But what about the supernatural stuff? Do you think a vampire is going to get you?"

She laughed without humor. "The monsters are metaphors for real-life horrors." She lifted a finger. "Though my jury is still out on ghosts. And it sounds weird, but horror is often about hope. We want to believe we can be the final girl. That the good guys or girls can still beat evil despite it all. I mean, Laurie Strode in *Halloween* is a badass. The kids in *IT* are terrified but determined to win. They never stop fighting."

Hill set down his beer on the side table, a thoughtful look on his face. "I never thought about it that way."

"Yeah, well, lots of people dismiss the horror genre as exploitative and cheap. But it's been around so long for a reason. We get something out of being scared. It's important." She laid her head back against the couch. "And Andi will now step off her why-people-should-respect-the-horror-genre soapbox. Sorry."

"Don't be," he said, his deep voice like distant summer thunder. "It's good that you're passionate about what you do."

She lifted her head, trying to determine if he was being sarcastic or serious. "You have feelings on horror?"

"Not really. By the time I was old enough to be interested in exploring any of that, I lived with my aunt and uncle. They didn't allow me to watch or read that kind of stuff." He reached down and grabbed the handle on the recliner to lift the leg support. "Partly because of their religious beliefs, but more because I think they worried it would warp my brain or something."

She wrinkled her nose. "Bummer. Did you go out and watch or read all the things once you were a grown-up?"

He reached down, absently massaging the knee above his prosthesis. "Not really. I guess I didn't feel like I was missing out on anything. Plus, I used to see a lot of real-life horror at my job. Why come home and see more of it?"

Her lips parted. "So, wait, you're telling me you've never really watched horror movies?"

"I watch thrillers sometimes," he said, an unsure note in his voice. "Do superhero movies count?"

She sat up fully now, setting her beer aside, the shock of this new information making her voice rise. "Those don't count. Thrillers are adjacent to but different from horror. So no *Nightmare on Elm Street* or *Poltergeist* or *The Ring* or *Misery* or—"

He laughed at her overt shock. "No. I guess I'm a horror virgin."

He didn't look like a virgin of anything. Those old-soul eyes of his looked like they'd seen the world a few times over. But she believed him on this one. "Unacceptable. We have to fix this."

He shook his head. "We do not. I promise. I'm good."

"Nope. This cannot stand." She frowned. "Unless you're scared of the movies, because then I wouldn't force them on you and—"

"It's not about being scared," he said, cutting her off. "I don't think anything in a movie would be scarier than some of the stuff I've seen on the job."

"Then we're fixing this. You have no idea what you're missing out on." She got up and walked to her shelves of DVDs, already scanning, determining. "We need to break up all that rom-com brainwashing you got. Plus, watching movies gives me much-needed writing inspiration, and it will be more fun to do that with company. I need to put together a syllabus."

"A syllabus?" he asked, amusement in his voice. "Andi..."

But it was too late. The starter pistol had been fired. She was off and running. "This could be a great series for the podcast. Me introducing a horror virgin to the classics. It could be—"

The chair squeaked as he shifted. "Whoa there. You went from zero to podcast series in two point three seconds."

She turned to him, her mind moving too fast for his protests. "You said you had some free time on your hands, right? This could be a fun project, and my podcast could really use an injection of something new and lighthearted. I've been wanting to put something fun in the Friday slot."

"Andi."

"And have you *heard* your voice?" She put her hand on her bookcase of DVDs. "I mean, it's like melted butter and molasses had a baby. I would listen to anything in your voice. You could read me the ingredients on the cereal box and I'd be enthralled."

His eyebrows arched. “Uh, thanks?”

She rolled her lips together, realizing she’d let a little more than she’d planned slip out. “It’s just, your voice is made for radio—or in this case, a podcast.”

“Andi, I don’t know anything about podcasting or being a guest on one,” he said, his voice calm but firm. “I think this is one of those late-night ideas that will look ridiculous in the morning.”

She put on her best pretty-please expression. “Come on. Don’t shoot it down yet. Late-night ideas can be the best ideas. It’s why I keep a notebook and a lighted pen next to my bed. This could be fun. It wouldn’t feel like a podcast. It would be watching movies and then talking about them afterward—just us. Like going out for a drink with your friends after a movie to discuss.”

“Right. Just us. And the world listening to *just us*.”

Just us. The two simple words coming out of his mouth sent a little zap of pleasure through her. Unbidden images flashed through her mind—nights curled up on the couch with Hill, watching scary movies with his big, warm body next to her, her sliding her hands beneath that T-shirt and feeling exactly how furry the werewolf was. *Nope. Stop that.* They were dangerous visions, ones that were way too tempting. This was about the *podcast* and *friendship*. She *could not* get involved with her neighbor and landlord.

She didn’t get involved with guys at all. She didn’t slide her hands beneath their T-shirts. She didn’t do the things she fantasized about late at night. She’d tried that in real life a few times, trying to get past her hang-ups, but it’d been a disaster every time. She’d learned sex could only be good in her fantasies and with a vibrator. In reality, with another human being, it was a terror fest for her and an exercise in confusion and frustration for the guy.

No matter what fantasies Hill stirred up, the only thing they could be was friends. She would need to keep the boundaries clear.

“We could do a few practice runs. If you hate it, we can stop.

I would never post anything without your permission," she said. "You'd have full veto power."

Hill ran a hand over the back of his head, considering her. "How about we start with a movie? Because you've got me curious about the genre. But no podcast promises. I'm a pretty private person and that seems very not private. I don't know if I want comments from listeners about tying me up."

She grinned. "Oh, you'd get some comments, but I bet they'd be date proposals, not death threats." She pointed at him. "Molasses and melted butter, Hill."

He snorted dismissively.

"But I hear you and agree to your terms," she said, meaning it. "We'll start with a movie night. I'll curate a list and provide the movies. You can provide snacks with your mad cooking skills. It will be fun. And educational. And life-affirming because you should not be deprived of the best genre that ever existed in the world."

His expression turned amused. "Not that you're biased or anything."

"Course not." She rocked forward on her toes. "So..."

He released an audible breath, and she sensed victory. "So, I agree to a movie-night trial run. I could hate the genre."

She smirked. "Or get nightmares from it."

"True," he said with a solemn nod. "If I start having to leave the lights on at night, I'm out."

She rolled her eyes. "Yeah, I'm sure you're the scaredy-cat type." She flicked her hand toward him, indicating his general size. "You ooze frailty."

He smiled a truly wolfish grin. "Delicate like a flower."

"Uh-huh."

"I do have a hard line though," he warned. "No bug movies, especially spiders."

She lifted her hands. "Got it. My hard line is torture movies."

He looked surprised. "So the horror writer is afraid of some things, huh?"

She scoffed. "Hill, the horror writer is afraid of *all the things*. That's why I can write it so well. You can't write horror if you don't know fear."

He frowned at her attempt to be flippant. But before Mr. FBI Profiler wannabe could dig deeper on that, she began to list movie categories they should sample first—slasher classics, possession movies, teen horror.

But she only made it halfway through the list before she could feel exhaustion hitting her. Hill got up to grab them another beer, and she settled back on the couch, but she didn't remember him bringing it back.

By the time the sun started to peek through the blinds, she'd dozed off on the couch, a half-written list in front of her, and Hill had zonked out in her way-too-comfortable recliner.

He'd broken her rule. He'd slept over.

She'd broken her own. She'd let him.

chapter **eight**

Something warm touched Andi's shoulder, and she vaguely registered that she should look into that, maybe open her eyes, but right now she was floating on a boat in the middle of a lake, the sun warm on her, the sound of lapping water in her ears. She couldn't remember where she was. A vacation? Summer camp? She hoped it wasn't summer camp. The scene suddenly felt a lot like the final scene in *Friday the 13th*. No. That couldn't be it. She was fine. She was safe...

Wait, was she *naked*?

"Andi." A deep, melodic voice floated into her ears. Pressure on her shoulder.

She clenched the side of the boat, the thing rocking beneath her, fear leaking in. "No."

"Andi." Louder this time.

She opened her eyes, the bright sky blinding her for a moment, and then a hand burst out of the water and grabbed her, tipping the boat, and—

A scream ripped out of her, and her body jolted upright, the sky disappearing and her head whacking into something hard.

"Shit," the deep voice said.

"Ow." Andi's vision cleared as she reached for the stinging

spot on her head, and a handsome, wincing face came into view. No lake. No hand. No summer camp. "Hill?"

Her neighbor looked chagrined, sitting there on the edge of her couch cushion, as he rubbed his forehead. "Sorry. I didn't mean to scare you. You all right?"

She shifted to sit up fully, the whole thing still feeling like a dream. The sun shining through the curtains. Her neighbor's hip pressed up against her thigh. "My head hurts."

"I've heard headbutting people has that side effect." He lowered his hand, revealing a reddening spot on his forehead.

She hissed in empathy and reached out to push his hair away from the spot. "Oof, sorry. I think I was having a nightmare."

"Yeah, you were mumbling. I wouldn't have woken you, but I need to get back to my place, and I didn't want to leave you without letting you know. Or leave your door unlocked."

Andi lowered her hand, the night coming back to her along with a ripple of anxiety. "Oh. Right."

Hill shifted to the other side of the couch so his hip was no longer pressed against her. "Your head okay?"

She touched the spot on her forehead again to make sure she wasn't bleeding. "I'll live. I'm sorry I headbutted you. What time is it?"

"Almost eight. I wanted to get on the phone early to make sure I can get the locks changed and maybe the alarm installed today," he said, his voice still groggy from their late night.

Their late night. Jesus. The reality of that rushed over her. She'd fallen asleep with a stranger in her house. *A guy had slept over.* "You stayed the night."

He scrubbed a hand over his bearded jaw. "Yeah, sorry about that. You nodded off, and I didn't want to wake you, but I also didn't want to leave without telling you. I guess I fell asleep eventually, too. My night-shift muscles must've atrophied. I used to be able to pull all-nighters with no problem."

She tugged her afghan around her shoulders, chilled. "I'm sorry. I didn't mean to keep you here all night."

His lips lifted at the corner. "It's fine. I wish it hadn't been under these circumstances, but I enjoyed hanging out. Plus, I got a fake girlfriend out of it."

A little laugh slipped out at that. *Girlfriend.* The word being directed at her sounded both foreign to her ear and enticing in his voice. "Should we take a pic together with our bedheads so you can put it on your Facebook? Because dollars to doughnuts your ex still follows you there."

"Nah. We're good."

She shifted on the couch. "Did I dream that you agreed to do a few podcast episodes with me?"

He gave her a don't-try-it look. "I agreed to watch horror movies with you and to bring snacks. That is the extent of our contract."

"Right, right, right," she said, nodding firmly. "Of course."

He touched his head gingerly again. "Well, I better get going. You need anything before I head out?"

"Let's see, Chef. A three-egg cheese omelet with sliced tomatoes and sprinkle of chives on the side. A glass of freshly squeezed orange juice. Maybe some biscuits with fresh churned—"

He laughed and pushed up off the couch. "Goodbye, Andi."

She stood, letting the afghan fall away. "Wait."

He turned to her.

Before she could think better of it, she stepped forward and wrapped her arms around him, giving him a hug. Hill froze for a moment, arms stiff by his sides, but then his muscles relented and he returned the embrace.

"Thank you for last night." She squeezed him, finding the guy didn't have any give. He was solid as a wall. "It was above and beyond."

He cleared his throat and patted her back awkwardly. "It was no problem."

She released him and stepped back, meeting his gaze. "No. You turned a horrible night into something much less horrible. If you hadn't stayed, I'd have been a ball of anxiety all night and wouldn't have slept a wink. So, thank you. Also, I appreciate you not murdering me in my sleep. Bonus points for that."

He nodded once and tucked his hands in the pockets of his sweats. "You're welcome. And I'll let you know about the locks and the alarm," he said, holding the eye contact. "I'll make sure you feel safe tonight."

The promise and the way he said it in that sleepy sex voice of his sent a hot shiver through her. Part of her hated discovering that one of her hell-yeah buttons was this alpha-male protective thing he did. She'd never been attracted to that before. Her crushes tended to be on artsy, laid-back types. But with Hill, that modern cowboy vibe did something to her.

She felt her cheeks and neck growing warm. "Thanks. And I'll let you know what I choose for our first movie da—experiment."

A little smile peeked through. "Looking forward to it."

With that, he headed back over to his side, giving her a brief wave before he stepped through the door.

....

Hill walked inside his place with his head pounding and his cock half-hard, wondering what the fuck had just happened. All night, he'd kept himself in check with Andi. He could hang out with an attractive woman and not make it about attraction. But seeing Andi there in the morning sunlight, wearing his shorts, her skin flushing a pretty pink for whatever reason, he'd imagined an entirely different kind of night taking place.

What else would turn her skin rosy like that?

No. He didn't need to let his brain go down that path. Andi had called what they were doing with the movies an experiment. Not a date. They were neighbors. He was her landlord. She was too young for him both in age and spirit. Plus, she'd straight up told him that she didn't have guys sleep over. He didn't understand exactly what she'd meant by that, but he understood enough. Ms. Andi Lockley wasn't looking for sweaty sheet time with the neighbor. What she'd offered was an invitation to become friends. Buddies.

Of course that would be all she wanted from the "grumpy werewolf" with the disability and the cheating ex. He was kidding himself if he thought he'd sensed anything more than that between them. And what could he offer her anyway besides a good time or two in bed?

He was in no place to be someone's boyfriend. Opening himself up to someone like he had with Christina was never going to happen again. It had taken so much to get to that point with her, to finally trust that love could be good, that it didn't have to hurt or be dysfunctional like it had been between his parents. But he'd stupidly left himself without armor. Finding out about Christina and Josh had ripped through him like a chain saw. It'd hurt so much worse than losing part of his leg. It'd shredded every fairy tale he'd told himself, proving what he'd known from the start. Love was fucking dangerous. It was walking into a gunfight without a bulletproof vest.

The price was way too high.

He hoped to have sex again one day. But falling in love? They could fucking keep it.

Feeling clearheaded for the first time since Andi had banged on his door last night, Hill went to the kitchen to brew some coffee and then pulled out the ingredients to make a quiche. He needed something else to occupy his brain. He didn't need to worry about how beautiful his neighbor was. He didn't need to wonder what it'd be like to kiss her or touch her. All he needed to worry about was making sure she was safe. He couldn't offer her much, but he could offer her that.

....

Andi set a venti cold brew on Eliza's desk late that afternoon, her unspoken payment for a makeshift therapy session with her friend. Andi had stopped seeing her official therapist a year ago because she couldn't afford it anymore. But when her friend Eliza, who rented space at WorkAround for her therapy practice, found out, she'd offered to be an unofficial sounding board for Andi. *Not your therapist but an educated opinion.*

"Ooh, thanks." Eliza grabbed for the coffee with a smile. "I'm in desperate need of caffeine."

"You and me both, sister." Andi yawned and collapsed onto the giant red couch Eliza had found at an estate sale and just *had to have*. She'd called Andi, so excited about the find, and had asked her to help gather troops to move it into the office. When Andi had seen the overstuffed monstrosity, she'd thought it had to be the least therapy-like couch ever—too bright, too big, too much. But then she'd sat on it. The thing was like a hug in couch form. And though the dirt-cheap price Eliza had gotten it for meant someone had *definitely* been murdered on it, Andi didn't care. That couch was magic.

Andi needed some magic today.

"So, hey," Andi said flatly.

Eliza's dark eyebrows lifted as she sipped her coffee. "That is the least Andi-like 'hey' ever." Her brown eyes narrowed. "And you're so pale I can see your freckles. What's up, *chica*?"

Andi blew her bangs away from her eyes. "I'm pretty sure someone broke into my house last night."

Eliza set her cup down, her lips parting. "Oh my God. Are you all right?"

"I'm not hurt," Andi said, slipping off her flats and swinging her legs onto the couch. "I'm not exactly all right either."

"Oh, honey," Eliza said, tone gentle. "I'm so sorry. Did they take anything?"

"Besides my already-shitty sense of security?" Andi huffed. "No. Not that I can tell. The police think the door might've blown open, but I *know* I locked it. They're not going to gaslight me about it."

Eliza nodded, frowning. "Good. Don't let them. You know what your habits are."

Andi rubbed her forehead, a vague headache lingering at the spot where she'd headbutted Hill this morning.

"So I'm guessing you didn't get any sleep," Eliza said, leaning back in her chair, her curtain of dark hair framing her concerned face. "You could've called me, you know. Stayed at my place."

"I know. I would've, but my neighbor ending up staying with me," she said, the image of Hill sitting next to her this morning coming back to her. "I ran over to his side of the house when I discovered the back door was open. He stayed after the cops left to help me calm down."

"Wait. The retired firefighter?"

Andi pulled her knees to her chest, wrapping her arms around them. "The very one. Though 'retired' doesn't seem like the right word. He's got a below-the-knee prosthesis from what I assume was an on-the-job incident. He was taken off duty."

Eliza's expression sparked with interest. "Oh. I was picturing an old guy."

"Oh no. This guy is definitely not old. Probably around thirty. Could definitely pose shirtless in the firefighter calendar."

"Oh."

It was the kind of *oh* that meant *tell me everything.*

"He slept over." The words fell out. Flat. Still slightly shocking even to her ear. She'd let a stranger *sleep in her house.*

Eliza blinked as if Andi had started speaking another language. "Wait, what? Holy shit, Andi—"

She lifted a hand. "Don't get too excited. I don't mean he slept in my bed or anything. *I* didn't even sleep in my bed. It wasn't some breakthrough. It was inadvertent. He offered to stay a while so I could calm down. We got to talking, and I eventually dozed off."

Eliza took a slow sip of her coffee. "Wow. Inadvertent or not, that's still a pretty big deal. You were able to let your guard down enough to fall asleep with him in the room."

Andi shook her head, still searching for an explanation—like she'd been doing all day. "I think I was just exhausted."

"I'm sure, but don't you think you had to trust him on some level to even let yourself doze off?" she asked, that probing therapist tone entering her voice. "Normal Andi would've sent him out the door the minute she felt sleepy."

Andi rubbed the bridge of her nose, her head *pound, pound, pounding.* "Yeah, I don't know. Nothing about last night was normal. Hill seems really nice, but he's also kind of hard to read. He's quiet. But that kind of observant quiet where you can see he's thinking all these things he's not saying. He could have all kinds of secrets. He could have bodies in his freezer next to the ice cream for all I know. But..."

Eliza cocked her head a little. "But?"

"Ugh, I don't know." Andi blew out a frustrated breath. "He made me feel safe last night—which I guess, as a firefighter, is in his skill set. But it wasn't that 'We've got everything under control, ma'am' thing. Instead, it was almost like he was wary of *me* instead of the other way around, and *that's* what made me feel safe. Like when he offered to stay over, I got the vibe that he didn't really want me to say yes."

Eliza set her chin in her hand, her pondering face on. "Hmm, interesting. It wasn't an attempt to be coy?"

Andi laughed at that. "Not even a little. I don't think he's interested in me like that. Honestly, I think I freak him out."

"Really." Eliza looked thoughtful. "Huh. What's he look like?"

Andi gave her a sly smile. "If you were really my therapist, you wouldn't ask that."

"Good thing I'm not," she said, giving a conspiratorial look. "So?"

Andi tipped her head back and examined a water spot on the ceiling. How to describe Hill? Normal words didn't seem to fit but she tried. "He's over six feet tall. Dark, shaggy hair. Brown eyes, maybe hazel, because there's some green mixed in. In good shape."

"Sounds like a police description," Eliza said, clearly unimpressed. "Tell me what he looks like *to you.*"

Andi lifted her head and gave Eliza a pointed look. "Bearded, broad, probably prone to growling in bed."

"Oh shit," Eliza said with a laugh. "So he's hot."

"*So hot.* So not my type." Andi sighed. "And I can't tell if what I felt when I woke up this morning and saw him sitting next to me was a result of him making me feel safe last night or if it was something else. I was like...happy to see him there. What the hell is that?" She groaned. "Ugh, I can't get a crush on a guy just because I think he'd be a good bodyguard. That's so fucked up."

Eliza considered her, expression neutral. "Is that such a bad quality to want in a partner? Someone who makes you feel safe?"

"It sounds like my trauma stuff getting twisted up and masquerading as attraction. And I'm not looking to hook up with someone. You know what will happen if I try anything."

Eliza gave her an innocent look. "I do not know what will happen."

"Come on. Don't give me that."

"No, I'm serious. You haven't tried anything physical with anyone in what, three years? Just because it didn't go well the last time doesn't mean that's how it will always go. Hill is a new person. You're a different you than you were three years ago. Maybe the fact that he isn't your normal type is a sign of progress. Your brain is willing to consider someone who physically could be a threat. Normally, you would've dismissed someone like that out of hand."

Andi frowned, a new thought coming to her. "Oh hell, do you think I'm feeling this way because he's got a disability? Like that's some insurance policy? Because that is majorly fucked up and my subconscious needs to be put in time-out if that's the case."

Eliza gave her a ghost of a smile. "Do you think this guy is weak or incapable of physically overpowering you?"

Andi pictured Hill, that wall of muscle, the way he handled everything last night, the way he'd been ready to charge next door to see what was going on. "He could take me down in a hot second."

Eliza pointed at her. "There you go. It's not about his disability. If anything, I suspect it's the opposite."

Andi turned fully toward Eliza. "The opposite."

"Yeah. He's everything you've forbidden yourself to indulge in. He embodies your biggest fears—he could overpower you, could probably throw you over his shoulder and save you from a burning building. But something about him is telling you that he's not there to hurt you. So instead, you can imagine him channeling all that big, aggressive energy into really great sex. It's the very thing you've forbidden yourself from having."

The images those words conjured in her mind—big, aggressive

sex—sent heat rushing to her face. "That doesn't make sense. Why would I want the scariest kind of sex?"

"Because, think about it, it's not actually the scariest type to you," she said. "Your sexual encounters with Evan Longdale were gentle. He used those sociopathic powers of his to manipulate a young teenage girl by being sweet and loving. That was his weapon with you. The wolf in sheep's clothing. So you're not going to trust sweet and gentle because you know the level of violence that facade was hiding."

Andi grimaced. Evan *had* been sweet and gentle. He'd picked up on his little sister's best friend's neighborly crush and had done exactly what he needed to do to keep Andi from looking too hard, from saying anything she shouldn't about all those times she'd watched him come in late, from telling his secrets when she'd seen things in his room she shouldn't have. He violated her with false words and fake romance and gentle sex, saving his sadistic side for the people he stalked and murdered at the nearby college he attended. "That makes me sound so screwed up."

"Absolutely not," Eliza said, her tone sharp. "Don't put that label on yourself. The range of what turns people on is vast. As long as there's consent on all sides and it's legal, who cares? There's no rule that says gentle, sweet sex is the healthy kind. I have clients in the kink community. Some of the things they do would make most people's eyes fall out their heads, but they're perfectly wonderful, well-adjusted people." She shrugged. "Maybe it's time you let yourself feel what you feel and trust that. Your gut is more accurate than you give it credit for."

"My gut had me give my virginity to a serial killer," she launched back.

"You were a vulnerable teenager with a crush who trusted someone you thought was a friend. And you were still a child. You have to forgive that girl for that. You are not her anymore. Your bullshit detector is much more refined now."

Andi sighed. Tired.

"If this guy gets you hot and bothered, let yourself feel hot and bothered," Eliza said, making it sound so simple. "Enjoy that rush of attraction. If you want to try something with him and he's into it, be honest with him. Tell him that you sometimes get anxiety and that you might need to take it slow or stop completely."

Andi groaned and put her hands over her face. "I can't even imagine that conversation. I don't want to dump my past in his lap." She dropped her hands and pasted on a smile. "Hi, I'm Andi. I think you're really hot. By the way, if we get naked and I dissolve into a panic attack, don't worry, it's not you. It's only because my last actual relationship was with a sociopath who murdered people for fun and used me to hide evidence. Wanna make out?"

Eliza gave her a sympathetic look. "You don't have to tell him everything up front. If he's not a complete idiot, he knows that lots of women have suffered traumas at the hands of men. Just tell him you've had a bad experience and need that assurance. If he's not cool with that, then that's all you need to know about him and can move on. And if it makes you feel safer, you can always call me to let me know: *Hey girl, I'm with the sexy neighbor and this lucky bitch is about to have some filthy hot sex*. You know, so he knows someone knows where you are and who you're with."

Andi snorted and threw a couch pillow at Eliza. The pillow hit the edge of her desk and flopped to the floor. "Pervert."

"Sometimes," she said with a laugh. "But really, don't talk yourself out of being open to the possibility. Vibrator technology is great, but there's nothing quite like being skin to skin with someone, naked and sweaty and frantic for each other. That shit is rejuvenating."

Andi squeezed the back of her neck, trying to work out the tension there. "I don't even think it's a possibility. Even if he were interested, I have no idea what I'm doing. I'm like an inexperienced teen trapped in a grown-up's body."

"Probably another reason why this guy appeals to you. He sounds like the type who would take more control in bed. And you know more than you think. You know what makes you feel good. If you can show him what you like, you're all set. Making sure the guy has a good time is the easy part."

Andi snorted. "Nothing about this is easy."

Eliza's expression turned empathetic. "I know, honey. But for what it's worth, I think you're a badass. And you're fucking brilliant. I know that there's no way to guarantee one hundred percent safety out in the world, but I truly believe that your gut is worthy of your trust. It will tell you if this guy is bad news. So maybe see if you can be friends with him. Feel him out. Then, if you're still picturing him naked, make a move. See what happens."

Andi couldn't picture herself making a move, but she also didn't see her attraction abating anytime soon either. "I will get the chance to get to know him better. He's a horror virgin, so he's agreed to watch some movies with me."

A smile brightened Eliza's face. "Oh, that's great. Like watching movies at your place?"

"Pretty much."

"Andi, you sneaky vixen. Getting the hot guy to agree to scary movies. Couch cuddling is almost inevitable. I'm so proud of you!"

Andi laughed. "It's not some grand master plan. I just feel it's my duty to introduce him to the best genre in cinema. Plus, he recently had a bad breakup and seems a little lonely."

Eliza nodded. "Right. He's the lonely one."

Andi rolled her eyes. "Yes. I'm not lonely. I have tons of friends."

"You do," she agreed. But in that therapist way. Like she was saying ten other things, too. "Either way, I'm proud of you.

Inviting a guy over to your place to hang out—whether anything romantic happens or not—is a big step for you."

"Thanks." Andi glanced at the clock. "I better get going. Your next client is probably already here. They pay better than I do."

"I don't know. This coffee is like magic." She stood and smoothed her blouse. "Are you going to be okay tonight? Do you want to stay over at my place?"

"Part of me wants to say yes because that would be so much easier, but I'm afraid if I do that, I won't ever want to sleep at home again. I need to get this first night out of the way." Andi stood and rolled her shoulders, trying to work the tension out. "Hill is getting the locks changed and is looking into getting an alarm installed, so there should be extra protection. Plus, I can't imagine whoever broke in would want to come back the next night."

Eliza nodded. "Good. I'm glad you'll have a few extra layers of protection to help you feel safe. Plus, you know, a hot firefighter neighbor."

Andi laughed. "And there's that."

Eliza came around to the other side of the desk to hug Andi. "I'm glad you're okay."

"Me too. Thanks for the chat," she said, releasing her friend.

"Of course." She wiggled a finger at Andi. "And keep me posted on Operation Hot Neighbor."

Operation Hot Neighbor. Sounded like a bad porn movie from the eighties. "Will do."

chapter **nine**

Hill was eating lunch at the same place he'd been going every nonworking Friday for years. They served thin fried catfish at Lola-Ann's on Fridays, and it was the best fried fish in the state. He used to make a version of it at the firehouse, but he never had the energy to make it for himself, so this was a treat. He could vaguely hear the phones ringing for takeout and the general bustle of the restaurant but otherwise was totally focused on enjoying his food and reading the words in front of him.

On the way to the restaurant, he'd ducked into The Dog-Eared Page, the little independent bookstore on the corner. Usually if he was in the mood to read, he went for travel or food memoirs, but today he'd found himself wandering past those aisles, through the large romance novel section, and finally to the corner in the back where Stephen King had an entire bookcase dedicated to him. But Hill wasn't looking for a King novel. He scanned through the K's and finally found what he'd been hunting for: A. L. Kohl.

He picked up the two books the store had and bought them without reading the descriptions. Now, at his table in the corner, most of his lunch consumed, he was ten chapters into Andi's book, *Thirsty*, a story about an ostracized teen girl who gets humiliated by a viral video calling her *thirsty*, which apparently meant desperate. The girl is devastated, but the night she plans to end her life, someone sends her a mysterious computer program that lets her hack into her classmates' phones and webcams to see their secrets. She starts using the secrets against them, but strange things are starting to happen to the people she's watching.

Hill suspected some supernatural shit was about to go down. He picked up his iced tea, his eyes glued to the page, and sipped. But the sound of his name made him jolt, almost spilling his drink into his lap. "Shit."

He set his glass down, annoyed that he'd startled like a damn cat, and turned toward the sound. His jaw tightened at the sight.

Christina was standing there in uniform, arms crossed. "I figured I'd find you here. I've been trying to call you."

And he'd been trying to ignore that. "What do you want, Chris?"

Without asking, she took the spot across from him. She glanced at the novel in his hand and snorted. "What in God's name are you reading?"

He tore off a piece of his napkin and tucked it between the book's pages to save his spot. Despite purchasing the book at a place called The Dog-Eared Page, he was staunchly anti-dog-earing. He set the novel down. "You need something?"

She picked up the book and eyed it, her brows arching. "High school horror? Since when do you read this stuff?" She flipped it over to read the back. "Or is this thinly veiled porn? Are there lots of big-boobed cheerleaders at this haunted high school?"

His jaw tightened, and he reached out to take the book from her. "It's not porn. Andi wrote it."

Christina's gaze flicked to the name on the cover. "Ah, the neighbor girl who's a horror writer."

Hill sniffed at her insistence on calling Andi a girl. "A multi-published author."

"Well, that explains why she can't admit that she didn't latch her door all the way. Maybe she thinks a ghost did it." Chris wiggled her fingers and made a spooky ghost sound.

"Chris," he warned, his patience thin. He was not in the mood to deal with his ex right now—or ever really.

"So, you dating her or something?" she asked.

"Not sure how that's your business," he said, a nonanswer if ever there was one.

"It's not, but I'm nosy. And if you are, I think that's...good. She seemed...colorful."

His fist curled against his thigh. "Why are you here?"

Chris sighed and ran a hand over her braid, a nervous gesture she'd had since he'd known her. "Yeah, fine. God forbid we try to have a civil conversation. I'll get to the point. I just wanted to let you know that Josh and I are getting married."

Hill's stomach dipped, but he kept his expression smooth. "Okay. Am I supposed to say congratulations?"

She rubbed the spot between her eyebrows like she was the adult trying to deal with a petulant child. "You don't have to say anything. I only wanted you to hear this from me instead of one of the guys at the firehouse." She took a breath and lowered her hand, something shifting in her gaze. "I also wanted to tell you that I'm pregnant."

If the first confession had pushed him back a step, that one knocked him flat on his ass. When he and Christina had gotten engaged, he'd lain in bed that night next to her, imagining their life-movie montage. One where he pictured them getting a house together, babies being born, him running around with his kids. The kind of family life he hadn't experienced as a child. A happiness he'd never experienced in his whole life.

He'd let go of Christina when he'd found out she was cheating with Josh—anger making the breakup quick and sharp—but now those other visions came rushing back. The realization that he'd not only lost her in that moment, but he'd lost that movie montage, that future. But she hadn't. She was going to do it with someone else. He was going to have to watch her have kids with someone else.

Christina was staring at him, not gloating, not smirking. Instead, she looked…sad for him. "I just wanted you to know."

He cleared his throat and tried to cover whatever emotion he'd revealed. The pity in her voice made him want to break things. He grabbed his straw and stabbed the ice in his cup. "Well, that's… good. I mean, good for you. I know you've always wanted kids."

She let out a breath and looked down. "Thanks."

"Yeah," he said, not knowing what else to say.

She glanced up, her eyes a little shiny. "I hate this."

"What?"

She flicked her hand between them. "This. How things are between us."

He scoffed. "Chris, I don't know what you expect. You and my best friend screwed behind my back. While I was still recovering from a catastrophic injury. The minute I wasn't Captain America anymore, you jumped ship. It doesn't leave a guy with great feelings."

She rolled her lips together and shook her head. "I know. I'm so sorry for how things happened. In no world is that okay. I know you'll never believe me, but what happened with Josh had nothing to do with your injury and everything to do with how I felt when I started spending time with him. It made me realize that what I felt for you was affection and friendship but not that turn-your-world-inside-out kind of love. If we had gotten married, it wouldn't have lasted. We didn't have that *thing*, that thing that gets couples through all the hard stuff. In the end, this was best for both of us."

The words stung like vinegar over a cut. Maybe she hadn't loved him, but he'd loved her. "Right. So you're the heroine in this story? Saving us from our doomed fate by cheating on me? Got it. Where's that medal of honor? Let's schedule the award ceremony."

Her jaw flexed. "I'm trying to be honest with you, but I guess you don't want to hear it. You want to be the victim." She stood. "You know, I hope one day you realize I'm right about how we would've turned out and stop feeling sorry for yourself. It's not a good look, Dawson."

He kept his expression mild. "Are we done here?"

She crossed her arms. "Yeah, I guess we are."

He smirked. "I look forward to my wedding invitation. I'm assuming you'll toast me for bringing you two together."

"God, you're such a dick sometimes." She grabbed her phone off the table and strode out.

"One of my finest qualities," he muttered as she left.

When he was alone again, he leaned back in his chair and rubbed a hand over his face, exhausted by the exchange. He didn't want to fight with Chris. He didn't want to share *any* emotion with her anymore. But every time he saw her, it reminded him of who he was now, of the life he'd lost. She was moving on. Marriage. A baby. She was heading toward the future he thought would be his.

And what the fuck was he moving toward?

Another night at home alone with a stack of cookbooks and no one to cook for.

He couldn't face that solitude tonight. He glanced at Andi's book, and without thinking too hard about it, he grabbed his phone. It'd been almost a week since the night he'd slept over. He'd gotten an alarm and new locks installed. He'd checked on her a few times, but they'd both been busy and hadn't talked much. She'd said to let him know when he was ready for a movie. He'd responded vaguely.

He was tired of being vague.

He found her name in his contacts.

She answered on the second ring. "Hey, Werewolf, what are you doing awake during daylight hours?"

Just the sound of her upbeat voice smoothed some of the jagged edges his conversation with Christina had caused. "Shh. I'm in my human form during the day. Don't tell anyone my secret."

She laughed. "Your secret is safe with me. What's up?"

He picked up his fork and stabbed at his napkin, steeling himself for a no. "I was wondering if you wanted to make tonight our inaugural movie night? I know it's last minute and if you have plans or work to—"

"I'm in," she said, cutting him off.

"Yeah?" His shoulders relaxed and his lips curved.

"Absolutely. That sounds perfect actually. I've edited two podcast episodes today and spent last night wrestling with writer's block. I could use a break." She made a sound like she was covering a yawn. "You have any special requests for the first movie? Ghosts? Slasher? Monsters? Trashy? Sophisticated?"

"I'm a true horror virgin, so maybe let's start out with something you consider foundational. I might not appreciate a later movie as much if I haven't seen what came before."

"Ooh, foundational," she said, enthusiasm in her voice. "Is it nerdy that you saying that totally makes me want to build a lesson plan so I can school you?"

An image of Andi with glasses, a ruler, and a stern teacher expression flashed through his brain. Blood rushed south. He cleared his throat, trying to push away the pervy thoughts. "I'm fully prepared to be schooled."

"Yay!" she said with glee.

He closed his eyes and absorbed the exclamation points in her voice. Her unchecked enthusiasm was like inhaling a warm spring breeze after a long winter. He loved her utter lack of self-consciousness about how she was feeling. After what he went through as a kid, he'd spent his life honing his stoicism. When enough kids bait you with *Hey, freak, I heard your dad's a drughead*, you learn not to react to anything. To see someone so... *out there* like Andi was a novelty.

"I've got lots of movies I can pick from," she went on. "Why don't you come over around seven?"

They had plans. He already felt buoyed. "Tell me what I can bring."

"An open mind and your drink of choice." Something squeaked on her end, and he pictured her rocking in her desk chair. "Do you like pad thai? I can pick up some takeout on my way home, my treat."

"How about I make some and bring it over?"

"Really? You know how to make that?" she asked, sounding impressed.

"Yeah, I used to make it sometimes at the firehouse. It's quick if you've got the ingredients. Are you pro-tofu or anti-tofu? Because I can make it vegetarian or with chicken."

"Vegetarian sounds great. Thanks." She paused. "And I'm glad I'm not a betting woman because I would've lost this bet."

He picked up his unused fork and twirled it between his fingers. "What bet?"

"I would've bet the farm that you were going to back out on our movie project. So, this is a nice surprise."

He *had* almost backed out. He didn't trust himself around Andi. She made him want things he'd taken off his list of options. But right now, he didn't want to think that hard about it. He'd been overthinking his whole life since the day of the accident—maybe even before that. Tonight, he wanted a break from it all. Good movie. Good food. And a pretty woman who made him smile.

"I'm glad the invitation still stands," he said.

"I'll double-check it's not a full moon," she teased. "Don't want to get bitten."

He laughed, but the words conjured images he *definitely* didn't need to be picturing sitting in a restaurant. His mouth on Andi's creamy smooth skin. His teeth grazing her neck. Her red-glossed lips wrapped around his... He shoved the images from his brain, searching for something to say. "Waxing crescent tonight. You're safe."

"Phew," she said with a dramatic flourish. "Wait, should I be concerned that you know the moon stage? Who knows that off the top of their head?"

"Andi."

"Werewolves, that's who," she declared.

He chuckled. "I was only guessing. I have no idea what the moon phase is tonight."

"Uh-huh. Don't think I'm not going to google it now." He heard typing on her end. "All right, we're good. It's a new moon—the moon of new beginnings—so it's perfect for our inaugural movie night."

New beginnings. That sounded nice, even if he'd learned new beginnings were impossible. Life didn't really give you redos. The past didn't get undone. Like when he'd moved in with his aunt and uncle, his life had improved dramatically, but living in a new place with a new family didn't erase the marks his old life had left on him. "Sounds great. I'll see you tonight."

"I can't wait to eat food that doesn't come from a takeout container or a can," Andi said, sounding genuinely excited. "Later, neighbor."

Andi's enthusiasm was catching. Hill hung up the phone with

a dumb grin on his face and turned back to the book, forgetting all about the exchange with Christina.

On his way out of the restaurant, he texted Ramsey.

Hill: I'm having movie night with the neighbor.

Ramsey responded within seconds with a GIF of Will Ferrell yelling "Awesome!" and punching boxes in the grocery aisle. Followed by:

Ramsey: Inertia plan activated. Bring condoms.

Hill: This is a just-friends movie night.

Ramsey: Buzzkill. But good luck, brother.

Hill sent a GIF of a fist bump. He had no idea what to expect tonight, but he knew he definitely wouldn't need condoms. Either way, he already felt better. Maybe Ramsey's inertia theory was more accurate than Hill had given him credit for.

He'd never tell him that, though. The guy's ego was big enough.

....

Andi pondered her closet and shook out her arms, nerves making everything tingly. She'd been shocked to hear Hill's rumbly voice in her ear when she picked up her phone this afternoon. She'd gotten the sense he'd been avoiding her since the night he stayed over, but today on the call, he'd sounded downright eager to get together. She wasn't sure what to think about the change.

She'd happily accepted the plans on the phone, but afterward, she'd been racked with a bout of anxiety. She was having a guy over. It wasn't a date, but it wasn't...not a date. And he was her *neighbor*. For anyone else, that would simply mean potential for awkwardness. For her, it was triggering as hell. All her old demons were nipping at her heels like rabid hyenas, trying to take her down. And that was before she even contemplated the fact that he was also technically her landlord.

She grabbed her phone off her nightstand and dialed Eliza—again. She'd already updated her on the situation when she'd seen her at WorkAround today. As soon as Eliza answered, Andi barked out, "What should I wear? What says 'Hey, we're just friends' but also 'Look how pretty I am'?"

Eliza laughed. "Be comfortable. Look casual. Show some skin."

"Jeans and my purple *Save the Chubby Unicorns* tank top it is," Andi declared.

Her friend snorted. "What's a chubby unicorn?"

"It has a drawing of a rhino." Andi grabbed the shirt from her closet.

"Perfect, that will show skin and personality." Eliza paused. "You gonna be okay? Do you need me to call and check in with you?"

Andi blew out a breath, so thankful for her friends that she could barely contain the gratitude. "I'll text you by nine to let you know how I'm doing."

"You've got this, girl," Eliza said, utter confidence in her voice. "Try to relax and have a good time. Listen to your gut. Or you know, parts lower than that if the situation arises."

Andi rolled her eyes. "Goodbye, Eliza."

"Love you."

"Same."

Andi ended the call, stripped out of the clothes she'd worn to the office, and changed into her outfit. She eyed the result in the mirror. Casual and cute and her boobs really did look great in this top. Winner.

She barely had time to pin her hair into a messy bun before the doorbell rang. A little zing went through her bloodstream, a mix of anxiety and anticipation. She took a breath, nodded at herself in the mirror in a silent he's-probably-not-a-serial-killer pep talk, and then headed to her front door.

She checked the peephole, typed in the code on the newly installed alarm, and swung the door open. She'd anticipated that she'd feel nervous letting Hill inside. What she hadn't anticipated was the rush of pleasure she got at the sight of him. *Helloooo there.* His dark hair was still damp at the ends like he'd just showered, and his black V-neck T-shirt clung enough to remind her what he'd looked like with his shirt off. The impact of all that gorgeous maleness was enough to rock her back on her heels a little.

"Hey," he said with a small smile.

She wet her lips, feeling nervous energy—part giddy, part anxious—move through her. "Hey, yourself."

He lifted the plastic container he was holding along with a grocery bag. "Food is fresh out of the pan. And I brought margarita fixings—not a traditional pairing with pad thai but usually a crowd favorite. I hope that matches well with losing my horror V-card."

"Margaritas go great with everything." She stepped back to let him in, waving her arm with a flourish. "Welcome, virgin. This will only hurt a little, I promise."

He chuckled and stepped inside. "I'm officially terrified."

She closed the door behind him and took a breath.

Me too.

But there was no turning back now.

chapter **ten**

Andi led Hill into her kitchen, and he set the container and bag he'd brought on her counter. The spiced scent of pad thai filled the room, and her stomach growled. "God, I'm starving."

"Yeah, lunch seems like a long time ago." Hill pulled out a bottle of good tequila, limes, agave nectar, and something called citrus jalapeño salt, setting it all on her little rollaway kitchen island.

Andi eyed his offerings. "Well, la-di-da, neighbor. Those are fancy fixings. No cheap margarita mix for you?"

His lips hitched up at one corner. "I did a bartending stint at a high-end Mexican restaurant before I became a firefighter. Once I had this kind of margarita, I couldn't go back to the other stuff. I hope you're okay with on the rocks."

"Hey, that's where my writing is right now, so it's fitting," she said with chagrin.

His gaze flicked up to her as he arranged his ingredients. "That bad, huh?"

"Hasn't been great." She grabbed glasses and a measuring jigger and set them in front of him. Then she took out some dishes to plate the pad thai. "The word factory is very unreliable. You put in an order and have no idea if and when those words are going to show up and if they're going to be any good or not. Yet you have to keep showing up at your doorstep every day, hoping for their arrival."

He opened the bottle of tequila and poured some into the jigger. "What's your current story about?"

"Slasher genre, meaning some type of crazed killer. Summer-camp setting à la *Friday the 13th*. I'm trying to take the cliché of that and twist it into something new, but I haven't found the right direction yet. Honestly, I don't even know if it's the right concept to start with." She watched him measure out the alcohol. "I'm hoping our movie watching will fill the creative tank with some fresh inspiration."

"Are we watching a summer-camp slasher?" He lifted a lime. "Knife?"

She stepped around him, opened a drawer, and handed him a paring knife. She had the brief thought that this could be the opening to a horror scene. She frowned.

"What's wrong?" Hill asked, ever observant, as he took the knife and sliced into a lime.

"Huh?"

He drew a circle in the air around her face with his finger. "You look concerned."

She blinked and waved a dismissive hand. "Sorry. My mind goes to weird places sometimes. Don't mind me. No, we're not watching a summer-camp movie, but we are watching a foundational slasher classic. *Halloween*."

He eyed her as he adeptly made their drinks, his hands moving in a dance he'd clearly done many times before. "Tell me where your mind went. I'm curious."

She shook her head. "You don't want to know."

"Now I *really* want to know," he said with a little laugh. "Come on. Lay it on me."

She sighed and leaned back against the counter. "You know, I had trouble imagining you as a bartender because you're kind of quiet, but now I see it. Bartenders get people's stories without them realizing it by being friendly yet chill enough to coax it out of them."

He smirked. "Easier to get people's stories as a bartender. Alcohol makes for a loose-lipped interviewee." He rubbed the lime around the rim of the glass. "Should I wait until you've had a drink before asking again?"

She sniffed. "No, it's fine. You want a peek inside my brain? Well, here you go. I handed you the knife, and I had this vision of a horror scene. Guy is making a girl's drink, asks for a knife, and when she turns her back, he slips something into her drink. She then turns and hands him the weapon he's going to torture her with later when she's too drugged to fight back. Then I got the image of a margarita glass rimmed with blood instead of salt, the villain drinking from it with a smile on his face."

Hill had stopped mixing the drinks and was staring. "Wow."

"Yep," she replied, emphasizing the *p* at the end of the word. "I can pretty much turn anything into something sinister. It's like my personal Instagram filter—one I can't always turn off. Aren't you sorry you asked?"

"No. I find it fascinating," he said, no jest in his voice. "I'm sure that kind of brain helps you write great books. But I also could see how it'd be a hard thing in other situations." He set down the knife, concern in his eyes. "Are you worried I'm going to do something to your drink?"

"Logically, no." She shrugged. "But also, I didn't turn my back while you poured. I made sure the tequila bottle had a seal on it when you opened it. Not because I'm suspicious of you personally but because I've done the *What Can We Learn from This?* podcast long enough that those habits are ingrained."

He nodded. "Smart. I'm sorry that we live in a world where you have to worry about things like that."

The words were simple but helped something unwind inside her. "Thanks."

"And truly, I won't be offended by any safety precautions you take, even if it means being suspicious of me," he said, going back to the drinks. "I know women have a lot more to worry about than guys even consider." He looked over at her, meeting her eyes. "You're safe with me, but feel free to test me on that."

She smiled, the offer warming her from the inside out. "How do you know *you're* safe *with me*? I'm the one picturing blood-rimmed margarita glasses."

"Oh, I don't." He handed her a drink with a wry smile. "You scare the hell out of me, Andi Lockley."

She laughed and accepted the glass. "Good. Be afraid. Be very afraid." She sipped the drink, the delicious tart-sweet combo making her hum with pleasure. "Ooh, that's tasty."

He nodded slowly. "Yes. Arsenic does go down easy. Sweet on the tongue."

She snort-laughed and almost choked on her drink. She shoved him in the shoulder. "Oh my God. You're awful. No poison jokes!"

He grabbed her drink from her and sipped it from the other side, a playful glint in his eye. "There. Now we're both in trouble."

He handed the drink back to her, but her laugh quieted in her throat. She hadn't seen this side of Hill before—this confident, flirty side. The man was damn sexy on any day, but this? This was fan-herself-and-find-the-smelling-salts swoonworthy. She held his eye contact and sipped her drink where he had. He watched her mouth.

That focused gaze felt like a touch.

Worried she'd show how she was feeling all over her face, she pushed off from the counter. "We should eat. Otherwise, this is going to go straight to my head. And drunk Andi will not be a good movie buddy."

Hill's attention jumped back to her eyes and he nodded. "Lead the way."

Andi calmed herself while she plated the food and set up the TV trays so they could eat in front of the television. Hill brought the drinks into the living room, and before long, the two of them were set up side by side on the couch, the DVD in the player.

She took a quick bite of the pad thai and closed her eyes, the sweet-salty-sour combo making her groan in approval. "Holy crap, this is amazing. This tastes like what my takeout aspires to be when it grows up."

Hill's expression transformed, obviously pleased. "I'm glad you like it. It's been a while since I made it, so I was hoping I remembered the recipe."

"It's freaking fantastic. I'm supersmart for making friends with a chef. I don't know why I didn't think of this before." She took another bite before setting her plate down to cue up the movie.

"So," Hill said between bites as she scrolled through the menu. "Why DVDs? Wouldn't streaming be easier?"

"I watch a lot of newer stuff on streaming, but you don't get the extra features that way," she said. "So I try to get my favorites on DVD."

"Makes sense." He took a sip of his drink. "Tell me why *Halloween* is my first lesson."

A rush of enthusiasm went through her, and she realized how much she wanted him to enjoy this. She wanted him to *get* it. So many people didn't. "Well, first, it's a great introduction to a horror staple—the slasher film. The original *Halloween* was, in my opinion, the start of the golden age of slashers. We get the crazed killer who may have a motive, but his kills are mostly random. Random makes it scarier because it means anyone can be at risk. We get the masked killer who can't seem to be killed—which pops up again in movies like *Friday the 13th* and *Scream* and *The Strangers*. We have the final-girl trope—meaning the one woman who either defeats or escapes the killer and is the last left standing—and this movie has a great final girl." She looked over at Hill. "Her journey from sweet to badass is awesome."

"You like the final-girl aspect," he said, taking in her expression.

"It's one of the things I like most about horror movies. People seem to think horror is anti-woman, but I think a lot of it subverts gender dynamics. In most cases, you don't want to be the dude in the horror movie. The dudes get dead. They ride in like the hero to save the ladies and the villain is like—nope. The women save themselves."

....

Hill had stopped eating and was listening intently, watching the sparkle in Andi's blue eyes. This woman wasn't only beautiful, she was fucking smart. He'd sensed that from the start, but hearing her talk about her passion brought that intelligence to the forefront. He bet a lot of people discounted her as the "quirky, cute girl" with her bright hair and nose ring and silly T-shirts. But that outer image was smoke and mirrors.

She stopped talking and smiled when she caught him staring. "What?"

"Nothing. I just feel like I should start calling you Professor," he said. "You probably really could teach a class on this."

She sipped her drink, looking pleased. "Maybe I will one day. Lucky you, you get to be my guinea pig and listen to me wax poetic."

"I'm here for it. So horror movies aren't anti-woman," he said. "I'm taking mental notes."

"Well," she said. "Let's watch. They have their pro-woman moments but also some problematic ones. Like the women who have sex are more likely to die—slut-shaming at its finest. Final girls, especially in older movies, are virgins. That changes over time as culture shifts on premarital sex, but still." She made a sour expression.

"What?"

"I just realized I forgot to ask if you were okay with nudity," she said.

His brain didn't compute for a second. Hearing her ask if he was okay with nudity made his mind go in a decidedly unneighborly direction. *Yes I am. Very much so. How about right now?* "Huh?"

She cocked her thumb toward the television screen. "This movie has boobs. Is that going to make it awkward to watch with your neighbor?"

His mind clicked back into place. "Oh. Boobs. No, it's fine. I've seen those before."

She grinned and reached out to pat his knee. "Good for you, Hill!"

He laughed at her unexpected reaction. "You're weird, Lockley."

She nodded and turned back to the TV. "Yeah, I get that a lot. All right, now that we know you're not going to clutch your pearls over the R-rated parts, we're good to go."

She leaned over and clicked off the lamp, plunging them into near darkness, and hit Play. The iconic fast-paced music even he was familiar with started up, a glowing jack-o'-lantern appearing on the screen. He watched intently as the movie opened with the view of a house, presumably from the killer's point of view.

The killer was spying on the couple inside as they were making out. Hill swallowed a bite. "Uh-oh. Guess *she's* toast."

"Poor nonvirgin," Andi agreed.

Hill sipped his drink, his muscles tightening a little as the killer snuck inside and up the stairs, stalking the girl.

"And here are the previously promised boobs," Andi said, gaze on the screen, fork paused halfway to her mouth.

"Right out of the gate with the nudity. Hello, seventies cinema." Hill winced when the killer attacked the girl. "This music is intense."

"Music can make a horror movie. And the use of silence, too. This movie does both really well." She kept her eyes on the screen, and he watched her profile in the blue-silver light. "It's a tool filmmakers have that I don't get to use in my books. I wish I could force people to listen to a certain soundtrack while they read my books."

"Your books are scary enough on their own," he said before he could think better of it.

She turned her head, confusion there, and hit Pause on the movie. "You know my books?"

He groaned inwardly. If he was worried about her thinking he was a stalker, he'd just given her a checkmark in the YES column. He forced a shrug. "I saw one of yours when I was walking through The Dog-Eared Page earlier today. I figured I'd give it a try. I'm about halfway through *Thirsty*. You're good at what you do. It's creepy as shit."

"You're reading one of my books," she said as if still processing that.

He narrowed his eyes, trying to pin down her tone. "Is that bad?"

She pursed her lips as if her frown got caught halfway there. "No, it's not...bad. It's... I don't know. I feel a little strange when someone *I* know is reading one of my books. It's this weird vulnerability thing. Like you're seeing my secrets or something—even though I know that's dumb when the book is out there for any stranger to read."

"I can stop."

She waved her fork at him. "No, no, it's fine. I know I'm being weird. Just don't tell me if you hate it. I won't ask you what you thought when you're done."

He smiled at her flash of insecurity. "I already know I'm not going to hate it. It's really good—and darkly funny. And if it helps, I don't know you well enough yet to recognize any secrets that may be encoded in there. Except that maybe you got really pissed at someone in high school and secretly wish for some serious revenge."

Her expression flattened.

"Oh no," he said with a laugh. "Did I actually guess right?"

She stared at him for a second and then scoffed. "Who didn't get pissed at someone in high school?"

He lifted his drink. "Truth."

She gave him one last look and then turned back toward the TV. "Okay, stop trying to distract me with flattery to get out of the scary movie. We're doing this." She hit Play. "Let's meet baby Jamie Lee Curtis and her fashionable tights."

chapter **eleven**

Hill is reading my book. Andi was trying not to pick that apart but...she was totally picking it apart. Was he just curious? Or was he trying to impress her? What did he think of the gory scenes in the book? Or the sex scenes? The story was about a teen but was definitely an adult book. Her cheeks grew warm at the thought of him reading some of the explicit stuff she'd written. Her actual sex life was nonexistent, but her imagination was quite the wild child. Did he think she was into the stuff she wrote about?

More than anything she found herself wondering if this was a date in his eyes or just a friendly thing. She no longer knew what answer she wanted.

Eliza had told her that if she wanted to make a move, to make one, but the thought scared the hell out of her. She didn't make moves on guys. She could be reading Hill all wrong. He could be completely uninterested. Or faking nice. He could be here for a quick hookup. He could be a dangerous guy who was fooling her like she'd been fooled before.

She frowned. That didn't *feel* like what was happening. She peeked over at Hill who was setting aside his pad thai while not taking his eyes off the movie. He sipped his margarita and she watched his throat work as he swallowed. The guy was fucking gorgeous.

Hill startled, a barely there tensing, but she'd caught it because she'd been staring. Even without looking at the screen, she knew what had happened. Michael Myers had appeared, complete with sharp, sudden music.

He glanced over, finding her looking. He smirked. "You didn't see that."

She smiled. "Not many people are immune to the jump scare. No shame. I still jump sometimes, even when I've seen a movie a hundred times and know it's coming."

He considered her, his dark lashes making shadows on his cheeks in the blue-gray light of the television. "But you like that feeling?"

"Being scared in a safe way is a rush." Feeling bold, she reached out and grabbed his wrist, placing her fingers against his pulse point. His arm tensed beneath her touch, but he stayed very still. "Your heart is beating fast. You probably have already gotten a small dose of adrenaline. You're breathing a little harder. It's riding a roller coaster without having to leave your house or risk throwing up."

His heartbeat picked up speed beneath her fingertips, his skin warm and solid under her touch.

She swallowed hard. "It can even make the person you're watching the movie with more attractive," she rambled on, her own heartbeat racing. "Studies have shown that your body mistakes the fear response to the movie for attraction to someone you're with."

His gaze held hers, the movie rolling on in the background. "Is that right?"

She wet her lips and pulled her hand back, feeling ridiculous but unable to stop talking. "Yeah. The arousal response system kicks in."

"I guess I've been doing movie dates wrong all my life then," he said with a half smile. "I thought taking dates to a romantic movie was the way to go. I missed the opportunity to appear more attractive."

She scoffed. "Right. Like you need the help."

A look of surprise crossed his face, and she instantly wanted to take back the slipup.

"I mean, I'm sure being the tall, dark, and fit firefighter who cooks was a real burden," she added.

"Right." Something closed off instantly in his expression as his gaze shifted back to the movie.

She didn't know what she'd said wrong, but clearly he didn't want to continue this conversation. She needed to turn back to the movie, focus on why they were here, but her mouth had other ideas. "Did I say something wrong?"

Hill reached for the remote and paused the movie, turning to her with a frown. "What?"

"You were with me and then you weren't," she said. "Usually that means I've stuck my foot in my mouth again."

He let out a breath and shook his head. "No, sorry. You didn't do anything wrong. It's nothing."

"Which is code for it's obviously something," she said, apparently unable to keep from prodding. "I crossed the friendly line, didn't I? With what I said? I'm sorry. I ramble. I didn't mean—"

"I know you didn't," he said quickly. "You've been clear about what this is—that this isn't a date. I just needed a second to remind myself of that. My lines got blurred for a minute, but I'm good now. We're good."

A whoosh of some unnamed emotion went through her. "Oh." She watched him watching her, a realization coming over her. "Wait—do you *want* this to be a date?"

His jaw flexed like he was ten kinds of uncomfortable. "That's not why I came over. I'm not trying to pull a bait and switch on you. I came over here to hang out with you and watch a movie. No ulterior motives."

She considered him. "That didn't exactly answer my question."

He sighed, weariness on his face. "Because there's no easy answer to it. It's more complicated than that."

She tucked her legs beneath her, turning more toward him. "Try me."

His throat worked and his gaze met hers. "In some ways, yes, I'd like this to be a date. You're an interesting, smart, and beautiful woman. I'd be lying if I said there wasn't attraction on my end. But you're also my neighbor and tenant and a good bit younger than me. And even if there weren't those factors in play, I'm in a weird place in my life right now, so I'm not dating. I promise I came here tonight for the friendship and company. This wasn't some scheme to turn it into something it's not."

Her mind spun at all the information. Hill was attracted to her but currently not dating. In a weird place. She could relate. "Wow, well, okay. That wasn't what I was expecting. I...appreciate your honesty."

"I've made this completely awkward, haven't I?" He scrubbed a hand through his hair. "I'm really good at doing that these days."

She smiled, endeared. "I *should* feel awkward, but for some reason, I think you made me more comfortable. Honesty is my favorite quality in a friend." She gave him a pointed look. "And, for the record, in the spirit of honesty, I think you're superhot."

His eyebrows shot up.

She groaned. "Don't look so surprised. Have you looked in a mirror? Have you tasted your food? But I bet I could out-weird you in the weird-place zone. So I'm glad we're on the same page. We're here to be friends. To watch horror movies. And to possibly boost the ratings on my struggling podcast."

His lips curved at that. "Beautiful yet so pushy."

"That's my tagline." She searched his gaze. "So we're cool?"

His shoulders seemed to relax. "We're cool."

"All right, back to bloody murder."

But before she could hit Play, he put his hand on her forearm, stilling her. She looked over at him.

"Thanks," he said with a little nod.

"For what?"

He gave her arm a gentle squeeze, sending a shimmer of awareness through her, and then released her. "For being pushy. I need that right now. I've been too good at saying no to everything and everyone lately."

She gave him a conspiratorial look. "Oh, if it's pushy you're in need of, you've picked the right new friend. I'm your worst nightmare." She cocked her head toward the TV. "Now pay attention because some day this week, you're coming with me to WorkAround and we're doing that tour."

"Andi."

She reached out and pressed her fingers over his lips. "Nope. You've given me the green light to be pushy. Contract has been signed. You're doomed. So just say yes, Hill. I promise I'll take good care of you. It won't hurt at all."

He stared at her for a long moment but then nodded.

She lowered her hand. "Good."

"But that doesn't mean I'm agreeing to any podcast," he added.

"Of course not." She shifted, turning her body back toward the movie, but landing a little closer to Hill. She could feel the heat coming off him. So much of her wanted to lean in to him, to have him put his arm around her, bend down, and kiss her with those lips she'd just been touching. But now that she knew he wasn't interested in starting anything up with her, that took the weight out of the thoughts. She could indulge in her little fantasies about him without playing the what-if game or trying to read if this was a date or not a date, if he was going to make a move or not, if she was going to panic if he touched her. Boundaries had been set.

She was safe.

....

Hill was engrossed in *Halloween II* after he and Andi had decided to go on to the sequel, but in a quiet part of the movie, deep breathing caught his attention. He turned, finding Andi with her cheek against the back of the couch, her eyes closed, fast asleep.

He reached for the remote and hit Pause, afraid a jump scare would wake her, and checked the time on his phone. Damn, how was it almost one in the morning? After watching the first movie, they'd taken a break and Andi had thrown some premade cookie dough in the oven. Somehow, over warm cookies and cold milk, they'd ended up deciding to make the night a double feature. But his movie buddy had apparently run out of steam.

Of course she had. She'd told him earlier how much work she'd done today. Unlike him, she had actual jobs with actual responsibilities. He should've left after the first movie and given her time to rest instead of selfishly wanting to soak up more time with her.

After she'd admitted that she was attracted to him, the whole night had taken on a different glow. When he'd first gotten there, he'd felt tentative and unsure about what the situation was. Then when she'd made the comment about how he had to have been attractive when he *was* a firefighter—past tense—he'd gotten the message. But then she'd quickly corrected his assumption. She thought he was superhot *now*.

That simple compliment had stirred up something inside him that had been dormant for a long damn time. He hadn't lost his ability to feel desire after everything happened, but *feeling desired* was something he hadn't felt in this new version of his life. It'd been like a shot of adrenaline.

He'd wanted to take back everything he'd said about not dating and being in a weird place and had wanted to pull Andi to him, to kiss her, to show her how he wanted her, to feel her wanting him. To forget that there were any complications with her being his tenant and neighbor, to forget he was in no place to date anyone, to ignore that sex would be all he was capable of offering. But Andi had laid down her own honesty. She had said she was in a strange place, too. She hadn't told him why or what that meant, but he remembered her statement from the night of the break-in. She never let guys sleep over.

There was a story there, and he had a feeling it was an ugly one. He would respect her boundaries.

Careful not to jostle her, he got up from the couch and grabbed the empty plates and glasses from the coffee table. He went to the kitchen and flipped on the light. Andi's kitchen was a mirror image of his on the other side, but hers had a lot more color. A bright aqua toaster, a yellow bowl of apples on the counter, and a collection of Super Mario Bros. fridge magnets complete with turtles, redbrick blocks, and green pipes.

He set the dirty dishes in the sink and glanced up. The window above the sink had a small ledge, and Andi had a line of little, round metal bells sitting on it. He'd noticed another set like it on the windowsill in the living room. They didn't match the rest of her style, so they'd stood out, and he'd wondered if she was one of those people who left Christmas decorations out year-round. He touched one of the bells, but it rolled off the ledge, and he caught it before it could hit the sink. Sensitive little things.

Only then did he realize what they were there for. *Noise.*

If someone tried to break in through a window, it would send the bells rolling and clanging. He glanced over his shoulder back toward the living room, concern moving through him. Was Andi that frightened? He'd had an alarm installed, and the new dead bolts were top quality. He'd wanted her to feel safe, but obviously, she was still worried. He hated that she felt so insecure in her own place.

A floorboard creaked behind him, and he turned, bell still clutched in his palm.

Andi stood in the doorway, arms crossed like she was cold, and her hair askew from her nap. "I fell asleep on you again."

"It's fine. I hadn't realized how late it'd gotten. I was just picking up the dishes." He set the bell back on the windowsill carefully and then turned back to her. "I was going to wake you before I headed out."

Her gaze went to the window, and she rubbed her arms as if chilled. "I see you found my silly security measure."

He tried to gauge her expression. "You still don't feel safe."

She stepped inside the kitchen and shrugged. "I'm not sure I ever feel truly safe, but those were there before the alarm was installed. I left them in case I forget to turn on the alarm."

"Is there anything I can do? To make you feel more secure here?" he asked, stepping closer, concerned about that haunted look in her eyes.

Andi gave him a wan smile. "It's not about the house or the neighborhood or anything like that." She tapped her temple. "It's all up here, unfortunately. There's part of me that knows no one is ever one hundred percent safe, that there's only so much you can do. There is no foolproof plan. But I still try."

His jaw flexed, her tone saying everything she wasn't. "Someone hurt you."

She looked down, her posture closing. "Yeah. Inside a house with the best security system money can buy. So I honestly don't know why I think Christmas bells would help anything."

His lungs deflated as a sharp kick of anger went through him. Someone had *hurt* Andi. Sweet, upbeat Andi. Hurt her badly enough that she never felt safe, that she expected dates to spike her drink and murder her in her sleep, that she spent her life immersed in horror to prepare herself. He wanted to ask all the questions, but he could tell she'd said more than she wanted to.

He moved into her space and reached out, putting his hands on her upper arms. "I'm sorry."

She looked up, black liner smudged. "For what?"

"That you had to go through whatever you've been through. That some pathetic excuse for a human hurt you. I'm sorry you don't feel safe."

"Thanks." She blinked, her eyes going a little shiny. "If it makes you feel better, I feel safer right now."

His chest filled up with relief at that. "I'm glad. You can feel safe with me, Andi. I swear. I've got shit I'm dealing with and my life is kind of a dumpster fire right now, but I would never harm you—or anyone. I became a firefighter because I wanted to be one of the good guys."

She stared at him for a long moment and then stepped forward, bringing her fully into his space. Before he realized what was happening, she slid her arms around his waist, put her cheek to his chest, and hugged him. The feel of her against him was a shock, but his reflexes finally caught up, and he wrapped his arms around her, holding her to him. Her head tucked right under his chin and the smell of her fruity shampoo filled his nose. He closed his eyes and gave himself over to the moment.

But what started as comfort seemed to morph into something else as the hug went on, the air crackling with it. His body began to take notice of Andi's curves, her softness, her warmth. His heart picked up speed. He stayed very, very still.

Her hold on him eased after a while, and she leaned back a

little, looking up at him, so close he could see the dark-blue ring around her pupils. She wet her lips. "Hill?"

"Yeah?" he said, his voice suddenly hoarse as he worried she could read his thoughts on his face. In his previous life, he would've labeled Andi's expression as an invitation to be kissed. But he didn't trust his instincts on that anymore, so he stayed stock-still.

However, he didn't have to worry about misreading things for long because Andi pushed up on her toes and leaned in. He closed his eyes, anticipation rushing through him, but instead of feeling her mouth against his, he felt the soft brush of her lips against his cheek.

"Thanks for coming over," she said softly and then her warmth was gone.

He let out a breath and opened his eyes as she stepped back, trying to get his brain back on track. "Sure. Thanks for the invite. This was fun."

She nodded and gripped her elbows again, looking more closed off than he'd seen her all night.

"You okay?" he asked, frowning.

She gave him a humorless smile. "Yeah, I'm fine. Just tired. I think I pushed past my limit tonight."

He had a feeling her limit wasn't only about the late hour, but he got the hint. "I'll head out. Let you get some rest."

She nodded and they made their way to the front of the house. When he stepped out onto the porch, she said, "I still plan on giving you that tour."

"Look forward to it," he said, the awkwardness growing. "G'night, Andi."

"'Night."

Before he made it to his door, he heard the lock turn on her side and the beep of the alarm.

A sense of loss moved through him as he stepped into his empty half of the house, but he was thankful that at least he hadn't acted on his stupid instinct to kiss her. He really would've ruined things then. He needed to get it through his head that Andi wasn't looking to kiss him or touch him or do anything else with him besides hang out. Hell, she might have just been making him feel better by telling him she thought he was attractive.

His stomach turned at the thought.

Either way, he needed to keep his head on straight around her.

chapter **twelve**

Andi was lying in bed two hours after Hill left, still wide awake. She'd almost *kissed* him. When he'd held her, had been so kind and gentle about her fear instead of dismissing it, that frazzled part inside her had settled for a moment. She'd had the thought, *Maybe him*. Like maybe this was the guy who could finally help her push past her anxiety about getting physical with someone. That maybe she could have a normal night where she'd had a cute guy over and ended the date with a kiss.

But the minute she'd pushed up on her toes, intending to kiss him, a surge of panic had nearly knocked her on her ass. Flashes of terrifying things had flickered through her mind like a horror movie on fast-forward. She was alone in a house with a man—one she barely knew. She'd stopped checking in with Eliza hours ago, so no one knew he was still there. If she kissed him and he wanted to take it further than she did, she'd have no way to physically stop him. All of it had flooded her brain, dousing any desire she'd had with cold water.

She'd kissed his cheek and backed away, hoping to God he wouldn't be able to see the panic coursing through her. She'd been stupid to think she could just *decide* that she could do this now. That she could handle interacting with a guy in that way.

She'd been telling herself a story that when she felt ready, when she found a man she was comfortable with, she could do this. Like it was an actual decision she had control over. Her brain and nervous system had reminded her tonight who was really in control. Anxiety was a fucking dictator, not an elected official. You couldn't simply vote it out of office. Anxiety grinned its evil grin and told you to take a seat.

And that realization had made her...*furious*.

Furious with herself. Furious with the situation. And furious with the disgusting bastard who had broken these things inside her. Even in jail, Evan Longdale was still stealing things from her—her sense of safety, her chance at a normal life, the simple pleasure of being able to kiss a man she'd shared a nice night with.

It made her want to throw things.

It made her want to cry.

It had her feeling trapped in a way that made it hard to breathe.

If she were the star in her own horror movie, the villain was winning. He had been for a really long time. She often liked to think of herself as the badass final girl—that was the kind of heroine she wrote in her books—but she'd been faced with the hard truth tonight. She was no Laurie Strode or Ellen Ripley or Sidney Prescott. She wasn't standing up and facing her fears and telling those fears to fuck off. She was carefully orchestrating a life around them.

And she was fucking tired of it.

She sat up, pushed her blankets off, and got out of bed to grab her laptop. By the time the first rays of dawn started to peek through her windows, she'd already consumed two cups of coffee and had finished a long email to Eliza. Then she took a breath and opened up a new document in the program she used to outline her novels. She clicked to the spot meant for the title of the book.

Here goes nothing.

Before thinking too hard about it, she typed in *The Revenge of Andrea Lockley.*

Time to write a story no one else would see, a new story for herself.

....

Eliza flipped through the mostly blank pages Andi had plopped in front of her at their favorite Mexican place a few hours later. Andi was bouncing her knee beneath the table, hyped up on lack of sleep and too much caffeine. She put another tortilla chip in her mouth, trying to absorb some of the coffee she'd had.

"Well," Eliza said, finally looking up, "I always knew you were smart, *chica*, but you just inadvertently outlined a type of therapy that already exists—with what I'm guessing is no prior knowledge of it."

Andi swallowed her mouthful of tortilla chip. "What do you mean?"

"You wanting to rewrite your own story—making yourself an external character and writing her book—it's a version of something called narrative therapy. I'm not trained in it, but I know the general overview."

"You're shitting me," Andi said, leaning forward on her forearms. "This is a thing?"

"I shit you not," Eliza said with a little smile. "I should've thought of it before. You're a writer. Telling stories is what you do. Recasting yourself as the heroine in the story, modeling yourself after those heroines in the books and movies you like so much, might be really powerful for you."

A little spark of hope went through Andi. "I was lying in bed last night after everything and I was so mad, Eliza. So freaking mad."

"Mad is good," she said, dragging a chip through the salsa.

"And I realized that if I were reading the book of my life, I'd be really frustrated with the heroine. She's overcome a lot, but she's letting what happened to her as a teenager define her life. If I turned in that kind of story to my editor, she'd send it back with red marks about a weak lead who doesn't transform. She's not on the hero's journey."

Eliza gave her an empathetic look. "She's not weak, Andi. Maybe she's just in the early part of her story. Maybe this is only Act One."

The thought buoyed Andi, and she appreciated Eliza talking about her in the third person like she was a separate person, a character. That was the flash of insight she'd had last night. If she could step outside herself and see herself as a character in one of her books, it would be easier to map out a plan. Easier not to get caught up in the anxiety of imagining those moves for herself. "So, do you think this could work?"

Eliza considered her, a little wrinkle in her brow. "I think... that you're capable of anything. Let's get that out of the way first. But"—she flattened a hand against the table as if bracing herself—"I really worry about you doing this without a therapist to guide you. Part of the narrative-therapy thing is that sometimes we tell negative stories about ourselves that aren't necessarily true. A therapist can offer another perspective."

Andi frowned and sagged back in her chair. "I see what you're saying, but therapy is out of the question right now. What little insurance I have doesn't cover it, and this is the first time in a long time I've felt motivated to tackle this, so I don't want to wait until I can afford therapy."

Eliza rolled her lips together and nodded, then a little smirk peeked out. "Well, therapist me will tell you to be careful and that you know you can always talk to me. But friend me is really proud of you and pulling for you. I think you already are a badass movie heroine."

Andi reached out and gave her friend's hand a squeeze. "Thanks, girl. But I was definitely not a badass last night. I had a hot, sweet man who knows how to cook in my kitchen, and I sent him off with a kiss on the cheek and a don't-let-the-door-hit-you-on-the-way-out goodbye." She took a long sip from her margarita—one that wasn't nearly as good as Hill's had been last night. "I wish I could rewrite that chapter for sure."

Eliza lifted a brow. "So do it."

"What?"

Eliza slid the pages Andi had given her across the table. "You're the author. Delete last night's chapter and start over. What would Book Andi do?"

"Is that like WWJD—what would Jesus do?" she asked. "WWBAD? Ha, it spells 'bad'."

"I definitely don't think Book Andi would do what Jesus would do in this situation," Eliza said with a knowing look.

Andi inhaled a deep, fortifying breath and grinned. *WWBAD?* She pulled a pen from her purse and scrawled something on the page.

When she held it up for Eliza to read, Eliza picked up her mojito and clinked it with Andi's margarita glass. "I can't wait to read this book."

"Me too. Hope it doesn't totally suck."

"I hope there are dirty parts."

Andi laughed. "Same, girl. Same."

....

Hill pulled into his driveway after a grocery run and was surprised to see Andi sitting on their shared porch, reading a book in the weather-beaten rocking chair that had come with the house. When she noticed him pull up, she stood and lifted her hand in a wave.

He returned the greeting and took in the view. She had her Doc

Martens on again, but today she was wearing aviator sunglasses and a blue flowery sundress that was fluttering in the breeze. *Damn it all.* He groaned, his mind going to places it shouldn't—like what her skin would feel like beneath his fingertips, like what flavor her lip gloss was, like how easy it would be to unbutton that dress and find every spot that made her sigh. She was temptation personified.

And she'd kissed him on the cheek. *Fucking hell.*

He schooled his expression into one of neighborly appropriateness and climbed out of the car. After grabbing his grocery bags, he headed up the walk.

Andi slid her sunglasses to the top of her head and smiled. "Hey there, neighbor. Need some help?"

His knee-jerk instinct was to say no, that he needed no help, but he stopped himself. Help meant more time with Andi. "Yeah, sure."

She set her book down on the rocking chair and then met him at the top of the stairs. He off-loaded two bags to her and then unlocked the door. She followed him inside, trailing him to the kitchen.

He set his bags down and took the others from her. "Thanks."

"No problem." She leaned over and peeked into one of the bags. "Cooking anything interesting, Chef?"

"Just got the basics today. I keep it pretty straightforward. It's not as fun cooking for one." He started pulling out the things that needed to be refrigerated.

"You know, I'm happy to be your test subject," she said, leaning against the counter and smiling. "I mean, I can probably find time in between my gourmet dinners of grilled cheese and frozen burritos to fit in a meal or two."

He put a carton of eggs in the fridge and peeked back over his shoulder, surprised by the comment. "That can be arranged, but

I hope you're not really surviving by grilled cheese and burrito alone."

She winced. "Boxed mac and cheese makes an appearance sometimes, too. And hot dogs if I'm feeling fancy."

He shut the fridge and turned fully to her, trying to read if she was joking. She wasn't. Knowing that she was living on cheap, food-type products disturbed him more than it should. "No one in your family ever taught you how to cook for yourself?"

She shrugged. "This is going to sound super pretentious, but my parents had hired help, so meals just appeared. If I went into the kitchen while Ms. Jenkins was cooking, she'd shoo me out. Even she knew what a hazard I was in the kitchen."

"Well, of course you were a hazard if no one ever bothered to show you how to cook. It's not something anyone's born knowing how to do." He pulled a few other items from the bags, an idea poking at his brain. He cleared his throat. "I could teach you a few things if you want."

Her expression brightened. "Really? Do you have a death wish?"

He laughed. "I have full faith that I could teach you how to cook something other than boxed cheesy things without anyone dying in the process. It's an important life skill. Cooking and not dying, I mean."

She cocked her head in a playful tilt. "The Horror Virgin teaches the Cooking Virgin?"

"Sounds like a fair exchange to me," he said, glad to hear she still wanted to meet up for movies. "We could add a cooking session to our movie nights."

"So I get food *and* a movie buddy?" she asked. "I'm in."

"Yeah?" The answer pleased him more than he wanted to admit, a buoyant feeling moving through him. "Great."

"But that actually wasn't what I wanted to talk to you about." She bit her lip like she was fighting a cringe.

"Oh? I didn't realize you wanted to talk. I thought you were just a benevolent grocery-carrying neighbor." He quickly put the rest of the cold things in the fridge. He'd organize them later. Right now, he felt like whatever she wanted to talk about was something he needed to pay full attention to.

She scuffed the toe of her Doc Martens on the floor, stalling. He got the impression he was seeing a flashback of what Andi had looked like as a teenager—Andi without her trademark self-assurance. "So about last night. Specifically, about how it ended."

He braced his hands on the small butcher-block table he used for an island, his knee aching. "What about it?"

This was the part where she was going to say he acted weird or inappropriately, that he'd let the lines blur with that hug.

"I think I may have given you mixed signals."

He shook his head. "No, that was my—"

"Because I was," she said, cutting him off. "The signals *were* mixed because I was mixed up."

He swallowed down his retort, not fully understanding. "Okay."

She took a breath, her shoulders lifting and falling with it. "We talked about how it wasn't a date. We set up expectations. Neither of us are dating. We're both in weird places. All true." She wet her lips. "But when we hugged last night, I... Well, I wanted to kiss you."

The floor seemed to tilt beneath him. So he *hadn't* read her wrong. That had been a kiss-me expression. His brain gave a little fist pump. "Oh."

She looked down, color coming into her cheeks. "I wanted to kiss you, but I freaked out at the last minute." She glanced up, her gaze serious. "I panicked. That's what happens when I try to get close—physically—with a guy."

A pang went through him at her somber tone. "Did I do something to scare you?"

She shook her head. "No, it wasn't you. I... It's aftereffects from what I went through in my past."

That knocked the wind out of him. Last night he'd suspected what she'd been through, but now she'd practically confirmed it. At some point in her life, she'd been abused or assaulted. *God.* "I'm sorry, Andi."

She wouldn't look at him. "It's okay."

But it wasn't. And he needed her to hear that from him, not to have her feel so alone and vulnerable. "I don't know what you've been through, but if it helps, I can tell you that I'm not unfamiliar with post-traumatic stress." He swallowed past the dryness in his throat. "I'm dealing with that, too."

Her attention snapped upward. "You are?"

He pointed at his prosthesis. "I lost my leg and suffered some serious burns when a building collapsed on me during a fire rescue. I get flashbacks if I hear anything that sounds like snapping wood. And I wake up from nightmares pretty often. It's why you hear me moving around here so late at night."

He left out the part about his crushing depression. He didn't want her to see that side of him. Andi made him act more like his old self, and he wanted to keep it that way.

Empathy crossed her face. "I'm so sorry, Hill."

He lifted a shoulder. "I'm dealing with it and am seeing someone about it, but I'm only telling you because I don't want you to feel like you owe me some kind of explanation. You wanted to kiss me and then decided you weren't comfortable doing that. That's okay."

She rocked back on her heels. "Would you have kissed me back? We talked about just being friends."

The question sent a ripple of electricity through him. "I stand by wanting to be friends. But that doesn't mean that friends don't sometimes add benefits to that relationship."

She held the eye contact. "So..."

He let out a breath. "Of course I would've kissed you back, Andi. I'd been stopping myself from kissing you all night."

Her shoulders seemed to sag in shared relief. "I don't know what to do with this...this attraction thing. Friends with benefits sounds like such a cliché, and I don't even know that I won't freak out if you did kiss me, but..."

"But what?" he asked, voice quiet, heartbeat loud.

She gave him a helpless look. "But I still want to kiss you."

The words were so honest and raw, so familiar to him. He knew what that feeling was—wanting something but not knowing if you were capable of having it without your demons getting in the way. He fought those wars, too.

"Maybe it doesn't have to be so complicated or defined," he said, the words tumbling out.

"Maybe." She wet her lips, and he found himself transfixed as she pushed away from the counter and stepped closer. "Maybe it could be two people in a weird place who could keep each other company until they find their way out of it?"

Hill swallowed hard and stepped around the island, stopping an arm's length away from her. "I'd like that."

He watched as Andi's throat worked. She was nervous as hell, but there was a determined look in her eyes. She moved into his space and put her hands on his waist. "I think I can work with that."

Hill gave in to the urge to touch her and gently cupped the back of her neck. He felt like he was holding a robin's egg in his palm—something beautiful and special but fragile. He wanted to kiss Andi so badly he ached, but he also sensed if he made one wrong move, he'd crush the egg in his fist. He needed her to be clear. "Tell me what you're asking for."

Her hands were resting lightly on his hips, and her fingers twitched against him. "I need something fun and light with no pressure of any kind. Taking it slow with someone I can feel safe with. A friend. That I can watch movies and cook with but also maybe kiss and touch sometimes." She met his gaze. "And honestly, I don't know if it would move beyond that. I need you to know that. This is basically going to be...an experiment. I may freak out sometimes. Will probably freak out sometimes."

"Experimenting." Enticing images flooded his mind, and he traced his thumb in the tender spot behind her ear. "That sounds kind of amazing."

"Really?" Her gaze widened, and he almost laughed at her surprise.

"Why do you look so shocked?"

"Because most guys are down for a hookup or even friends with benefits, but that's because jumping in bed is implied. I'm telling you I may not get to that point. I'm telling you I'll probably panic sometimes and flat-out reject you."

He released a breath. "Then most guys are dicks. Andi, someone hurt you and violated your trust. You're dealing with the aftermath of that."

She closed her eyes.

"You don't owe me anything," he went on. "A kiss can just be a kiss. A touch can just be a touch. I understand it's not a promise or an invitation for more than that. I understand the word 'no.' I understand the concept of slow. Have you seen me walk? I'm a goddamned master at slow."

She finally opened her eyes and smiled at that.

"Plus," he said, "kissing, touching, making out like teenagers—those things can feel pretty fucking good all on their own."

She bit her lip and nodded. "They can."

"I miss those things," he admitted, revealing probably more than he should. That he hadn't kissed anyone since Christina. "It's been a while."

"Me too," she said softly.

He searched her expression. "So, are we doing this, then?"

Resolve came over her expression.

"Yeah, we're doing this." Her hands went to the front of his shirt, and then she pushed up on her toes like last night, only this time her lips landed against his mouth. She pressed her lips gently to his. He closed his eyes.

The kiss was sweet and soft, tentative. He kept his hand on her neck, feeling the quickening of her pulse and letting the pleasure of the contact suffuse through him. It'd been forever since he'd experienced that first blush of attraction with someone when everything was new. And it'd been so long since he'd been touched that even the simple kiss threatened to make him hard and hot.

Luckily, she pulled back before he embarrassed himself. She looked up at him, her lips shiny, and she smiled a triumphant smile. "I kissed you."

He laughed under his breath. "I'm well aware. Every part of me is aware, I think."

"And I didn't freak out." She tipped her chin up, clearly pleased, and patted his chest. "Go, me."

"Gold star." He pressed his thumb gently to her forehead like he had a sticker to award her.

"My first werewolf kiss." She lifted a brow. "Does this mean I'm going to turn at the full moon now?"

He smirked. "Nah, I think I'd have to bite you for that."

"Don't get ahead of yourself." She playfully poked him. "This has got to be a Crock-Pot experiment—cooked low and slow."

He chuckled. "That's the least sexy analogy I've ever heard. We're a pot roast."

She sniffed, affronted. "Pot roast can be very satisfying."

He leaned down and kissed her gently, needing to take his own step forward, but he didn't linger or push it further. "Yes, it can."

She rubbed her lips together and gave him a look that damn near melted his insides. “You’re pretty good at that, neighbor.”

“I try.”

She gave his T-shirt a little tug and then stepped backward. “Well, I’m going to get out of your hair. My people will be in touch with your people to arrange our next cook-and-watch. And we still need to take that WorkAround tour.”

“You don’t need to leave, you know.” He jutted a thumb toward the grocery bags. “I could cook us something now.”

She gave him a little smile. “No, I better go. Today’s been a big day. I need some time.”

“Understood,” he said with a nod.

She stepped forward and gave him another quick kiss. “Bye for now.”

He watched her walk out, hips swaying, dress dancing around her legs, and marveled at the turn of events. He didn’t know what strange universe he’d landed in, but he hoped to stay a while.

chapter **thirteen**

ANDI PERUSED HER DVD COLLECTION, TRYING TO FIND THE perfect follow-up to her and Hill's *Halloween* marathon. There were some obvious choices if they wanted to stay in the foundational zone—*Psycho*, *Nightmare on Elm Street*, *Carrie*, *The Shining*. But she was in the mood for something different tonight. She was already feeling a little anxious because this would be the first movie date after their kissing-is-now-allowed conversation a few days ago. She needed something lighter.

Horror comedy.

She smiled. That could be perfect. Nothing slapstick but something that played with dark humor. She didn't want to rewatch *Scream* yet. Hill wouldn't appreciate that one fully since there was a lot of winking at tropes from previous horror movies. Her finger slid over the DVD cases. *Gremlins* was a possibility, but she liked to reserve that one for Christmastime. *Jennifer's Body*. Maybe. *Cabin in the Woods*. Too meta. *Ready or Not*. Could be fun. Her finger stopped. *Happy Death Day*. "And we have a winner."

Lately, Andi felt like she was trying to reinvent herself, so it'd be appropriate to watch a horror movie with a *Groundhog Day*–inspired premise about a girl who needed to do some transforming to move forward. Plus, it was a good mix of scary and funny. She pulled the DVD out and set it on the coffee table. Only then did she realize her hands were trembling. She clenched her fists.

"Ugh." She shook out her hands and rolled her shoulders. "Be cool."

She closed her eyes and breathed through the wave of anxiety. Hill had said he understood she needed to take it slow, that he knew the word *no*. He'd shown her no reason not to trust that. If she didn't feel comfortable doing anything more than holding hands on the couch tonight, he would respect that.

WWBAD—what would Book Andi do? That's what she needed to be asking herself.

She opened her eyes, new resolve moving through her. Book Andi would definitely not stand here and let a panic attack ruin the night before it even started. She headed to her room to change into something cute. Hill would be giving his first cooking lesson tonight, so she needed something practical, but the old yoga pants she was wearing said *working writer* and not *hot date*. She searched through her stuff, settling on a pair of skinny jeans and an oversize dark-blue, off-the-shoulder top. Then she went into the bathroom and braided her hair in a face-framing Greek braid that Nessa, a beauty blogger at WorkAround, had shown her how to do. Finishing things off, she swiped on some lip gloss and freshened up her mascara. Staring at her reflection in the mirror, she imagined Book Andi looking back at her. *Let's do this.*

A few minutes later, Hill knocked on the door right on time. Bonus points for him. Andi was a fan of people who knew how to be on time. She did a quick scan of the living room to make sure she hadn't left anything embarrassing out, and swiped a bra she'd draped over the back of the couch. She stuffed it behind the couch cushion.

When she made it to the door, she checked the peephole and

then turned off the alarm before opening the door with a smile. "Hello, neighbor."

Hill was loaded up with two bags of groceries from Whole Foods, but he smiled over the top of them. "You sound like Mr. Rogers."

"Hashtag Life Goals. Here, give me one of those." She reached out and took one of the paper sacks, and Hill followed her inside, shutting the door behind him. She peeked into the bag as she headed to the kitchen. "What delicious things did you bring me?"

"You'll see," he said, a few steps behind her. "I figured we'd start off basic."

She grinned back at him. "The Basic Bitch cooking show. I'm here for it."

He snorted. "The alternative to Julia Child."

Andi set the bag on the counter, and Hill placed his next to hers. Before she could think too hard about it, she took his hand, stepped into his space, and kissed him quickly. "Hi."

He squeezed her hand and brought it to his mouth, kissing her knuckles, and then gave her a warm look that made her stomach flutter. "Hey, yourself." He glanced down at her outfit. "You look…wow."

She took a breath, her heart quickening, and stepped back. "Thanks. You get date wear tonight."

"I'm honored." He released her hand.

"You look great, too." She took in his dark jeans and lavender T-shirt, the light color making all his dark features stand out. "Of course, we're probably about to ruin both our outfits when you let me cook. Prepare for splatters."

He smirked. "I'm prepared for anything."

The words landed and sank in. She believed him. Whatever she wanted to happen tonight, he'd let her lead—whether that was nothing at all or kissing or more than that. "So," she said, going to one of the bags and pulling a few items out. "What's on the menu?"

"Steak tacos with homemade salsa and guacamole."

"Ooh, yum," she said, her mouth already watering at the thought. "What made you choose that? Besides the fact that tacos are the best."

Hill started unloading the other bag and spreading the ingredients out on the counter. Tortillas, steak, jalapeños. "One of the first skills you need to learn if you're going to cook for yourself is how to use a knife the right way. This meal will give you lots of chopping opportunities."

She set a bundle of cilantro on the counter. "Or opportunities to end up at urgent care."

He laughed and pulled a box out of the sack. "Let's hope not. I brought you a new set of knives. The best way not to get hurt is to have good, sharp knives."

"Ooh, thanks for that, but that logic doesn't track, Hill," she said, taking the box from him and eyeing it. "Sharp knives are less dangerous?"

"Dull knives make you push down with more force and fight the knife, which can make things slip out from beneath it. I learned that the hard way when I first started cooking at the fire station. They had a crappy set of old knives that made everything challenging." He set a red onion and limes on the counter. "I nearly took a fingertip off one Thanksgiving shift, trying to cut through a butternut squash."

"Ouch." She took the wooden knife block out of the package, examining the shiny silver handles of the knives, making note that she needed to hide this in a cabinet. If someone broke in, these were too at-the-ready for handy murder weapons. "You need to tell me how much I owe you for this. You agreed to teach me how to cook, not outfit my kitchen."

"You don't owe me anything even if I had bought them, but I didn't. I had an extra set at my place." He cleared his throat and focused on the groceries. "They were an engagement party gift. I'd rather someone be using them than have them sitting in my hall closet."

Andi frowned and set down the knives. He could've lied to her that he'd bought them, but she appreciated that he'd gone for the awkward truth instead. "How close were y'all to getting married?"

He looked over at her as he flattened the grocery sack. "My accident happened a little less than three months before the wedding date."

Andi leaned back against the counter, considering him. "Wow, that close."

"Yeah." He started organizing the ingredients, dropping the eye contact. "After that, we kept pushing the date back, waiting for me to fully recover. But then...everything else happened."

Everything else. Meaning, Officer Christina had slept with someone else. "I'm sorry."

He glanced over at her and gave a tight shrug. "It is what it is. Neither of us held up our end of the deal. I thought I was marrying someone who took the in-sickness-and-health thing seriously. She thought she was marrying the invincible firefighter. We were both wrong."

Andi's jaw clenched at that. "That's bullshit, though."

"What?"

"If you marry a firefighter, you know there's an inherent risk in that job. If you love that person, you're taking on that risk with them. You don't get to bail when they need you most because it's hard or upsetting."

"I wasn't the easiest patient."

She scoffed. "Who would be? You'd been through major

physical and mental trauma. No one else gets to dictate to you what the proper way to respond to trauma is. Screw that."

He eyed her, his gaze holding hers. "Did someone try to do that to you?"

She sighed. "Some people in my family would argue that what I went through wasn't a trauma at all. So yeah, been there."

He frowned, deep lines cutting in around his mouth. "That's... I'm sorry. You know if you ever want to talk about what happened, I'm a pretty good listener."

She nodded, the offer hitting her in a tender spot. "Thanks. I'll let you know." She forced a smile. "But enough about all that. I was promised tacos."

His eyes crinkled at the corners. "And tacos the lady shall have." He held out a container of grape tomatoes. "After she learns how to cook them for herself."

She smirked and walked over, taking the container from him. "I have a feeling we're going to be ordering pizza after this."

"Nope." He placed a hand on her shoulder and gave her a knowing look. "I have full confidence."

"In me?"

He winked and patted her shoulder. "In my teaching skills."

She rolled her eyes. "Ha."

"Go ahead and wash those tomatoes and the rest of the produce," he said, cocking his head toward the sink. "I'm going to get everything else set up."

"Washing vegetables, I can do." She grabbed a colander and went to work on the tomatoes, limes, cilantro, and peppers.

When she was done, he patted the spot next to him at her rollaway island. "Join me, sous chef."

He'd grabbed the butcher-block cutting board that she'd bought on impulse at HomeGoods one day just because it looked pretty and set it atop the island along with the knives and some other items he'd gathered from her kitchen. She took her spot next to him and set the bowl of clean produce off to the side.

His arm brushed against hers, the hair tickling her skin, as he grabbed the tomatoes, and goose bumps chased up her arm. "For tacos, you could make traditional salsa, which would involve a blender or a food processor, or you could make pico de gallo, which leaves it chunkier. Tonight, we'll tackle pico." He pulled a knife from the block. "For most vegetables, you're going to use a straight-edged knife, but for soft-skinned things like tomatoes, serrated is better."

She eyed the pile of tomatoes. "We have to cut each one?"

"Yes. They're more work, but cherry tomatoes tend to be sweeter than regular ones—unless you stop at one of the roadside stands and find some locally grown Creole tomatoes, which are pretty much the tomatoes all other tomatoes aspire to be."

She laughed. "The grand pooh-bah of tomatoes."

"Without a doubt, but these little ones will be good practice for you. They're slippery little suckers and have a tendency to roll away, which can cause you to cut your finger."

She gave him a skeptical look. "Maybe we shouldn't start here. These sound like the villains of the tomato world."

"Not if you know how to handle them." He grabbed two white plates he'd taken out of her cabinet. "Here's the trick."

He flipped the plate over and then put a layer of tomatoes onto the bottom of the plate where the rim kept them from rolling off. Then he took another plate and set it atop, trapping the tomatoes between.

He took her elbow gently and guided her in front of him. "Now, they'll stay put and you can slice a bunch in half at once."

His arms came around each side of her, and his body pressed gently against her back. A hard wall of muscle. She sucked in a breath at the heat and feel of him.

"This okay?" he asked.

She swallowed past the tightness in her throat. Part of her recognized she was caged in by a guy with a knife, but the other part of her felt every inch of strong, beautiful man behind her. The two sides warred for control of her thoughts. The better side won. "I'm good."

"Great," he said softly. He placed the knife in her right hand. "Put your left hand on top of the plate to keep the tomatoes from escaping. Then take this knife and slice horizontally between the plates. Use a small sawing motion back and forth."

Andi wet her lips and placed her hand on the plate. Hill's breath coasted against her neck. She took the knife and placed it sideways between the plates. Her first attempt, a tomato rolled out.

"Push down a little more," he said in a quiet voice. He put his hand over the one that held the knife. "Like this."

He guided her hand in a gentle sawing motion while she increased pressure on the plate, and soon the knife had made it to the other side of the dish. But she couldn't remember how it had gotten there because all she could think about was how good Hill felt against her, around her, how he smelled like mint and fresh-cut grass.

"There you go," Hill said. He lifted the plate, revealing a bunch of perfectly halved tomatoes. "And we didn't draw any blood."

Andi smiled down at their handiwork. "Score."

"Now they'll be safe to quarter with the smaller serrated knife," he said. He handed her a different knife. "They won't roll away now."

He showed her how to protect her fingers while she was chopping. He guided her through dicing an onion, and laughed along with her when she promptly ruined her mascara with onion tears. He taught her that she could ignore when recipes said to pick off individual cilantro leaves, that the stems could be chopped up with the leaves and it all tasted good. Before long, they were squeezing lime into brightly colored pico de gallo. And all the while, he hadn't stopped touching her. Not aggressively. Not with innuendo. But in a way that made her feel more and more comfortable.

Hill stepped from behind her and grabbed a spoon. He scooped up some of the pico and held it out to her. "Now for the fun part."

Andi smiled. "I feel like we've already been having the fun part."

His eyes sparked with pleasure at that. "Truth. But go ahead and taste the fruits of your labor."

She stepped closer and let him feed her a bite. The fresh, tart taste hit her tongue and she groaned. It was so much better than that jarred salsa she bought.

"So?" Hill asked, looking sweetly anticipatory, as if he was afraid she'd hate it.

She swallowed her bite and grinned. "It tastes like summer on a spoon. We're amazing at cooking."

He laughed and took a bite. "We definitely are."

She grabbed a jalapeño that was still on the cutting board. "What about this guy?"

"That guy needs some extra attention, and we have to decide how hot we want the pico to be."

She eyed the pepper. "Extra attention?"

"Gloves," he explained. "If you cut a chili pepper without protection, the oils get in your skin and it can burn for hours. And it will make everything you touch burn, too—your eyes, your lips"—he raised a brow—"other things."

She pressed her lips together to stanch a laugh. "Sounds like you're speaking from experience."

"You only make that mistake once," he said with a sage nod.

"Ouch."

"Yeah. We also need to taste a little because some jalapeños are as mild as bell peppers, and some are really hot. You can't tell by looking at them."

He gave her a pair of disposable kitchen gloves and then walked her through the process of stemming, seeding, and mincing the pepper.

When they were done, he took a small piece of the jalapeño and held it up to her. "Now for the test."

She opened her mouth and let him place it on her tongue. The heat of it hit her almost instantly, warming her tongue and sending an almost fruity taste along her taste buds. She chewed and swallowed, the spice potent but not overbearing.

"Well?" he asked, pulling off his gloves.

"I think it's the perfect amount of spicy," she said, picking up another piece and holding it out to him. He let her feed it to him, his gaze locked with hers. Her face was only inches from his.

"Just right," he said softly.

She should step back now, give them space, but she didn't move.

"I want to kiss you," Hill said in warning.

The words were what she needed to hear. He was giving her a chance to opt out. "I'm going to let you."

He smiled and she peeled off her gloves, tossing them somewhere on the counter without looking, and then her hands were splayed against his chest. Hill wrapped his arms around her and dipped his head down to kiss her. Her eyes fell shut. This time it wasn't a sweet peck or a gentle press of the lips. His hand squeezed her waist, and when her lips parted, his tongue grazed against hers, spicy heat from the pepper sparking along her taste buds again. She groaned into it, and her arms slid around his neck.

He made a sound of pleasure in the back of his throat and deepened the kiss, tasting her fully and making her legs feel like jelly beneath her. Before she knew it, she was pressed up against the opposite counter, his hand slipping beneath the hem of her shirt and pressed hot against her rib cage, not moving but sending heat straight to the center of her, making things wake with awareness. Her body arched against him.

"Andi," he said between kisses. Her name sounded like a prayer and plea all at once.

His tongue stroked hers, and her hips rocked against him, seemingly of their own volition. When he pushed close again, hard heat met her belly, sending electricity through her like a shock wave. Hill's arousal stoked her own, made her want to touch him, explore, make him even hotter, but it also sent up a warning flare in her brain. The last time she'd gotten to this place with a guy, he'd seen it as an automatic invitation to her bed. When she'd stopped him, he'd been pissed and called her a fucking tease. His anger had scared the hell out of her, setting off her anxiety like a forest fire.

She didn't want to stop, but she also didn't think she was ready for more than this yet. She broke off the kiss, pressing her forehead to Hill's. He stayed in that position, panting softly.

"Sorry," he whispered.

She lifted her head. "For what?"

His eyes met hers, his pupils dark. "I should be able to kiss you without getting a hard-on. I wasn't trying to push you into something further. My body just…really appreciates you. On a survey, it would give you five out of five stars."

She grinned at the unexpected response. "You don't need to apologize for getting turned on. Just because my response isn't visible doesn't mean my body's not a big fan of yours right now, too."

His eyebrows arched and a wicked little smile touched his lips. "Yeah?"

"Andi's girl parts give you two thumbs up." She slid her hands to his shoulders. "But Andi's brain is hitting the Pause button for the moment."

He nodded and cupped her face, placing a kiss on her forehead. "Understood." He stepped back, giving her space, and headed back to the kitchen island. "Let's make some steak. I'm starved."

The thick outline in his jeans was goddamned distracting, but something tight and nervous in her chest unfurled a little more. Hill was keeping his promise. He was obviously turned on, clearly wanted her, but he was going to respect her boundaries with no judgment or cajoling.

That felt...magical.

She took a steadying breath, her body still coursing with her own arousal, and headed back to him. "I'm ready to learn, Chef."

He reached out and took her hand. "Let's talk about how flank steak is your friend."

chapter **fourteen**

Hill draped his arm over the back of Andi's couch as they watched *Happy Death Day*. He couldn't remember the last time he'd felt this content being in the moment. Normally, his brain was filled with images from the past or grim thoughts of the future. But right now, he was just happy to be there, having a movie night with Andi.

He'd always enjoyed movies, but watching a movie with Andi was a whole different experience. He had no doubt that she'd seen this film countless times and already knew what happened in the plot, but she watched it with such full-body commitment that a stranger observing would've sworn this was her first time.

Andi was currently biting her thumbnail, her knees to her chest, sock-covered feet on the couch, and her gaze glued to the screen. He was starting to recognize this as her pre-jump-scare position. She shook her head. "Don't do it, girl. Don't go in there."

Hill bit his lip, trying not to laugh. Andi was a talk-to-the-screen person, which he found enormously entertaining. "She's totally going to do it."

Andi turned to him, eyes glittering with light from the screen. "Yeah, they never listen. They really need a best friend like me to warn them. But I don't wanna be a best friend in a horror movie. Things usually don't end well for the BFF."

"No?"

"You have to be the star or, at the very least, the love interest, or you're screwed."

"At least she'll get another do-over." The heroine of the movie kept dying over and over and reliving the same day. "I'll hold out hope for the love interest."

"I'm sure he appreciates your support." Andi glanced at the arm Hill had draped across the back of the couch and then back to him. He could almost see her mental *Should I or shouldn't I* wheels turning. After a beat, she scooted closer and settled against his side. The little vote of trust sent a dart of pleasure through him. He moved his arm, curving it a little so that he was holding her. He could feel her shoulders tighten a bit, but then she rolled her lips together and seemed to breathe out the tension.

A sharp pang went through him at her reaction. Even something as simple as an arm around her made her tense up.

What did he do to you, Andi?

The question whispered through his mind—not for the first time tonight. Hill didn't know who the *he* was or what specifically had happened, but in that moment, he wanted to physically harm the scumbag who'd hurt her. Whoever had made this smart, vibrant woman so frightened of even a simple cuddle on the couch deserved to have the shit beat out of him. Twice.

"Do you need me to move my arm?" he asked.

She reached over and patted his thigh. "I'm good. Thanks for asking, though."

"Just let me know." He turned back to the screen, and the heroine was waking up in the same day again. "That really is a true horror premise," he said as the heroine's phone started playing "In

Da Club" again. "Imagine having to live the same day over and over again. And not just any day, but your worst day."

That was what his nightmares felt like—waking up in the same day over and over. In the same horrible moment. Roof beams splintering, fire raining down. Unable to escape and forced to relive it.

"Yeah," she said, leaving her hand on his thigh. "But if it gave you the chance to change something, maybe it'd be worth it?"

"Right." His mind went to the day of the fire. He'd been filling in for someone who was sick. What if he hadn't answered the call to come in that day? What if he and Christina had gone on a road trip that day like they'd planned and turned off their phones? Where would he be right now? Still a firefighter, two fully intact legs, married. Not depressed. Not waking up soaked with sweat from nightmares.

"I have a day like that," she said, still looking at the screen. "I'd go back in a second if I could change it."

He squeezed her shoulder. "Me too."

She gave him an empathetic look and then rested her head against his shoulder. The solid comfort of having her against him smoothed the sharp edges of the memories that had surfaced.

They finished the movie in comfortable silence. When the credits started to roll, Andi turned off the TV and shifted her body to face him. "So, what'd you think?"

"I think that you, Andi Lockley, are a great curator of movies," he said, meaning it. "This one was really different from the *Halloween* ones even though I assume it'd still be considered a slasher."

"Yep. Definitely in the slasher genre." She smiled and patted his cheek. "Look at you, learning and shit."

"I have my moments. I also liked that it was darkly funny." He gave her a mock serious look. "But...let's talk about the true horror ramifications of that movie."

She cocked her head. "Which is?"

"I'll never be able to get 50 Cent's 'In Da Club' out of my head ever again." He tapped his temple. "Burned there. Permanently. Forever and ever, amen."

She laughed. "Oh yeah, you'll be stuck with that for days."

She started humming and rapping the line "It's your birthday." He playfully put his hands over his ears.

She grabbed his wrists and pulled them away from his head. "Sorry not sorry."

He smiled, his wrists still cuffed by her fingers. "I'm not sorry either. I like watching movies with you."

"Yeah?" She narrowed her eyes. "You don't find it annoying that I talk to the screen? My friends often throw popcorn at me."

"Nope." He noticed she wasn't letting him go, and he shifted his body to face her fully. "It's highly entertaining. I think half the time I was watching the movie, and the other half I was watching *you* watch the movie."

Rosy color dotted her cheeks, bringing her faint freckles into relief. "I'm insufferable in a theater."

"Nah. I can't imagine you're insufferable under any circumstance."

"Don't count those chickens yet. I'm bound to annoy you at some point," she teased.

"Too late. Chickens counted." She looked so pretty in the lamplight, her dark-red hair braided like some Renaissance woman, her blue eyes full of mischief, and her shirt sliding off her shoulder, giving him a peek of smooth, creamy skin and a thin purple bra strap. He wanted to kiss her right there, where her neck met her shoulder, wanted to know if the skin there felt as soft as it looked. He swallowed hard, trying to rein in the pictures his mind was weaving. *Crock-Pot experiment.*

She looked down at her hands, which were still holding his

wrists. After a long moment, her voice was soft when she spoke again. "Hill?"

"Yeah?" he asked, his voice coming out tight.

She peeked up from under her lashes, worry there. "I want to kiss you some more, but...could you keep your hands by your sides?"

The request made his gut twist. He hated—*hated*—that Andi had been victimized, that she'd been saddled with this fear by some selfish, malicious asshole. He wished he could wave a wand and take it all from her, make her feel safe and powerful and in control. But there were no magic wands. He knew more than anyone how deep trauma cut, how lifelong those wounds could be.

What he could give her, though, was his word. "I won't touch you unless you ask me to. I promise."

She inhaled deeply, her shoulders rising with it, and then nodded. "Thank you."

"Don't thank me. I've been wanting to kiss you again for the last hour. You're giving me exactly what I want."

She smiled at that. "Benefits for both sides then." She tucked her knees beneath her and lifted up, pressing his wrists down at his sides and against the couch cushions, bringing her breasts precariously close to his face before sitting back on her calves again. "You stay right there."

"Yes, ma'am."

She bit her lip, still smiling. "Okay, the way you say 'ma'am' is kind of hot."

He laughed under his breath. "Andi Lockley, author, podcaster, budding sexual dominant."

She cocked a brow and then swung her knee over, straddling his thighs and surprising the hell out of him. "Don't give me any ideas. I do enjoy being in charge in other areas of my life."

His tongue pressed to the back of his teeth at the feel of her straddling him, her hands on his shoulders, giving him a delicious view down her loose shirt. "Andi, feel free to get any goddamned ideas you want."

Her fingers curled into his T-shirt, her gaze meeting his. "To be one hundred percent honest, my experience is extremely limited. So even though I've figured some things out on my own, I don't know a lot about what I like and don't like yet with guys."

On my own. Aaaand he was done. Picturing Andi getting herself off was enough to send his starved libido into a seizure. All his blood rushed south, and his cock pressed against the zipper of his jeans. He felt his ears go hot, embarrassed that he was on such a hair trigger. "Sorry. Obviously, I'm happy to be your test subject."

Andi glanced down, her eyes widening slightly. But when she looked back up, instead of her expression saying *Dude, control yourself*, it seemed to be saying *Well, hello there*. She braced her hands on his shoulders and leaned down, putting her mouth a breath away from his. "I have to say, knowing I can do that with just words does feel pretty damn powerful."

He wanted to reach out and touch her so badly, slide his hands beneath the hem of her shirt, feel her skin, kiss her neck, find out what sounds she made. But he kept his palms glued to the couch cushions. "It's not just your words, Andi. If you haven't noticed, you're fucking gorgeous. And smart. And—"

Her lips touched his, cutting him off and making his eyelids fall shut. Her hands went to his jaw, holding him where she wanted him, and her tongue touched his. The kiss was hungrier than the ones earlier, more urgent, like she was daring herself to take it a little further. She deepened the kiss and shifted on his lap, settling against him, the hard ridge of his erection pressing at the apex of her thighs. He groaned into her mouth, the heat of her body apparent even through his jeans, and she made a delicious noise in the back of her throat. He lifted his hands, wanting to grab her waist, to angle her where he could make her feel even better, but he caught his mistake just in time. He planted his hands against the couch again.

Trust. Above all else, that was what she needed from him. To be able to trust his word.

He refused to let her down.

She broke away from the kiss, still holding his face in her hands. Her blue eyes were a little dazed, and she was out of breath. "I want your shirt off."

"Then take it off," he said. "I've been told not to use my hands."

She bit down on her bottom lip, eyes smiling. "So you have."

She reached for the bottom edge of his T-shirt and then lifted it over his head before tossing the shirt somewhere behind the couch. Her palm pressed against his chest, a hot brand of skin-to-skin contact.

A flash of insecurity went through him. In the past, he'd been proud of his body, working hard to keep in top shape for the fire department, but he didn't look how he used to. He had scars from the fire, places where hair would never grow again, raised pink stripes where the edges of a burning wooden beam had landed on him.

But when he looked up at Andi's face, the sharp edges of self-consciousness softened. He never claimed to know a woman's mind, but right now, Andi's poker face was nonexistent. That wasn't the look of revulsion or pity. It was the look of a woman who wanted things. Who wanted *him*.

....

Andi had been prepared for the scars. She'd gotten a brief look that day she'd surprised Hill at his house, but what she hadn't been prepared for was the full-body kick of arousal that shot through her at the sight of him without his shirt. She was already running hot, the feel of his erection pressing between her legs about to drive her mad. But now she wanted to touch him everywhere, kiss him everywhere, see all of him.

However, even in the haze of arousal, she knew she wasn't ready for that step. She'd made that mistake the last time she'd tried something physical with a guy. She'd rushed, trying to outrun her anxiety, but it was faster and more cunning than she'd given it credit for. She needed to be careful not to go too fast too soon. If she got spooked, she could ruin this whole thing and set herself back.

That didn't mean she couldn't do *some* things, though.

She let her fingertips travel down the solid muscles of Hill's chest, over the smooth, raised patches of scars, and then lower to the ridges of his abdomen. His belly flexed beneath her fingers as he hissed out a breath. "Andi."

She loved the ache in his voice, the need. She liked knowing that she was getting to him as much as he was getting to her. And the fact that he hadn't touched her, had kept his hands at his sides, gave her a burst of confidence. She reached down and pulled her top over her head, tossing it to the side, and leaving her in her lacy purple bra.

Hill's gaze ate her up as he groaned softly. "Jesus. You're perfect."

His voice was pure sex. She could imagine it against her ear as he stretched out on top of her, pushed inside her. But the image was too much right now. If he lay on top of her, she'd panic for sure. So instead, she reached down and took his wrist in her hand again. She lifted his hand, her heart beating like a hummingbird's wings against her ribs, and pressed his palm against her lace-covered breast. "You can touch me here."

His eyes flared with heat, and he cupped her breast, the warmth and weight of his palm waking up every nerve ending there. His thumb brushed across her nipple, and her flesh tightened and pushed against the lace, sending a shudder of need through her.

"Can I kiss you here?" he asked, his voice a soft rumble.

Andi swallowed past the knot in her throat and nodded. "As long as you promise to stop everything if I say stop."

"Always." His gaze bore into hers, his liquid brown eyes reflecting the lamplight. "I mean it. You say stop, slow down, back off, I'm going to listen. Nothing happens that you don't want to happen, okay?"

She rubbed her lips together, the words winding their way through her, and she nodded. "Okay."

"Come 'ere," he whispered, bringing his other hand to her back and gently easing her forward. "Let me make you feel good."

She let him guide her forward, pushing up on her knees and putting her breasts at eye level for him. Her heart was ready to pound out of her chest, but Hill started off gentle, brushing the tip of his nose against her skin, kissing her lightly along her collarbone, making her nerve endings strain for more. He kept his other hand loosely against the small of her back, giving her the ability to back off if she needed it, but that was the last thing she wanted to do in this moment. He murmured her name against her skin, his breath tickling her, and she arched against him, seeking more.

When his mouth closed over her lace-covered nipple, sensation sparked through her and she gasped, her fingers threading into the hair at the back of his head, holding him in place. His mouth was hot and wet around her, the pressure sending tendrils of arousal straight downward. "*Hill.*"

He tugged gently, and it felt as if he'd touched her everywhere, her whole body going sensitive and hungry. Without thinking, she reached behind her and unhooked her bra. She needed more of him, skin to skin. Hill lifted his hand without pulling away and slid her bra strap down her shoulder, freeing one arm and exposing her fully to him. She was trembling. She didn't know if it was fear or anticipation but probably both.

However, when his tongue stroked against her bared breast, any fear trying to break through vaporized. "Holy shit."

Hill hummed against her skin in clear approval and teased her nipple with his mouth, while cupping her other breast and stroking with his thumb. His beard tickled her skin, just the right amount of soft and abrasive to set her nerve endings aflame. Her head tipped back, and her body rocked against him, pressure building deep inside her. Yes, yes, *this*. Colors danced behind her eyelids, and her pulse felt as if it was pounding between her legs.

It'd been years since she'd been touched by someone else and never like this, never with this much focused attention. Hill wasn't just kissing her body as a means to an end or a journey to the big event. This *was* the event. He made wherever he kissed the center of the universe. Like if that square inch of skin was all he had to work with, by golly, he was going to slay it.

"Hill," she panted, the pressure building hot and urgent, "I need…but… *God.*"

He pulled away for a moment and looked up at her, his lips shiny and his pupils black with lust. "Do you need to come, Andi?"

Yes. Yes. Yes. Her throat tightened. "I'm not ready for sex."

"That's not what I'm asking," he said, voice full of confident promise. "I can help. You don't even have to take your jeans off, but you'd have to trust me to touch you."

She considered him, her body aching for what he was offering, and finally nodded. "Okay."

"Thank you." He took her face in his hands and kissed her gently, soothing some of the nerves that were trying to surface. When her body relaxed again, he let go of her face and kissed down her chest. She was dizzy with arousal, trying not to overthink things and get in her head. But she didn't have to worry long because while his mouth was occupied with her breast, his hand slid down, and he pressed the heel of it between her legs over her jeans. The simple pressure shouldn't have been intense with a layer of denim between them, but lightning streaked down her thighs as his hand put pressure against her clit.

Oh. *Oh.*

He rocked his hand against her, and she matched his rhythm, her fingertips digging into his shoulders. It'd been so long since any hand had touched her but her own that the sheer novelty of sensation had her rocketing toward climax.

"Hill," she gasped. "Please."

His teeth grazed her nipple, and he circled the heel of his hand against her. That was all it took. Her orgasm burst through her, making her cry out and surprising her with the blunt force of it. She held on to his shoulders, angling her body against him, riding out the delicious relief and losing all sense of where she was for a few blissful moments.

When every ounce of her energy was sapped, she sank back onto his thighs, panting, the cool air of the room rushing along her overheated skin and her clit pulsing along with her heartbeat. Her head dipped between her shoulders, and she gripped her thighs, trying to regain her balance.

Hill squeezed her knee gently. "You okay?"

She took a steadying breath and lifted her head, finding Hill with searching eyes and a furrowed brow. She nodded. "I'd say I'm very okay. That was... Thank you."

The corner of his mouth lifted and his brow softened. "Thank you back."

Her gaze tracked down to the very obvious erection pushing at the fly of his jeans. Only then did she remember that she had gotten her pleasure, but she hadn't done a thing for him. "I'm not sure you should be thanking me. That looks uncomfortable."

He shrugged. "Worth it. That was sexy as hell, Andi. *You* are sexy as hell."

"Do you need me to..." She didn't know exactly what she was offering. Part of her wanted to touch him, make him feel good, but reality was starting to creep in. She could feel the first fingers of anxiety trying to reach into her brain.

He took her hand and kissed her knuckles. "I don't need you to do anything. I'm a grown man. I won't die from a hard-on." He reached to the other side of the couch and grabbed her shirt. He handed it back to her. "Here, you're shivering."

Gratitude moved through her. Somehow he'd sensed she needed some armor back. She tugged her shirt on, not bothering with finding her bra. "Thanks."

He helped her climb off his lap and found his own shirt hanging off her shelf of DVDs. He pulled it over his head and then joined her back on the couch. He gave her an evaluating look. "You sure you're okay?"

She lifted her hand and pinched the air between her thumb and forefinger, offering him a small smile. "I may be freaking out just a little bit. But not because of you. You were... That was... great. You're an excellent...experiment buddy."

He laughed, his eyes crinkling with it. "Your dirty talk is on point, Lockley."

She snorted, but the little joke eased some of the tension coursing through her. She didn't need to overthink this. Hill had made her feel good, and he'd kept his promise, letting her take the lead on things and not pushing for anything more. She leaned over and kissed him gently. "Thank you."

"My pleasure. Thank you for trusting me. And for a great movie night."

"What movie did we watch again?" she asked. "I can't seem to remember a thing that happened before the last half hour."

He smirked. "Good. That's called a job well done."

"We should do this again," she said, forcing herself to be brave. "The movie and the making out. And possibly you cooking more things for me."

He lifted a finger and pointed. "I didn't cook. You did. Your taco-making skills are top-notch now."

Her lips curved. "That's because you're a great teacher." She lifted a brow. "You know how I get when I talk about horror movies and books? How I get all fast-talking and excited?"

He gave her an affectionate look. "Hard to miss."

"Well, that's how you are when you're talking about food," she said. "You're a complete cooking geek. It's kind of adorable."

"Nah," he said dismissively. "Horror's your passion. Cooking's just something I learned how to do."

"Bullshit." She poked his shoulder. "You waxed poetic about tomatoes and flank steak. You don't just like cooking. You nerd out about it. And you like teaching other people about it."

He grabbed the finger she'd poked him with and kissed the tip of it. "Maybe I just like teaching *you*. You're pretty and a very good student."

She put her hand to her chest. "Well, obviously I am an absolute joy to teach, but I think this has much less to do with my charming ability to start fires in the kitchen and more with your natural ability to teach." She nodded toward him. "You should do more of that. You could do online videos or something."

A wrinkle appeared between his brows. "Of me cooking?"

"Yeah, teaching people to cook. Lord knows a lot of people are in need of it." She gave him an up-and-down look. "Plus, you'd look damn good in an apron. People would watch you."

He scoffed. "No, they wouldn't. I'm not a chef. The TV and internet are full of professionals showing people how to cook. I'm just some dude who used to cook for his fellow firefighters."

"But that's what makes you perfect. You're self-taught. You break it down for people like me because you used to be someone like me. And you make down-to-earth food."

He gave her a skeptical look. "Thanks for the suggestion. But how about I stick to teaching you for now?"

She narrowed her eyes, an idea coming to her, but she tucked it away in the For Later Consideration folder in her brain. "Fine. I will accept my own private chef lessons *for now*." She tucked her knees beneath her. "But give it some thought. Life's too short not to do the things that make us happy. If cooking makes you happy, you should do that."

He propped his elbow on the back of the couch, leaning his head against his fist and looking at her. "How about right now I teach you how to make the perfect hot fudge sundae?"

"An orgasm *and* ice cream? This night keeps getting better." She climbed off the couch and put her hand out to him. "Hell yes. You are definitely the best research buddy ever."

He put his hand in hers and let her pull him to a stand. "I try."

A rush of warmth went through her. Hill did more than try. He *listened*. He hadn't pushed or rushed her. He hadn't cajoled. But more than that, he hadn't made her feel wrong or broken for being the way she was. He'd simply been with her in that moment, meeting her where she was and seeming to enjoy what they were doing as much as she did.

That didn't feel like *trying*. That felt special.

And dangerous.

This was a guy getting over a bad breakup and a catastrophic injury. He wasn't here for anything more than a friendship and some physical connection. He'd told her as much. She needed to remember that.

She needed to be careful with this one.

More than that, she needed to be careful with herself.

chapter **fifteen**

Hill set his giant salad bowl on the table and took the spot across from Ramsey, who was already grinding pepper over his salad concoction. On their weekly lunch rotation, they tried to alternate the junk-food places with restaurants that were conceivably healthy like this build-your-own-salad joint. Ramsey's dad, who'd also been a firefighter, had died of a heart attack two years ago, and it'd spooked Ramsey about his own health. It hadn't made him stop eating french fries, but now he at least inserted some greenery in between.

Ramsey handed the pepper grinder to Hill and then started splashing hot sauce on his salad. The guy put Tabasco on everything. "So," Ramsey said when he was done with his salad doctoring, "how's the cookbook coming?"

Hill gave him a look as he swallowed a bite of his salad. "It's not. I never agreed to write one."

"Right," Ramsey said with a sage nod. "Because you're so busy and all, you just can't find the time."

"I'm not…not busy," Hill said grumpily. "I'm rehabbing. Jogging. Strength training. Doctors' appointments."

"Uh-huh." Ramsey shoveled more salad in his mouth, looking wholly unimpressed.

"I've been giving my neighbor cooking lessons," he added. "And she's teaching me about horror movies."

Ramsey's brows went up, and he swiped at his mouth with a napkin. "No shit? You're still hanging out with your hot neighbor?"

Hill shrugged, aiming for nonchalant. "Yeah. Some. We got together for a movie night last week."

Ramsey grinned wide and leaned back in his chair. "Well, goddamn, you should've led with that. I'm impressed—you know—with myself. My inertia pep talk totally worked. I should definitely get into motivational speaking. *How to Win Friends and Occasionally Get Laid.*"

Hill snorted and went back to his salad, spearing a chunk of avocado. "I said I was hanging out with her. I didn't say I was sleeping with her."

And even if he had been, he wouldn't be blabbing about it. Not anyone's business.

"Hey, man, baby steps," Ramsey said, forking a piece of kale and eyeing it like he wasn't sure why he was eating such a thing. "Are you into her? Or is it strictly a friends thing?"

"We're friends," Hill said, not meeting Ramsey's gaze.

"Friends." Ramsey leaned forward on his elbows, obviously trying to get more out of him. "Which doesn't mean you're *not* into her."

Most of the time Hill appreciated that Ramsey could read him so well. It saved him having to explain himself and had been indispensable when they were fighting fires together. But times like these, he wished his friend wasn't so damn observant. Hill took a big bite of salad.

Ramsey laughed. "Yeah, you're into her. But, let me guess, feel too out of practice to ask her out?"

Hill swallowed his bite and took a swig of his iced tea. "More complicated than that."

Ramsey went back to his food. "What do you mean? She with someone?"

"No."

"Then it's not that complicated." He pointed his fork at Hill. "It's that fear of getting back on the horse blocking you. I get it. You just need some practice after being out of the game so long." He smirked. "Which is perfect because I'm about to solve your problem."

Hill gave him a cease-and-desist look. "There is no problem, Rams."

"Sure, sure. You're fine. Everything's cool. You're totally not a hard-up, grumpy shut-in. You're absolutely not on a one-way trip to becoming the get-off-my-lawn guy in the neighborhood."

Hill sniffed derisively. "Get off my lawn."

Ramsey chuckled. "See. You're way too good at that. But listen, I'm being serious. I have something that will help. I was going to talk to you about this today anyway, but now you have even more reason to say yes."

"No."

Ramsey lifted his glass and frowned from behind his Diet Coke. "You don't even know what it is."

"I know that look," Hill said, going back to his salad. "Last time I saw that look, we almost got arrested for public indecency."

Ramsey lifted his hands, palms out. "I swear this is not like that. Hear me out. This is right up your alley because I know that my friend Hill is a man of the community." He put his hand on his chest. "He is a hero who sacrificed himself to save others. He is selfless and brave and wise."

Dread was building in Hill. This kind of hand-over-heart, saccharine speech would lead to nowhere good.

"And he believes in charitable causes," Ramsey said in his preacher voice. "And he would never *ever* leave his best friend hanging with two unfilled spots at a charity event he's in charge of for the firehouse."

"And there it is," Hill said with a groan. "What'd you get yourself into?"

Ramsey cleared his throat and suddenly took an interest in stabbing more kale. "I may have volunteered to be in charge of this season's charity event for burn victims. And I might have promised a firefighter bachelor auction. And I may have been blindsided when multiple guys got engaged in the last two months and are no longer available. Impatient assholes."

Hill stared at his friend, the information slowly falling into place and clicking. "Oh, fuck no. You better not be asking what I think you are."

"Retired firefighters are eligible to participate," he said quickly. "And dude, you're a hero. You'd bring in big cash. And—"

"No," Hill said with a tone of finality. "Not happening. I am not going up there as some pity case to get people to open up their wallets."

"Pity?" Ramsey frowned. "That's not what it would be. You remember women used to like you, right?"

Hill didn't answer.

"Look, man, I guarantee you'll get bids that have nothing to do with pity. And really, it's not even a true bachelor auction anymore. The chief put all kinds of limitations on the event because she thinks the auction tradition is in poor taste. She told us we have to come up with a new tradition next year. So you don't even have to go out on a date with the winner. All you'd have to do is take the person to the party we have planned afterward in the same building. A little conversation, a little karaoke. All in good fun."

Hill shook his head. "You're bent if you think I'm going to do this."

"I'm a genius actually," Ramsey said, undeterred. "Beyond helping the charity, this could help with your problem with your neighbor. Hanging out with some woman at the auction who doesn't mean anything to you can be a good practice run. Because the woman is going to know it's just for fun and that there are no expectations. You'll just part ways after the party."

Hill grimaced. The thought of being onstage, his story being paraded out in front of a crowd made his stomach twist. "I will pay you what you think I'd get at the event, and you can donate it directly to the fund. I'm not up for more than that. Having to make small talk with some stranger who paid for time with me sounds like a special kind of torture."

Ramsey pressed his lips together, clearly frustrated now. "I don't just need the money. I need the slot filled." He gave Hill a no-bullshit look. "This is the first time the station has trusted me with such a big event, and I know everyone is probably expecting me to screw up something because…I have a reputation. But I want this charity to have the best event possible and as many donations and press as I can drum up. That fire at that elementary school last year left a lot of kids with scars and injuries that require a lot of additional surgeries, and all those medical bills are draining their parents' bank accounts. I want to hand all of them a big pile of money. And I'm not going to be able to do that if I don't have a solid list of eligible firefighters and a sold-out event."

Hill's breath sagged out of him at the words and the honest desperation on his friend's face. This charity did mean a lot, and families were counting on Ramsey to pull it off. *Fuck*. How the hell was he supposed to say no to that?

But how could he say yes to being onstage, being paraded around like a hero, being expected to be energetic and upbeat and positive at a party with some stranger when it took almost every ounce of energy he had some days just to get the hell out of bed?

He ran a hand over the back of his head, anxiety trying to take over, but then an idea came to him. One that might at least solve part of the problem. He ran the scenario in his head, trying to imagine it. Yeah. Maybe he could do that.

He'd need help, though.

Ramsey looked at him expectantly. "Come on, man."

Hill lowered his hand to the table and sighed. "You are going to owe me so big."

Ramsey broke into a huge smile and set his chin in his hands, fluttering his eyelashes like a starstruck cartoon character. "You're my hero, Hill."

"Oh, go to hell."

Ramsey chuckled. "Auction's next Saturday. Wear something cute."

Hill flipped him off.

....

Andi leaned closer to her microphone and adjusted the angle of it. The door to the podcasting room at WorkAround was sealed tight, and the room as quiet as a tomb. "*Gina Holiday thought the new guy in her life was too good to be true. He treated her like no other guy she'd ever met. Polite. Respectful. Good listener. David was a breath of fresh air. She thought she had finally found the one.*

"*But she had no idea that David was simply setting the trap. He would spend the next few months expertly brainwashing her, isolating her from her friends and family, and getting her more and more tied to him and less and less tied to things and people who could help her get away. What felt like falling in love ended up being falling into the hands of a sociopath.*"

Andi paused the recording and took a sip of water, her throat dry. Gina Holiday's story was a little too close for comfort to

Andi's own story. While reading through the events of Gina's life, instead of imagining the face of the victim, Andi was picturing her own. That innocent, wide-eyed girl who'd been high on the feelings of a teenage crush. That feeling of *He likes me, he really likes me!* coursing through her like a drug.

Ugh.

She hit the record button again. "I'm going to pause here in Gina's story for a second. I just want to say to all of you who are out there listening to this, especially those of you who are still teenagers, that you should never feel…lucky that some guy or girl loves you—like they are somehow above you and, wow, are giving you a shot to be with them. You, whoever you are, are amazing and worthy of love. See the people you date as equals." She took a breath. "This is not to blame the victim. I've been that girl who felt 'special'—I'm putting air quotes around that—because some 'cool' guy deemed me worthy of his attention. It didn't work out well. So this is meant to be more of a PSA on the importance of nurturing your self-esteem. Love doesn't work if both people aren't on even ground. We're all human with good qualities and flaws. No one gets to be on a pedestal. Putting someone high up on one in a relationship makes it too easy for them to crush you."

Andi's phone screen lit silently with a text. She paused her recording and grabbed her phone.

Hill: Hey there. I know you've been swamped, but on the off chance that you still require food, want to get together for dinner tonight? I can make dragon noodles and bring them over.

Andi smiled at the invitation. She and Hill chatted or texted daily now but hadn't had a chance to get together since their movie night almost two weeks ago because she'd been so busy. Hanging out with Hill would be a welcome respite from what she'd been doing, but then she glanced at the notes and papers in front of her and sighed.

Andi: Ooh, dragon noodles sound intriguing. But I'm still at WorkAround and have two hours left on my rental time for the podcast room. It's booked solid tomorrow so I'm stuck here for a while.

Hill: Bummer on the late night. Maybe tomorrow then.

She started to type back that tomorrow sounded good, but then another idea hit her.

Andi: How would you feel about coming here? I'll order some delivery and we could have dinner. I could give you that tour, too.

Hill: Yeah?

Andi: If you're willing to come out this way. Dinner with you would be a nice carrot at the end of this stick. This podcast episode is wringing me out. Really sad story.

Hill: :(I'm sorry. And yes, I can come to you. What time?

Andi: 7:30? I'll send you the address.

Hill: Great. See you then.

Andi texted him the address and set her phone down. She still had hours of work ahead of her and the most gruesome part of

Gina's story to get through, but suddenly, she felt ten times lighter than she had a few minutes ago.

Not only was Hill going to come out here and have dinner with her, but this also told her something she'd been wondering about in the back of her mind. He was coming here simply to hang out with her. She'd been worried after movie night that now that they'd taken semi-naked steps, it would become an expected part of their get-togethers—which may have been one reason why she'd used her busyness to turn down the last few invites—but Hill was proving that her fears were unfounded. Because they certainly weren't going to be getting naked at WorkAround.

Andi glanced over at the spongy acoustic tiles on the soundproof walls, and unbidden images flooded her brain. Hill pushing her up against the soft wall, his mouth on her neck, his hands sliding beneath her dress, his fingers finding the edge of her panties.

A full-body flush cascaded through her, and she leaned back in her chair, her body liking the images too much.

Nope. Down, girl. Not happening.

She closed her eyes and shoved the dirty movie from her mind. She needed to keep her head together. Starved libido or not, she couldn't afford to let her hormones fog her brain when it came to Hill. "Blinded by lust" was a saying for a reason.

They were friends.

They were going to have dinner.

That was it.

Back to work.

chapter **sixteen**

Andi grabbed two Topo Chicos from the coffee-bar counter and thanked Dwight, the new WorkAround barista, before turning to Hill, who'd arrived right on time looking like a sexy mirage in the desert after the marathon of finishing her podcast. She handed him his drink. "When you rent space here, you get two free drinks a day. My friend Jasper used to make the best iced coffees, but he's leveled up and bought an improv theater, so now I'm working on training Dwight. He's a sweet guy, but if you don't watch him, he puts too much milk in everything. Luckily, he can't mess up mineral water."

"Thanks." Hill accepted the drink and glanced around the bottom floor of WorkAround, his gaze bouncing from one thing to the next in the high-ceilinged, industrial-style space. The sound of clicking keyboards filled the air, and many of the hot desks were still occupied with people wearing headphones or AirPods and nursing coffee drinks even at this late hour. "So all these people are just doing their own thing?"

Andi walked alongside him, matching his slower, methodical pace and continuing her mini-tour. "Many are one-person operations, entrepreneurs, that kind of thing. Some may work for a company but work remotely and don't want to or can't work from home. Some have day jobs and rent a hot desk for a few hours at night or on weekends for a side hustle." She pointed. "Alyssa over there is a social media manager for a number of popular online sites." She nodded toward someone else. "That guy with the fedora—he's got a YouTube channel about board games—but during the day he's a dental hygienist. Tyra, the gorgeous woman with the messy bun, she's got a popular beauty-based Instagram channel, but comes here a few days a week to work on the behind-the-scenes aspects of her business. She's got a ridiculous number of sponsors, so I'm sure getting that all coordinated each week takes a lot of time."

Hill listened intently as they walked. "You know all these people?"

Andi sipped her drink, the glass bottle already sweating even in the air-conditioned space. "Not all of them. I try to meet as many people as I can, but the hot desks rotate so much that there are always new faces. Some people's ventures fail and they can't afford the rent anymore. Some move on to more permanent arrangements or move into an office upstairs. Some go off the grid and hike for a year. Whatever. The first floor is very transient."

Hill shook his head. "This makes me feel really old."

She laughed and gave him a quick once-over. He'd gone for his standard uniform of a T-shirt—green this time—and well-fitting jeans for this visit, and was looking like all her best fantasies of him. "Yes, Hill, you're ancient. You're what? Thirty?"

"Thirty-one," he said, "but in spirit, I feel ancient compared to these people—to *you*. I can't imagine flying by the seat of my pants with my job. That seems terrifying."

"Oh, it is," she said with a humorless laugh. "I pretty much live with the daily fear that it will all crumble beneath me at any time. As my landlord, you didn't hear that."

His lips tipped up. "Of course not."

"But when I think of doing something else? Some nine-to-five thing that I don't feel passionate about? I just... I'd rather eat ramen and wait tables until I got on my feet again if what I'm doing now stops working." She pushed the button for the elevator. "I grew up in a family where money was basically everything. My parents have a lot of it, but it's never enough. They always want more. Status is everything. Appearances are more important than reality. I want no part of that."

He glanced her way. "What do they think of what you do?"

She rolled her eyes as the elevator doors opened, and they both stepped inside. She pressed the button for the second floor. "They tell people I'm studying literature at Tulane."

"What?" He leaned back, grabbing the rail on the wall behind him, and flexed his knee as if loosening it up. "You're a published author."

"Of utter trash, Hill," she said patiently, using her mother's heavy Georgia accent. "Not of respectable books an educated young woman should be writing. There's *violence* and *blood* and *sex*, oh my. Things a proper young lady shouldn't speak of, much less put in print. What did we send her to college for anyway? What a waste."

He grimaced. "That's messed up."

The doors opened on to the second floor, the blast of air-conditioning hitting them in the face. "Yeah, I know, but I'll never convince them they're wrong. They think I write what I write because of what happened to me—an incident they'd like to pretend never occurred—so it's a constant reminder. Thanksgiving is fun. We get to play pretend."

He frowned as he followed her out. "I'm sorry."

"Thanks. It's okay. I'm used to it. I can't live up to their expectations, and they can't live up to mine." She shrugged. "We're at an impasse."

"Well, for what it's worth, I think you're a badass," he said, falling into step beside her. "I finished your book this afternoon. I never saw the twist at the end coming. You're really talented."

The compliment pleased her more than she would've expected, warming her from the inside out. She stopped in the hallway and turned to him, hand on hip. "You sure you're not saying that just because you want to make out with me?"

He leaned down as if he were going to whisper a secret to her. "I'm saying it because it's true. And I also want to make out with you. Those two truths can exist together, you know."

"Oh." A hot shiver went through her. "Well, thank you. On both."

"You're welcome."

She took his hand. "Come on. I want to show you something."

"Your office?"

"Later. First, I have a little surprise," she said, sending him a cryptic smile as they began walking again.

His expression shifted into one of concern. "Now I'm worried."

She laughed. "Don't be. Trust me. This won't hurt a bit."

She led him down the hallway, stopping at Hollyn's door. She knocked, and she could see her friend wave her in through the narrow window next to the door. Andi opened the door and tugged Hill in with her.

Hollyn smiled, her gaze jumping briefly to Hill and then back to Andi. "Hey."

"Hey," Andi said cheerfully. "I wanted to introduce you to my friend, Hill. He's the neighbor I was telling you about." She released Hill's hand. "Hill, this is Hollyn. She's a local entertainment writer and podcaster. You may know her as Miz Poppy."

Hill's brows lifted. "Miz Poppy. I used to read your posts on the *NOLA Vibe*. They were great." He stepped forward and put out his hand. "Nice to meet you."

Hollyn's facial tics went through a little dance, but she

maintained her smile and shook Hill's hand. "Thanks. Nice to meet you, too."

A bolt of pride went through Andi, seeing her friend so much more at ease than when she'd first met her. Hollyn had done a lot of hard work to manage her social anxiety, and it was goddamned inspiring. If her friend could make that much progress, surely Andi could figure out how to take some steps of her own. "So," she said, catching Hollyn's eye, "everything arrived okay?"

Hollyn sat back down and nodded. "Yep. All arrived as planned. You should be good to go."

Andi leaned down and gave Hollyn a little side hug, being careful not to spill her Topo Chico. "Thanks, lady. You're the best."

Hill looked between the two of him, clearly growing suspicious. "What was planned?"

Andi popped up. "Welp. I think we better get out of here and let Hollyn get back to work so she can get home."

Hill sent Hollyn a look. "Should I be scared?"

Hollyn's nose scrunched. "With Andi, you should always be a little bit scared. But in a good way. Like a roller coaster."

Andi laughed. "She's not wrong." She grabbed Hill's hand again, liking that she could do so without overthinking it. "Thanks again, Holls."

"Have fun," she said as Andi and Hill walked out.

Hill went willingly, but a few steps down the hallway he asked, "Are you going to tell me what's up?"

"Better to show you." She turned a corner and went down a hallway she rarely had reason to travel. The double doors on the right had a clipboard hanging outside of them with the printout of who had reserved that room for which times.

When she stopped in front of it, Hill turned with her and read the label above the door. "The Test Kitchen."

Andi bit her lip and turned to him, hoping he would be happy instead of frustrated by the surprise. "So, I know I said I was going to order takeout, but I may have asked Hollyn to book the test kitchen for us tonight, and I may have had some groceries delivered."

He tilted his head. "May have?"

She gave him her best don't-hate-me smile. "I was thinking maybe we could still have a cooking lesson tonight. And maybe I could video it to share with my readers and podcast listeners? I try to mix in some fun content in between all the murdery stuff."

Hill's expression went flat. "Video it."

"I know you nixed the idea of being the horror-movie virgin on my podcast, which is totally fine, but I thought this may be more up your alley. You love to cook, and you're really good at teaching it. I think if you gave it a shot, this could be a fun project for you." She rocked back on her heels, bracing for him to shut her down. "I just know that, for me, when I'm going through a tough time, the best thing I can do is direct my energy toward something creative. I wrote my first book when I was in a really dark place, and it helped get me out of it. And I started the podcast when my anxiety was starting to overwhelm me because it gave me a small way to fight back against the bad guys."

Empathy filled Hill's brown eyes.

"I'm not going to pretend to know what you're going through," she went on. "My trauma was different from yours, but I know that finding things—even little things—that gave me joy helped me build up my energy again so that I could tackle bigger things. Maybe teaching other people to cook could give you that little boost."

Hill let out a breath and ran a hand over the back of his head. "This is you being pushy."

She swallowed hard. "Yes. Which you said you appreciated and, frankly, kind of asked for."

He glanced toward the closed doors of the test kitchen and set down his mineral water on a table by the door.

"If you hate it, I won't post the video, but I think this could be fun," she rambled on. "I ordered some ingredients, and Hollyn made sure they were put away in here for us. I also thought you might enjoy cooking in the fancy kitchen they have here since my kitchen is kind of bare bones."

Hill turned back to her, and she braced for him to be annoyed, but instead, he lifted his hand and cupped her jaw, his gaze searching hers. "Thank you."

She brightened. "Really?"

His thumb brushed lightly against her cheek. "Yes. I don't know if I've ever met anyone who's so...sweet."

She grimaced at the word.

He smiled. "Don't make that face. I don't mean that in a dismissive way. I just mean that it's rare to find someone who spends their time thinking of ways to help someone else or make their life better. That's sweet. And kind. And sexy." He bent down and kissed her gently. "So I will cook for you on video, but no promises on if I'll give the go-ahead for you to post it. I'll have to make that call afterward. I'll probably be awkward as hell on-screen."

The simple kiss and his words had sent goose bumps chasing over her skin. She smiled. "Deal."

He swept an arm out in front of them. "Lead the way, pushy one."

She grabbed his hand. "Great. I'm starving."

For dinner. But also for more time with Hill. So many times in her life, she'd pushed her friends a little too far, her "help" sometimes perceived as being overbearing, as annoying, as Andi being *too much*. Her family had always thought she was too much. Still did. She realized that she'd expected Hill to react the same way.

Instead, he'd called her sweet and kissed her and said yes to her plan. He was going to step out of his comfort zone and trust her. That vote of confidence filled her up. She wasn't going to let him down. This was going to be the best damn cooking-lesson video ever created.

Or at least the most fun.

She would make sure of it.

chapter **seventeen**

HILL FOLLOWED ANDI INTO THE TEST KITCHEN AS SHE flipped on the lights. The space was bright and modern, with an all-white kitchen and professional-grade stainless-steel appliances on the left and an area for a camera and chairs for spectators on the right.

"They keep things pretty neutral so that people can dress up the kitchen how they want for their videos," Andi explained. "Or for live demos. That's why the chairs are there. Sometimes Lucinda, the head of WorkAround, will bring in a local chef to teach us a few things as a perk for renting here."

"This is a really great setup," Hill said, taking it all in and running his hand over the white quartz countertops. The appliances alone were a cook's dream. At the firehouse, the outdated equipment had required a hope and a prayer that something wouldn't break down in the middle of a cooking session.

"I'm going to put my phone on a tripod," she said. "Why don't you double-check that we have what we need. I looked up the recipe for dragon noodles and got those ingredients, but they also stock staples here in the fridge and pantry if you need other things."

"Thanks." Hill went to work checking what they had and tried to ignore the fact that Andi was setting up a camera.

He hated the idea of being on video and was sure he'd be about as smooth as sandpaper on film, but he wasn't going to think about that right now. Andi had arranged this in an attempt to do something nice for him, and the sentiment of that had hit him right in the gut. He'd meant what he'd said to her. The woman was *sweet*. In a way he'd never experienced.

From the very beginning, before the hanging out and the kissing and the touching, she'd set her sights on cheering him up. Bringing brownies over. Offering to plant flowers. Inviting him to watch movies with her. He'd initially perceived it as charity, as her feeling sorry for him, but the more he was around her, the more he realized that notion was misguided. She hadn't straddled his lap and came against his hand as charity. She hadn't invited him tonight to be nice. She *wanted* to spend time with him. But she also *saw* him.

Even when he tried to fake being okay, she saw through it. She knew he was fighting some demons, and she was showing him she wasn't scared of that. She'd stand by his side as a friend and help him fight. And she did it without acknowledging what an extraordinary thing that was—to do that for someone she'd only met two months ago.

But maybe that was because she had been there—was still there on some level—with her own demons. He saw the shadows cross her face when she talked about her past. He'd seen the fear bubble up when she talked about sex. Maybe she saw through his bullshit facade because she knew how to wear one, too. They were shopping at the same costume shop.

He vowed in that moment that this wouldn't be a one-way street. She was trying to help him, but he was going to be there for her as well. She wanted to learn how to trust a man again? Well, he was going to be the most trustworthy guy who ever lived. No more holding back with her. Honesty about who he was and what he was going through. Even if it was ugly or embarrassing. That was what he could give her.

"Are we all good?" Andi asked from behind him.

He shut the double-door fridge and turned around. "You did great. Everything's here, plus some extras."

Andi grinned and did a little fast clap. "Yay. I'm ready to learn. And I hope it's a quick-cooking thing because oh my God am I hungry." She cocked a thumb toward the tripod. "I'm already recording."

He eyed the phone like it was a bomb ready to go off. "I can't promise I'm going to get this right on one video take. Or twelve."

She waved a hand. "Oh, don't worry about that. I'm going to record us in one long take, and I'll edit and piece it together. So if we mess something up, we'll just pause and do it again. This is just for fun. My followers aren't going to expect it to look like a show on the Food Network."

He nodded. "Got it."

She grabbed a blue-striped apron off a hook on the wall and looped it around his neck. "Let's do this, Chef."

He smirked as he tied the apron around his waist. "I don't know why you're putting the apron on me. You're the one who's going to be cooking."

"True." She peeked over her shoulder at the camera. "Pray for us, y'all."

And with that, they were off and running.

Andi talked to the camera while Hill set things up. "Hey, everyone, today I have something a little different for you. After a long night of recording a podcast about a really sad case, my friend Hill offered to come by and feed me to cheer me up." She looked over at Hill and gave him a little wink. "Isn't he the *sweetest*?"

Hill chuckled under his breath. Andi wasn't going to let go of that word. "I'm downright adorable."

"Yes," she agreed, looking pleased that he was playing along. "Yes, he is. And lucky you, I'm going to share him and his skills with you tonight because I'm sure I'm not the only one who could use a little help not setting her kitchen on fire."

"I'm prepared for that, too," Hill said, arranging items on the kitchen island next to the thick butcher-block cutting board.

Andi reached out and put her hand on Hill's shoulder, making him pause in front of the camera. "Yes, this handsome guy is also a retired firefighter, so no one need worry for the surrounding villagers. We're all safe here."

A wave of awkwardness crashed over him at the thought of anyone watching this, but he took a breath and tried to center himself. *This is just cooking.* He finished laying out all the ingredients on the counter and tried to imagine he was teaching an impromptu class at the firehouse, that there were only friends in the audience.

He turned to Andi, giving the camera a side view. If he focused on her, he'd be all right. "Before you start cooking, you want to make sure you have everything you need for the recipe. If you're missing something, you can google substitutions so that you're not caught off guard when you get to that step."

Andi opened a spice bottle of red pepper flakes and gave it a little sniff. "Whoa." She blinked. "That's going to be hot. How do you know if it's okay to substitute something?"

Hill took the bottle from her. "Don't inhale those or you're going to be hating life." He set the bottle down. "With substitutions, you'll develop a feel for that the more you cook. Unless you're baking, most of the time, substitutions won't be catastrophic, but they may change the flavor profiles, so look for things that keep the heart of the dish." He picked up a bottle of sriracha sauce. "For this dish, your key flavor profiles are sweet and spicy and Asian-inspired. So if you don't have sriracha, you can experiment with a different hot sauce. If you don't have brown sugar, you can use white sugar or honey. But something like the soy sauce is more integral, and it will change the profile if you switch it out."

Andi smiled. "Sweet and spicy. I think that should be our cooking team name."

"You're not going to let me live down calling you sweet, huh?" he asked with a smirk.

"Nope." She scooted between him and the counter to grab the pasta pot. "And I would obviously be the spicy one in that equation."

Without thinking, he braced his arms on the counter on each side of her, caging her in, and bent down and kissed the spot where her shoulder met her neck. "Maybe we could take turns. I'm not always sweet."

She stilled for a moment, her back brushing against his front, and he quickly moved his hands off the counter. He hadn't been thinking. He didn't want her to ever feel trapped in any way.

"Sorry—" he started, but she spun around before he could continue.

She looked up at him from beneath those dark lashes of hers and gave him a little smile. "Forgot the camera was there?"

"Maybe just for a second," he admitted. "But I was saying sorry about caging you in. I wasn't thinking."

"Caging me in?"

"With my arms," he said, doing the motion again but lowering his arms quickly. "I know it might make you nervous to have someone in your space like that, blocking you from moving."

Her lips parted as awareness dawned. "Oh. Right." She glanced back at the camera. "Give me a sec."

She stepped around him and headed back toward her phone. She touched the screen, presumably stopping the recording, and then walked back over to him.

"Everything okay?" he asked.

She gave him a considering look, and then she stepped between him and the kitchen island and hoisted herself onto the counter so that she was closer to eye level with him. "I'm okay. But maybe we should talk."

He hooked his thumbs in his pockets. "All right."

She took an audible breath, and a line appeared between her brows. "I know I've been vague about what happened to me. I hate talking about it. I rarely tell anyone. Hollyn doesn't even know."

"You don't have to—"

She lifted a hand to gently halt him. "I know I don't have to, but if we're going to attempt this kind of friends-with-kissing relationship, we'll need an open line of communication. I don't want you to feel like you're walking on eggshells around my triggers, and I also want you to feel comfortable being open with me about what's going on with you. I'm not sure this works otherwise."

"I think you're right," he agreed. "I'm really worried I'm going to do something to scare you."

"Right. So maybe we should talk a little bit more about what may or may not freak me out and why," she said, resolve in her voice even though she looked worried.

He nodded. "That's probably a good idea."

She looked down at her hands, which she'd pressed flat against her thighs, and took a breath before looking up at him again. "I'm going to have to do this rip-the-Band-Aid-off style, okay? This is not a fun story to tell."

"Whatever you need," he said gently.

"So, I know you're assuming I was sexually assaulted."

The words were like a punch to his gut, but he managed to nod. "Yes."

Her throat bobbed as she swallowed. "Well, it's probably not in the way you're thinking." She smoothed the loose fabric of her dress along her thighs in a slow, repetitive motion. "When I was fifteen, I had a huge crush on my neighbor, my best friend's older brother, Evan. He was twenty-one."

Hill kept his expression neutral, not wanting to scare her off talking, but the fact that this story was starting with her being a young teen made his fists curl. Someone hadn't just hurt Andi, they'd hurt Baby Andi.

"I followed him around like a goddamned puppy dog when I went over to their house," Andi said, derision in her voice. "He was always nice to me but mostly just being polite. Putting up with his little sister's chatty friend, you know?" She glanced up. "I thought he would never actually notice me or see me as anything but a kid. But then one night, I was having a sleepover with his sister, and I went downstairs in the middle of the night to get some water. Evan was just getting home, and I ran into him in the kitchen."

Hill noticed goose bumps prickling her arms, making the fine hairs stand up. He resisted the urge to reach out and warm her up, to soothe her in some way.

"He was as surprised to see me as I was to see him. But he couldn't exactly ignore me, so he had to talk to me. His clothes were dirty, and he had a cut on his arm." She looked off beyond Hill's shoulder and rubbed her lips together, like she was seeing the memory. "Of course, I asked him what had happened. He told me he'd been out by the lake because he had trouble sleeping and had drunk a little too much and had fallen down and cut himself on a bush."

Hill frowned, not understanding where she was going with all this.

"I helped him clean up the cut, and he made me promise not to tell anyone because he wasn't supposed to be out and he'd sworn to his parents that he'd stopped drinking," she went on. "I swore

I'd never tell because I was so desperate for him to like me. And it seemed to work. After that night, he started paying attention to me, flirting with me when no one was looking, and just generally making me feel special.

"I started sleeping over there more often because it would give me some alone time with him in the middle of the night. He always stayed out late, and I'd sneak out of my friend's room and wait for him. A lot of times, he'd come back looking like he'd been through something. But I figured he was battling a drinking problem and going through some emotional stuff. I wanted to make him feel better, be there for him."

Hill's shoulders were growing tense.

"Eventually, he started telling me that I was the only one he trusted because I kept his secrets and that he adored me and all kinds of romantic nonsense." She huffed a disgusted sound. "I bought it because it was everything I wanted to hear, and it made me feel more adult. He told me he wished I was older so that we could be together. So, trying to prove the point that I was plenty old enough, I kissed him one night. That gave him the green light he needed—that I was willing and wouldn't tell. We started sleeping together." She looked up to meet Hill's gaze. "He was my first."

Hill's throat was tight but he nodded for her to go on.

"My teenage-crush feelings for him made me blind," she said, tone grim. "So when news stories started popping up about people being murdered in a nearby city, it never even crossed my mind that the dates matched up to some of those times I'd seen Evan come in late."

Hill's stomach dropped. *Oh, fuck.*

She rolled her lips together and gripped the counter, her eyes a little shiny. "And when cops eventually started asking questions, Evan told me what to say, that the whole thing was bullshit and a misunderstanding, that he'd never hurt anyone." She shook her head. "And I believed him because he'd always been so gentle with me, and I couldn't imagine him doing those horrible things. So when the cops asked me questions, I lied for him."

Jesus. Hill's heart broke for the young, innocent girl Andi had been.

"And his family was loaded, so they hired the best lawyers, and the cops couldn't charge Evan with what little they had. So, they moved on to other suspects. And I figured it'd all been a big misunderstanding." She closed her eyes for a moment before opening them again. "But another victim was killed a month later, and I knew for a fact that Evan had been out that night. I didn't want to believe it was possible, but I decided to ask him."

"God, Andi," Hill whispered, fear welling in him even though all of this had happened many years ago.

She made a sound of disbelief. "That's how dumb I was. It didn't even occur to me that it could be dangerous to approach him about it. I just didn't really believe it was possible, but I had to ask. So the next time I met up with him, I let things proceed like normal. He took me to bed, and I told him that he could tell me anything, that I wouldn't hold it against him, that I loved him." She grimaced.

"I know now that it made him angry, me questioning him. But he played it off. He smiled and said, 'Don't be silly.' But then once we started to have sex, his expression changed. He whispered against my ear, *If you tell anyone what you know, I will tell the world that you helped me. Because you have. I could never have done this without you. You've known the truth for weeks and didn't say a word. You've already lied for me. To the police. You're in this with me, so let's not pretend otherwise.*"

All the air left Hill's chest.

A tear tracked down Andi's cheek, and she met Hill's gaze. "I had to stay calm and let him finish. I had to pretend that yes, I'd already known and that no, I wouldn't tell on him, that I loved him. Because I knew if I didn't say that, he'd kill me right there. I could see it in his eyes—the monster that had been hiding behind the facade." She swiped at her tears.

"I waited for hours until he fell asleep, his arm over me, thinking I'd die if I made a move too soon, and then I finally snuck out. I ran to my parents and told them everything. Evan had already taken off by the time the cops got there, but they tracked him down a few days later two states away, and he was arrested."

"Thank God," Hill whispered, his mind reeling.

"My parents and their lawyers made sure my name was kept out of everything since I was a minor, and Evan got convicted on six murder charges and is in jail in Georgia for life." She met his gaze. "But I spent the next few years having flashbacks, not just of that night and the way it had felt to lie there, knowing he was a killer. I also started picturing his victims, feeling like I was responsible for what had happened to them."

Hill put his hand over hers. "Andi, of course you weren't responsible. You were a kid. Being manipulated by a sociopath."

She gave a humorless smile. "My logical brain knows that. The emotional one, not so much, but I've come a long way—with lots of therapy. I still have trust issues, and sex got knotted up with all that terror, which has made it hard to untwine, but I'm working on it." She patted his chest. "With you."

His heart broke for her. "I'm so sorry that happened to you."

"Thanks." She sniffled and gave him a quivery smile. "Aren't you glad you signed up for this disaster?"

He frowned. "You're not a disaster. You're an amazing woman who has survived something not many could. And you went straight to your parents even while being terrified for your own life, and I'm sure worried what they would think. I'm in awe of you, actually."

She looked down. "I shouldn't have worried about what my parents would think. They didn't surprise me. They were obviously horrified by what Evan had done to those poor people and that I'd been with him, but they never saw what happened to me as an assault. In their eyes, I'd chosen to be with Evan. They didn't see me as a victim. I was just a dumb teenager making bad decisions."

Hill's jaw flexed. "But you know that's not true, right?"

She nodded. "I do. Now. That took some work. But it's left me with a bad case of not being able to trust my gut. I'm apparently a really shitty judge of character. Evan sold me a mirage about who he was, and I bought it hook, line, and sinker."

"Andi...you can't... That's what sociopaths do. That's not a statement on your judgment."

"Isn't it, though?" She shook her head. "But that's why I'm telling you all this even though I hate telling anyone about my history. I don't want to be tied to that girl anymore, and because my name was held out of the news, I can keep it in the past. But if we're going to continue getting together, you should know what my real fears are."

He took her hands in his. "I'm listening."

She met his gaze, her blue eyes clear and resolute. "You caging me in against the counter and kissing me? That didn't scare me. The scariest sex I've had was sweet sex. Evan manipulated me with loving words and gentleness, made everything feel like my idea and like I was coaxing him into it." She pressed her lips together and paused as if choosing her words carefully. "I would almost rather you be the take-charge type—as long as you stop immediately if I say no to something—because that feels safer, more honest. Then it's about sex and desire and not manipulation. But if you go the sweet, gentle route, whispering loving things into my ear? It may trigger me."

Hill absorbed that for a moment, processing her words, and

then laced his fingers with hers, stepping into her space. She parted her knees, making room for him to stand between them. He held her gaze, needing her to hear him, to understand. "I can promise you without a shadow of a doubt that I will *always* listen to no. Or stop or slow down or whatever directions you throw at me. I've told you that and I mean it." When she gave him a little nod, he went on. "Beyond that, whatever you need from me to feel safe or comfortable, just ask. I know I'm not the most talkative guy, but my past is an open book. You can background check me. The fire department does an extensive one.

"I can give you my ex-fiancée's number, and you can ask her anything you want about me. She doesn't like me these days, but she will tell you I'm not dangerous. As for my own background, my mom left when I was young. She passed away a few years later, and my dad has been an addict since I was old enough to remember. My aunt and uncle took me in when I was twelve and are good people. They would tell you anything you wanted to know about me."

She looped her arms around his neck, her expression soft.

"And I'm not in a great place," he went on, going for the honesty he'd promised himself he'd give her. "I'm dealing with PTSD from the fire, a disability, and depression that makes some days hard, but I'm working on it. I have a pushy neighbor who's making me."

She smiled.

"But I know one thing for sure." He met her gaze. "I would never, ever harm you. Your gut is not wrong about me. You *are* safe with me."

....

Hill's words cascaded over Andi, and she closed her eyes, absorbing them. Everything inside her said she could trust him, that he meant it. She wanted to question that internal assuredness. Had taught herself to *always* question it. But in that moment, she couldn't muster doubt no matter how much she tried.

The realization hit her hard. She believed him. Truly *believed* him.

She opened her eyes, Hill's brown-eyed gaze intent on her. She could smell the scent of his shampoo, fresh and minty, and feel the heat of his body wafting against her. She'd looped her arms around his neck and decided now that she didn't want to let him go. She had never, as an adult, felt this gut-level trust in a man she was attracted to. The possibilities of what she could do with that rolled out in front of her like the most enticing buffet. If she trusted Hill, if she didn't have to be scared with him, if there was no pressure to make this something romantic, they could...have a whole lot of fun.

"Hill."

"Yes?" he asked, tucking a lock of her hair behind her ear.

"I believe you."

Relief crossed his face, the lines in his forehead smoothing. "Thank you."

She slid her hand to the collar of his T-shirt and tugged him down. When he was eye to eye with her, she said, "Now let's get this cooking lesson over with because if I don't eat, I'm not going to have the energy to show you just how much I believe you. And I really, really want to show you."

A slow smile spread over his face. "Yes, ma'am."

Yes, ma'am.

Good Lord. Just that slow-honey voice of his had her skin going hot. This was going to be the longest cooking lesson ever.

chapter **eighteen**

Andi's heartbeat quickened as she turned off her car's ignition. Hill had parked on his side of their duplex, having left WorkAround a few minutes ahead of her, and by the time she pulled into her driveway, he was leaning against the side of his car, arms crossed casually but expression intent. He lifted a hand in silent greeting. He looked so tall, broad, and confident in the golden light shining from the porch, and her body gave a kick of appreciation. *That guy* was the friend she now had permission to touch. How the hell had she landed here? She'd somehow hit the friends-with-benefits lottery. Now she had to find the guts to cash in that ticket.

They'd had a great dinner in the WorkAround kitchen and had laughed their way through the video despite the somber conversation beforehand. Hill had given her approval to post a video, but she had no idea if she'd even have enough usable material to share with her followers. At this point, she didn't care if she had a single shareable minute. She and Hill had cooked together, joked around, and she'd manage to make a delicious bowl of spicy pasta with his guidance. It'd been like an exorcism, chasing the demons out of the room with a relentless commitment to having a good time.

But now they were back home, and she was going to have to face one of her biggest fears—taking this to the next level. She knew without a doubt that Hill would end the night right now if she asked him to. If she told him she wasn't ready for anything tonight, he'd walk into his side of the duplex. But she didn't want to tell him to do that. After the playful kissing and touching they'd done in the kitchen tonight, she was aching for more of that connection, that feeling of normalcy with a guy. She wanted to touch him without fear, wanted to be touched without panicking.

Her nerves were pushing at the edge of her brain, an army always on call, but she refused to let them take over this time. If panic showed up to the party, she'd deal with it when it came. Right now, she wasn't going to overthink this. *You're okay. You're safe.*

Hill headed over to her and pulled open her car door, ever the gentleman. Or maybe he was afraid she'd never get out on her own—a distinct possibility if she let her panic take over. Andi smiled, grabbed her purse, and took his hand as she climbed out. "Why, thank you, kind sir."

He gave a little bow and shut her car door. "My pleasure. You okay?"

"Yep," she said a little too brightly. She glanced toward the front porch, reality rushing in and making her hesitate, the weight of this decision heavy on her. "I'd offer you a glass of wine, but I'm all out. I might have beer. Or hard liquor. I'm not sure. But—"

He squeezed her hand, gently cutting her off. "You're nervous."

She cringed. "That obvious?"

He gave her a pointed look. "It's okay, you know. To change your mind."

She swallowed past the lump in her throat, frustration welling. "Ugh. I don't *want* to change my mind. That's not what this is. It's just...old habits die hard. I'm getting in my head about it. I trust you, and still, my mind wants to overthink every little thing.

I mean, look at you." She flicked her hand toward him. "Who *wouldn't* want to have sex with you?"

Hill laughed. "Lots of people, I'm sure, but I'm real glad you're not one of them."

She tipped her head back. "I'm sorry I'm being weird."

"Hey." He tugged her closer, tucking her hand against his chest. "I love your weird. No apologies needed for that, but maybe I can help with the overthinking."

She lifted her head and eyed him. "How?"

He reached down with his free hand and pulled her phone out of the front pocket of her purse. He handed it to her. "Call your friend. The one who knows about our situation and your past. Tell her you're with me and that you're spending the night at my place. Send her a photo of me. Cover all your bases."

Andi wet her lips. She knew doing all of that was unnecessary. She really did trust Hill, but the fact that he didn't mind that she went over the top with her safety measures made her breathe a little easier. She took her phone from him, snapped a photo, and then texted it to Eliza. Once it had gone through, she hit the button to call her friend.

Eliza answered almost immediately. "Hey, girl." A pause. "Whoa. Who's the dude?"

"Hey, Eliza," Andi said, staying close to Hill. "That's my neighbor, Hill Dawson."

"Oh, wait, *the* neighbor?" she said with delight. "Damn, you've got good taste. Hot werewolf, indeed."

Hill smiled, and Andi realized he could hear every word. Her cheeks heated. "I'm going to be staying at his place tonight, next door to mine. He wanted me to let you know so that I feel better, having a friend know where I am and who I'm with."

"*He* wanted you to call me?" she asked. "I'm impressed. You feel good about this?"

Andi let out a breath. "I do."

"Hallelujah, praise Jesus," Eliza said. "Give him the phone."

"Wait, what?" Andi asked.

"You heard me," Eliza said impatiently. "Come on, I promise I'll be nice. Let me talk to him."

Hill had heard all of that because he lifted his hand. She reluctantly handed him the phone.

Hill stepped back a little. "Hello."

Andi couldn't hear at the increased distance, and she frowned because Eliza was apparently going to say more than hi.

Hill nodded. "I understand... Yep...of course." Then he laughed, his gaze darting to Andi. "I promise. Happily."

He said goodbye and then handed the phone back to Andi. Andi put it to her ear. "What the hell did you say?"

She could almost hear Eliza grinning over the phone. "Hot damn. Even his voice is sexy. You have fun, girlie."

Before Andi could respond, Eliza ended the call. Andi groaned and slipped the phone back into her purse. Hill was still smiling.

"What's with the look?" She put a fist on her hip. "What did she say?"

"Not much," he said with a little shrug. "Just that if I hurt one hair on your head, she'd personally cut my balls off and use them for Christmas ornaments."

Andi's eyes widened. "Oh my God."

"And that I better give you the best sex of your life and not be some selfish asshole in bed because her friend, Andi, is a goddess who deserves to be worshipped."

Andi put her hand over her eyes, mortified. "I love her, but I'm going to kill her."

Hill grabbed her wrist and tugged her hand down gently, his gaze twinkling with amusement. "Don't be mad. I happen to agree with her. I promised I'd give it my all."

Andi let him pull her into an embrace. "My nerves have now shifted into mortification. I sound like a charity project. 'Please sleep with my poor friend. She needs all the help she can get.' Someone should make signs: *Orgasms for Andi. Please Donate.*"

"Stop." His hand slid down to her waist and squeezed. "You are *not* a charity project." His voice was quiet and deep when he spoke again. "You're a fucking fantasy, Andi. *My* fantasy. I've wanted you since that first night you opened your door wearing your Wonder Woman pajamas." The words sent a ripple of heat through her. "And I know this is scary for you, but maybe it will help you to know it's scary for me, too." He touched his forehead to hers. "I haven't been with anyone since my accident. The thought of you seeing me naked, without my prosthesis..."

She lifted her head to look at him, surprised. "You don't have to be afraid of that. I think you're gorgeous."

There was vulnerability in his eyes. "Thank you, but that doesn't mean the fear's not there."

She nodded, understanding that better than anyone. She pushed up on her toes and brushed her mouth against his, suddenly less afraid. "Ready to go inside?"

"I am," he said, holding her gaze. "Are you?"

"I'm ready," she said, quiet firmness in her voice. "Stop me from overthinking this."

A little smile touched his lips. "I can do that."

He took her hand and led her to his door. Her heart was pounding as he unlocked it and let them inside. But the minute he shut the door behind them, he turned to her, pinning her with a look of resolve that had her breath catching. "I'm going to do what you asked—what you told me earlier that you'd prefer—but know that the minute you say stop or slow down, I'm going to listen. Every time."

What she'd asked. For him to take charge. For him not to treat her like Evan had. Her mouth was dry, so she nodded.

"And all those sweet things you don't want to hear?" he said, bracing a hand on the door next to her and leaning close. "I'm going to keep them to myself after this. But know upfront that I think you're beautiful and smart and I feel honored that you're trusting me."

She closed her eyes and a shiver went through her. "Thank you."

"Now," he said, pressing a kiss to the tender spot behind her ear and slipping his hand beneath the hem of her dress, his thumb tracing over her outer thigh. "I'm going to keep my promise to your good friend Eliza. You stay just like this for me, neighbor."

She opened her eyes at the softly spoken command and found Hill's gaze sparking with heat. He dipped his head to kiss her, his mouth meeting hers with tender urgency. His tongue teased against hers as his hand traced along her bare thigh up to her hip, sending tingling awareness through her and coaxing her out of her head and into her skin. Her fingers gripped his left bicep, the muscles thick and unyielding. Lord, the arms on this guy. She wanted to rub herself on him like a cat.

But the idea burned up in a flash of heat as soon as Hill's other hand tracked to the top edge of her panties. *Oh, God.* Before she had time to contemplate the gravity of what was happening, Hill had broken away from their kiss and was dragging the lacy fabric downward. She could stop him. She knew she could. But she found herself complying instead. She slipped off her sandals, a tremor working through her, and he pulled her panties down and off, tossing them to the side. Her gaze zeroed in on the little puddle of lacy fabric that was now five feet away.

Cool air drifted over her heated skin as Hill traced his hand upward from the soft part of her knee and along her inner thigh.

Her body prickled with awareness and anticipation, a sheen of sweat dampening her skin. Hill kept his attention on her face when he moved his hand higher and higher and then finally brushed his fingers over the tender skin of her labia. A full-body shudder of need went through her, and she sucked in a deep breath.

He watched her like she was the most interesting movie ever made, desire flaring in his eyes as he stroked her and found her slick and needy from his touch. He groaned under his breath, the strained sound sending pleasure through Andi, and he eased his finger inside her, thick and callused and hot.

She gasped, the delicious friction making her feet arch with an electric sensation that shot down her legs. Her body clamped around him like a fist.

"God, you feel so good, Andi," he said, his voice full of grit as he guided another finger inside her, stretching her a little and providing a toe-curling fullness. "So fucking sexy."

She reached out blindly, gripping his wide shoulders to keep her balance. She suddenly worried her knees wouldn't make it through this.

Hill leaned down and kissed her again, his fingers pumping slowly inside her in a rhythm that had her hips rocking along with it. His tongue stroked against hers in the same pattern, slow, deep, taking his time. He tasted like the sweet, spicy dinner they'd had and a whole lot of promise. She couldn't get enough. The fear that had haunted her earlier had been chased into the shadows by Hill's touch. All she could think about now was how amazing he was making her feel, how much she wanted all of him stretched out over her, pushing inside her, skin to skin, the full experience.

The scent of her own arousal drifted around them, and she moaned softly into his kiss, his fingers like magic. He broke away from her mouth, his eyes hooded, and then just when she thought he was going to come back for another kiss, he lowered himself to his knees, his fingers still working her.

"Hill," she whispered, not sure what she was telling or asking him.

He looked up at her, face half-lit in the lamplight, and with his free hand gathered the fabric of her dress in his hand. "Hold up your dress, gorgeous. I want to see what this is doing to you."

Oh. God.

She took the skirt of her dress in her hand and watched as he braced himself on the knee of his uninjured leg. Then he was gazing right at the place where he was touching her, his breath tickling her sensitive skin. He circled his thumb on her clit, his fingers still inside her, and she thought she was going to lose it right there, but then he shifted forward, moved his thumb away, and put his mouth on her.

Some unintelligible sound slipped from her throat at the feel of his hot tongue and soft lips. Her body lit on fire with a new cascade of sensations. His beard brushing against her tender skin. The ends of his hair tickling her thighs. She tried to process it all, wanting to remember every moment, but then his tongue circled her clit and he rocked his fingers into her, obliterating all chance of organizing her thoughts. Pleasure shot through her veins like a drug, her nails digging into his shoulders and her head tipping back against the door, rattling it. She worried she might scale the damn thing like Spider-Man. Because somehow it was too much sensation to manage all at once. Her body didn't know how to deal with it. This was so much different than her own hand or her vibrator.

But before she realized what she was doing, she'd draped her leg over his shoulder, silently begging for more. Too much, yet she still wanted more.

"Fuck, Andi," Hill said after a few minutes of using his tongue to drive her wild, his panting breaths a cool caress against her overheated skin. "I could spend all night right here, hearing those needy sounds you're making. I know you're on the edge of coming, but I'm enjoying this too much to rush." He kissed her inner thigh. "You taste so fucking good."

She groaned, and she could almost feel him grinning at the torture he was meting out. "Hill..."

"Yes?" He dragged his tongue along her crease, making her fingers ball into a fist.

"Please."

"Tell me what you want," he said, slowly pumping his fingers inside her.

"I need to come," she gasped, barely resisting the urge to grab his hair and guide his mouth back to the place she needed it.

She waited, expecting him to give her the orgasm now that she'd asked, but instead, he slipped his fingers out, guided her leg off his shoulder, and stood. "I know you do."

Her lips parted, his movements not making sense in her brain. "What are you doing?"

Hill gave her a roguish smirk and brushed his thumb over her bottom lip, letting her taste herself. "You're going to get what you want...eventually. But after an orgasm is when the fear rushed in last time. So this time, we're not going to let the fear get its way." He slipped his arms around her, letting her dress fall back into place, and pulled her against him. His erection pressed against her belly, hard and thick.

"Wanting to come has a way of blocking out almost all other thoughts. That's why sex gets so many people into trouble." He slid his hand down to her ass, gripping her gently. "I want you so out of your mind with need that nothing else has room. No space for overthinking or worrying. So all you're thinking about is pleasure and fun and feeling good. Then, when I fuck you," he said with utter masculine confidence, "it will be because you begged me to, not because you're trying to white-knuckle your way through fear."

Her heartbeat was pounding in her chest and between her legs, but the words were weaving through her with erotic promise. As much as she wanted relief from the tension he'd built within her, what he was suggesting sounded way better. Sex without fear. Sex with a quiet mind. Sex with Hill.

"Sounds tortuous," she said.

"It does, doesn't it?" His smile was playfully wicked. "You game?"

She laughed and slid her hands up his chest, finding that his heart was beating quickly, too. Only then did she remember that it'd been years for him. She wasn't the only one dealing with demons and an empty bed. "I'm game under one condition."

He cocked his head. "And what's that?"

She slid her hand down and pressed her palm against the hard length in his pants. Her inner muscles clenched at the thought that he might be inside her sometime soon, filling her, making her feel good. "I get to torture you back."

Desire sparked in his eyes, and his cock flexed against her palm. "Game on, neighbor."

"Game on." She rubbed her hand along his erection, loving the groan he made, and she kissed him. "Show me your bedroom, Hill."

chapter **nineteen**

Hill wanted to pick up Andi and carry her into the bedroom like he was saving her from a fire, toss her onto the bed, strip her naked, and get back to making her gasp. But before he gave in to the instinct, he stopped himself. Even though he'd worked hard to keep his upper body strong, he couldn't trust his balance to carry another person with his prosthesis yet. Dropping Andi on the way to the bedroom would be quite the buzzkill.

He could just imagine explaining to Ramsey how he'd ended up putting his date in the emergency room. That metaphor would be way too appropriate for the state of his sex life. So instead, he grabbed Andi's hand and led her to his bedroom.

He switched on the overhead light by habit, but when the harsh light filled the room, his stomach clenched. He wanted to see all of Andi in full technicolor detail, but if things went well, he'd be getting naked, too. Even though Andi had assured him that she was attracted to him and his disability wasn't an issue, anxiety and self-consciousness still crept up his spine. There was a reason Christina hadn't slept with him after his accident, a reason she'd found someone else to go to bed with, and he couldn't help but think the amputation had a lot to do with it. It was an unavoidable visual reminder that he wasn't the same man he used to be.

Andi hadn't known him before, but he didn't want the spotlight on his disability. He didn't want her thinking about anything but her own pleasure. Unfortunately, as he glanced around, all he saw were reminders of how he was different. His room was neat, but he hadn't put certain things away. Like the crutches he kept by the bedside to use if he had to get up in the middle of the night. Or his running prosthesis, which was lying on the dresser. At least the wheelchair he sometimes used around the house when his muscles were aching was tucked away in the closet. Even so, he wished he could steer Andi back out and take a minute to put some things away.

"Wow," Andi said, oblivious to the internal crisis he was having. "This is how clean you keep your room when you're not expecting company? I thought boys' rooms were supposed to be messy. Where are the half-empty beer cans and dirty underwear? The big bottle of lube? I feel cheated."

Andi's comment broke him out of his circling thoughts, startling him into a laugh. "The big bottle of lube?"

She looked over at him, amusement in her eyes, and he realized what she was doing. Somehow she'd sensed his discomfort over her seeing his personal space and was trying to distract him. *This woman.*

"I'm not an animal," he said with a playfully affronted tone. "I keep the lube put away in a drawer like a gentleman."

She laughed. "Well, aren't you fancy."

He walked over to the side of the bed and turned on the lamp before coming back and flipping off the overhead light. The softened lighting took the edge off some of his nerves and made Andi's fair skin look like porcelain. He wanted to lick every bit of it.

He took her hand in his, trying to gauge how she was doing, and kissed the inside of her wrist. Her pulse jumped against his lips.

When she'd told him her story in the WorkAround kitchen, he'd wanted to personally castrate the sick fuck who had used her and hurt her so badly. But he knew he couldn't undo what she'd been through. All he could do was show her how different sex could be with someone she could trust. She'd told him it would be easier if he took control, was assertive instead of sweet, which he was one hundred percent down for. He'd always liked being bossy in bed, but he didn't want to push her further than she wanted to go.

"Still with me?" he asked, keeping his voice low.

Andi's gaze held his, her pupils dark in the low light, and she wet her lips. "Totally with you. Truly."

Something tight unlocked in his shoulders at her assurance, and he leaned down to kiss her. She relaxed into the kiss, her hands splaying against his chest, and he took the opportunity to reach around her and unzip her dress. The sound of the zipper was loud in the quiet room, but it only made his cock harder. It was the sound of Andi's trust.

When he pulled back from the kiss, he reached out and slipped her dress off her shoulders and down her arms. The light cotton fell into a cloud around her feet, leaving Andi standing there in his bedroom in a pale-pink lacy bra and nothing else.

His breath left him in a rush as he took in the sight of her. "Fuck, you're beautiful."

"Back at ya, neighbor." Andi's lips curved a little, and she reached back to unhook her bra. She let it fall away.

Her small, pert breasts made Hill's tongue press to the roof of his mouth. He lifted his hand to cup her breast, running his thumb over her dusky nipple and loving the way she shivered at his touch.

"My turn," she said, her fingers taking hold of the bottom edge of his T-shirt.

He lifted his arms and let her pull off his shirt. Cool air touched his overheated skin, and he watched her expression change as she took in the view. One of the things he liked so much about Andi was that she didn't play it cool. She didn't employ a poker face. She wore her feelings proudly, and right now, that look said she wanted him. That look made him forget to be self-conscious about the scars on his chest.

"I've had dirty dreams about you that started like this." Andi tossed his T-shirt onto the floor and stepped fully into his space. "Ever since you opened your door that day without your shirt on."

Her breasts pressed against his bare skin, and the feel of that silky feminine softness nearly did him in. He cupped her ass, fitting her against his erection. "Yeah? What happens next?"

Her fingers found the waistband of his jeans, making a little space between their bodies, and she unfastened the button. The zipper came down next and she tucked her hand inside his boxer briefs, the velvet touch of her hand wrapping around his cock making him shudder with need.

"You take off the rest of these clothes and show me how to make you feel good," she said, sounding a little breathless. "You got to taste me. Seems only fair I get afforded the same opportunity."

Show me. Taste me. He closed his eyes, a roll of *hell yes* moving through him. When he opened his eyes again, she was watching him, waiting. Part of him wanted to be the nice guy, tell her she didn't need to do anything for him, having her in his bed was enough. But the way Andi was looking at him told him what he needed to know. She wouldn't be asking if she didn't want to try it. She wasn't offering this as a favor. She said she wanted to torture him back. He wasn't going to stop her.

He slipped her hand out of his pants and walked backward toward the foot of the bed. "I can do that."

He sat on the edge and pulled off his shoes and socks. When

he shifted to take off his jeans, it took an inner pep talk before he could go for it. But after a few seconds of mental gymnastics, he bit the bullet and pulled his jeans and underwear down his thighs and off, exposing the insistent state of his cock but also revealing his residual limb and prosthesis.

He looked up, bracing himself for Andi's reaction. Her gaze tracked over him, gliding along his abdomen, lingering on his erection, and then continuing downward where his lower leg transitioned from flesh to mechanical device. Her attention glided back up to his face, her eyes unreadable, and she lowered herself to her knees. She braced her hands on his thighs and leaned in to kiss him. The kiss was long and deep, and he lost himself in it for a moment, his hand going to the back of her neck.

When she pulled back, she met his gaze. "I know this is hard for you, but you're luscious. Every bit of you. I would pin your photo on my wall and draw hearts on it."

He glanced away. "Andi, you don't need to—"

"No, I want you to really hear me." She slid her fingertips over the scars on his abdomen, tracing the raised skin there. "When I look at you, I see strength and bravery." Her hand tracked lower, wrapping around his cock and making him forget everything else for a second. "I see a man." Her hand moved down to his thigh, making its way over the sock that protected his limb below his knee to where his prosthesis connected. "I see a superhero who risked his own life to help others. Who literally gave up part of his body for it." She braced her hands back on his thighs. "And I think you're sexy as fuck."

He released a breath and cupped her face. "Thank you."

Her mouth tipped up at one corner. "You may want to hold that thanks for later. I'm about to do more than compliment you." She glanced down pointedly and then back up to him, heat in her eyes. "Show me what you like."

His stomach muscles flexed in anticipation as Andi lowered her head, hovering above his cock. He didn't want to blink, afraid to miss one second of this beautiful woman giving him pleasure. "It's hard to mess this up. Touch me wherever you want," he said, his voice a croak in his throat. "While you use your mouth. Don't do anything you're not into."

She gripped the base of his cock with her hand, her breath hot on the damp head, and smiled. "That, I can guarantee you."

The words were exactly what he needed to hear. He got off knowing his partner was enjoying herself, that she wanted to be doing what she was doing because it gave her pleasure, too. He damn sure had enjoyed going down on her.

Hill watched as Andi's lips closed over the head of his cock, the warmth of her mouth and tongue nearly making him cry out. It'd been so long. So. Long. Since a woman had touched him like this, tasted him, and the fact that it was Andi made it all the more intense. Her trust in him was the ultimate aphrodisiac. He threaded his hands in her hair, the soft red strands cascading over his knuckles, and he watched her.

She was taking her time, sucking him slowly, using the tip of her tongue to tease the crown, driving him out of his mind, and just when he'd get on the edge of orgasm and his grip on her hair would tighten, she'd back off. She pulled away briefly, sending him a wicked look, and then she dipped down and ran her tongue along his balls.

"Fuck," he groaned, his belly dipping as he tried to maintain control. "I'm not sure you needed instruction. You're going to kill me."

She laughed softly and peeked up at him. "I don't have a lot of experience with this, but I read *a lot* of dirty books. A single girl can't survive by vibrator alone."

He smiled. "God bless dirty books."

"Amen. Hallelujah," she said right before taking him into her mouth again and making his eyes roll back in his head.

He couldn't hold himself up anymore. He fell back onto his elbows and closed his eyes, the wet heat of Andi's mouth putting him into some trancelike state. But when she cupped his balls and took him deep to the back of her throat, he nearly levitated off the bed. He reached out, cradling her face, and easing back. "On the bed, Andi."

She sat back on her calves, lips slick and eyes a little dazed. He liked that look, like she was blissed out, too. He reached for her, helping her to her feet. Goddamn she looked like a fantasy—hair mussed, beautifully naked, skin flushed. How the hell had he gotten so lucky? The sweet, funny woman who'd baked him brownies, the one he'd try to scare off with rudeness, had just given him the blow job of his life and now was going to be in his bed.

He didn't know what he'd done to deserve this moment, but he wasn't going to question the universe and his good fortune right now.

He stood, pulling Andi against him and kissing her, their bodies pressed together skin to skin, and then he guided her down on the bed. She stretched out against his pillows, her hair fanning out, and her gaze tracked over him with hungry heat. He sat on the edge of the bed and reached down to remove his prosthesis. He didn't want anything in the way with Andi.

He made quick work of it, leaving the sock on that covered his residual limb, and set his prosthesis next to the bed. He pulled open the bedside table's drawer, grabbed a condom, checked the expiration date, and set it on top of the comforter. When he turned his body back toward Andi, she was watching him, biting her lower lip. He reached out and brushed her hair away from her face. "Still with me?"

She gave him a soft smile. "You better not leave me hanging this time."

He laughed. "Promise."

....

Andi's skin was burning up. She was so turned on, she was afraid spontaneous human combustion might actually be a thing, but seeing the condom also made this feel very real. She was going to sleep with Hill, have sex with her neighbor.

Yes, they were only friends. No, this was nothing serious. But that didn't mean it wasn't a monumental thing for her. The last time she'd tried to have sex with someone, she'd panicked the minute the guy had rolled on the condom. Flashbacks had hit her hard and fast, yanking her into the past and killing every ounce of sexual interest she'd had.

This felt different than that time. She felt safe with Hill. Present in a way she hadn't before.

Hill shifted closer. She could feel him watching her, gauging her mood. Honesty. She needed to be honest. She reached out and squeezed his bicep. "I'm getting in my head."

He nodded, expression serious. "Need to stop?"

"No. I want this. I just..." She didn't know how to articulate it.

He scooted closer and put his hand on her hip. He traced a finger right above her pubic bone, making her inner muscles clench. "How about this? You let me make you feel good. If you want to stop after that, the lube you suspect I have will make an appearance, and I'll take care of myself with my hand. There is no pressure to have sex tonight."

The thought of him stroking himself next to her wasn't exactly a deterrent. That sounded hella hot, but she also ached for the full experience, feeling him inside her, getting past this hurdle. She didn't want to back out. But she also knew that sometimes her anxiety won despite her best intentions. This would give her an out. The fact that Hill intuitively knew how to give her an option that wouldn't make the night feel like a failure if she had to tap the brakes made her want to kiss him again.

"That sounds perfect," she said, putting her hand over his and guiding it lower, dragging his fingertips over the hot, wet part of her.

Hill smiled that sinful smile of his and shifted into position. He braced his arms on each side of her and climbed between her legs. "Put your legs over my shoulders."

She did as she was told and watched as he lowered himself down and dragged his tongue over her aching flesh. Every feminine cell in her body clenched, and desire flooded her anew, a squeaking sound escaping her throat. He smiled up at her with smug confidence as he tucked two fingers inside of her. It was a smile that said *I got this*. A smile that said *fuck you* to her anxiety. A smile that said they were going to win the battle tonight.

Hill went back to work, laving and sucking and teasing her clit, and rubbing that sensitive spot inside her, bringing her to the edge of orgasm again in minutes.

"Oh, God." Her heels dug into his back and her fingers gripped his comforter. "Hill, I'm gonna—"

This time he didn't back off, though. He doubled down. Her head tipped back, and her back curved as she rocked against his mouth, the pleasure seizing her and forcing her body to move without her permission. Then every ounce of tension that had been building exploded into a million bits of light behind her eyes and she cried out, loud enough that she startled herself with the sound of it.

Holy shit. Holy shit.

Hill didn't stop, and the orgasm climbed higher, higher than she realized it could go, making her babble nonsense and squirm on the bed. She slapped her hand against the mattress not sure if she was asking for mercy or for more. She gasped Hill's name.

His hand gripped the back of her thigh as he lifted his head. "Tell me what you want, Andi," he said, breathless and urgent. "I need to hear it."

She was out of breath, panting, her body still quaking with aftershocks, but she still wanted more. She wanted Hill. "Use the condom," she managed to get out. "Please. Now."

The bed bounced as he moved. "Are you sure? You want this. I need to hear you say that."

She opened her eyes, her vision clearing in the low lamplight. She found him braced on one hand and knee, condom between his fingers, his cheeks flushed. She licked her lips. "I want you."

Relief crossed his face, and he tore open the condom. He rolled it on. "Get on your side, gorgeous," he said, stretching out next to her. "It will be easier this way."

She did as she was told and soon he was behind her, spooning her. He guided her top leg to bend at the knee, opening her body to him, and the head of his cock nudged her. Hill slid his hand between her legs, stroking her clit, sending sparks through her again, and then he eased inside. The feel of him stretching her was both foreign and delicious. She wasn't a virgin and knew her way around a sex toy, but this wasn't silicon. Hill's cock was thick and hard and hot, filling her in a way that made all her inner muscles clench and squeeze tight.

"Fuck, Andi," Hill groaned against her ear, his fingers still working her as he slowly pumped inside her. "You feel like a dream."

"Please don't let this be a dream," she murmured.

He pressed his lips against the curve of her neck and fucked her slow and deep, ramping up her body again. "You're going to come again for me."

She didn't think that was possible after the blinding orgasm she'd had. When she was alone, she was a one-and-done girl. But the confidence in his voice had a shiver of pleasure shooting straight downward, and her inner muscles twitched again.

Hill picked up the pace, his heart beating against her back, and he stroked her with expert fingers as he rocked his hips against her. Her breath quickened, tension building fast and low. The mattress squeaked beneath them.

"Put your hand between your legs," he whispered. "Feel what I'm feeling."

She listened without thinking and found his fingers, slick with her own arousal, moving over her clit. He took her hand and pressed her own fingers against herself. His cock slid against her fingertips as he fucked her, and the images that conjured in her brain sent her over. She cried out, her orgasm striking like lightning.

He groaned against her, a grinding, primal sound, and he pumped into her harder and faster, their bodies now sticky with sweat. She gasped, the feel of it all stealing her breath, and just as another wave of pleasure rolled through her, his body tensed against her and he cried out. His shout reverberated through the room, and she ate up the sound, his obvious pleasure filling her with pure feminine satisfaction.

They'd done it. They'd won. At least for tonight. Their demons were stuck out on the porch without an invitation to the party. Andi wanted to throw a goddamn ticker-tape parade.

Fuck you, Evan Longdale. Look what I found.

A few minutes later, when she and Hill were both quietly panting, their hearts still racing, Hill pressed his face into her hair. "Tell me you're okay, Andi."

She closed her eyes, a smile stretching her lips, and she snuggled back against him. "I'm very, very okay."

She could feel his body relax in relief. "Me too."

The simple admission that he'd been fighting something too made her heart squeeze, made something altogether *not* neighborly move through her. She shook the feeling away.

Careful there, Lockley.

chapter **twenty**

Hill stepped out of the bathroom after a quick shower and found Andi dressed again and sitting cross-legged on his bed as she scrolled through her phone. He would've invited her into the shower with him, but he didn't feel comfortable having her see what he referred to in his head as his old man's bathroom with the bench and handrails he'd had to install on the wall.

She hadn't noticed him yet, so he stood in the doorway for a moment, watching her as she scrolled. She'd gathered her hair into a messy bun atop her head, and her cheeks still wore the flush of a night well spent. Effortlessly sexy. He had no idea how a woman like her was sitting there on his bed in front of him right now. Part of him kept expecting to wake up from an erotic dream.

She turned finally and caught him staring. An indulgent smile lit her face. "Hey there."

"Hey." He stepped inside the bedroom. "You're dressed. I can lend you a T-shirt to sleep in if you need it."

She set her phone on the side table and pulled her knees to her chest, hugging them. "I'm not going to sleep over. Since this is a just-friends thing, I thought we should maybe not blur lines." She glanced at the bed with a little frown. "Plus, to be honest, I'm not sure I could fall asleep with a guy next to me."

He sat on the edge of the bed, facing her. "Because you're a bed hog or something else?"

She sighed and looked up. "The last time a guy slept next to me was that last night with Evan. He wrapped an arm over me, and I've never felt so scared or so trapped as I did those few hours. I'm afraid if I wake up in the middle of the night with your arm around me or something, I'll freak out."

The admission made Hill's heart twist. This sweet, lovable woman couldn't even be held without being reminded of the terror she went through. He reached out and squeezed her foot. "I'm sorry."

She gave him a little nod, a humorless smile touching her lips. "Me too. You'd be fun to cuddle with. Maybe some other time, on the couch."

"Deal," he said, trying to keep his voice light. "I can walk you back over to your side, make sure you get in safe."

"I'd like that," she said, taking his hand and letting him help her to her feet.

He walked her out of the bedroom, and she snagged her shoes from where she'd left them, the spell that had woven around them tonight already receding. Reality was a pushy sonofabitch. She leaned into him with easy affection, softening some of the unease moving through him. He had the overwhelming urge to say *Don't go*, but he knew that wouldn't be fair. He needed to give her the space she was asking for. And she was right, it probably was best not to blur boundaries. Sleeping over, waking up next to someone, could be more intimate than sex.

He unlocked the front door, the humid night air and the sound of crickets enveloping them, and walked Andi over to her side. She turned to him, shoes hanging from one hand, and smiled at him. She pushed up on her toes and kissed him—a soft, lingering kiss that had his blood heating again. When she pulled away, she gave his T-shirt a little tug. "I had a really great time tonight."

"Me too," he said, tucking her hair behind her ear.

"We should do this again sometime soon," she said, her smudged mascara making her blue eyes even brighter.

"We should." He considered her, an earlier idea creeping back in. "You wouldn't happen to be available Saturday night, would you?"

She gave him a flirty look. "I could be. Why? What'd you have in mind?"

He cringed. "A completely cheesy, embarrassing firehouse event that I somehow got roped into participating in. It's going to be horrible."

She laughed. "Well, with a sales pitch like that…"

"I know. Sorry."

She leaned back against her front door, gaze curious. "What kind of cheesy event?"

"My best friend, Ramsey, is in charge of this year's charity event for burn victims, and he got the brilliant idea to do a bachelor auction," he said, dread in his voice. "And somehow he guilted me into agreeing to participate."

Andi's expression lit with interest. "A bachelor auction? Like people bid on firefighters to take on dates?"

"Well, to take to that night's event, which apparently will involve food, booze, dancing, and karaoke." Hill braced himself for a *hell no*. He would say *hell no* if he could.

But Andi bit her lip, her eyes smiling. "Tipsy firefighters and karaoke? This sounds amazing."

He laughed at her enthusiasm. "It's going to be a nightmare. But I was thinking if you wanted to go, maybe I could give you the money to bid on me? Save me from a night of awkward conversation with a stranger?"

She snorted. "You introverts are so adorable. Stranger danger means a whole different thing to y'all. And of course I'll go and bid on you." She tilted her chin up haughtily. "As if I'd let some other chick or dude get their hands on you. No way. I'm an only child. I don't share."

Relief moved through him, and he cupped her face to kiss her soundly. "Thank you. You're a lifesaver."

"Don't thank me yet. You haven't seen me with a few drinks in my system and a karaoke machine within reach. It can get ugly real fast." She gave him a knowing nod. "I'm talking show tunes and power ballads."

He chuckled. "I'll take my chances."

"Then I will happily agree to join you on Saturday." She patted his chest and yawned. "But right now, I'm going to collapse face-first on my bed. Someone wore me the hell out."

He leaned down and kissed her forehead. "Get some rest, neighbor."

"Sweet dreams, Hill."

She went inside, and he waited until he heard the lock click and her alarm activated. For the first time in a while, he didn't dread the night. His body was sated, his sheets smelled like Andi, and he had a date Saturday night. Things were looking up.

....

Andi woke up early the next morning and edited the cooking video she'd made with Hill, grinning through the whole process. She knew they'd had fun together, but seeing it on-screen underlined how right she was. Hill would be great at teaching people to cook. He was so patient with her, gently guiding her through the process without making her feel inept when he had to step in and help. Plus, he looked fantastic on camera.

She posted the video to her readers and podcast followers and then went back to working on her manuscript. Over the last two weeks, she'd hit a bit of a stride with it and felt like if she kept it up, she'd have something sellable to present to her agent. Today, she'd decided to put in a love scene between the heroine and the guy who was helping her evade the killer. She hadn't planned for a romance between the two, but somehow, there it was.

She blamed her neighbor.

An hour and a half into writing, she took a break to get a refill on coffee and opened up the video again. Comments had poured in.

> **shura_blaese:** Whoa, who's the hot chef?
>
> **HorrorBelle4Life:** Omg, y'all are so cute together!
>
> **Dariaduzdetecting:** What dis? More murder pls.
>
> **marvinasakitas00:** Never trust a man who knows how to handle a knife that well.

Andi smirked at that one. Her followers were her people—always looking for the murderous potential in others.

> **Lizzy_Boredom:** Get it, girl. I hope dragon noodles were followed by canoodling. Ha. See what I did there?

Andi snorted, recognizing the screen name Eliza used on her nonprofessional accounts.

> **TruCrymDiva:** Where can I find his channel? And his number? :-p

Andi texted Hill the link.

> **Andi:** You're a star, dahling. Everyone wants a taste of what you're cooking.

He didn't immediately respond so she continued to scroll the comments, knowing she needed to get back to work but the pull of the internet was too strong to resist. It was too much fun reading what people thought of Hill.

Andi skimmed along a few more comments, smiling to herself, but then her gaze snagged on one.

> **KingXLeer:** Ooh, Man-Hater let a guy near her. Don't get 2 close, dude. She'll cut ur dick off & serve it 4 breakfast.

Andi's jaw clenched. "What the hell?"

A few of her followers had commented back to the guy with a few STFU's and orders for him to run back to his troll cave. But supporters had also chimed in for him.

> **ShanetheReaper67:** Inorite? All she does is whine about how horrible men are. A dude probably can't hold dis bitch's hand without being called a rapist. Prediction: this guy will be charged with something b4 she's done with him. Run, man!
>
> **KingXLeer:** I'd like 2 give Man-Hater something to cry rape about.

A sick feeling rolled through Andi. She was used to people being assholes on the internet. Being a woman online meant creepers and haters thought they had a right to come at you, especially when you were traipsing around in the male-dominated land of horror fiction. But the anger and threat behind these comments stirred a different kind of unease. This felt more personal than the garden-variety trolls who sometimes popped up.

Her phone rang in her hand, making her jump, and Hill's name lit up the screen. She swallowed past the anxiety the comments had sparked and answered the phone, trying to sound upbeat. "Hey."

"Hey," he said, tone clipped. "I got your text. Those comments—"

"Yeah, I saw," she said, cutting him off. "I didn't see the bad ones until after I texted you the link. I'm about to flag them and delete them."

"What the hell was that about?" Frustration filled his voice. "Who the fuck thinks it's okay to say shit like that?"

"Idiots on the internet," she said tiredly. "I'm mostly used to it. The Man-Hater guy has been in my comments before but never with a direct threat. He seems personally affronted that I try to help women learn how to protect themselves. I mean, how dare I tell women how to stay safe. The nerve of me."

"I guess you're really getting in the way of his date-rape plans," Hill said grimly.

"God, I hope he's not out there in the world dating actual women," she said, leaning back in her desk chair and pinching the bridge of her nose, a headache forming. "I'm hoping he's got all this anger because people sense what a disgusting human he is and no women come near him."

"Yeah, but either way, that sounds like a time bomb," Hill said, tone concerned. "He outright threatened you. Is there any way to report him?"

"Not really. I mean, I'll flag the comment, but that just means he'll pop up again with a new name or when he's let back on the platform." Her computer screen went dark, her book disappearing from the screen. "He probably lives in some dank basement far away. If I had to worry about every person who made a creepy comment to me on the internet, I'd literally never leave my house. And I use a pen name so people online can't just look up the real me."

Hill sighed. "I know you're smart and watch out for yourself, but I still wish I could get some time alone in a room with this guy. Teach him some manners."

"The best thing that I can do is continue my podcast," she said, appreciating Hill's protective instincts but knowing there was nothing to be done about it. "People like him want me to stop. That's why they come for me. They want to shut me up." She smirked. "But I won't. Instead, I'll probably put him in my next novel and have him murdered in a really humiliating way. Ooh, maybe I'll write an internet-troll-hunting vigilante. That actually could fit in the book I'm currently working on."

Hill laughed. "I like this evil, vindictive side. I'll be sure to be on my best behavior so I don't make it into one of your books."

She smiled. "Well, I wrote a love scene this morning, so you're already serving as great inspiration. But I promise, I won't murder you in a book—or, you know, in person, man-hater that I am."

"A love scene inspired by last night, huh? And how can I preorder this book?" he said in a mock-formal voice. "I need to write this down."

She snorted. "No one's going to be able to preorder it if I don't get back to writing it, but I promise both characters were very satisfied. Now they have to outrun a crazed killer so they don't get hacked into little pieces."

"Well, at least they had some fun beforehand," he said genially. "I'll let you get back to writing. Thanks for sending me the video."

"No problem. You got some great comments—and some flirty

ones. I better not post where this firefighters' auction is taking place. I think I'd have to get in line to make a bid on you," she teased.

"Don't even joke. I only want one karaoke partner Saturday night," he said firmly. "But I didn't hate watching the video like I thought I would, so thanks for making me do that. It's given me some things to think about."

"Really?" she asked, delighted.

"Don't get too excited," he warned, his voice a low rumble against her ear. "Thinking is different from doing, but it reminded me how much I like being in the kitchen."

A warm, sunny feeling moved through her, but if she gushed too much, she'd scare Hill back into his shell. "Noted."

She could almost hear him smiling patiently over the phone, like he sensed she was holding back. "Good luck with the writing. We'll talk soon."

She told him goodbye, still grinning, and went back to her book, completely forgetting about the internet threat still sitting on her account.

chapter **twenty-one**

HILL STOOD ACROSS THE STREET FROM THE POLICE station, the bland edifice familiar, the dread in his stomach new. He used to pop into the station regularly when he and Christina were together because the fire station wasn't that far from here, but now it seemed like a lifetime ago. He no longer felt welcome in Christina's world. However, he wasn't going to let his sour feelings for his ex stop him from doing what he'd come here to do.

Ever since the call with Andi the day before, Hill had been filled with unease. He'd watched the comments on his and Andi's video blow up. Andi's followers had jumped to her defense, aiming vitriol at the trolls, but there had also been more comments from the offenders and new ugly ones added to the mix. Hill couldn't get over how disgusting the comments had gotten. Why were these guys so *angry*? By late afternoon, the comments had been removed, but he'd taken screenshots of everything he could beforehand.

Andi seemed to be able to shake off what had been said. But he couldn't. In no world should a woman—or anyone for that matter—be expected to accept that people could threaten them and suffer no consequences.

Hill checked to make sure no traffic was coming and then made his way across the busy street. The minute he opened the door to the station, he was greeted with the sound of ringing phones and the stale smell of burnt coffee. His relationship had changed but the station hadn't. It was like walking back into a former version of his life. He headed toward the main desk, where Officer Bernice Winters was searching through a stack of papers, an annoyed look on her face.

"Hey, Bernie," Hill said, trying for casual, like he still came in here all the time.

Bernie looked up, her glasses sliding down her nose, and then a smile broke out, making her brown skin glow. "Hey, yourself, stranger." She stood and braced her elbows on the high counter, giving him an up-and-down look. "Lookin' good, Dawson. You lost weight."

He snorted. "Yeah, half a leg's worth."

"Ha," she said with a grin. "Pretty extreme diet plan. I'm just trying to give up carbs." She drew a circle around her chin. "I like the beard, too. Suits you."

"Thanks," he said, meaning it. The last time Bernice had seen him, he'd been laid up at home, recovering. "You're stunning as always."

"I know." She slicked a hand back over her gray hair, which she always wore in a low bun. "It's a burden."

The tight knot between Hill's shoulder blades eased a little. Just because he and Christina weren't together anymore didn't mean the old friends he'd made here would treat him any differently. He needed to stop avoiding all the Before people like he'd done something wrong.

"So, what can I help you with?" Bernie asked.

He glanced toward the door that led to the main part of the station. "Is Christina here?"

Her eyebrows arched ever so slightly. "Yeah, she's in the back. Let me see if she's free." She picked up the phone, and after a moment of murmured conversation, turned back to Hill and hung up the phone. "You can go on back."

"Thanks, Bernie."

"Y'all play nice," she said.

"Of course." Hill took a breath and headed through the door and toward the little office Christina used when she wasn't out on her beat.

She was waiting for him, leaning against the doorjamb when he turned the corner of the hallway, arms crossed, expression unreadable.

He cleared his throat when he reached her, and she didn't step aside to let him into the office. "Hey."

"Hey," she said with a brief nod. "What's up?"

Her expression was cool, which wasn't surprising, and his instinct was to react in kind, but he was suddenly tired of fighting with her—of being angry. It took so much goddamned energy to hold a grudge. He could feel it eating away at him, a cancer that grew each time he fed it.

Yes, she'd cheated. Yes, she'd left him for his best friend. There was no excuse for what she'd done. But would he have been better off if she had stuffed down the fact that she wasn't attracted to him anymore and stayed? Would that have done either of them any good? He wished she'd broken it off without the lying, but the end result would be the same.

"I was hoping I could get your help on something," he said, keeping his tone even.

"My help," she said flatly.

He sighed. "And maybe that we could talk."

Her eyes narrowed like she was gauging from what angle he was going to verbally attack her, but whatever she saw had her stepping back and letting him into her office. "Come on in."

Christina shut the door and then slid into the spot behind

the desk. As she sat, he noticed the slight roundness of her belly starting to show. The sight was weird—Christina pregnant. He'd imagined that a few times after they'd gotten engaged. That belly had been part of the future he'd pictured for himself, but now he realized he had no wistful feelings about that loss. This wasn't the person he was supposed to be with.

She clasped her hands together, leaning onto her elbows, and giving him the cop stare—the look that said *Start talking*.

Hill had come in for one reason but now realized he had something else to take care of before that. He rubbed his palms on his jeans. "First, I want to say I'm sorry."

Her brows shot up. "You're sorry."

"Yeah. Just because our relationship ended how it did doesn't give me the right to be an asshole to you indefinitely," he went on. "I'm going to stop doing that."

She blinked, obviously caught off guard. "Oh."

He hurried on, afraid he'd lose the nerve. "I realize now that while I was dealing with my injuries and the trauma, you were dealing with your own loss and trauma. You signed up to marry a healthy, active firefighter, and suddenly, you were having to be a caretaker of an angry guy with a disability. You went to someone else for comfort. I wasn't there to give you that."

Christina looked down at her hands. "Hill..."

"I just want you to know that I wish you the best. Truly," he said, realizing he meant it. "I hope you and Josh and the baby have a happy life."

Christina's gaze jumped to his, her eyes shiny—a rarity since Chris wasn't a crier. "Thank you." Tears slipped out and she swiped at them hurriedly. "Ugh. Fucking hormones. I'm crying over everything lately."

He laughed softly.

"And for what it's worth, I'm sorry, too," she said, frowning.

"For all of it. I know it's hard to believe, but I didn't do any of it to hurt you. I went about things in the most horrible way. I was lonely and upset and scared. But I'd known for a while—even before the accident—that I was drawn to Josh in a way that wasn't just friendly, that was different from anything else I'd ever experienced."

Hill stiffened. "What?"

She turned the engagement ring on her finger round and round, her face pensive as she stared at it. "I never acted on anything until after the accident, but I had already been thinking about canceling the wedding to pursue something with Josh. I'd talked about it with him." She looked up. "But then after the fire..."

The news that she'd already wanted to leave him before the accident had his brain spinning, pieces he'd thought he had in place repositioning themselves into a different picture. "You would've looked like a real dick bailing on me."

She bit her lips together and nodded. "I ended up being worse. I should've been upfront with you from the start. I'm sorry I wasn't."

Hill didn't know what to think. She hadn't left him because of his injury or the burden it had brought into the relationship. She'd left him because...she'd been drawn more to someone else. "Wow. I guess I was more blind than I thought."

She gave him a sympathetic look. "Not blind. Hopeful," she said. "I think you were so determined to have an idyllic relationship like your aunt and uncle and prove you weren't going to be like your dad that you shoehorned us into something more storybook than it was. We enjoyed each other, but looking back, I realize now that we were never in love, not the kind of love that would survive a lifetime. It was just new love. The first time we were with someone who wasn't a casual date, so it felt more important. But when push came to shove, neither of us were willing to fight to be together. We both gave up on each other when adversity hit."

Hill stared at her, absorbing her words, and then ran a hand over the back of his head. He hated the picture she was painting, him forcing their relationship into something it wasn't, but the truth of it rang through him. Hadn't he always done that? Tried to create the storybook? Even his chosen profession had been the classic hero role. No one would question the heart of a firefighter. He'd done everything he could to wash off the dirty shadow of his father.

"Fucking hell," he murmured.

Chris gave him a little smile. "I won't take credit fully for that insight. It's taken months of therapy to understand why I did what I did."

Hill made a wry sound in the back of his throat. "When each relationship ends, a therapist gets their wings."

"Right? But I'm glad you came here today and we talked this out," she said, expression more relaxed than he'd seen her in years. "I hate how things have been between us. I honestly wish the best for you, too."

"Thanks." He leaned forward in his chair. "Which means you're going to be happy to help me with why I came here today, right?"

She gave him a no-promises look. "Depends on the request. What've you got?"

"Are you still studying cybercrime stuff?" he asked, hoping Christina hadn't given up on her interest in eventually applying to the FBI to investigate cybercrime.

Her expression shifted into business mode immediately. "Yeah. Why?"

"I'm not sure if there's anything to do about it, but I wanted to give it a shot." Hill pulled a few folded sheets of paper out of his pocket and placed them on her desk. "My neighbor, Andi, the one you met."

"The girl who thought someone broke in?" she asked, reaching for the papers.

Hill grimaced. "Can you please stop calling her a girl? She's a grown woman. Only a few years younger than us."

Christina glanced up, amused. "Oh, so you're sleeping with her."

"Chris..." he warned.

She lifted a palm, still smiling. "No judgment. I'm glad to see you putting yourself back out there. So what's going on?"

Christina started to unfold the pages.

"Andi's a writer and a podcaster, so she posts content online as part of her job. She runs a true crime podcast called *What Can We Learn from This?*"

Her attention snapped upward. "Wait, I know that podcast. I've listened to it. It's good."

"Well, that's Andi's podcast and today, when she put up a video, she got some threatening comments." He pointed at the papers. "Those are screenshots."

She peered at the papers, lines bracketing her mouth as she read through the comments. "Jesus. What was in the video?"

"It was a video of me teaching her how to cook something. She wanted to do it for fun bonus content," he explained. "But then these assholes jumped into her comments, threatening her. Andi said she's used to it and that there isn't really anything to do about it, but I wanted to bring it to you in case there is."

Christina's frown deepened. "Unfortunately, she's mostly right. At least, legally speaking, but maybe..."

"Maybe what?" he asked, leaning his forearms onto his thighs.

She swiveled her chair toward the computer on her right. "I know a few tricks. I might be able to search some of these screen names, see if I can cross-reference them on other sites and figure out who these guys are. At the very least, if we can figure out where they live, she can rest easy knowing they aren't local."

"Local." The thought made his stomach flip over. "Let's hope to God that isn't the case."

"I highly doubt it," she said. "Most trolls never come out of the dark. They like wielding power on the internet because that's all they've got. But let me do some poking around, and I'll see what I can find."

"Really?"

She shrugged. "Yeah, sure. I mean, it will be unofficially. It's not police business. But no one should have to put up with that kind of abuse, especially when all Andi's trying to do is help women keep themselves safe."

He reached out and put his hand over hers. "Thanks, Chris."

She smiled and pressed her other hand over his. "She seems like a really interesting gi—*woman*. I wouldn't have predicted you'd go for someone who writes horror novels and looks like she could be in a punk band, but I'm glad you found someone who's helping you get back to your old self."

He slipped his hand from between hers. "My old self?"

She nodded, gaze going serious. "Yeah, the guy who doesn't hide himself away and let the world go by. The guy who doesn't cut off all his old friends. The guy who was good at being the hero."

His jaw flexed. "Andi doesn't need a hero."

"No, I'm sure she doesn't," she agreed. "But sometimes fighting on behalf of someone else helps us remember that our own life is worth fighting for, too." She gave him a pointed look. "I've been worried about you, Hill. Mad at you. But also worried."

The bald truth in her tone had him standing up. "I'm okay. Better than I was."

She stood and stepped around the desk. "Yeah. I see that. I'm glad."

He cleared his throat. "Well, I better get going. Thanks again for being willing to help with this. Call me if you find anything useful?"

"Of course."

Before he realized what she was doing, she stepped forward and put her arms around him, hugging him. On instinct, he returned the hug, the familiar scent of her shampoo drifting upward. It smelled like another lifetime.

"I'm glad we don't have to hate each other anymore," she said, a little catch in her voice.

He released a breath and gave her back an awkward pat. "Me too, Chris."

She let him go and stepped back, straightening her uniform, her cheeks reddening. "God, I'm sorry. Now the hormones are turning me into a hugger."

He chuckled at her dismay. "Oh, the horror."

"Don't tell anyone on your way out." She pointed at him. "I have a reputation to protect."

He winked. "Your secret's safe with me. We'll talk soon."

Hill left her with the screenshots and headed out, feeling lighter than he had in a long time. Hate really did take a lot of energy. He wished the best for Chris, but she no longer got to take up space in his head or his heart. He walked out of the station and finally—*finally*—let go of what they'd had. It'd only been a story he'd been telling himself anyway. That fairy tale had never been real.

No more stories.

No more turning things into what they weren't.

Eyes wide open from now on.

chapter **twenty-two**

Andi traced Hill's scars gently with a fingertip, her cheek against his chest, her body sated and heavy after an afternoon of seeing who could give the other the more powerful orgasm. He'd won—or she had—depending on how she looked at it. "This hooking-up-with-the-neighbor plan is going to be hell on my daily word count."

Hill's fingers glided along her scalp, combing lazily through her hair. "But think how many realistic sex scenes you can add to your book."

She laughed. "I'm going to end up shelved in the erotica section at this rate."

"Nothing wrong with that."

She let her fingertips follow the trail of hair down to his navel, enjoying the way his belly dipped under her touch and how the sheets twitched where they were draped over his naked bottom half. She loved having this languid time after sex. She'd always known that she was missing out on some level by not having a sex life, but she'd focused on the actual physical act. She'd reasoned that she could give herself an orgasm, so she didn't need a partner to provide that. But she hadn't thought about the before times or the after times, those moments of intimacy that could bookend the sex. This felt luxurious.

"I love this," she said, her thought slipping out. She winced, wishing she could call it back.

Hill kept playing with her hair. "What?"

She watched her fingers map his abdomen. "The full access to touch you," she said, trying to find a way to explain herself. "It's a big deal for someone to give another person permission to touch them. That can kind of get lost in the franticness of sex. But that kind of trust is a gift. Not one I give out easily, and I suspect not one you give away freely either. So, I'm...enjoying my season pass."

He pressed a kiss to the crown of her head. "I like you touching me."

"Same." She closed her eyes and took a fortifying breath, his reaction giving her a little boost of boldness. "Hill?"

"Yeah?" he said, a sleepy note in his voice.

Gathering her bravery, she pushed herself up onto her elbow to look down at him. His eyes were at half-mast in the lamplight. God, he was handsome. It wasn't even fair. How was she supposed to maintain clear boundaries when he was so beautiful and sweet? "Can I be totally honest with you?"

His eyes opened fully, concern there. "Of course."

She rubbed her lips together, nerves fluttering in her belly. "I'm starting to wonder why we're going the friends route instead of trying to date for real."

His forehead wrinkled. "Because we agreed we both weren't in the right headspace to date someone right now."

"Right, I know, but is there *really* a perfect headspace?" she asked. "Like, will there be an actual day when I'm like... *Oh, I'm totes over that trauma and now I'm ready for my real life to start. Hurrah!* I mean, what would that even look like or feel like?"

"Andi..."

"And what if in order to heal from the trauma, I have to

take action instead of waiting?" She pulled the comforter up to wrap around her chest. She couldn't have this conversation with her boobs out. "What if this could be something, and we're not even giving ourselves a chance to find out? We're like boxing it in instead of letting it have the freedom to explore."

Hill frowned as he shifted to sit up and lean against the headboard. "Andi, you *are* taking action. This—what we're doing—is action. And that urge you're feeling to turn it into something more, it's probably because it's new and you feel safe with me." Something flickered in his eyes, maybe sadness. "Because of what you went through, you skipped over those first-time experiences, so this is yours. First-time stuff feels intense and more monumental. It's easy to get attached quickly."

"Hill—"

"I've been there," he said, quietly cutting her off. "It happened to me with Christina. She was the first serious relationship I had, and I made it into something it wasn't. I'm proof that it doesn't lead anywhere good."

"That's not what this is," she said, but doubt was creeping in. "This isn't because you're first."

He grabbed her hand and brought it to his mouth, kissing her knuckles. "I'm enjoying this time with you. I can't even tell you how much. But I'm very aware of what this is. I know I'm just the practice guy."

"The *practice* guy?"

"Yes. With me, you're learning what you like, how to be comfortable with a guy, how to have fun in bed, how not to be scared. But you're young and have put your love life on hold a long time," he said, his eyes searching hers. "You have so many experiences ahead of you—terrible first dates, one-night stands, heartbreaks that teach you what you want, and eventually, the kind of guy you deserve."

His words made her throat feel tight. "And you can't be that guy?"

He shook his head. "I'm not that guy."

She looked away, feeling stupid that she'd put her feelings all out there like that when they'd agreed this was only a friends-with-kissing arrangement.

Hill squeezed her fingers. "I'm not the guy, but I *am* your friend. And I love spending time with you, and I love what we're doing. I don't want to end this, but I also promised you one hundred percent honesty."

She closed her eyes, letting those words roll over her. "You did." She turned her head and looked at him. "And I appreciate that, but I also am not going to let you tell me how I feel. I don't feel close to you because you're first. I feel close to you because you're you. But I can respect that you don't want more than what we have going right now. I know I'm trying to change the rules of the agreement we made."

He reached out and cupped her face. "I don't want to end this yet, but I understand if you do."

She stared at him for a long second, considering the possibility of walking away right now, of saving herself a heartbreak, of giving this a clean ending. But she couldn't form the words. She wasn't ready to walk away yet, and she knew she wasn't ready to go out into the dating world at large. If he was her practice guy, then she definitely needed a lot more practice. "I'm not ready to turn in my season pass yet."

Relief crossed his face and he smiled. "Thank God."

She shifted her body and straddled his waist. "But be careful. You better not fall for me. Keep spending time with me, and you'll find out I'm pretty fucking awesome."

Hill smiled but his eyes remained solemn. "I already know that. I've known it from the start."

....

Hell. Andi didn't know how on the mark she was. Looking up at her, brazenly naked, her red hair falling around her face, that knowing smirk on her lips... Hill was already sunk. He'd realized it when he'd walked out of Christina's office. He'd been falling for his neighbor since that first night he'd rushed over to her place. But he'd been telling himself a story again.

Andi was on a path to her own healing, and he was just a step along the way. It may take her a while to realize it, but he didn't want to say yes to dating and then have her look up one day and realize she'd settled for the first guy who hadn't treated her like shit. He didn't want to be the default choice. He didn't want to worry that she'd walk away like Christina had when she found a guy who really lit her up.

He needed to focus on what he could offer her—a friendship and a good time in bed. He slid his hands up her thighs and to her waist. "When do you need me to leave so you can get some writing done?"

She snorted, making the silver ring in her nose glint. "An hour ago."

"Well, if you're already late..."

She leaned over and braced her hands on his shoulders, putting her breasts enticingly close to his mouth. "Good thing I'm my own boss."

He leaned forward and pressed a kiss between her breasts, loving the way she shivered. "Someone definitely deserves a personal day—and a personal night."

Andi shifted down his body, pulling the sheets with her and straddling his upper thighs. "I can grant you the afternoon, but I'm having girls' movie night tonight." She dragged a finger over his quickly stiffening cock. "No penises allowed. And you, my friend, definitely have one of those."

He groaned at the barely there touch, already starved for her again. "Guess we'll have to make good use of our time then."

"Yes, yes we should." She arched a brow at him. "And this time, I need you to stay just like this. If you're my practice guy, I'm ready to get some practice in."

His blood heated at the seductive warning in her voice. Andi's confidence in bed was growing. It was a sight to behold. "I'm all yours, neighbor."

"Keep your hands at your sides. For now."

"Yes, ma'am," he drawled.

She looked at him from beneath her lashes, and he watched intently as she lowered her head and licked across the tip of his cock. Electric awareness radiated outward from the point of contact. He ached to reach out for her, but he wasn't going to break her rule, so he kept his arms against the bed.

Andi held the eye contact, bold and brazen, as she took more of him into her mouth, the hot, wet heat of it making every muscle in his body tense with arousal. He couldn't stop watching her watch him, the connection wildly intense and so fucking erotic that he could barely keep still. This woman was smart and talented and funny, but goddamn, he wouldn't have suspected that bubbly persona hid a siren.

He hated knowing that all these years, she'd had to bottle up that part of herself, that someone had hurt her so completely that she couldn't allow anyone to touch her but herself. He wanted to give her ten years' worth of pleasure to make up for it.

Andi lifted her head, releasing him with a soft pop, and then she shifted lower, pulling the sheet with her. Hill tensed when she shoved the covers all the way off, leaving him fully exposed. His heartbeat picked up speed, anxiety creeping in. He'd gotten comfortable enough with Andi to take off his prosthesis when they were in bed, but he'd kept the lights low, and the covers draped in certain ways. "Andi..."

"Please," she said softly, her gaze tender. "Let me touch and explore you everywhere."

He closed his eyes, inhaled, exhaled. He could feel his cock softening.

She kissed his thigh. "Trust me, Hill. I think every part of you is sexy." She pressed her lips to the spot right above the sock that covered his residual limb. "I'm not the only one who needs practice."

He opened his eyes at that, found her looking up at him. "Andi, it's hard…"

Her expression softened with empathy. "That's what we do, Hill. The hard things. I know what that pit in your stomach feels like. I felt it the first time you braced yourself over me. But then you made me feel good and safe, and the fear started to fade." She licked her lips. "You don't need to be scared of me."

"I'm not," he said, honesty slipping past his lips. "I just… I like the way you look at me. Like you want me. Like I turn you on. I can't stand the thought of you looking at me with pity."

"I *do* want you. I *am* turned on—like a lot." She gave him a pointed look. "I promise this is not about pity. This is about having sex without our elephants."

He blinked, the non sequitur throwing him off. "Our elephants?"

"Yeah, the big ones that tend to hang out in the room with us as soon as we get naked." She glanced toward her bedroom doorway. "We've sent mine into the hall to think about what he did, but yours is still here, knocking things around, making you do acrobatics to keep your leg covered. You need to throw some peanuts out the door and lure his big ass outside."

He had the brief vision of a giant elephant swinging its trunk around her bedroom and knocking him and Andi off the bed, which made him forget himself for a second and smile. "That's quite the visual."

"Send him packing, Hill," she said, cocking her head toward the hallway. "I'm ready to do dirty things to my neighbor."

A slow roll of bravery moved through him and he nodded. "Okay."

"Yeah?" she asked, gaze searching his.

"I trust you."

"Thank you," she said, voice soft.

He let out a breath. "Peanuts have been thrown."

Andi bit into her bottom lip, a little smile hiding there, and then instead of going back to his leg like he expected, she braced her hands on the mattress and took his softened cock into her mouth. The feel of the hot cavern of her mouth around him was enough to make all his blood rush south again and away from his spinning brain. His cock swelled against her tongue as she licked and sucked and basically made him forget his own name.

When his fingers curled into the mattress and he was on the edge of coming, Andi pulled back. He gasped at the loss, but then he sensed her shifting around again. He was afraid to look, but he felt when she put her fingers on the edge of the sock. After a beat, she gently rolled it off, exposing his residual limb and the scars.

His mouth went dry, but then Andi kissed his knee, her hands gliding over him, caressing lightly down his residual limb, tracing over skin and scars that no one but him and medical staff had touched in a year. Everything went hypersensitive, and a soft moan slipped past his lips, surprising him. His cock flexed, hardening further and aching.

He forced himself to open his eyes, bracing for what he'd find—a look of concern or disgust or worse, pity. But when his gaze landed on Andi, her eyes were on his face and her cheeks flushed, an obvious look of pleasure lighting her expression. She stroked the tender skin behind his knee and kissed up his other leg until she was back at his straining erection. She cupped his balls, making his back arch, and then she tasted the bit of liquid that had gathered on the head of his cock. She licked her lips and smiled. "Permission to use your hands now."

All his breath whooshed out of him, and he reached for her, hungrier for her than he'd ever been. He settled her above him, straddling him, and then blindly reached out for the strip of condoms he'd put on the bedside table. He quickly rolled one on and then he was guiding her to lift up on her knees.

The sight of her above him made more than his cock ache. His chest felt like it was going to crack open with all the things he was feeling. But he focused on the moment, on having her as close as possible. She sank down slowly, taking the length of him inside her inch by inch. She was so slick and hot, so obviously turned on by what they'd done, that any niggling doubt he might have had washed away. She couldn't fake this. This was real. She wanted him, scars and all. When he was seated deep inside her, they both sighed in relief.

His hands spanned her ribs, and he guided her into a slow, grinding motion that would hopefully drive them both wild. "You're so fucking beautiful, Andi," he said between breaths. "You feel so perfect."

The words had slipped out, and she tensed, briefly losing her rhythm.

Too late, he realized he'd said something sweet. He didn't want anything about this to remind her of the man who'd hurt her. "I'm sorry, I—"

"Shh. It's okay." She planted her hands on his chest, and her head dipped between her shoulders, the ends of her hair tickling his skin as she rocked over him. "I know when you say it, you mean it."

Relief moved through him. "I do. I absolutely do."

She lifted her head briefly to give him a ghost of a smile and then canted her hips in a way that made them both gasp with pleasure. He held her tighter, guiding her into the move again, and she made soft, needy sounds like she no longer had space left for words.

He savored the steady build of pleasure, loved the feel of her squeezing him, her body begging to come. Loved that she trusted him enough to let go with him like this. But soon, his own need was eclipsing any control he had left. He put his fingers between her legs, finding her clit and stroking as he pumped inside her. Soon, she was moving faster, her head tipped back and her small breasts bouncing with the effort. Hill couldn't remember ever seeing a more erotic sight than Andi lost to her own pleasure.

"Come for me, Andi," he said, the words coming out in panted breath. "Take what you need, baby."

He slid his fingers firmly over her and buried himself deep. That was all it took. Andi cried out, her entire body going taut above him and her inner muscles gripping him and sending him over with her. His eyes fell shut, and he fucked her hard and fast, spilling into the condom and crying out so loud he could feel his vocal cords strain.

Andi kept moving as she rode the wave of aftershocks, sharp, sexy sounds falling from her lips, and then she draped herself over him, sweat-glazed and sapped. After their breathing had returned to some semblance of normal, she pressed her lips to the crook of his neck. "I hope my grumpy neighbor didn't hear any of that and call the police."

Hill laughed and wrapped his arm around her. "Good thing he's not home. And last I checked, he's not so grumpy these days."

"Wow. Miracles do happen."

He closed his eyes and cuddled her closer. *Yes, they definitely do.*

chapter **twenty-three**

"WE ARE *NOT* WATCHING *THE TEXAS CHAIN SAW MASSACRE* for girls' night. I'm drawing the line there." Eliza gave Andi a don't-try-me look as she placed a bowl of caramel-and-cheese popcorn mix and a bottle of wine on the coffee table. "You are now hooking up with your hot neighbor and getting properly laid. That means you should be open to a romantic movie." She looked to the other woman in the room. "Don't let her sway you, Hollyn. Every time she promises a fun movie, she's lying. It's just a ploy to scare the bejesus out of me." She put her fist in the air. "I demand a romantic comedy!"

Hollyn rolled her lips together—obviously trying not to laugh and probably a little overwhelmed by Eliza. Andi was trying to introduce Hollyn to more people because she hadn't really met a lot of other women since she'd moved to the city, but Eliza could be a lot for an introvert. Hell, Andi could be a lot for an introvert. Poor Hollyn.

"Did I say anything about a massacre?" Andi asked, hand to chest as she tried to school her face into an innocent *who-me?* look. "Give me some credit. I wasn't going to suggest *Texas Chain Saw Massacre.*" She pulled one of the beat-up cases from her shelf of DVDs and held it up for her two friends with a toothpaste-commercial smile. "But *Let the Right One In* is sort of…sweet."

Eliza narrowed her eyes at the DVD cover. "Isn't that the one with the kid vampire?"

Andi winced. She hadn't accounted for Eliza's steel-trap memory. She thought she'd grabbed a movie Eliza hadn't seen yet.

"And a love story," Andi said with a serious nod. "She kills for him. It's sweet…in a murderous way." She looked over to Hollyn, who had claimed the corner spot on the couch and appeared to be regretting accepting her invitation to movie night. "Come on, Holls?" She waggled the DVD in her direction and batted her eyelashes. "Teen vampire love story?"

Hollyn's nose wrinkled, but Andi couldn't tell if the look of distaste was one of her friend's facial tics or if she was giving her opinion on the movie option.

"Oh, no you don't," Eliza said, reaching out and plucking the DVD from Andi's fingertips. She tossed it onto the coffee table. "You're not putting Hollyn in the middle of this. She's too nice to say no to you. And don't sell it like it's *Twilight*." Eliza looked to Hollyn as she picked up the bottle of wine and started pouring it into stemless wineglasses. "It's so not. There are zero werewolf abs. Zero. Just creepy pale kids and subtitles."

Hollyn smiled at Eliza as she twisted her mane of curly blond hair into a bun and secured it with a ponytail holder she'd been wearing on her wrist. "No abs is a big mark against it," she said to Andi. "Plus, you have to watch and read horror all the time for your job. Maybe you should take a break from work-related viewing tonight."

Andi groaned. Normally she'd be all for watching whatever her friends wanted to, but right now, the last thing she needed was a romantic comedy. She was already feeling too many feels after her afternoon with Hill. She didn't need anything making her feel *more* sappy and starry-eyed. He'd straight up told her it couldn't turn into something more, but all afternoon she'd been imagining what-ifs. *Ugh.* She needed to keep her head on straight.

She was not going to be that person. She refused to *pine*. But she also wasn't going to force her friends to watch something they weren't in the mood for.

She grabbed two glasses of wine and then collapsed next to Hollyn on the couch, handing her one of the drinks and sending a playful look her way. "Traitor."

Hollyn laughed and readily accepted the drink. "I should also admit I'm terrified of creepy kids, so you had no shot."

"Creepy kids are why I have an IUD," Eliza declared. "So, it's settled. My dating life is in the shitter, and I have to live vicariously through fictional characters, which means tonight is for sappy love stories. No monsters or murderers allowed. Bonus points for a hot guy taking his shirt and/or pants off."

Andi blew out a breath, ceding defeat. "Those are super-restrictive rules."

"You've got us covered on Halloween, though," Hollyn said, lifting her glass to Andi's to toast her.

Andi clinked her glass and settled in. "Fine, fine. I am at your sappy mercy."

Eliza tucked herself into the cozy chair Andi thought of as her reading spot and grabbed the remote. She signed in to one of the streaming services with her own credentials and pulled up her playlist of romantic movies. "I say we pick one of these. I'm in the mood for a rewatch of a classic."

Andi eyed the screen. *Sleepless in Seattle*, *You've Got Mail*, *Clueless*, *Overboard*, *Grease*. She laughed. "So we *are* watching horror."

Eliza pointed the remote at her in warning. "Don't go there, Lockley."

Andi bit her lip, smiling, and lifted her palm in acquiescence. "I'm just saying. Each of those is horror in its own way."

Hollyn shifted on the couch to look at her. "What—"

"Don't ask. Don't ask," Eliza chanted from above the rim of her glass. "Don't encourage her."

Hollyn smirked and her nose scrunched again. "Sorry. I can't resist. Tell me. How are those horror movies?"

Andi tucked her legs beneath her, bouncing the couch a little, and grinned at her friends. She took a long sip of her wine, preparing her arguments. "Let's go down the list, shall we? *Sleepless in Seattle*—Lady hears a dude on the radio talking about his dead wife and then totally stalks him and his kid while she's engaged to someone else. Creepy. Reverse the genders on that one, and it would've been a horror movie for sure."

Eliza rolled her eyes.

Andi flicked her wrist dismissively. "Next, *You've Got Mail*—Tom Hanks catfishes Meg Ryan and destroys her business. Total dick move. Then he basically gaslights her into thinking that was a good thing."

Hollyn frowned. "Damn, I hadn't thought about it that way. Her store *was* supercute."

Andi nodded. "*Clueless*—Eww, she falls for her stepbrother and she is underage."

"But young Paul Rudd!" Eliza protested. "I'd totally step-incest for young Paul Rudd. He was so...earnest-eyed and adorable."

Andi snorted but wasn't going to let a Paul Rudd—hot or not—discussion derail the master thesis she was laying out. "Moving on from Eliza's step-incest... *Overboard*—He gaslights the shit out of her and makes her think she's *his wife and mom to his horrible kids.* Huge nightmare scenario. And *Grease*? She literally has to give up who she is to win the guy. That's messed up." She shrugged and sipped her wine. "The movie I suggested has a much more solid love story."

Hollyn blinked a few times. "Wow."

"Aaaand she ruins all romantic movies for us," Eliza said with a sigh. "Your mind is a scary place."

"Truth," Andi agreed. "But I can't believe more people don't see it. Horror stories and love stories are two sides of the same coin. Both can involve obsession. Being overtaken by feelings you can't control. Being driven to doing crazy, out-of-character stuff. Being at someone else's mercy. Both involve death."

Hollyn's eyebrows went up. "Death."

"Sure. Horror involves actual death, but love stories threaten emotional death if the person doesn't end up with the one they love. Or that's the theory they're selling us." Andi lifted her glass toward the TV. "Take any one of those movies on the screen and change one little thing, one motivation, and you have a horror movie. Meg Ryan creepily spying on Tom Hanks and his kid, trying to figure out a way to capitalize on his grief and worm her way into his family. Then it goes from lighthearted rom-com to *Fatal Attraction*. The line between the two is very thin." She reached toward the coffee table and grabbed a handful of popcorn. "In real life too. There's a reason why people refer to dating as a nightmare."

"Andrea Lockley, true romantic," Eliza said with a tilted smile. "Does the neighbor know about your dark view of love? That you're going to break his heart after you use him for his hot bod?"

The popcorn Andi had put in her mouth stuck in her throat, and she coughed. After another sip of wine, she sent Eliza a look. "I'm not going to break his. He'll break mine."

Eliza frowned.

"What do you mean?" Hollyn asked. "Are things getting more serious with him?"

Andi eyed her two friends, wondering how much she should

share. Embarrassment made her want to wave off their concerns, not reveal what she'd gotten herself into. But Eliza knew her secrets, and Hollyn would never shame her for anything, so she took a breath and let the truth come out. "Things aren't more serious—at least not on his end. But I may have let my guard down and developed some feelings."

Eliza smiled like this was the best news she'd ever heard. "Really? That's great! Opening yourself up to that is like a *whoa* big deal for you."

"Yeah," Hollyn said, reaching out and giving Andi's arm a little squeeze. "He seems like a good guy. I'm happy for you."

Andi shook her head. "Y'all might want to hold off on the congratulations. I slipped up and talked about feelings with him today. We're not on the same page. He reiterated that this is strictly a friends thing and he isn't interested in dating in any real way."

Eliza cringed. "Eww. So, like, I'm cool having sex with you but don't want to have to actually buy you dinner in public?"

Andi frowned and shook her head. "No, not like that. He wasn't a dick about it. He just thinks that since I don't have a lot of dating experience, I'm only getting the feels because it's new. He called himself the practice guy."

Hollyn sipped her wine, her gaze concerned.

But Eliza looked pensive. "Practice, huh? I don't know the guy, but therapist me thinks that may be more about him than you. Maybe he's trying to protect himself. Sounds like he expects you to move on before long."

Andi tapped her fingernails against her glass, considering that angle. "Maybe. He is going through his own stuff, too."

Eliza's expression turned empathetic. "Girl, aren't we all? But regardless of how it turns out, I'm proud of you for putting yourself out there. Even if it turns out to be practice, it's been good for you. You've gotten something positive out of it. That's more than I can say about most of my relationships."

Andi sighed. "I know. This experience has been worth it. And I have gained a new friend, which can't be discounted."

Hollyn shifted to fully face Andi. "Also, I'm definitely not experienced enough in relationships to give advice. Jasper and I are figuring it out as we go along. But"—her tics pulled at her face—"nothing is written in stone. Neither of you really know how this is going to turn out. Jasper and I weren't planning for things between us to turn into a serious relationship, but it happened. Despite our best efforts to screw it up." She gave a chagrined smile. "So, as clichéd as this is going to sound, I'm a believer in if something's meant to be, it will happen. If it's not, then he was meant to serve some other role in your life and that's okay, too."

Andi reached out and patted Hollyn's knee. "Thanks, lady."

"And if nothing else," Eliza said with a sly grin, "you're having some fantastic sex."

"How would you know?" Andi said, throwing popcorn at her friend. "I have given you no details on the sex."

"Oh," Eliza said with a smug look. "You don't need to tell me. I watched that cooking video. *Girl.*"

Hollyn laughed and gave Andi a look. "The chemistry was pretty obvious."

Andi's face heated. "Fine. The sex is spectacular."

Eliza sighed and leaned back in the chair with a dramatic slump. "I'm *so* jealous. Happy for you, but a jealous bitch. I swear, this online dating world is going to kill me. The last guy I swiped right on met me for a drink and admitted that he'd only agreed to meet me because he needed free therapy."

"Ugh," Andi said. "He better take a seat. I'm the only one who gets free therapy from you."

Eliza laughed. "Damn straight."

"You're braver than I am," Hollyn said to Eliza. "Those dating apps and the whole scene would've sent me straight into social-anxiety meltdown mode. Like would I have had to put 'has Tourette's' in my profile or something? God." She shuddered. "Jasper almost had to literally fall into my lap for what happened to have happened with us. And it still almost didn't work out."

Andi smiled, remembering how adorable Hollyn and Jasper had been around each other in the beginning. They had both been clueless, but Andi had seen the sparks early. The memories gave her a little flutter of wistfulness.

"Sometimes I think I should take a break from the apps altogether," Eliza said. "Go old school. But I work so much, and I don't live in a romantic comedy. Mr. Wonderful is not going to randomly show up on my doorstep." She grabbed more popcorn. "I don't even need someone to love. Just someone to make out with would be nice." She got a dreamy look on her face. "I wonder what Paul Rudd is doing these days..."

Andi snorted. "Mrs. Rudd, I imagine."

"So does this mean we're watching *Clueless*?" Hollyn asked.

Andi flicked her hand toward the TV. "Eliza's choice."

"Yassss." Eliza pumped her fist in victory. "It really should be a rule that the lady not getting exceptionally laid gets to pick the movie. I need all the fantasy fodder I can get."

Andi frowned Eliza's way, even though her friend's tone had been joking. She'd been around Eliza long enough to hear the glimmer of sadness behind the words. Eliza was lonelier than she was letting on.

All this time Andi had thought she was the one who was most screwed up about relationships, but avoiding them was one thing. Wanting one and not being able to get one was another. Both had their own kind of pain attached.

"Hey," she said before Eliza could hit Play.

Eliza turned her head. "Yeah?"

"Next Saturday, Hill's old fire station is having a charity event. A bachelor auction."

Eliza's dark eyebrows arched. "Like with firefighters?"

Andi smiled. "Yep. I'm going so that I can bid on Hill, but why don't you come with us? Maybe you'll see someone who will inspire a charitable donation."

She laughed. "So paying for a date? Is that what it's come to?"

"For a good cause. And you get a firefighter to hang out with. Plus, there will be karaoke. And free drinks."

Eliza's eyes lit with interest. "This is sounding better and better. I'm in." She put her hand over her heart. "Because I'm a super-charitable person."

Andi nodded emphatically. "Of course. It's for the children." She bumped her shoulder into Hollyn's. "You and Jasper should come, too. No bidding on single firefighters, but I bet Jasper would have fun with karaoke."

Hollyn smiled. "Sure. Sounds fun. I'll ask him."

"Sweet." Andi settled back against the couch. "Now, bring on the completely inappropriate love story with the awesome clothes."

chapter **twenty-four**

Hill contemplated the emergency exit with a yearning akin to a kid watching the ice cream truck roll past. He wanted so badly to be out of this room, but there was no way he could sneak out. Still, he found himself glancing at the door more often than not.

The staging room of the venue that Ramsey had shuffled all the "bachelors" into was loud with conversation and laughter, firefighters from two different stations already drinking beer and getting ready for the big show. Some of the female firefighters were hanging out, too. The ladies were auctioning off spots in a fitness boot camp, clearly smart enough to not have agreed to Ramsey's ridiculous buy-a-karaoke-date idea. Next year, Hill needed to catch Ramsey early in the planning process and float new ideas to replace this awkward and outdated tradition.

Hill knew some of the people milling around, though a number of the bachelors were rookies who'd joined after he'd retired, and he'd chatted with a few old friends, but being there just felt... like he was looking in at a life he was no longer a part of. A *family* he was no longer a part of. The only thing keeping him from walking right out the emergency door was the fact that Andi and her friends were in the ballroom, waiting for the event to start.

Hill pulled out his phone and leaned back against the wall, scrolling through recipes he wanted to try. After watching the video he and Andi had made, he'd started pondering the idea of a cooking blog. He didn't think video was the right fit for him. He liked what he and Andi had put together, but the magic of the video was their interaction. If he had to talk straight to camera the whole time on his own, he didn't think he'd enjoy that as much. But a blog where he could put up new recipes, maybe learn how to take good photos, and break down the process of cooking to people in print—that sounded intriguing.

He'd done a little research over the past few days and had found that most cooking blogs were by women. The ones with guys tended to be professional chef situations or healthy living bodybuilder types who were super into green smoothies and grain-free everything. He thought maybe there was space in between for what he could offer—easy, budget-friendly recipes that single people could make for themselves or cook for their dates or friends. Recipes a novice cook like Andi wouldn't be intimidated by and that wouldn't cost a fortune to make.

"Hey, it's almost time for the show. You ready, my man?" A hand landed on Hill's shoulder. "Have you practiced your Magic Mike moves yet?"

Hill glanced up from his phone to find Ramsey grinning and looking way too enthusiastic. "Can I just have Andi give you the money now and save myself the stage?"

Ramsey laughed and squeezed Hill's shoulder. "And forgo my opportunity to shamelessly pimp you? Where would the fun be in that?"

Hill flipped him off.

"Come on," Ramsey said, leaning in. "Josh and Christina are supposed to be here. Don't you want to have them witness your pretty neighbor throwing money at you?"

Hill smirked, enjoying Ramsey's mean-girls vindictive side even if it wasn't needed at the moment. "Chris and I are actually on okay terms now. We talked."

"Oh yeah?" Ramsey asked, head cocked. "Wow. That's good, man. Glad to hear it. But Joshy?"

Hill sniffed derisively. "He can go to hell."

"That's the spirit!" Ramsey said. "Now be ready to go. You're going first, so I can put you out of your misery." He ran a hand over his head, a cocky look on his face. "And I will, of course, be last because I'm the grand prize."

"You're a prize, all right," Hill said with a droll tone. "Let's get this over with."

"Eager, huh?" Ramsey teased. "I love it."

A few minutes later, Hill stood off to the side and out of the view of the crowd as Ramsey went to a podium on the other side of the stage and talked about the charity they were raising money for tonight. Hill could see some of the audience, but he couldn't find Andi. He knew she was there. She'd texted him when she and her friends had arrived. He hadn't asked her to do that, but he'd appreciated the extra assurance. Getting up there and not seeing her familiar face in the audience was a nightmare that had woken him from a dead sleep last night. And of course, in the nightmare, he'd been on stage naked because...nightmares loved nudity.

"And now for our first bachelor," Ramsey said into the microphone, bringing Hill's focus back.

His heart was already pounding, and he wiped his damp palms on his jeans. *Please let this be over quickly.*

"Our first bachelor is a true hero," Ramsey went on. "Hill Dawson was a valued member of our station for eight years. Beyond being a guy you could always trust to have your back in an emergency situation, he was also our favorite firehouse cook." Ramsey leaned closer to the mic. "Which means he can cook, ladies."

There were claps and whoops from the crowd.

"During a five-alarm fire at an apartment building, Hill was helping evacuate families when he heard the roof starting to give way," Ramsey went on. "Though the danger was clear, Hill rushed back in and saved three additional people and the family dog before the roof caved in and a beam landed on him."

There were murmurs in the crowd. Hill closed his eyes, trying to breathe and forcing himself to count the breaths so that he didn't let his mind go to the memory. Ramsey had promised him that he wouldn't go into anything but the most basic details so as not to trigger Hill. *Breathe. One. Two. Three. Four.*

"So, though he's now retired from the station, Hill is the guy I look to when I need lessons in being a badass. He is my friend. He is a hero. And tonight, for the right price, he can be your karaoke date." Ramsey looked toward the side of the stage where Hill was standing in the shadows. He waved him forward. "Everyone, please welcome our first eligible bachelor of the night, Hill Dawson."

The crowd erupted in applause. Hill's throat was tight and his shoulder muscles locked, but he forced himself to move forward. The spotlights aimed at the small stage were blinding for a moment, but Hill made his way toward Ramsey and then turned to face the audience, pasting a half smile on his face.

When his eyes adjusted to the lights, he caught sight of red hair off to the left. Andi was smiling and clapping, her gaze a little shiny as it locked on him. The wash of relief and delight that went through him from seeing her there almost knocked him backward. The world felt lighter when Andi was around. She was like the human version of an Instagram filter, making everything a little softer and a lot more beautiful. His forced smile grew into a real one.

"So," Ramsey said. "Let's open up the bidding at fifty dollars."

Hill kept his eyes on Andi. They'd given everyone little cardboard auction paddles with numbers on them. He waited for her to lift hers but before she could, a voice from the right side of the crowd shouted. "I bid fifty!"

"Fifty dollars to the lovely lady holding number twenty-two," Ramsey said.

Hill found the bidder, a pretty woman with light-brown skin and long, dark hair—Amir's sister. Hill remembered meeting her once at one of the events for firefighters' families, but it'd been a while. Amir was another of his friends being auctioned tonight.

"Seventy-five," someone shouted from somewhere near the back wall. A blond with a group of laughing girlfriends.

The quick bids surprised Hill. He glanced toward Andi. Her face was half-turned, an annoyed look on her face. She raised her number fourteen sign. "One hundred!"

"We have one hundred from the front row," Ramsey said, sending a knowing smile Hill's way.

"One fifteen," Amir's sister announced.

"One twenty-five." This from a new voice near Andi.

Oh shit.

Andi was looking truly perturbed now, and Hill was trying to keep the worry off his face. He'd only given Andi a hundred and fifty bucks. He hadn't expected the bidding to go this high.

"One fifty," the blond in the back said.

Hill's stomach flipped over. She'd topped out what Andi had.

"I love this," Ramsey said. "A battle with a good cause as the winner. Let's throw some more money at him, ladies!"

Andi looked at Hill with wide eyes. A different version of his nightmare was coming true. He never should've agreed to this or made this plan to outwit the system, but how could he have guessed that anyone would spend that much money just to sing karaoke with some washed-up firefighter?

"Two hundred!" Andi announced, waving her sign.

Hill let out a breath. *Thank God.*

"Two twenty-five," the blond countered.

Andi turned her head, a you've-got-to-be-kidding-me look on her face. Hill knew she didn't have a pile of available cash to throw at this. Panic that he'd be stuck with some stranger tonight grew. But as he watched Andi, her friend Eliza grabbed Andi's wrist to lift the sign in the air. "Five hundred!"

"Whoa," Ramsey said, sending Hill a delighted look. "Five hundred to the ladies up front."

To Hill's great relief, that over-the-top donation quieted the competition. Andi grinned and put her arm around Eliza and kissed her cheek.

"Going once, going twice," Ramsey said, thankfully not drawing it out. "Number fourteen, you have won yourself an evening of karaoke and drinks with Mr. Hill Dawson. Thank you for your generous donation!"

Andi let out a whoop, and the rest of the crowd clapped. She hurried to the steps at the edge of the stage and Hill headed down to meet her. He wrapped his arms around her, picked her up off her feet, and kissed her, forgetting people were still watching.

There were a few sounds of encouragement from the crowd.

Ramsey cleared his throat. "And just to clarify. These two know each other, so please don't kiss your firefighter when you win him. Boundaries, y'all."

There was a ripple of laughter, and then Ramsey moved on to the next introduction, taking the spotlight off of them. Andi grabbed Hill's hand and led him away from the front and toward a spot where her friends had gathered. "Look, everyone," she announced. "We've bought ourselves a firefighter!"

The guy who had his arm around Hollyn—a lanky dude with

dark hair and glasses—smiled. "Wow, I've always wanted one of those. Does he come with his own fire truck and Dalmatian?"

Hill laughed.

The guy stepped forward and put out his hand. "Jasper Deares. Hollyn's fiancé."

Hill shook his hand. "Nice to meet you. Hill Dawson, Andi's purchase."

Andi snorted. "I hate to break it to you, but you're a shared purchase tonight. Eliza here contributed to the fund."

Hill turned to Eliza. "You're my hero. Thank you. I can pay you back."

Eliza laughed. "You don't have to do that. It was my pleasure. No way someone else was getting my girl's date." She shrugged. "Plus, it's a good cause. I've spent money on worse things."

Andi leaned her head on Eliza's shoulder. "My friends are the best. They buy me men."

"Men?" Hill teased. "Who are these other men?"

Andi sidled up next to him and hooked her arm in his. "Kidding. I'll just take the one." She glanced at the stage where bidding was firing up again. "So, do y'all want to go next door to the party area or do you want to see more of this part?"

"I'm ready for a drink," Hollyn said, and Jasper nodded.

"Girl, me too," Eliza agreed. "Come on. Let's head over and get a jump on all the best finger foods."

Jasper took Hollyn's hand, and Eliza walked alongside them, leaving Hill and Andi behind. Andi let them get a few steps ahead before she started walking. She glanced up at him. "You okay?"

"I am now," he said, meaning it. "Seeing your face in the audience got me through that."

Her lips curved. "Well, if you were nervous, it didn't show. You looked super sexy up there. Very broody and mysterious. That's why all the ladies were fighting over you."

The compliment warmed him, and he chuckled. "That wasn't broody and mysterious. That was awkward and slightly terrified. But thank you." He lifted the hands they had clasped together and kissed her knuckles. "I'm glad I'm all yours tonight."

"Same." They maneuvered around the back of the crowd, nearing the blond who'd bid on him. Andi sent her a saccharine smile as they passed.

A rush of affection moved through him. Andi was being playful, but he found he liked that little spark of possessiveness, liked being the guy holding her hand, liked *her*.

No. More than liked.

Fuck. His breath whooshed out of him.

They were almost to the door that led to the party room, but Andi glanced at him and stopped. He must've been wearing his thoughts on his face.

"Hill," she said, concern entering her voice. "What's wrong?"

"Nothing," he managed to say.

"You sure?" She put the back of her hand to his cheek. "You look pale."

He swallowed hard, trying to shove the thoughts that had escaped back into the mental closet he needed to keep them in, and forced a small smile. "I'm fine. I got a little light-headed for a minute. I ate an early lunch and haven't had anything since."

Mostly the truth. He was definitely light-headed.

She pressed her lips together and nodded. "Well, let's get some food in you, okay? Maybe being onstage and fought over by multiple women was too much for an empty stomach."

"Maybe so."

Andy hooked her arm in his again and steered him toward the party room. Inside, the room was already filling up with people. Some were in line at the tables of food. Others were getting drinks from the bar, which was where Andi's friends had gone. Karaoke wasn't supposed to start until the auction was over, so CJ the DJ, a female firefighter from the other firehouse, was playing "Light My Fire" by the Doors.

Andi looked to the DJ booth and then to Hill. "Interesting song choice."

He nodded. "Yeah. She did this at a barbecue once. She has a playlist of all fire-related songs. It will be fun watching people try to dance to 'We Didn't Start the Fire' by Billy Joel."

She laughed. "Don't worry. I've got dance moves for every beat." She playfully swung her arms in a move that looked suspiciously like the Carlton. She looked at his face, her silly smile sagging, and stopped. "I didn't say they were *good* moves."

"It's not that," he said with a frown. "It's just...I won't be dancing."

"Oh. Right," she said, her tone bright but awkward. "I didn't mean to imply—"

"That's not something I've practiced yet with the prosthesis," he said, feeling like a rain cloud on her parade. "I'm not going to test that out in front of a crowd. A slow dance, maybe, but nothing fast."

"It's fine," she said, with a wave of her hand. "I doubt there will be much dancing anyway. Karaoke is the main attraction."

She didn't look bothered, but the knot in his stomach was growing.

"Let's get some food." She took his hand. "I'm starving and there's nothing I love more than tiny crustless sandwiches."

....

Andi was trying to keep her attitude upbeat as she and Hill filled their plates and headed over to her friends, but alarm bells were going off in her head. Hill had been fine when he'd met her by the stage. Hell, he'd been so happy, he'd picked her up off her feet and kissed her in front of everyone. It was like one of those moments in Eliza's romantic comedies. The sweet move had made Andi's heart swell. But then just as quickly as the moment had happened, it was as if a switch had gone off in Hill.

For a few seconds, he'd looked so pale she'd thought he may pass out, but she sensed it was more than low blood sugar. His entire expression had shut down. It'd been like when she'd first met him and he'd worn that steel-wall expression, the one that obscured everything from view. Like a door slamming in her face. She hoped maybe it was because he was back among his fellow firefighters. She knew things were kind of awkward with some of them, but it felt like more than that.

They joined her friends at a table, and she managed to keep up with the conversation as they drank and ate. Luckily, Eliza was regaling them with stories, so it gave her time to reset. Eventually, after a glass of wine and too many finger sandwiches, Andi had shaken off most of the worry and was enjoying spending time with the people she cared about. Hill seemed to be loosening up a little, too. She reached out and grabbed his hand under the table. He gently squeezed her fingers.

The room had filled up and was echoing with conversations and laughter. The DJ had Andi grinning with all her fiery song choices, but when Katy Perry's "Firework" ended, CJ didn't blend it into another track. She spoke into the microphone instead.

"We're going to kick off karaoke in a few minutes, so start making your choices. But before then, let's play a few slow ones. Ladies, get those firefighters you bid on out on the dance floor. And don't let them claim they can't dance. Anyone can do the high-school-prom penguin." CJ mimed the stiff side-to-side swaying slow dance that high schoolers often did. "Let's do this."

James Taylor's "Fire and Rain" started up, and Jasper pushed his chair back from the table. He put his hand out to Hollyn. "May I have this dance, milady? I do a fine penguin."

Hollyn gave him an adoring look and took his hand. "I'd be honored."

Eliza scooted her chair back as well. "Y'all go dance. I need to go to the little girls' room."

"Oh, we aren't going to—" Andi started, but Hill tightened his grip on her hand.

"I can probably manage a penguin," he said, lifting her hand. "If you're willing to join me."

Andi's belly did a little flutter. She knew Hill didn't have the sudden urge to dance. He was doing this for her. "I'd love to." She let him pull her gently to a stand. "I actually don't know if I can penguin. I never went to prom."

Hill frowned, and she could tell that he'd read between the lines. She hadn't gone to prom because prom had happened post–Evan Longdale. No way would she have been in any state to be held by a boy and not have a compete panic attack. She'd spent her prom night watching *Prom Night*, parts one, two, and three.

Hill led her out to the dance floor, where a number of other couples had already started to sway under the twinkle lights that had been strung from the ceiling. They found a spot, and she looped her arms around his neck. "You don't have to this if you don't want to, you know."

He squeezed her hip, a slightly sad look on his face. "It's not that I don't want to. I love being close to you like this."

"I love it too," she said softly and then leaned in to kiss him lightly.

She laid her head on his shoulder and closed her eyes. Hill didn't talk, allowing the music to sweep her away a little, and he guided her gently into movements that were definitely smoother than a penguin waddle. Soon, she felt herself sinking into the moment, imagining this was her prom and this was the guy and this was a real date and a real relationship.

They were dangerous thoughts, but she let herself indulge in them for now.

The song ended and blended into Sarah McLachlan's "World on Fire" and the beat picked up a little. She lifted her head, looking into Hill's eyes as he guided her into a turn. Sarah sang a line about not being alone in this story's pages, and Andi felt a surprising urge to cry. She'd always had friends but, on some level, had always felt alone. No one could understand what she'd been through. No one could relate. But what she saw in Hill's eyes told a different story. The guy knew pain, too. He knew that separate-from-the-world-but-still-living-in-it feeling. He saw her, not the armor she tried to put on each day. He'd known she needed this dance.

Andi reached up and stroked the hair at the nape of his neck, trying to keep her tears in check. "Thank you for this," she said. "Waiting all these years for my first prom dance was worth it. *You* were worth the wait."

He closed his eyes, and she could feel him take a deep breath. When he opened them again, he leaned down and kissed her. Not like the light brush of lips from earlier. This was a *kiss*. Soft and slow, his hands on her face and her palms sliding down to his chest. They were still moving to the music but not leaving their spot on the dance floor.

She lost herself to the feel of him, the music fading, and all her senses homing in on their kiss. She forgot they were in a crowd, on a dance floor, that her friends were here somewhere. She forgot everything.

But too soon, Hill broke away from the kiss and stepped back. The song rushed back into her ears. A lyric about the world being on fire and it being more than the person could handle. She expected to find Hill smiling or maybe a little embarrassed at the public display. But instead, his expression was stark, his eyes impossible to read.

Dread snaked through her. "Hey, you okay?"

The song was too loud. Hill looked away. "I'm fine. I need a break."

Something about his tone set off her alarm bells. "Want to step outside and get some air?"

He wouldn't look at her. "Yeah. Let's do that."

chapter **twenty-five**

"Hey," Andi said to her friends when she and Hill walked back to the table. "We'll be right back. We're going to get a little fresh air."

Eliza fanned herself and gave them a knowing grin. "Yeah, I can see why."

Hill's heartbeat was in his ears, panic digging its claws into him. *You were worth the wait.*

Before Hill realized what was happening, Andi had grabbed her purse and was leading them along the edge of the dance floor and out into the humid night air. The door clicked shut behind them, leaving them on a quiet street, a line of parked cars their only company. They walked a few more steps and around the side of the building to the parking lot, shielded from anyone who may go in or out of the venue.

Andi turned to him before he could get a word out. "You look like you saw a ghost. What happened in there?"

"Andi..." He didn't want to do this.

Had to do this.

"What?" she said, standing in front of him, searching his face. "Tell me. I can feel something's going on with you."

He stared at her, everything welling up to the surface, all the things he'd been trying to keep down punching through. He leaned back against the brick wall of the building, dipping his head and closing his eyes.

"Tell me," she repeated softly, her hand going to his bicep.

Honesty. He'd promised her honesty. It was all he could give her right now.

He lifted his head. "I'm falling in love with you."

Andi's eyes widened and her lips parted, her bright-red lipstick making the expression even more dramatic. She blinked. "You're..."

He let out a ragged breath. "I knew it the second I stepped out onstage tonight and saw you in the audience. I didn't just feel happy to see you. I felt..." He searched for the right words. "Lit up inside. Like, 'Oh, there she is. I've been waiting for her.' I tried to shake it off. But just now...when we kissed..."

Andi stared at him in wonder, and her blue eyes turned shiny with tears. She grabbed his hands. "Hill..."

He shook his head before she could say anything. "But I can't do this."

A line appeared between her brows, her fingers cold against his. "Do what?"

"I meant what I said about being the practice guy," he said, the words like knives in his throat. "How I feel about you doesn't change that."

"Of course it does," she said, exasperation in her voice. "Hill, don't be ridiculous. I already told you I wanted to date you, that I've developed feelings for you. And you think I didn't feel something with that kiss? Knowing you're feeling things back..." She squeezed his hands. "That's... I want that. I want to be in a relationship with you."

He swallowed past the pain in his throat. What she was offering him was like the ripest, brightest fruit on the tree, but he couldn't grab it. He knew better. "Andi, I can't. I can't be the default guy or someone's comfort-blanket choice again. What happened with Christina…" He released her hands. "It ripped me apart."

Andi was shaking her head slowly, silently.

"She told me that she'd already been tempted to cheat before my accident. She'd already realized her mistake," he said, the words echoing inside him with shame. "I was just the good-enough guy, not *the* guy. She didn't recognize that initially because she didn't have enough experience to know what a true soul mate felt like."

"I'm not her," Andi whispered.

"No, you're not," he said. "But I also think you've been put in a position where you can easily mistake safety for feelings. I'm the safe guy." His eyes burned. "I'm glad you feel safe with me, but I don't want you to look up in a year or two and realize that what we have isn't setting your heart on fire, that you should've dated around and determined what you're looking for in a guy beyond 'guy who won't hurt me.'"

She blinked, quiet tears escaping down her cheeks. "You're hurting me now. You're telling me I don't know my own heart, my own mind."

His ribs cinched, a sick feeling moving through him. "Andi, you've never even had a slow dance with a guy. You don't know what you don't know yet."

"Who the fuck cares if I've slow danced or not? And you're right," she said, frustration in her voice. "I can't guarantee you that a relationship between us will work out. No one can promise that up front. But I *can* guarantee you that if we don't try, we're promised a zero percent chance. The only way to protect yourself from a broken heart is to never let yourself love anyone. And wow, that sounds like a fun life."

He looked down.

She sighed at his nonresponse. "Come on, this isn't you. Your heart told you the truth in there on that dance floor. This—whatever this is—is your depression telling you lies."

His attention flicked upward at that.

"I know about those kinds of lies," she said, earnestness in her voice. "I know what it's like for your brain to tell you it's safer not to try at all. Mine used to tell me not to leave the house, that nowhere was safe. Once I fought those back, it told me to trust no man, that evil lurked everywhere, that any guy would hurt a woman if given the chance. I still fight those demons, but I do *fight.*" She shook her head. "Your fight looks different, but it's still a fight. Your demons tell you that no one could possibly want to be with you. That once I come to my senses, I'll bail on you. They tell you that you're somehow less than because of what you've been through. They tell you that you're doing me a favor by pushing me away. And it's *bullshit.* You're an amazing man, Hill. Smart and sexy and brave. You think those women earlier were throwing around money at the auction for you because they were feeling charitable?"

He heard what she was saying, but she wasn't seeing all the experiences she hadn't had yet. She was like the girl who'd always lived in the small town who'd never been to the city. He was the boy who lived down her street in that small town. He would not tie her to him, would not hold her back from the world.

He took a deep breath and gathered up the guts to say what needed to be said. "We need to end this. It's not good for either of us anymore."

Andi gasped like she'd been hit in the stomach. "You can't be serious. Are you hearing me at all?"

The betrayed look in her eyes gutted him. "Andi..."

"You give me a movie-worthy kiss, tell me you're falling in love with me, and then *break things off*?" she asked, looking up to the heavens as if answers from on high would be forthcoming. "Why would you give me that only to take it away?"

He winced. "We promised we'd always be honest with each other."

"But you're not being honest with yourself." She gave him a frustrated look. "You're breaking up with me because you're falling in love with me? Listen to that statement. That doesn't make any sense."

The words stabbed at him. "You deserve more than what I can offer you."

She stared at him for a long moment, like she was trying to figure out a puzzle, testing out different pieces and none fitting. "You know," she said finally, shaking her head, her tone changing almost as if she were talking to herself. "Maybe that's true."

He frowned, her agreement stinging.

Her throat bobbed, and her chin tipped up in that way he'd learned was her defense mode. "I deserve someone who's willing to risk a broken heart to be with me. Who's willing to gamble that things may not go perfectly. Someone who doesn't require a guarantee."

He opened his mouth to respond, but she beat him to it.

"That's what being open to love looks like," she said. "I was willing to risk all of that for you. I was willing to face down whatever demons I had to because it meant I got to be with you."

The confession tore him open, the past tense in her words hitting home. He wanted to reach for her, to take it all back, but he forced himself to keep his hands at his sides.

Something closed off in her expression. "You're so concerned that you're my practice guy, but maybe you weren't *my* practice at all. Maybe I was yours. You tried things out and realized you'd rather be alone."

He stepped forward, shaking his head. "No, that's not—"

She lifted a hand, halting him. "Please, don't. You said what you needed to say. I'm hearing you. This is done. Got it." She made a quiet sound of disbelief in the back of her throat and gave him a sad-eyed look. "But you know, what I told my friends on movie night was right. Love isn't romantic. It's a goddamned horror show. Just when you start to trust that it can be good, it punches you in the face again. I should've known better."

His stomach twisted, hating that he was causing her any pain. "I'm so sorry, Andi."

She shook her head and hiked her purse up higher on her shoulder. "I know you are. I wish that made it better." She nodded toward the building. "I'm going home. Tell my friends I wasn't feeling well."

"You don't have to—"

"No, I really do." She gave him one last look, her mascara making streaks along her cheeks. "Goodbye, Hill."

With that, she turned and walked away. Hill leaned back against the wall and closed his eyes, knowing he'd done the right thing, but his heart breaking into a thousand pieces anyway. *I was willing to risk all of that for you.* Her words were going to haunt him.

He waited until he saw Andi pull out of the parking lot, and then he steeled himself to go back inside. He would make sure to pay back Eliza, and he would tell her friends to go find Andi, that she'd left upset. He didn't want her alone tonight.

Hill schooled his face into a blank expression and headed back into the party room. Karaoke had started. Some dude he didn't know was singing a country song he hated. He saw Andi's friends gathered on the far side of the room, flipping through a binder of karaoke choices. He took a breath and turned to head that way.

But before he'd taken three steps, Christina stepped into his path. "Hey."

Hill instantly halted, narrowly avoiding knocking her drink out of her hand. "Hey."

"I'm glad you're still here," she said, pushing up on her toes to get closer to his ear. "I just got here and thought I'd missed you."

"I was outside, getting some air," he said against her ear, trying not to shout. "Can we catch up in a second? I need to—"

"Where's Andi?" she asked, cutting him off.

"She left. Wasn't feeling good."

When he leaned away from her ear, he found Christina's expression pinched with concern. She jerked a thumb toward the left. "We need to talk. Come next door with me for a second."

"I'm supposed to let Andi's friends know where she is." He glanced their way again, but they hadn't noticed him yet.

Christina grabbed his elbow. "In a minute. This is important."

Hill sighed. He didn't have the energy for another conversation. He wanted to go home and forget this night ever happened. But Christina looked like she wasn't about to be put off. He nodded and followed her back into the room where the auction had taken place.

When the door shut behind them, the off-key singing blessedly turned to a dull throb. Christina let go of his elbow when they were a few steps away from the door and turned to him. "I tried to call you earlier."

He frowned. "My phone's been on silent since I got here a few hours ago. Ramsey's orders for the auction. What's going on?"

Christina was in a black, dressy jumpsuit thing, and after setting her drink on a nearby table, she put her hand into some hidden pocket and pulled out her phone. "I've been digging into Andi's trolls for you, and last time we talked, I hadn't really found anything. But this afternoon, one of the searches I set up pinged with a hit." She touched her phone screen, entered a code, and then found what she was looking for. "There's this obscure message board where a few people were discussing Andi—people who hate the podcast, people who don't like her or what she stands for. Typical toxic shit."

"Okay..." he said, her tone making him nervous.

She looked up, her expression the one she used when she told people bad news. "Hill, they doxed her."

His heart dropped. "What? When?"

"A few days before that night she called us out to the house for the break-in."

The words took a second to register, the gravity of them. But when they hit him, they hit hard. "Jesus. You mean..."

Christina nodded, face grim. "Someone from that message board broke in." She handed him her phone. "Someone posted that he'd been in her house."

Fear crawled up Hill's spine. He stared down at the screenshot Christina had taken.

> **KingXLeer:** Bitch thinks she's so safe. SO SMART. But guess who was able to jimmy her door open and LITERALLY stand in her house while she was home with her never knowing. The things I could've done to her stupid ass. For those wanting to visit, here's where you can find Ms. *What Can We Learn from This?* Maybe we can teach her some things.

The guy then posted Andi's full address.

Hill went cold all over, the idea that one of these psychopaths had been inside Andi's kitchen shaking him to the core. "These sick fucks."

"Yeah," Christina said, taking her phone back. "I'm so glad you installed an alarm. That's probably deterred more visits. But Andi needs to be made aware that her information is out there.

This is going to become part of the break-in investigation now, so if I can find out who this asshole is, I can charge him. But until then"—she gave him a pointed look—"she needs to keep an eye out. And maybe you could put in some motion lights or a camera or two outside the house just to be safe. Someone could be creeping around in the dark."

Creeping around in the dark. When Andi went home alone. *Oh, God.* "I have to go."

"What?"

"Andi just headed home—alone. I need to go," he said, already turning toward the door.

"Do you want me to come for backup?" she asked.

He wanted to say yes, but Chris was dressed up and here for a fun night. The chances of something happening to Andi when she got home were slim. Her information had been on the board for a while. If they were going to make a move, they probably would've already. "No, you go have a good time. I'll text or call if I need anything."

She crossed her arms and nodded. "Okay. Be careful."

"Thanks, Chris. For doing all of this."

"Of course," she said with a brief smile. "Andi seems great and you seem happy with her. I'm pulling for you guys."

The words stung like vinegar in an open wound, but he forced a nod. "Thanks."

With that, he was out the door. His heart was pounding fast, and electricity was moving through his veins. He knew it was unlikely Andi was in trouble at this very moment. And she wouldn't be happy to see him on her doorstep, but something in his gut was telling him that he needed to get to her.

Right. Now.

chapter **twenty-six**

Andi was a goddamned mess by the time she pulled onto her street. She'd mostly held it together in front of Hill, leaning into her anger and frustration instead of into the heartbreak she was experiencing. But as soon as she'd turned out of the parking lot of the event, all of her bluster had given way to the helpless feeling of knowing what she wanted and it being impossible to get.

Hill had danced with her, kissed her in front of everyone, and then told her he was falling in love with her. It'd been the most romantic evening of her life. She could tell none of it had been part of his plan. He'd seemed so overwhelmed by all of it, like the feelings had blindsided him. Knowing that she'd done that to him, that the stoic firefighter had been taken down by emotion for her had felt like magic, like she'd been filled up with helium and could fly.

She'd suddenly understood what the heroines in those romantic comedies felt—like yes, *this guy*. Not because the guy was handsome or funny or brave or whatever it was that made him stand out at first, but because he made the heroine feel seen and understood in a way no one else ever had. That he saw the good stuff and the ugly stuff and loved all parts of that mix. But as quickly as she'd gotten to experience those emotions, they'd been ripped away.

Yes, Hill could love her. No, he wasn't going to let himself.

They were done.

Just like that.

And the worst part was that he had convinced himself that he was doing it for Andi's own good. Like he was saving her from the fate of being with him. *God.* She could shake him and his hard head.

She wasn't experienced at relationships or love. She could admit that much. But she wasn't a sixteen-year-old girl anymore either. Hill saw her as inexperienced because she hadn't had relationships, but he wasn't counting every guy she hadn't trusted, every dude she'd passed up, every date she'd turned down. She hadn't *wanted* to say yes to anyone until she met him. That had to mean something. That had to be more than seeking the "safe guy."

She scoffed as she turned into her driveway. *Safe.* What a fucking joke that was. Hill wasn't safe. He was the most dangerous guy out there. He was the one she was falling in love with, the one who had the power to crush her heart with a few choice words. The one who was so wrapped up in a cloud of depression that he couldn't see what they could have, what the possibilities were, how great they could be together.

She wanted to wrestle that monster off his back, to stop it from putting its claws over his eyes and blocking his view of what was really there, but it was bigger than she was. She couldn't will him out of that state. Her feelings for him couldn't magically cure his trauma, just like his couldn't take away what had happened to her. That was his fight.

In one respect, he was right. They wouldn't last. Not if he believed that he wasn't worthy of her. Not if he thought he was holding her back or that she was one second away from some other guy catching her eye.

The way he viewed himself made her heart hurt. All those people in that room tonight had looked at him as a hero, as someone who'd sacrificed for the good of others. She'd nearly had to challenge other women to an arm-wrestling contest to win the bidding war. But none of that admiration seemed to penetrate Hill's armor.

Eliza had once told her that until you can learn to love yourself, no one else can love you enough to make up for that hole. As much as Andi wanted to be with Hill, she didn't want to spend her life shoveling dirt into a hole only he could fill. Which meant...

She was going to have to let him go. Even if her heart wanted him. Even if this connection with him felt special and right in a way nothing had before.

The cold reality of it was like a fresh kick to the gut.

She parked in her driveway, ready to get into her yoga pants, curl up on the couch with a pint of ice cream, and watch a movie where everyone was killed and no one fell in love.

She turned off the engine, grabbed her purse, and climbed out of the car. As she headed up the driveway, her heels clicked along the pavement and she mentally scrolled through a list of movies, trying to decide which would be the perfect post-breakup horror movie. But before she could pick one, something made her pull up short, yanking her from her thoughts. She halted one step away from the little path that would lead her to the porch steps and her front door.

Something wasn't right. She gripped her keys and stared up at the house, trying to place what was giving her pause.

The porch light.

It wasn't on. She was sure she'd turned it on before she'd left tonight. She always flipped it on when she knew she'd be returning home in the dark. She frowned at the darkened porch, the tree in the front yard throwing creepy, swaying shadows along the front of the house. She tried to think back to when she'd left, going through the scene in her head. Had she just forgotten to turn on the light?

She couldn't remember flipping the switch, but it was a habit. She also didn't remember grabbing her purse, but she'd obviously done that. She slid her keys between the knuckles of her left hand, pointy side out, and tucked her other hand in her purse, anxiety welling in her.

Breathe. Think through the logical explanations first.

Maybe the light bulb had burned out.

Maybe she'd forgotten to flip the switch since she'd been excited to get to the event.

She'd played this game with herself so many times, it was like second nature. She'd learned the technique in therapy early on—not going to the scariest, worst-case scenario first. But her brain was still trained to do exactly that. The horror writer was imagining all kinds of horrible scenarios.

She glanced back toward her car, which was now as far away from her as the front door. She let her gaze travel over the front yard and the side of the house she could see. There was barely any moonlight tonight, but she didn't see any lurking shadows besides the outline of the garbage cans and the bushes. The only sound was the breeze through the trees and the steady drone of crickets.

Only a few steps to the door, she told herself. *You have an alarm. No one is in the house.*

She swallowed past the lump in her throat, pulled her pepper spray out of her purse, and forced herself to move her feet. She tried to imagine the warm light of her living room, the safety of the locked door behind her. She tried to tell herself that she was fine. She was just on edge from the emotional night.

But as she made her way up the porch steps, her gut instincts were screaming at her. She stopped pretending she was calm and speed-walked to her front door. But right before she got her key in the lock, a board squeaked on the porch—and she hadn't moved her feet.

Panic was like a lightning strike within her—hot and instant. She spun to her right, pepper spray aimed, but before she could fire it, someone grabbed her wrist and wrenched her arm so hard, the canister dropped from her fingertips, clattering to the floorboards.

She yelped, the pain in her shoulder stealing most of her breath, and she tried to yank free. But whoever had her was bigger and stronger, twisting her arm behind her back. She parted her lips to scream, but a gloved hand clamped over her mouth, muffling the sound.

Her mind was on fast-forward, the whole thing taking on a surreal quality. This had to be a nightmare. She'd imagined this scenario so many times that it couldn't possibly be happening. *This isn't happening.*

Her attacker pulled her back against his body, her arm still pinned behind her, and laughed. His breath reeked of cigarettes and beer. "You stupid bitch," he said, sounding so damn proud of himself. "What can we learn from this? Obviously, you haven't learned shit. You made this too easy. Didn't even get your mace fired. Poor Andrea."

Evan.

Terror filled every cell of her body. *He's found me.* The feeling was old and familiar. Lying next to a serial killer, waiting for him to fall asleep, hoping to God she made it out alive. Her worst nightmare all over again. But she forced herself to push through the swirl of flashbacks, not to lose herself completely in the panic. Panic could lie.

This couldn't be Evan. Evan was in prison for the rest of his life. And replaying the words in her head, this guy didn't sound like him. *What can we learn from this?* He'd said that. This was someone who knew her podcast.

She closed her eyes, forcing her voice into something resembling calm. "What do you want?"

The words were muffled against his hand, but she knew they were loud enough for him to hear.

"To see you just like this," he said. "Terrified. Shaking. Ready to beg me not to hurt you. A useless little girl who thought she was soooo smart, who acts like she's tough shit online but is just a dumb bitch who could be grabbed right off her own front porch. Your minions would be so disappointed."

Online. Her minions. She couldn't believe it. This guy was a *fucking troll*? She'd been grabbed by some butthurt dipshit from the internet? Her body was trembling from the top of her head to her toes, but she absorbed his words, letting them become fuel. Anger was so much more productive than fear. Her teeth clenched.

No way was she getting taken out by this guy.

"Open your door," he said, shuffling them both forward. "We need to have a private conversation."

Never let them take you to a second location.

The words echoed through her head. They were from an old *Oprah* show she'd once overheard her mom watching. The words had stuck with her, and she'd talked about them on the podcast. She didn't know if inside her house qualified as an official second location, but there was not a chance in hell she was letting him in without a fight.

She stalled, jiggling her keys in her left hand like she was trying to maneuver them as she quickly ran through what she knew, her mind grasping at information. He had one hand holding her arm behind her back, the other over her mouth. Which meant he had no weapon—at least not actively in his hand. He was bigger than she was, so in a fight, she was at a disadvantage. Her best shot was a distraction and then either getting loose enough to get away and run to the neighbor's house or at least get her mouth free so she could scream bloody murder.

"Put the key in the fucking lock," he said, squeezing her jaw so hard it made her eyes water.

She nodded like she was the scared little girl he thought she was. But as she did it, she was getting her keys between her knuckles again. She lifted her left hand with the little range of motion she had as if she was going to reach for the lock, but then she quickly swung her hand back the other way and stabbed him as hard as she could in his thigh.

"Fuck!"

It wasn't enough to truly injure him, but it was close enough to his crotch that the element of surprise had him angling back to protect himself, and his grip loosened. She wrenched away and screamed like she'd never screamed before. Her arm came free from his grip, and she bolted toward the stairs. But before she could get there, he grabbed her hair and viciously yanked her backward. She fell and landed hard on her ass. Pain shot up her spine, and her scalp burned like it'd been lit on fire.

He called her a slew of names and tugged her hair again, but she was already scrambling, her hands searching. When they found what she was looking for, she didn't think, just turned and aimed. The hiss of the pepper spray was like a prayer going up. The high-pitched scream that followed was the prayer answered.

Her attacker released her hair to grab for his face, and the stinging burn of the pepper spray made them both cough. But Andi hadn't taken a direct hit, so she scrabbled backward like a crab toward the stairs, kicking off her shoes. Once she was out of his arm's reach, she got to her feet and ran down the stairs, screaming the whole way. Her phone was in her purse, which was somewhere on the porch, and she'd dropped her keys in the fray, but she'd bang on every neighbor's door until someone answered.

However, right before she reached the edge of the front yard, headlights blinded her. She put up her hands to shield her eyes, but then started waving both arms when it registered that this could be someone to help. The vehicle screeched to a halt in the street, and the door swung open.

When her vision adjusted and she recognized the truck, relief rushed over her like a tidal wave. *Oh God, oh God. Thank you, God.*

Hill climbed out with the headlights still on blast. "Andi!"

She ran toward him, the warm pavement rough against her feet. "Get in the truck! Someone's on the porch. He attacked me."

Horror filled Hill's face as he took in the sight of her. He grabbed her, pulling her to him. "Jesus Christ. Tell me you're okay."

The feel of his arms around her was the sweetest relief, but they weren't out of danger. "I'm okay. In the truck. Get in the truck."

"Right." Hill herded her over to the passenger side and got her into the seat.

"I got him...with the pepper spray," she said, her words coming in gasps. "Need to call...police."

Hill pulled his phone from his pocket and punched in 911. "Talk to them. I'm not going to let him get away."

Fresh panic zipped through her. She grabbed him by the belt. "No. Stay here. You'll get hurt. He could have a weapon."

The operator came on the line, asking what was her emergency. Andi quickly gave the lady her address and told her she'd been attacked.

As she was trying to describe what was happening, a figure appeared in the beam of the headlights. A lanky white guy in dark jeans, a black T-shirt, and a backward baseball cap. He was swiping at his eyes with one hand and still coughing. He started jogging in the opposite direction.

"Motherfucker," Hill seethed.

"Please," Andi begged, pulling the phone away from her ear. "Don't. Get in the truck. The police are on the way."

"Andi," he said, looking back to her like she'd lost her mind. "He'll get away."

"That's not your problem," she said, pleading. "You're worth more to me alive than your name in the paper for being the hero. Please, Hill. I love you and you love me, and though you don't realize it right now, we're eventually going to be together because we're supposed to be. So if you let some punk-ass troll take you out, I'm going to be super pissed."

He blinked, his expression stunned.

She had surprised herself with the love declaration, but she wasn't going to take it back. Seeing Hill in front of her at the exact moment she needed him was all the sign she needed. The universe wanted them to be together. She would keep fighting for this.

"And news flash," she went on. "Horror stories don't end well for the dudes. Don't go after him. I don't want to be a final girl." She released his waistband and whirled her finger in the air. "Get in the damn truck."

Hill stared at her for another second and then gave a curt nod. "Yes, ma'am."

She put the phone back to her ear. "I sprayed the guy with pepper spray. He's running down the street, heading north, but he's going slow because he can't see."

"We have officers on the way," the operator said. "Just stay on the line."

Hill got in the truck and put it in gear. He rolled forward slowly, keeping the guy in the beam of the headlights but not getting too close.

Andi reached out and grabbed Hill's hand, squeezing it.

He sent her a gentle smile that warmed her from the inside out and squeezed back.

She knew they had things to work through if they were going to be together, but him getting into the truck had told her enough. Hill had chosen to be *her* hero instead of *the* hero. He'd kept himself safe even when it went against his instincts. That meant he had hope for the future. For himself. For them. A belief that there was something bigger waiting for them that was worth protecting. That was all she needed to know.

She could work with that.

"If he walks into the street, you have my permission to hit him nonfatally with the truck," she said, her eyes narrowing on her attacker. "Fucker."

"Gladly." Hill's jaw flexed as he kept the guy in sight.

Sirens whined in the distance.

The guy took a sharp left, right out in front of them. Andi smirked.

Hill gave her a brief look and then accelerated just enough to make it hurt.

chapter **twenty-seven**

Hill sat in the waiting area of the police station while Andi gave her statement down the hall. The guy Hill had accidentally-on-purpose tapped with his truck—Jake something or other—was in another part of the station getting interrogated. Hill wished he could have a few minutes alone in a room with that piece of shit. When Andi had stepped under the harsh fluorescent lights of the police station, Hill had seen for the first time that her elbows and knees were scraped up and a patch of her hair had been ripped out, her scalp matted with blood. The thought that someone had hurt Andi, had thrown her to the ground with plans to assault her or worst… Hill couldn't even process that level of rage.

I could've lost her.

The realization was like being plunged into icy water. He didn't want to imagine a world that didn't include Andi. Though he'd only known her for a couple of months, she'd become part of the fabric of his days without him realizing it. He could clearly define the time before Andi and the time after. Even in his memories of the times before, everything seemed grayer, faded. Long days, an empty house, time stretching out before him with no idea what to do with the hours. The times after, in contrast, were painted with color—full of laughter and scary movies and cooking and tangled sheets. Mornings when he woke up and was actually excited about the day. Days when he remembered the person he used to be. Andi had been like a shot of adrenaline straight into the bloodstream of his life.

And she could've been taken from this world. Just like that. Because he'd pushed her away, hurt her. To protect himself. The coward's move. He should've been walking her to her door tonight. Instead, she'd had to face her worst nightmare alone.

But still, even after all that, when he'd gotten to her, she hadn't yelled at him or been angry for what he'd done. Instead, she'd knocked him flat on his proverbial ass. A talent she seemed to have.

When she'd declared she loved him—right before demanding he get his butt in the truck—his whole world had tilted under him. He'd known after their conversation earlier in the night that she was developing feelings for him, but the way she'd put it out there... *I love you. You love me.* Like that didn't take a shit ton of bravery. Like they were facts that just *existed*. That had made something inside him click into place.

Could it be that simple?

Everything in his life had felt so complicated for so long that he always looked for layers within the layers. Why had he gone back in to save those people even after the building was declared too dangerous to go back inside? Was it because he was brave or because he didn't care if he made it? Had Christina cheated on him because there was something wrong with him or because there was something wrong with the relationship? Had his mom left because she didn't think Hill was worth sticking around for, or was she just so depressed that she thought everyone would be better without her?

He'd searched for answers for so long, but maybe the answers didn't matter. The past couldn't be changed. The future couldn't be controlled or guaranteed. All he could do was deal with what was going on now—here, in the present. What did he want his life to look like now?

When he was with Andi, he was happy. And she seemed happy with him.

Maybe it *was* that simple.

Hill was broken from his train of thought when Eliza sat down next to him. She'd arrived at the station a little while ago, after Andi had called her to tell her what happened. She handed him a Snickers bar from the vending machine.

He took it even though he wasn't hungry. "Thanks."

"Do you think she's going to be in there much longer?" Eliza asked, opening a package of Reese's Cups. "I'm afraid when the adrenaline wears off, the reality of what happened tonight is going to settle in for her and she's going to need us."

Hill frowned. "I don't know how much longer it will be, but Christina's in there with her. She'll watch out for her and let me know if Andi needs anything."

"Christina the ex?" she asked. "That might be awkward."

"I don't think so. We're on good terms now, and she already met Andi a while back. She's the one who helped figure out that Andi had been doxed. I wouldn't have gone to the house when I did if Chris hadn't told me what happened." He leaned back and sighed. "I don't want to think about what would've happened if Andi had been forced to bang on neighbors' doors for help. If the guy had caught up with her..."

"God, me neither," Eliza said. "Though I suspect she would've figured something out. She's a warrior, that one."

He glanced over at Eliza. "One hundred percent."

Eliza looked down at her chocolate, a little smile touching her lips. "That's why you two make a good pair," she said casually.

"From the outside, it seems a weird match. You, the quiet, stoic type. Andi, the quirky, bubbly one. But underneath that, you've both experienced real trauma. The kind of stuff that distills life down to its most vital parts." She peeked over at him. "You both know how to cut through the bullshit."

"The bullshit?"

"Yeah." She peeled off the brown wrapper on one of the peanut butter cups. "Everyone says life's too short, but the two of you *know* it. Because you've each had to contemplate that yours was about to end. That matures a person real fast."

Hill stared at her, processing the words.

She smirked and took a bite of her candy. "Andi's like an eighty-year-old woman with a nose ring."

He chuckled. "I don't know about that."

Eliza swallowed the bite, and her expression went serious. "I do. And my unofficial advice to you—because I know something happened tonight at the dance to send Andi home early—is don't insult her by underestimating her. Andi is whimsical, but she doesn't do anything or feel anything *on a whim*. She's an overthinker. Every choice she makes is made with thought and purpose. Including the choice she made to spend time with you."

Hill released a breath, the words resonating. He *had* insulted Andi. He'd told her she didn't know what she didn't know. When the truth was, he was the one who didn't know shit about relationships. He'd never had one last. "I told her I was falling for her and then broke things off."

Eliza's brows arched. "Wow. That's a dick move, bro."

"I'm aware," he said grimly. "I thought I was doing it for her own good."

She snorted. "Oh, that's our favorite thing. When men do things for our own good. Super fun. I'm sure Andi loved that."

He groaned and tossed the candy bar onto the seat next to him. "I screwed everything up."

Eliza laughed and patted his knee. "Oh, honey, that's obvious. If you don't do something about it, she's definitely going to murder you in a book."

He gave her a droll look. "You must be a really encouraging therapist."

"I'm the best," she said, popping the second half of her peanut butter cup in her mouth and clearly not taking offense.

"Hold up. There is candy and no one brought me any?"

Hill's attention snapped to the left to find Andi standing there with her hands on her hips. He reached out for the Snickers bar and handed it to her. "Courtesy of Eliza."

Andi took the candy bar and smiled. "Thanks."

Eliza was on her feet and headed to Andi, wrapping her in a hug before Andi could open the candy. "Oh my God, hey."

Andi kept her eyes on Hill as she hugged Eliza back. "Hey, girl. Thanks for coming."

Eliza leaned back, tears in her eyes, her gaze scanning her friend. "Are you okay? For real, for real?"

Andi nodded and reached out to squeeze Eliza's hand. "I'm okay. I'm going to have to do some creative hairstyling for a little while to cover my newly acquired bald patch, but other than that and a few scrapes, I'm good."

Hill watched them. Eliza checking her friend over. Andi reassuring her and smiling like she hadn't just been through an assault. He could see every little scrape, every war wound, even though someone had helped her clean up a little. He wanted to soothe each spot, take her in his arms, make her feel safe.

Safe.

A feeling was filling him, slow and steady, making everything swell inside his chest. He'd told Andi he didn't want to be her safe choice, but now he realized how wrong he'd been looking at it. Feeling safe with someone was part of what made love *love*.

He wanted to be that person she could be with without worry, the person she could let all her guards down and be herself with. She had become that person for him. She got him talking when he was prone to quiet. She made him laugh when his depression tried to smother him. She was the one who had gotten him cooking again, giving him back something that had always made him happy. She saw him and loved him, and tonight, she'd shown that she wasn't going to let him off the hook so easily. The tools he'd used to push other people away since his accident—and maybe for his whole life—weren't going to work on her.

She was going to be his final girl.

The thought rang through him as loud as church bells.

There was knowing you felt things about a person. But this was more than that. This was...confidence. Confidence in the future. Confidence in himself. Something he hadn't tasted in a long time. He had a lot of work to do still, but he was going to do it.

Andi was a warrior.

Well, so was he.

He stood so quickly that he knocked the chair back against the wall. Andi and Eliza turned to him, both with questioning looks on their faces.

"Hill?" Andi asked. "Everything okay?"

He had no idea what his expression must be saying. He probably looked like a lunatic. There were too many feelings and words trying to come out at once. "I'm in love with you."

Andi stared, and Eliza grinned, taking a step back and giving them space.

"I know this isn't the right place or probably the right time," he rambled on, phones ringing in the background, police officers walking by. He stepped closer and took her hands in his. "And I know I've screwed this all up. I know I said all the wrong things earlier. I got scared. I'm still scared—fucking terrified, actually."

Andi's expression softened.

"But I've been sitting here and looking at you and thinking about the last couple of months... And I know it's quick and I know I have a lot to work on but...I don't want you to go off and look for other guys. I don't want to be practice. I want to be the guy. I *am* the guy."

Andi blinked, her eyes glittering with tears. "Yeah?"

He let out a breath, getting the words out feeling like an exorcism. "Yeah."

She squeezed his hands. "I already knew that you were. I just wasn't sure you were ever going to figure it out." She put her hands on his jaw, her teary gaze holding his. "I love you too, you hardheaded man. I'm glad you finally got a clue."

He laughed softly and then dipped his head, touching his forehead to hers. "You've completely ruined my life plan to be a grumpy hermit. I would've been so good at it."

"Sorry not sorry," Andi said, a smile in her voice. "You ruined my plan to be an eccentric horror writer who lives alone in a creepy mansion."

"You'll always be eccentric, neighbor."

"Thank God." She lifted her head, meeting his gaze and letting her hands lower to his shoulders. "So are we doing this?"

He cupped her jaw and brushed his thumb over her lips. "Yes. How about every day for the rest of our lives?"

Tears spilled over, her smile like sunshine. "Deal."

Light suffused through him, brightening all the dark corners that had gathered inside him over the years. *This one. This one. This one.*

"I'm going to kiss you now," he warned. "I don't care who's watching."

"I'm going to let you."

With that, he lowered his head and kissed her, finally knowing it wouldn't be the last. This was only the beginning.

In their movie, there would always be another sequel.

Epilogue

One year later

"To Andi and her sick, demented mind!" Eliza announced, raising her glass of champagne.

Andi laughed as Hollyn, Jasper, and Ramsey raised their glasses. Hill set the tray of sliders he'd carried out to the back porch onto the table and grabbed a glass. "May *Doxed* continue to climb the bestseller list and keep people the world over from getting a good night's sleep."

Andi grinned and raised her glass, clinking it to each of her friends' and then Hill's. "Thanks, y'all. I'll drink to reader insomnia."

Hill set his glass aside and put together a plate of food, getting a few of each of the finger foods he'd made for the party celebrating Andi's new book's success, and then handed the goodies to her.

"Thanks, babe," she said, setting her drink on the side table. "This all looks great."

"It does," Hollyn agreed as she chose items for her own plate. "This whole spread is gorgeous. Totally Instagram worthy."

"Right?" Eliza agreed. "Maybe Hill should do this for a living, huh?"

"What a brilliant idea," Ramsey said, piling mini-hamburgers onto his plate. "You should give that some thought, Dawson. I think a good friend of yours suggested that a long time ago. What was his name? He was the really smart and good-looking one?"

"Humble too." Hill smirked as he took the spot next to Andi on the pretty blue outdoor couch they'd bought for their new place and draped his arm across the back of it. "I hope it all tastes as good as it looks. I'm using y'all as guinea pigs for some recipe testing for the cookbook."

"Always happy to be of service," Jasper said, sharing a towering plate with Hollyn. "To be a guinea pig or just a pig in general."

Eliza grabbed one of the shot glasses Hill had filled with his version of gazpacho and plopped down cross-legged in one of the chairs. She took a sip and hummed her approval. "Yum. If everything tastes as good as this soup, I volunteer as tribute for recipe testing, too."

"Same," Ramsey said, taking down a slider in one bite. "Hey, Eliza, can I be your recipe-testing date?"

Eliza gave him the side-eye. "Stop trying to date me, fireman. I don't want to fight about who gets custody of the children"—she waved her hand to indicate Andi and Hill—"when we divorce."

Ramsey chuckled, this interplay with Eliza a common one these last few months as Hill's and Andi's friends came together. "Who's saying we wouldn't make it?"

Eliza rolled her eyes.

"So," Jasper said, clearly trying to save Ramsey from a conversation that would only continue to spiral, "when's the cookbook due?"

Hill took a gulp of his champagne. "We have about four months. The publisher only wants to use a few recipes from the blog so that it's mostly brand-new content, but they want me to keep the same kind of recipes that I do on the blog and in the videos. You know, keep it simple for new cooks, single people, busy couples, that kind of thing. Plus, Andi will be adding the movie recommendations."

Andi was smiling so hard as Hill talked that she was sure she probably looked deranged or drunk, but she never got tired of seeing her guy explain his new projects. The man lit up when he talked about cooking and food. She'd noticed it pretty quickly when they'd first started seeing each other, but since he'd decided to give a cooking blog a real try, she'd watched him transform. First, when the blog had started to gain some traction, then when he'd agreed to do some cooking lessons with her on video. In their videos, they'd feature a meal and a movie that matched the theme and dubbed the segments Netflix & Hill as a play on Netflix and chill.

The segments had turned out to be the tipping point. An editor had started following the vlog and then contacted Hill to see if he'd be interested in doing a cookbook with Hill providing the recipes and Andi matching movies to them.

"So does this mean lots of movie marathons?" Hollyn asked between sips of gazpacho.

"Yep," Andi declared. "And you ladies are always invited. I promise it won't be only horror." She bumped her shoulder into Hill's. "I've grown to appreciate a good romance these days, too."

Hill kissed the crown of her head, right over the spot where the hair had been yanked out by Jacob Alberts. Luckily, her hair had grown back with no permanent damage beyond her scalp sometimes tingling. And though her psyche would always have the mark of that attack along with what had happened to her as a teen, she'd gotten back into therapy and felt more in control of her anxiety these days than she'd ever been. Plus, she'd used the incident as fuel, which had helped her healing process tremendously. She'd poured all her anxiety, anger, and frustration into her book *Doxed*, and the joke was on Jacob. While he was sitting in jail, her book was on the bestseller list.

Fuck him.

Hollyn gave Andi a knowing smile and then sent Eliza a look. "Look at that. We've turned her into a romantic after all."

"Hush your mouth, Hollyn Deares," Andi said, tossing an olive at her. "You say that too loud, and you're going to ruin my reputation."

"It'll be our little secret. And don't worry, we'll still allow you to have the occasional movie where everyone dies at the end," Eliza said magnanimously.

"Except the final girl," Hollyn added.

"Thank you." Andi raised her glass. "To final girls."

Hill gave her a squeeze when everyone repeated "To final girls."

He leaned close to her ear. "To my final girl."

Warmth moved through her, and she turned to brush her lips against his. "To my final guy."

The words came out so easily because she knew them to be true. They'd been together for over a year, and not once had she doubted what she'd declared the night of her attack. She loved him. He loved her. They were meant to be together.

That hadn't meant there hadn't been work to be done. Both of them had issues they were working through in therapy. Andi still looked over her shoulder at night. She was still suspicious of strangers. Hill had to be vigilant to keep his depression from surfacing again, and he still had flashbacks to the fire if he heard certain sounds. But the difference was that they were a team now. They didn't have to fight those battles alone.

Love meant someone had your back. Love meant you didn't have to hide what you were struggling with. Love taught you that sometimes it was okay not to be okay.

But more often than not lately, Andi was so much more than okay. She was *happy*. Full-throated, screaming-into-the-sky happy. She'd worked really hard to get there, and she wasn't going to take one second of it for granted.

Andi settled in and enjoyed the evening with her friends, laughing a lot, drinking a little, and eating too much of Hill's bread pudding. But when the sky went full dark, her friends started the dance of *It's getting late, we better get going*. They gathered their things and headed out as if they'd mutually agreed on an exit time. After exchanging hugs with everyone and sending them all home with containers of leftovers, Andi shut the front door, locked it, and turned on the alarm. The sound of it activating was a comfort to her even in this quiet neighborhood. She spun around, leaned back against the door, and sighed.

Hill was standing in the middle of their living room, watching her with a look of affection that made her want to clutch her hands to her chest like an overdramatic actress.

"What's that sigh for?" he asked.

"Tonight was great. I love my friends."

"They're awesome."

"And I love you," she said, taking in the view of him—dark hair mussed from the breeze outside, T-shirt clinging just enough to give her dirty thoughts.

"I love you back," he said as he took a few steps closer. "In fact, you're my favorite. Like, in the world."

She closed her eyes and took in the sweet words, contentment winding through her like a drug. "Did you mean what you said about me being your final girl?"

He took her hands, and she opened her eyes, finding him right in front of her. "I did. Well, woman, not girl." His lips kicked up at one corner in a suggestive smile. "You're definitely all woman."

"I meant what I said, too."

He guided her arms around his waist and filled the space in front of her, his body heat radiating against her. "Good. Because one day, when you're ready"—he leaned down to kiss her gently—"I'm going to marry the hell out of you, Andi Lockley."

The words cascaded through her, filling her up to the brim. Her gaze jumped up to his. His brown eyes held her stare, saying everything she could ever want to feel from him. Sincerity. Love. Honesty. Forever.

"Is that right?"

"Absolutely." He pushed her bangs away from her eyes and cupped the back of her neck. "With your permission, of course."

A crazy thought snaked its way through her, whispering, daring her. "And what if I'm ready now?"

He didn't flinch. "Then I'd marry you now."

His lack of hesitation stole her breath, and an overwhelming sense of rightness flooded her. *I'd marry you now. Now.* "You're serious."

"I'm serious," he said, voice calm as ever. "But there's no rush. I'm not going anywhere. I just want you to know my intentions." He kissed her again and gave her a small smile. "I'm done for. You're it for me, neighbor. Ruined for all others."

Her throat tightened, emotion knotting there. "You're it for me, too." She took in the sight of him, letting herself feel exactly what she was feeling and not overthinking it. "So if I'm it for you and you're it for me, what exactly are we waiting for? What if you and I..."

"What if you and me, what?" he asked softly when she didn't continue.

"What if we did that?" she said, boldness making her spine straighten. "Got married. Like this weekend."

A slow smile spread across his face. "Like elope? Don't you want all the pomp and circumstance with your friends and family there?"

Images flashed through her mind. Her parents inviting all their friends. Picking out bridesmaids' dresses. Having her family dictate when and where things happened in order to stick with family tradition. Having to decide which state to have the wedding in. What food to serve. Which music to play.

None of that sounded appealing. She'd never been the little girl who dreamt of her future wedding. She'd been the little girl who imagined living in a real haunted house or meeting a vampire or solving a mystery in her neighborhood. And Hill had already been through wedding prep once before. Proposing, planning a wedding, only to have it all blow up in his face.

"I don't need all that unless you want it," she said, her heart picking up speed. "We can elope. We can do it in City Park under the oaks. Invite a few of our friends to witness and just do it." She slid her hands up his chest and looped her arms around his neck. "I don't need pomp and circumstance. All I need is you."

Hill's eyes sparkled in the low light of the living room, and he cradled her face in his hands. "I would love nothing more in this world than to be your husband."

The words sang through her like the best song she'd ever heard.

"Wish granted," she whispered, and that was the last thing she got out before Hill lowered his head and kissed her against the door until her knees went to jelly beneath her.

Somehow over the next few minutes, they made it to their bedroom, kissing along the way, without tripping over furniture. Items of clothing got dropped behind them like bread crumbs and no more words were needed. They were getting married. *Married.*

Andi had spent a long time not trusting her gut, not believing it when it gave her the green light on things. That intuition had let her down a long time ago. But in this moment, she'd never felt more certain of any decision in her life. The feeling deep in the pit of her stomach, at the very core of her, was like the clear ring of a bell on a quiet night resonating through her. What she'd thought was her gut feeling all those years ago when she'd trusted Evan Longdale hadn't been this, hadn't felt like this. This was what gut-level knowing really felt like. Her gut hadn't lied to her back then. She'd simply been outmatched—an innocent child who was victimized by a master manipulator.

As she and Hill stepped through the doorway into the bedroom, she let go of that old story, freeing that ghost who'd haunted her for so long. And silently she whispered to that little girl, *I'm sorry. None of it was your fault. But you're going to be okay.*

Andi walked backward into the bedroom, letting Hill unhook her bra and toss it to the floor. Yes. She was definitely going to be okay.

By the time Hill tumbled Andi onto the bed, she was fully naked against the dark-green comforter, her thoughts zeroing in on the man in front of her and her body buzzing with arousal. Hill flicked on a lamp, and she watched him watch her as he finished undressing.

She loved the privilege of seeing him completely bared. Exposing himself like that to her had once been so hard for him. He'd perceived his disability as a weakness, as something to hide. Even after they'd gotten together officially, it had still taken him a month before he let her see him in the wheelchair he sometimes used when his leg was aching too much from the prosthesis.

But now, now he trusted her to see every private part of him, body and soul. It was a gift she didn't receive lightly. She only wished that he could see what she saw when she looked at him. Strong shoulders, beautiful body, soulful face, a thousand places she wanted to kiss and touch and taste. Every bit of him turned her on.

Hill gave her a sly smile as he sat on the edge of the bed and removed his prosthesis. "I love how you look at me."

"Like I want to eat you?" she guessed.

He laughed and stretched out next to her, sliding his big hand over her belly. "Something like that." His hand drifted down between her legs, his fingers finding her slick and ready. "The feeling's mutual."

She bit her lip and hummed her approval as he dipped a finger inside her, the sensation of his callused finger sending tingling awareness radiating through her. He was always so focused and precise when it came to her pleasure, like a musician learning every nuance of an instrument. What will this do? What sound will this elicit? What music will this make? He'd also helped her unwind the knotted emotions she'd had about sweet sex, about romantic words in bed. She could enjoy the full range of options now because she trusted Hill without reservation. Romance was no longer a weapon of mass destruction in her world. Slowly, patiently, he'd shown her how good things could be—one sexy experiment at a time. She was more than happy to be his subject of study.

In fact, she was conducting her own experiments as well—a thesis on what made her sexy, quiet man lose all that artful calm. Even after more than a year together, she was still discovering new tricks and ways to drive him crazy. As he teased her, ramping up her arousal, she reached out and wrapped her hand around the smooth, velvet length of his cock, unable to go another second without touching him. She stroked him slowly, loving how thick and hot he felt in her hand, and he let out a soft gasp when she circled her thumb along his slit, spreading the fluid there.

Hill slipped another finger inside her and kissed along her neck as she continued to stroke him. She closed her eyes, relishing the lazy luxury of not having to rush. They could tease each other all night if they wanted. They had nowhere to go, nowhere to be, no pretenses to cling to. This bed was theirs. She could sleep next to him now. Wherever the finish line landed, they'd end up curled together under the covers tonight. This was their life now.

They'd earned this.

So they were damn sure going to enjoy it.

The ceiling fan above her whirled softly on low, sending a cool breeze over her hot skin as Hill continued to dip his fingers into her, his thumb finding her clit and his mouth finding her breast. Her hips rocked in rhythm against him, and she let herself explore him blindly with her hand—cupping him, teasing him, wrapping her fingers around his cock and then backing off when she sensed he was getting too close to the edge.

He did the same for her, bringing her to the brink and then easing her back down, until she was so wound up that her heels were pressing into the mattress and her back was arched. Begging words started to fall past her lips without her permission. She'd wanted to prove she could wait, prove she could be patient, but Hill was playing dirty.

He usually did.

"Please." Her hand slid off him, her brain no longer able to multitask. "Please."

He moved his fingers more quickly, his thumb working her sensitive flesh, giving her more pressure. Then, he was shifting on the bed and the blissful wet heat of his mouth landed on the spot where his thumb had been. She cried out, the shock of contact so delicious and overwhelming that she nearly launched herself off the bed. But Hill put a hand on her thigh and held her in place.

Mine, the action whispered.

He gave her pleasure with the focus of a man who had one mission in life, and before she could beg him again, her orgasm crashed through her like the crescendo of a symphony—all cymbals and screaming violins and rumbling drums. She cried out in panting, gulping sounds as she rode the wave of sensation. All thought blinked out of her mind, leaving only clenching muscles and heat and bliss behind.

She grappled for Hill, her fingers digging into the thick muscles of his shoulders. "Need you," she gasped. "Now."

She didn't have to beg this time. Hill quickly shifted on the bed, positioning himself above her and sliding deep, her orgasm still coursing through her. The feel of his cock, like heated steel inside her, was everything she needed in that moment. Her body tightened around him, the pressure and fullness ramping up her orgasm further. Hill murmured unintelligible words and began to rock into her with slow, grinding thrusts.

She'd learned the man had staying power, but right now, she wanted to feel him go over along with her. They'd ditched condoms after she'd gotten on the pill, and she loved the feeling of him coming inside her, the heat of his release, the sounds he made when it happened. She lived for that moment they were both lost to each other and riding the same high.

She dug her nails into his back, sweat glazing both of their bodies, and she kissed him. Hill groaned into her mouth with a primal sound and picked up his pace. The controlled, measured man was letting go. He buried deep and whispered her name, and then they were both launched into the stratosphere together. Clinging to each other, loving each other, promising each other.

Joined. For now. And soon, for always.

Afterward, both of them ended up splayed on their backs on the bed, wrung out and sated, and Andi couldn't stop smiling. "I feel like I owe you brownies or something."

Hill laughed and laced his fingers with hers. "That's how we got into this mess. You brought me baked goods. I never had a chance."

She pulled his hand up and kissed his knuckles. "I'm glad you opened the door to your pushy neighbor."

He rolled onto his side and looked down at her. "Best decision I ever made. Even if the brownies were terrible."

She gasped. "*They were not*, you food snob."

He grinned and kissed her. "I still ate every one of them because you had made them."

She harrumphed, playfully affronted, and he kissed her again. And somehow even though she'd thought she'd been totally spent a few minutes ago, she ended up on top of him and round two began.

She'd never get enough of this man.

Later, when they were finally settled beneath the covers, exhausted and cuddled up naked against each other, Hill tucked her backside against his body. She snuggled into his warmth. "I love you."

"I love you too." He pressed his face into her hair, his beard tickling her neck as he let out a soft sigh. "God. I can't believe I get to keep you."

Andi closed her eyes, a contented calmness she'd searched for her entire life coming over her. She'd never felt so loved.

So *safe*.

And when Hill fell asleep next to her, his arm draped over her, she didn't get a flashback to a night so long ago when she was trapped beneath another man's arm. In fact, she didn't think about the past at all.

All she could see was the bright, beautiful future.

Acknowledgments

Getting a book out into the world takes a lot of effort in a normal year, but writing, editing, and polishing a book during the upheaval of 2020 takes a special kind of dedication. Luckily, I have been blessed with a great team of people (and my family) in my corner to help make that happen.

To Mary Altman, my editor, who didn't panic when, after already having written a big chunk of the book, I told her I'd like to change a major aspect of my hero and would need more time. Thank you! Now I can't imagine Hill any other way.

To the whole Sourcebooks team, including Christa, Stefani, Rachel, and Jessica, your dedication and enthusiasm are top-notch. I know my books are in great hands!

To Sara Megibow, my agent, who has had my back for ten years. Happy author/agent anniversary!

To Dawn Alexander, my dearest friend and a badass brainstormer, who keeps me laughing even when I'm in the pit of writer's block.

To my parents, who are way cooler than I'll ever be. I love you.

To my readers, thank you for picking up my books even when I can't seem to stay in one place genre-wise. I am grateful to each and every one of you. Every. Single. Time.

And finally, to Donnie and Marshall, my rock stars. I wouldn't want to be quarantined with anyone else. Love you. Love you. Love you.

About the Author

Roni Loren wrote her first romance novel at age fifteen when she discovered writing about boys was way easier than actually talking to them. Since then, her flirting skills haven't improved, but she likes to think her storytelling ability has. She holds a master's degree in social work and spent years as a mental health counselor, but now she writes full time from her cozy office in Dallas, Texas, where she puts her characters on the therapy couch instead. She is a two-time RITA Award winner and a *New York Times* and *USA Today* bestselling author. Visit her online at roniloren.com.

YES & I LOVE YOU

First in the emotionally compelling Say Everything series.

Everyone knows Miz Poppy, the vibrant reviewer whose commentary brightens the New Orleans nightlife. But no one knows Hollyn, the real face behind the media star...or the fear that keeps her isolated. When her boss tells her she needs to add video to her blog or lose her job, she's forced to rely on an unexpected source to help face her fears.

When aspiring actor Jasper Deares finds out the shy woman who orders coffee every day is actually Miz Poppy, he realizes he has a golden opportunity to get the media attention his acting career needs. All he has to do is help Hollyn come out of her shell…and through their growing connection, finally find her voice.

"Absolutely unputdownable!"

—Colleen Hoover, #1 *New York Times* bestseller, for *The One You Can't Forget*

For more info about Sourcebooks's books and authors, visit:

sourcebooks.com

FOR YOU & NO ONE ELSE

Third in the emotionally compelling
Say Everything series.

Eliza Catalano has the perfect life. So what if her actual life looks nothing like the story she tells online? But when she ends up as a viral meme, everything falls apart. Enter the most obnoxious man she's ever met, and a deal she can't resist: if she helps Beck out of a jam, he'll teach her the wonders of surviving the "real world." No technology, no pretty filters, no BS.

Except what starts out as a simple arrangement gets much more complicated when their annoyance with each other begins to morph into an attraction that neither can resist. As complex feelings grow, this living-in-the-analog-world experiment threatens to get much too real.

"Absolutely unputdownable!"

—Colleen Hoover, #1 *New York Times* bestselling author,
for *The One You Can't Forget*

NEON GODS

He was supposed to be a myth...

Society darling Persephone Dimitriou plans to flee the ultra-modern city of Olympus and start over far from the backstabbing politics of the Thirteen Houses. But all that's ripped away when her mother ambushes her with an engagement to Zeus, the dangerous power behind their glittering city's dark facade.

With no options left, Persephone flees to the forbidden undercity and makes a devil's bargain with a man she once believed a myth...a man who awakens her to a world she never knew existed.

"Unspeakably hot."

—Entertainment Weekly

For more info about Sourcebooks's books and authors, visit:

sourcebooks.com

THE ONES WHO GOT AWAY

Only a few survived the Long Acre High School shooting. Twelve years later, the kids once called The Ones Who Got Away are back...and ready to claim the lives they never truly got to live in this emotional and steamy series by *New York Times* bestselling author Roni Loren

The Ones Who Got Away
Olivia Arias is ready to end the decade-long riff between her and Finn Dorsey and move on. But when her attempt at closure turns into a kiss that reignites their old flame, moving on proves tougher than either of them thought…

The One You Can't Forget
Chef Wes Garrett is trying to get back on his feet after losing his dream restaurant, his money, and his mind in a vicious divorce. But when he intervenes in a mugging and finds he's saved Rebecca Lindt, the divorce attorney who helped his ex-wife, his simple life gets a lot more complicated.

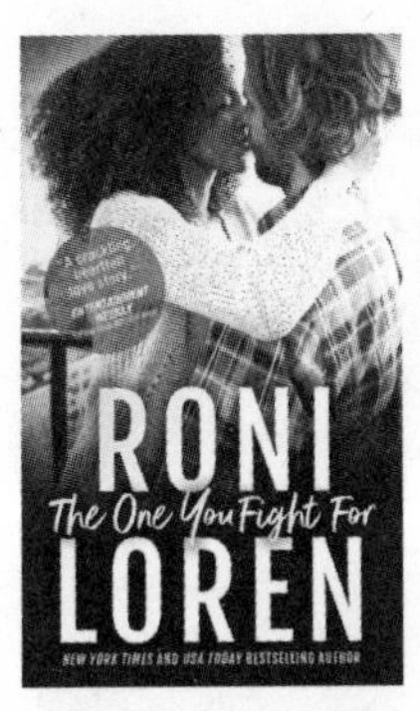

The One You Fight For

Shaw Miller and Taryn Landry weren't meant to meet each other. They weren't meant to fall in love. Now they're left grappling with undeniable feelings, both of them wondering: When the world defines you by a tragedy, how do you find your own happy ending?

The One for You

For Ashton Isaacs, Kincaid Breslin is the one who got away. For Kincaid, Ash is the one for her...she just doesn't know it yet. When fate throws them together, they'll have to deal with the ghosts of the past and decide who they are to each other now. . . and whether they can forge a future together.

"Absolutely unputdownable, delivers all of the feels! Roni Loren is a new favorite."

—Colleen Hoover, #1 *New York Times* bestselling author, for *The One You Can't Forget*

THE GIRL WITH STARS IN HER EYES

Her name's Antonia Bennette, and she's not (yet) a rock star...

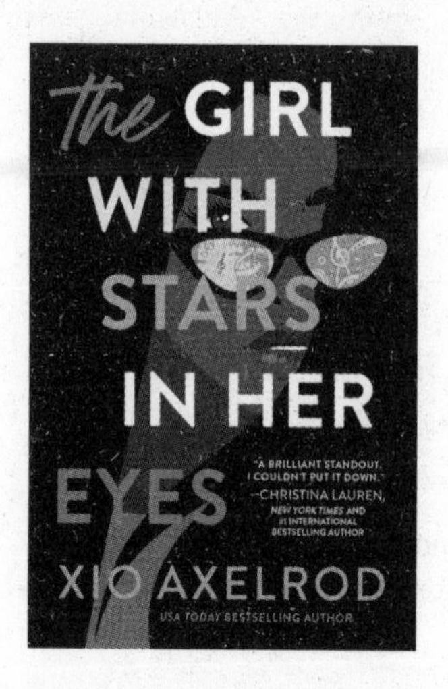

Growing up, Antonia "Toni" Bennette's guitar was her only companion...until she met Sebastian Quick. Seb was a little older, a lot wiser, and he became Toni's way out, promising they'd escape their small town together. Then Seb turned eighteen and split without looking back.

Now, Toni B is all grown up and making a name for herself in Philadelphia's indie scene. When a friend suggests she try out for the hottest new band in the country, she decides to take a chance...not realizing that this opportunity will bring her face-to-face with the boy who broke her heart and nearly stole her dreams.

"A brilliant standout."

—Christina Lauren, *New York Times* bestselling author

For more info about Sourcebooks's books and authors, visit:

sourcebooks.com

Hooray for the Stainless Steel Rat!

"The Rat can hold his head high amongst the most elevated superhero company—Bulldog Drummond, James Bond, and Flash Gordon included."

—*Times Literary Supplement* (London)

"Cheerfully larcenous and anarchic. . . . Long may the Rat run roughshod over the forces of law, order, and the square world."

—*The Orlando Sentinel*

"Fast moving, light-fingered entertainment from one of the masters of tongue-in-cheek parody."

—*New York Newsday*

"Pure entertainment. . . . Abounding in quick action and quicker jokes. . . . The Stainless Steel Rat series shows Harrison's talents at best advantage."

—*Science Fiction Review*

"Harrison is a superb comic author." —*Library Journal*

TOR BOOKS BY HARRY HARRISON

Galactic Dreams
The Jupiter Plague
Montezuma's Revenge
One Step from Earth
Planet of No Return
Planet of the Damned
The QE2 Is Missing
Queen Victoria's Revenge
A Rebel in Time
Skyfall
Stainless Steel Visions
Stonehenge
A Transatlantic Tunnel, Hurrah!

THE HAMMER AND THE CROSS TRILOGY
The Hammer and the Cross
One King's Way
King and Emperor

HARRY HARRISON

THE STAINLESS STEEL RAT GOES TO HELL

A TOM DOHERTY ASSOCIATES BOOK / NEW YORK

THE STAINLESS STEEL RAT GOES TO HELL

Cover art by Walter Velez

This book is printed on acid-free paper.

A Tor Book
Published by Tom Doherty Associates, Inc.
175 Fifth Avenue
New York, NY 10010

Tor Books on the World Wide Web:
http://www.tor.com

ISBN: 0-812-55107-9

Library of Congress Card Catalog Number: 96-19967

First Edition: November 1996
First mass market edition: January 1997

Printed in the United States of America

0 9 8 7 6 5 4 3 2 1

THE STAINLESS STEEL RAT GOES TO HELL

CHAPTER 1

I POURED A GOOD MEASURE of whiskey over the ice, scowled at it—then added a splash more. But, as I lifted the glass and drank it with glugging pleasure, my raised eyes drifted across the clock that was set into the wall above the bar.

It was just ten in the morning.

"My, my, Jim, you are hitting the sauce a little earlier each day," I growled wordlessly. So what? It was my liver wasn't it? I gurgled the glass empty just as the house computer spoke to me in rich, educated—and possibly sneering?—tones.

"Someone is approaching the front door, Sire."

"Great. Perhaps it is the booze shop delivery?" Venom dripped from my voice; but all computers are immune to sarcasm.

"Indeed not, Sire, for Garry's Grog and Groceries delivers by freight tube. I identify the person approaching as Rowena Vinicultura. She has stopped her popcar on the front lawn and is emerging from it."

My morale plummeted as the name slithered across my eardrums. Of all the beautiful bores on Lussuoso, Rowena was possibly the most beautiful—and certainly the most boring. I had to flee—or commit suicide—before she came in. I was already heading for the back of the house, to possibly drown myself in the swimming pool, when the housebot's computer voice stopped me in my tracks.

"Ms. Vinicultura appears to have fallen down onto the plastic mat outside the door that spells out WELCOME in six languages."

"What do you mean *fallen?*"

"I believe the description is an apt one. She closed her eyes and her body became limp. Then she descended slowly towards the ground and is now lying, unmoving, with her eyes still closed. Her pulse appears to be slow and irregular as detected by the pressure plate in the mat. Lacerations and bruises on her face . . ."

The thing's voice followed me as I ran back through the house.

"Open the door!" I shouted. It swung wide and I dived through.

Her cameo face was pale, her dark hair tousled gracefully, her ample bosom rising and falling slowly. There was blood on her cheeks and a darkening bruise on her forehead. Her lips moved and I leaned close.

"Gone . . ." she said, barely audible. "Angelina . . . gone . . ."

It felt as though my body temperature had dropped thirty degrees. This did not slow me in the slightest. While I was still reaching down for her I managed to tap the number 666 into my wrist communicator.

"Where is the home medical treatment center?" I shouted as I slipped my arms under warm thighs, soft back, and lifted her as carefully as I could.

"The settee in the library, Sire."

I ran, ignoring the cold knot of despair her words had punched into me. Since both Angelina and I were strenuously healthy we had never used the medical services in this house. I had glanced at the specs when I signed the rental agreement; with the price we were paying, the medical arrangements should equal that of a provincial hospital at least. By the time I had carried Rowena to the library the settee had vanished into the wall and an examining bed had risen in its place. Even as I laid her on the bed the detectors were snaking down from the med-bot that had popped out of the ceiling. An analyzer fastened onto the back of my neck and I slapped it away.

"Not me! Her, on the bed, you moronic machine."

I stepped back out of reach while it set to work with mechanical enthusiasm. A glistening row of readouts sprang to life on the screen. Everything from temperature and pulse to endocrine balance, liver function, hair-follicle growth and anything else that could be measured or assessed was there.

"Speak! Tell!" I commanded and there was a rustle of electronic activity as the various expert programs shuffled and sorted their input, compared and interacted and agreed on the results in a speedy microsecond.

"The patient is concussed and contused." The computer-generated voice was deep, male and reassuring. "The bruises are superficial and have been cleansed and sealed," there was a scurry of flashing apparatus, "and the appropriate antibiotics injected."

"Bring her to!" I snapped

"If you mean, sir, that you wish the patient restored to consciousness that is now being done." If a computer can sound miffed—this one was miffed.

"Whasha?" she muttered, blinking lovely purple eyes that were blurrily out of focus.

"You've got to do better than that with her," I said. "Stimulants, something. I must talk to her."

"The patient has been traumatized . . ."

"But not badly—you told me that. Now get her to talk, you overpriced collection of memory chips or I'll short-circuit your ROM, PROM and EPROM!"

This seemed to do the job. Her eyes blinked again and looked at me.

"Jim . . ."

"In the flesh, Rowena my sweet. You're going to be fine. Now tell me about Angelina."

"Gone . . ." she said. And fluttered her luxurious eyelashes.

I felt my teeth grating together and forced a smile.

"You said that before. Gone where? Gone why? Gone when—" I shut up since I was getting into a rut.

"The Temple of Eternal Truth . . ." was all that she said as her eyes closed again. It was enough.

I shouted to the housebot as I bolted out the door.

"Cure her. Guard her. Call an ambulance."

I did not mention the police since I didn't want their flat-footed presence interfering with my investigation.

"Switch on!" I shouted to the atomcycle as I jumped into the garage. "Door open!"

I landed in the saddle, hit full power and tore off the bottom half of the garage door, it wasn't opening fast enough, as we burst through it. I managed to miss a strolling couple on the pavement, shot between two vehicles and roared down the road. Shouting into the atomcycle's phone since it would be nice to know where I was going.

"AdInfo, emergency access. The Temple of Eternal Truth—coordinates."

A street map was projected onto the now-cracked windscreen and I screeched tires around the first corner. As I straightened out I saw that the com light was blinking. It could only be an answer to my emergency call since only Angelina, James or Bolivar could access this number after that call went out.

"Angelina is that you?!" I shouted.

"Bolivar here. What's up, Dad?"

I explained briefly and curtly, then repeated myself when James signed on. I had no idea where they were—I would find out later—but it was enough to know that they were informed and on the way. This was the first time we had used the 666 call. Major emergency. Drop everything and assemble. I had set it up when they had left home and both gone their individual ways. To help them in the future, I had imagined; now I was the one who was calling. They clicked off, not wasting my time or attention with needless comments. They were listening and would be here.

I blasted around the last corner and stood on the brakes.

Oily smoke was billowing into the air—already dying down as white spray from a fire copter played over the wrecked building. The cold clutch on my chest was physical now. I took a moment to regain control, to breathe carefully. Then ran towards the ruins. Two men in blue uniforms were in my way and both sprawled and bounced. Then there was a bigger one before me with lots of gold braid; massed minions closed ranks behind him. I got control of my adrenaline-zapped reflexes and put my brain into gear.

"My name is diGriz. I've reason to believe that my wife is in there . . ."

"If you will step back and—"

"No." I spat the word like venom and he recoiled automatically. "I pay taxes. Lots of taxes. To pay you. I am more experienced in police operations than you are." I neglected to add on which side of the law I had gained that experience. "What do you know about this?"

"Nothing. Fire and police have just arrived. There was an automatic alarm call."

"I'll tell you what I know. This is—or was—the Temple of Eternal Truth. A survivor just came to my house. Rowena Vinicultura. She said that my wife was here."

I could hear the police computer buzzing in his earphone. "Admiral Sir James diGriz. We will do everything we can to find your wife . . . Angelina. I am Captain Collin and I note that your status permits you to accompany this investigation under your own cognizance and responsibility."

Purely by reflex I had established my forged bona fides as an Admiral of the Fleet when we had first come to Lussuoso. Basic precautions always pay off.

We followed a large and well-insulated firefightbot into the ruins. It plowed a careful path, occasionally spraying a smoking remnant, recording for later examination every movement that it made, every obstacle it put aside. A hanging door screeched and fell and we entered the smoking interior of what had been a good-sized meeting hall. Roblights suspended from whirring blades floated by above us and illuminated the smoke-filled interior.

Destruction on all sides—but no bodies to be seen. The cold knot was still in my midriff. The room had been seriously decorated with carved wood paneling and—now smoking—draperies. Rows of pews faced towards the destroyed side of the room where the smoke was thickest. Precipitators soon cleared the air and the floating lights glinted from wrecked and twisted machinery.

"We'll hold it here," Captain Collin said. "The disaster team takes over now."

The disaster team was embodied in a single metallic gray robot. It was undoubtedly packed full of expert programs produced in collaboration with fire and forensic investigators, along with detectors and probes of microscopic efficiency. Logically I knew it would do an infinitely better job than we fumbling humans: I still wanted to kick it aside and rush in.

"Do you see any . . . bodies?" I called out.

"No living creatures. No corpses of humans or animals detected. No—yes. Correction. Red liquid on the floor. Detection processing. It is human blood."

My throat was almost closed. My voice grated and I had trouble talking. "Primary test. Blood type?"

"Testing. O positive, Rh negative."

I didn't hear the rest—nor did it matter. Angelina was a sturdy type B—and Rh positive. I relaxed, but only so slightly.

In a very few minutes two important facts were made clear. Other than the drops of blood, there were no visible human remains or traces of anyone living or dead. There was the ruined hall and next to it the burnt and crushed room that had held large amounts of electronic equipment. All of it now apparently—and deliberately—destroyed beyond any possibility of recognition.

But where was Angelina?

I waited until the ruined building had been examined and re-examined. Nothing new was discovered and I was just wasting my time at the site. The police had vetted every spacer that had left the planet since the explosion and would keep on doing so. Neither Angelina—nor even anyone who resembled her in the slightest—had been recorded as being aboard any of them. There was nothing I could do here.

I drove slowly home, obeying all traffic regulations. Stopping for pedestrians and waving them on. I rolled through the remains of the garage door and parked the bike. Went straight to the bar where I threw out the flat drink sitting there and prepared a small but stiff replacement before I dug into the E-mail printouts. The twins were on the way. Both were off-planet so it would be a few days at least before they arrived. They did not go into details but I knew that they were now buying, cajoling, bribing—perhaps stealing—the fastest means of transportation in the known universe. They would be here. Our little clan may have rejected the outside worlds and their values—but this made our own cohesion that much stronger.

But now we had to wait for plodding technology to sift, examine and assess the ruins of the Temple of Eternal Truth—and present a coherent picture of what had happened there. There was nothing I could do until I got the police report. I tried to contact Rowena in the hospital but was given the brush-off. Querying her more would have to wait until she had recovered a bit. Lussuoso was rich and technically efficient and would do the search-and-analyze job as well as—or better than—any other planet we had visited. I hated this place but gave it all credit for technical competence. My mind kept trying to numerate all the terrible possibilities of Angelina's disappearance. . . .

Don't dwell on it, Jim, I told myself firmly. You have chosen to lead what others might consider a strange and possibly criminal life. I began to wish I had stayed with crookery and away from the Special Corps. I was always uneasy on the right side of the law. Even more I regretted coming here. Yet it had seemed like a good idea at the time.

This was a paradise planet and unbelievably expensive. To move here I had had to tap into bank accounts untouched for years. I even had to draw in some long-overdue debts and that had not been easy to do. I mean not easy in the sense of heavy weapons and a number of people in the hospital before the accounts were closed. A life of crime is not always profitable—particularly when I had some unwelcome assignments from the Special Corps. Certainly my saving the universe had been exciting, but not money-making in the slightest. The same thing happened when I ran for president of Paraiso Aqui. Good fun, but again no money involved. So between these kinds of legal jobs, Angelina and I had done a number of other jobs that filled our coffers while depleting those of others. Enough had been stored away for a rainy day that had proved to be a sunny one here. It had all been well worth it since Angelina was happier here than she had ever been before. I even forgot how much I hated the place when she smiled and kissed me. It had all started simply enough.

"Have you ever heard of Lussuoso?" she had asked.

"A new drink—or something you rub onto the skin?"

"Don't always play the fool, Jim diGriz. I mean every day there is something about it in the news—"

"Vicarious thrills and sheer jealousy. There isn't one person in a trillion who could even afford a day's visit there."

"We could. I'm sure."

"Of course—"

Of course. Famous Last Words. Springing to my lips engendered by relaxation and mental sloth. By hindsight it was obvious that every word of that simple conversation was planned and orchestrated by my dearest. She was a woman who, when she knew what she wanted done, got it done.

Lussuoso. Famous in myth and legend and galactic soap operas. A paradise planet. Populated only by the very, very rich and those who were richer. I had been intrigued by this phenomenon at first and had done a bit of research. I was in an exotic enough income bracket to quickly discover why it was so attractive.

It was the galactic center for rejuvenation treatments. These were so hideously expensive that you had to be a millionaire to even see their price list. The treatments were painless but time-consuming. Depending upon the degree of customer decay this could take years. Since a clinic would be a bore, and there was no shortage of money in the project, an entire planet had been terraformed into a holiday world. Luxury villas rivaled each other in exuberance. Operas, theaters and entertainments of all kinds abounded. All the sports from deep-sea diving and fishing to mountain climbing and hunting were there for the taking. But hidden away from all this consumptive capitalism were the clinics and surgeries where the rich got younger and, if possible, poorer. This was the taboo subject and never mentioned—but was the real reason why the planet existed in the first place.

I had discovered all this and had instantly forgotten it. Angelina had not. I knew that my fate was sealed, my goose well-cooked, served and carved, when she stopped in front of the hall mirror one day just before we left for dinner. She patted her immaculately groomed hair as women are wont to do—then leaned closer. Touching the corner of one eye with a delicate fingertip.

"Jim—is that a line, right here?"

"Of course not. Just the way the light is falling."

Even as I spoke these polite, truthful and simple words my thoughts were briskly whirring forwards. Years of happy marriage had taught me one important fact—if not a lot of important facts. Women speak with many levels of meaning. As simple a question as *Are you hungry?* can mean *I* am hungry. Or have *you* forgotten we have a dinner appointment? Or I'm not hungry but I'm sure you will be bothering me about lunch soon. Or any other of countless convoluted interpretations. So a possible line in the corner of an eye, following soon after a simple query about Lussuoso and the chance appearance of a gilt brochure on the end table could mean only thing. I smiled.

"I am beginning to feel that this world has worn out its welcome and is starting to bore more than a little. Have you ever thought of passing a spell on, I don't know, some grander and more exciting planet?"

She whirled about and kissed me enthusiastically. "Jim—

you must be a mind reader! What do you think about . . ."

I really didn't have much to think about. Other than remembering long-forgotten bank accounts.

But it had been well worth it. For awhile. Angelina absented herself from time to time—but we never discussed the rejuvenation treatments. I am forced to admit that, after noting my touches of gray hair, as well as a slight tendency to be short of breath after serious exercise, I was not that adverse to a medical session or two myself. After all I was paying for it. And Lussuoso was as jolly and entertaining as the brochures had said. Our house was lovely and our friends lovelier still. I don't know how beautiful these people had been before they had become beautiful people—but they were sure good to look at now. Neither age shall wither nor time detract. They used to say that money couldn't buy everything, but this cliché had long been extinct. On Lussuoso they were all young, handsome and rich. Or rather rich first—therefore young and handsome.

It did not take me long to discover that they were also boring beyond belief.

Making a lot of money seems to produce people who care only about making money.

Now I am not a snob—far from it. My circle of friends and acquaintances contains weird and wonderful examples from all walks of life. Conmen and connoisseurs. Forgers and foresters, police and politicians, scientists and psalm singers. All of them entertaining and good company in a variety of strange and interesting ways.

Yet after a month on Lussuoso I was ready for anything but more of Lussuoso. Suicide perhaps, or back into the army again, maybe swimming in a lake of sulfuric acid; any of these would be preferable.

But I bided my time and increased my drinking for two reasons. Firstly I had paid a satellite-sized bundle for the medical treatments and I was going to get my money's worth. Secondly, and more importantly, Angelina was having an incredibly good time. Our lifestyle had previously prevented her from having female acquaintances or close lady friends. Her early and murderous life, before the psych treatments that had turned her into a more civilized, though still criminal, person, was far in the past and hopefully forgotten. We never discussed those early years when I—for a rare change!—was on the side of law enforcement. And she was a criminal on the run. A very nasty criminal indeed and I could not understand how one so beautiful could be so devious and cruel. Until she trusted me, perhaps she loved me even then, and had opened the locket with the secret of her past. Her beauty had been the product of the surgeon's knife. That had changed her from what she had been to how she looked now. Only her criminal existence had enabled her to pay for the operations. Because of this, and our extra-legal standard of living, we might have had a lonely existence in many ways. We had not led a solitary life, but it had certainly been a different kind of life from the normal ones led by the other 99.99 percent of mankind.

Having the twins had been a novel experience for both of us. One that I had not looked forward to with a great deal of enthusiasm. But I had changed, for the better Angelina always said, and she should know. When the boys were growing up we had seen that they had received the best education. We had discussed it a lot and had finally agreed that they could choose the style of life that most appealed to them. In all fairness, when they were old enough, we had introduced them to some of the more interesting aspects of our lifestyle. I am happy to say that they took to it instantly. All of this kept us busy enough and, since Angelina had never had any close friends, she apparently had never missed the acquaintance of those of the fairer sex. Now she had them in abundance.

They went out together and did things together. Just what I was never quite sure. But she—and they—did enjoy themselves. She had even mentioned lightly, and oh how I wish I had listened more closely, the Temple of Eternal Truth. She hadn't seemed terribly interested but had gone there at a friend's insistence.

Now this. I sipped long and hard at my drink and resisted a refill.

"DiGriz here," I called out at the instant the communicator buzzed.

"It is Captain Collin, Admiral. We have some more—and very puzzling—information about the Temple of Eternal Truth. Do you think you could come to my office . . ."

I was out the door even while he was still speaking.

CHAPTER 2

"WHAT HAVE YOU FOUND OUT?" I asked brusquely as I stamped into Captain Collin's office. He was speaking on the phone and he raised his hand signing me to wait.

"Yes. Thank you. I understand." He hung up. "That was the hospital. It seems that Mrs. Vinicultura is suffering from post-traumatic amnesia—"

"She's forgotten everything that happened?"

"Precisely. There are techniques that could get access to those memories but their application must wait until she has recovered from the shock."

"That's not why you called me here?"

"No." He ran his finger around inside his collar and—if it were possible for an overmuscled police captain to look embarrassed—he looked embarrassed.

"Here on Lussuoso we pride ourselves on our security and the thoroughness of our records . . ."

"Which means," I interrupted, "your security has been penetrated and your records are doubtful?"

He opened his mouth to rebut me. Then closed it and slumped in his chair. "You're right. But it has never happened before."

"Once is once too often. Tell me about it."

"It is this Temple of Eternal Truth. It appears to have been duly registered as a qualified religion. They kept accurate records and reported regularly on their financial position, though of course like all religions they pay no taxes. Everything seemed quite aboveboard. The directors are on record and, most discreetly of course, we know about all of its members . . ."

"*Know* about? Would you like to explain that?"

He looked uncomfortable. "Well, like any civilized planet we practice the galactic constant of complete freedom of religion. You have heard of the Interstellar Freedom of Religion Act?"

"Vaguely, in school."

"The Act is not vague. The history of religion is a history of violence. Only too often religion kills, and we have had enough killing. Therefore no state or planet can have an official religion. Neither can a state or planet make any laws controlling religion. Freedom of worship and assembly is essential to civilization."

"What about nut cults?"

"I was coming to that. Galactic law requires us not to interfere with any religion and to adhere to that rule sternly. But since the weak and the juvenile require protection so that, always legally and with the utmost caution, we do investigate all religions thoroughly. We make ongoing investigations to assure that religious rights are not violated, that each religion has the freedom to practice in its own way, that minors' rights are not violated, that parishioners have complete freedom of choice—"

"What you are trying to say is that you keep tabs on who goes to what church and how often and you know what they are getting up to."

"Precisely," he growled defensively. "The records are secure and can only be accessed at the highest level in case of emergency."

"All right. We have an emergency and they have been accessed. Tell me."

"Rowena Vinicultura is one of the first members of the Temple. She attends regularly. She brought your wife to exactly four seances or sessions or whatever they call them."

"So?"

He was beginning to look uncomfortable again. "So, as I have explained, our records are detailed and complete. Except, that the leader of the Temple of Eternal Truth, one Master Fanyimadu, is, well . . ."

His voice ran down and he stared at his desktop. I finished the sentence for him.

"Master Fanyimadu does not appear in any entry in any of your records."

He nodded without looking up. "We know his place of residence and have documented his attendance at the temple. However to preserve religious freedom we have done no more than that."

"No investigations? No cross-reference with Immigration or Criminal Affairs?"

He shook his head in silence. I glowered.

"Let me guess. You don't know how he came to this planet, or if he is still here—or if he has left. Is that correct?"

"There has been . . . a certain failure of communication, an oversight."

"Oversight!" I exploded, jumping to my feet and stamping the length of the room and back. "Oversight! Fire and blood and an explosion, a woman in the hospital and my wife vanished—and you call that oversight!"

"There is no need to lose your temper—"

"Yes there is!"

"—we are proceeding with the investigation and have already made some progress." He ignored my sneer. "The blood found in the temple has been subjected to analysis down to the molecular and subatomic levels. These results have been compared to those of *everyone* on this planet. We keep complete health and hospital records as you might imagine. Computers are accessing this immense data base at the present moment. When I called you earlier the search had been narrowed to less than twenty possibilities. As we talked I have been following the progress on this readout." He tapped the screen on the desk. "The exacting comparison has now been reduced to five. No—four. Wait—there are only three now. And two of them are women! And that remaining man is . . ."

As he tore the slip from his printout we turned as one and raced for the door.

"Who?" I shouted as we ran. He read without breaking his stride.

"Professor Justin Slakey."

"Where?"

"Under sixty seconds' flight from here."

At least he was right about that. The copter was airborne even as we fell through its door. The military must have had the news the instant that the police did because a cover of military jets roared by above us. Even before we began our descent we could see that copcopters were already hitting the ground and unloading troops to surround the house. Rotors roaring we dropped down onto the stone-flagged patio. Collin had produced a large gun and was a fraction of a second ahead of me as we kicked open the doors.

The house was empty, the bird flown.

A suitcase was obviously missing, a gaping hole like a missing tooth from what had been a row of four in the bedroom closet. The garage door gaped open. A commofficer strode in, saluting as he pulled a printout from his chest pack.

"Gone, sir," he said. Collin snarled as he grabbed the sheet. "Professor J. Slakey, passenger on the stellar liner *Star of Serendipity*. Departed . . ." He looked up and his face was grim. "A little over an hour ago."

"So they are already in warpdrive and cannot be contacted until they emerge." I considered the possibilities. "You will of course be in touch with the authorities at their scheduled destination. Which is an operation that might work normally—but this is not a normal situation. I have a strong suspicion that this suspect is ahead of us all of the way. Contacting the ship's destination will probably do no good at all because the spacer will arrive instead at some unscheduled chartpoint. If you ask me you've lost him, Captain. But you can at least tell me who—or what—he is supposed to be."

"That is the worst part. He really *is* Professor Slakey. I started a search as soon as his name appeared. I have just received a report directly from the medical authorities. He is a physicist of interstellar repute who was requested to come here by the Medical Commission, no expense was too great to acquire his services. Something to do with retarded entropy as applied to our hospital work."

"Sounds reasonable. Slow down entropy and you slow down aging. Which is what this planet is all about. Was he for real?"

"Undoubtedly. I had the privilege of meeting him at a function once. Everyone there, the scientists, physicists for the main part, were greatly in awe of his talents and the work that he did here. I am getting reports now," he touched his earphone, "that they all refuse to believe he had anything to do with the Fanyimadu personality."

"Do you?"

Before he could answer there was a shouted exchange outside, then the door was thrown open and a policeman ran in. Holding an insulated container.

"The search team found this when they were going through all the debris in the Temple of Eternal Truth, Captain—crushed under the machinery in the temple. We had no idea it was there until the wreckage was lifted. It's a . . . human hand."

He put it on the table and, in silence, we looked through the transparent side at the crushed and mangled hand inside. I had a long moment of panic before I could see by the size, the shape, that it was certainly male.

"Did anyone think to take the fingerprints of this?" I said.

"Yes, sir. They were sent for comparison . . ."

He was interrupted by the ring of the phone. Captain Collin put it to his ear, listened, replaced it slowly.

"Positive identification. This is—Professor Slakey's hand."

I pointed. "If you need proof, there it is. They were one and the same person. The blood tests, now this. Slakey was Fanyimadu. Keep me informed of everything. Understand?"

I did not wait around for an answer. Turned on my heel and left. Called back over my shoulder. "I assume that *all* details on Slakey will be in my commhopper when I get home."

So much for the police and the authorities. It was time to get to work. I radioed for a cab, told the driver to have my own car returned from the Central Police Station—one of the perks of the rich is letting the menials do as much as possible—and planned each step of the action that must be taken.

"Let me off here," I ordered while we were still a kilometer from my house. I was too jumpy to be driven around in luxury. I wanted to walk—and think. I had the strong feeling that the police were not going to come up with any answers for this one. They had been out-thought right down the line. But could I do any better?

The homes were luxurious, surrounded by brilliant gardens, the air rich with bird sound. I heard little, saw nothing. Though I was aware when I walked up the path to my home that the front door was slightly open. I had left it closed. Thieves? No way—at least they took care of the ordinary kind of crime on lovely Lussuoso. I was smiling as I banged my way in. James jumped to his feet and we embraced warmly. Or was it Bolivar?

"It's James, Dad," he said, knowing my weaknesses. "One day you better learn to tell us apart."

"I do. You usually wear blue shirts."

"This one is green—you have to do better than that."

He poured a drink for me, his already in hand, and I reported the progress or lack of it by the police. Then he spoke the words we had been both avoiding.

"I'm sure Mom is all right. Disappeared, yes. In trouble, undoubtedly. But she is the toughest one in the family."

"She is, of course, comes up aces always." I tried to keep the gloom from my voice, could not. He grabbed my shoulder, very hard.

"Something terrible has happened. But that Rowena

women said *gone*—not *dead.* So we get to work to find her and that is that."

"Right." I heard the roughness in my voice; a sentimental old gray rat. Enough. "We'll do it. If the diGriz clan can't do it—it can't be done."

"Damn right! I have a message from Bolivar. He should be here very soon. He was in a spacer doing a lunar geological survey. Dropped everything and should be in faster than light drive by now."

"Lunar geology? That's a change. I thought he had become a stockbroker?"

"He was—found it too boring. When he had stacked away his millions, more profits than those of his clients I am sure, he burnt his business suits and bought a spacer. What do we do next."

"Top up this drink, if you please." I dropped into a chair. "Fill it with one-hundred-proof Old Cogitation Juice. We have some work to do."

"Like what?"

"Like first forgetting about collaboration with the authorities. They have got this investigation completely wrong so far and can only get it worse."

"And we can do better." He said it as a fact—not a question.

"That's for sure. The bureaucrats are going to do an incredibly detailed and thorough search for this Slakey. We are not." I saw his eyebrows rise and I had to smile. "If their search is successful, which I doubt, we will hear about it quickly enough. Meanwhile we want to find out everything we can about the Temple of Eternal Truth. We go to the horse's mouth, so to speak. The church members will tell us what we want to know." I waved the membership list I had extracted from the police with not too much difficulty. "There are three of these ladies whom we are very closely acquainted with. Shall we begin?"

"As soon as I dipil my face and get a clean shirt. I'm a handsome devil and have a way with women."

I sighed happily. Some might have called this braggadocio, but I saw it as simply speaking the truth. In this family we do not condone false modesty. "You do that. Meanwhile I'll fire up the family car."

An expression empty of meaning since this healthy planet had what was probably the most rigidly enforced clean air act in the galaxy. You would probably get clapped in jail for even thinking about an infernal combustion engine. Vehicles were powered by atomic or electric batteries. Or, like our luxurious Spreadeagle, they ran on the energy stored in a flywheel. It plugged into the electricity supply at night and the motor was run up to speed. During the day the motor became a generator and the spinning wheel generated electricity for the driving wheels. All six of them. A heavy flywheel made for a big car—I had stinted on nothing. The robot driver tooled the thing out of the garage when I whistled, nodding his plastic head and smiling inanely. The gold plated door to the passenger compartment lifted heavenward while soft, welcoming music played.

I sat on the divan and the television came on. It was a news program with no news I wanted to hear. "Sports," I said and a high speed balloon race replaced it. The bar served me a glass of champagne just as James appeared.

"Wow!" he admired. "Real gold?"

"Of course. As well as diamond headlamps and a prescription windshield. No expense spared."

"Where to?" he asked, sipping his drink.

"Vivilia VonBrun is first on the list. On anyone's list I imagine. Incredibly rich, desirably attractive. I phoned and she awaits our pleasure."

She swept out to greet us, smiling compassionately. She had permitted a tiny rim of red to remain around her gorgeous eyes, to express her unhappiness at recent events. Which of course had been described in gruesome detail by the news programs. She was wearing something diaphanous and gray, which revealed enticing glimpses of tanned skin when she moved. She looked too good to be true, twenty-five years old, going on twenty-six maybe, and she was. Too good to be true, that is. I didn't dare think of her real age; the number was too large. She extended a delicate hand to me; I took it and kissed it lightly about the knuckles.

"Poor, dear Jim," she sighed. "Such a tragedy."

"It will all end well. May I present my son, James."

"What a *dear* man. How nice of you to come. My husband, Waldo, is away on one of those boring hunting things, blowing up wild animals. So if you need a place to stay . . ."

Vivilia wasted no time. While Waldo was destroying robot predators she was doing a little predation herself. And she was probably old enough to be James's great-great-grandmother. Which meant she certainly had some experience—I put the thought from me and got to work.

"Vivilia, you can help us find Angelina. You are going to tell us everything you know about the Temple of Eternal Truth."

"You are *so* forceful, Jimmy. I'm sure that your son takes after . . ."

"Facts first, lust later," I snapped.

"Coarse but to the point," she smiled, uninsultable. "I'll tell you *everything* that I know."

Enjoyable as that prospect was it would have taken far too long. I kept her memoirs to the point. A very interesting point as it turned out to be.

With boredom at Olympic intensity on Lussuoso, sports, escapism and cult religions were going concerns. Master Fanyimadu had begun to appear at various soirees and parties, his fascinating beliefs excelled only by the intensity of his gaze. Ladies of leisure looked in on the Temple of Eternal Truth and most went back a second time. It was easy to see why. Vivilia explained.

"It wasn't so much the consolation of his religion as the positive promise of eternal bliss. Not that he doesn't preach a good sermon, mind you, better than TV any day. It is what his sermons are all about. He tells you that if one attends often enough and prays with great intensity, as well as donating enthusiastically, one might get a little look-in on Heaven."

"Heaven?" I asked, trying to remember some rudimentary theology.

"Heaven, of course, you *must* have heard of it? Or perhaps in your religion . . ."

"Dad's an atheist," James said. "We all are."

Vivilia sniffed meaningfully. "Well, I suppose most people are in this age of realism and social equality. But there is a down side to that, to worshiping the nitty-gritty of society. It is boring to be so practical. Therefore you can understand why some of us with more sensitivity search for a higher meaning."

It was I who sniffed meaningfully this time but she graciously ignored me. "If you had studied more diligently in school and not ignored your Applied Theology class you would know all this already. Heaven is the place where we go after we die and if we have been good, there you will reside in happiness forever. Hell is where you go if you have been bad, to suffer intensely for eternity. I know it sounds very simplistic and illogical. I, as well as lot of the other girls, felt that way when we first heard of Heaven and Hell. But as I said, to add weight and gravitas to Heaven it is possible to visit the place, at least temporarily. So you see, having been there I have lost, shall we say, a certain amount of credulity."

"Hypnotic suggestion," I suggested.

"Jimmy, you sounded *just* like Angelina when you said that. She flared her nostrils and snorted lightly in exactly the same way. I told her that I had felt exactly the same way when other of my friends had told me about their Heavenly excursions. But I know hypnotism when I see it—and this was no trance. I can't begin to describe the process of going to Heaven. But I *was* there, with Master Fanyimadu holding one of my hands and that incredibly stupid Rosebudd holding the other. I don't think she has enough mind to hypnotize. Yet we saw each other in Heaven, experienced the same things. It was simply wonderful and too beautiful to explain in mere words. It was very . . . inspirational." She had the grace to blush when she spoke the word; inspiration not being her usual line of work.

"Had Angelina been to Heaven?" I asked. "She never mentioned anything about it to me."

"I know nothing about that. I would *never* think of snooping into another person's personal secrets."

She ignored my lifted eyebrow at this preposterous statement. Nor would she go into any more detail. Saying that if we had the faith we would see Heaven for ourselves. She was very determined and sure of that; a rock of belief. It was only after she had changed the subject and taken James by the arm to show him the house I knew that I at least had worn out my welcome. She was reluctant to let him leave, but a provident call from Bolivar from the spaceport supplied an inescapable reason to escape.

As we drove towards the spaceport I found myself scowling as I grew more and more angry.

"Rrrrr . . ." I finally said.

"That was a pretty fair growl, Dad. You wouldn't care to expand upon it?"

"I would—and I shall! I'm angry, James—and growing angrier by the minute. There are a lot mysteries here—but one thing is not mysterious at all. This con man and his fake church are raising the wrath in me."

"I thought you had a soft spot for cons and scams?"

"I do—but only when it comes to bilking the filthy rich. I don't con widows or orphans or those who can't afford it. And I work for money. Good old green, the folding and golden stuff . . ."

"I get you now," James said, his angry scowl matching mine. "You're for a good clean con, taking money from the rich and giving it to the slightly less rich. Namely you. But no one gets hurt in the process."

"Exactly! There is money involved in this con, sure, but there is also belief. This fake guru is trampling about where he doesn't belong. In people's beliefs, their most intimate feelings. In the matter of religion it is live and let live, I say. I tell no one what to believe. I even listen carefully to sincere beliefs, no matter how nutsy they sound. But Slakey-Fanyimadu is playing with fire. Preaching fakery, using machines to con the unsuspecting into believing in an afterlife that in this case can't possibly be true. If Heaven is the place you go after you die—well there is only one way of getting there. Guided tours for a quick inspection are just not in order. What is going on here is very dirty and could be very hurtful as well. If he were showing his unsuspecting marks a real Heaven they would go to, well fine. He would only be depriving them of their money, which is a wonderful and noble thing to do. But he is depriving them of their individuality and their trust. He is lying to them, preying upon their fear of death. When they discover what has been done to them they will be hurt, shattered, emotionally destroyed. Whatever else happens—he must be stopped."

We growled in unison as we pulled up at the arrivals terminal. Bolivar waved and opened the door. Tanned by UV and still wearing his spacer's gear, we brought him up to date during the drive home. Once in the house I felt a twinge of appetite. I glanced through the autocook menu with little enthusiasm, unadventurously punched up three of my usual aardvark steak and fries. Silently wishing that I had been ordering for four—a banquet of exotica had that been the case.

"Very well done, Dad, you're quite a cook," Bolivar said pushing away his plate and untouched glass of wine. "It has been dehydrated-rehydrated space rations for far too long. I have been thinking of eating their wrappings, which would probably taste better than their contents. So, time to get down to work . . ."

At this precise moment as the clock struck the hour, the central computer terminal buzzed, while its screen lit up with Angelina's image.

"I've left this recording for you, Jim," she said, and my heart, which had leaped up into my throat, settled slowly back to its usual position. "I'm off to church soon, for what promises to be an interesting experience. I don't believe any of the guff this meandering idiot Fanyimadu has been feeding us—but I do *know* that something most interesting is happening. Physical travel of some kind and, I suspect, it may be offplanet. I can't tell you more right now since I am going mostly on guesswork and, don't laugh, intuition. It will be dangerous, but I'm going prepared. So if you lose track of me for a bit—don't lose hope. Bye."

She blew a kiss in my direction and the recording clicked off.

"Did she say offplanet?" Bolivar asked. I nodded. "Let's play it again."

We did. And when it ended a second time my mind was made up. "She said offplanet—and she meant it. Any ideas?"

"Plenty," Bolivar said. "Let us forget Slakey, as you suggested, Dad. The police can search the police files without our help. But this recording tells us things they don't know. Offplanet covers a lot of space—and so will we. We must start searching the galactic records. We have to find this Temple of Eternal Truth when it surfaces again—under any other name or guise. We list the characteristics it must have and get our search agencies to digging into the records."

"Exactly so," I agreed. "We will be looking for the modus operandi."

"I'm not so great on the old dead languages, Dad," Bolivar said. "But if you mean we will track down this joker and that nutsy religion I am for it!"

"That's the idea. It may very well have a different name, and different ways of bringing in the suckers—but the operating basis will be the same."

"What is that?"

"I haven't the slightest idea. You'll have to work it out as you go along."

"And we search in the past as well as the future," James said. "There is no reason that this church should be confined to just this one planet, and every reason to believe that it isn't."

"Too right," Bolivar agreed. "That goes into the search plan."

I was proud of my boys. They were taking over, plowing ahead without a moment lost. As for me, I wasn't that rusty an old rat—not yet.

But it was nice to see a couple of shiny young ones sharpening their teeth.

They started at once, putting the search operation into effect. Dividing up the planets between them and working out in an ever-expanding sphere of communication and interrogation. I left them to it. Found a cold beer, took it to my study and whistled at my computer terminal to turn it on. I sipped the beer while I surfed through various data bases, zeroing in on Religion. I needed to know more about this Heaven and Hell business. I found what I needed under Eschatology. It was all about future life after death and was all very confusing. Down through the ages there have been a bewildering variety of beliefs held by an even more bewildering variety of social groups. Sometimes future life was seen as a continuation of present life, under more or less favorable conditions. Though at other times retribution for sins or evil deeds made this future life the very opposite of the one we know. I boned up on Heaven and Paradise, then went on to Hell, Hades, and Sheol. All very complex and very much at loggerheads, one religion with the other. Though not all of them. A lot of them were very derivative and borrowed bits and pieces from each other. My head was beginning to ache.

But out of all the confusing theorizing and philosophizing one thing was very clear. This was very heavy stuff. A matter of life—and then death. The earliest religions were obviously pre-science. They had to be because they made no attempts to consider reality, but were based purely on emotions. A desire to find some solutions to the problems of existence. When science finally appeared on the scene these religions should have been replaced by observation and reason. That they were not was sure proof of mankind's ability to believe two mutually exclusive things at the same time.

It had been a very long day and I found my eyes first glazing then closing as the multicolored aspects of future life passed before me. Enough! I yawned and headed for bed. A well-rested rat would be of far more use than an exhausted one with wilting whiskers.

I crashed and ten seconds—or ten hours—later I blinked up blearily at the figure shaking my shoulder.

"James . . . ?"

"It's Bolivar, Dad. We've found another Temple of Eternal Truth."

I was wide awake and standing next to the bed, almost in eyeball contact. "Not under the same name?"

"Nowhere close. This one is The Seekers of the Way. No names, books, or characters are the same as in the Temple of Eternal Truth. But they are identical if you do a semiotic comparison."

"Where?"

"Not that far. Planet named Vulkann. Mining and heavy industry for the most part. But it does have an attractive tropical archipelago that is devoted only to holiday making and retirement homes. Apparently so fascinating that it draws customers from all the nearby star systems."

"We leave—"

"As soon as you're packed. Tickets waiting at the shuttle flight. One hour to liftoff."

I checked my wallet and credit cards. "I'm packed. Let's grab some passports and go."

CHAPTER 3

EVER CAUTIOUS, WE TRAVELED UNDER new names with new passports; I had dozens of them, all genuine, locked away in the safe. The only equipment we took was a brace of electronic cameras—which I had improved far beyond their manufacturer's wildest dream. I of course had my diamond dress studs, as well as a few bits of jewelry and other innocuous items in a small sealed case.

Our arrival on Vulkann was most dramatic. As we stepped out of the space shuttle, along with a gaggle of brightly togged tourists, a brass band began to play lustily. Everyone cheered—and cheered even louder when the Corps of Guides marched up before us. Black-booted and high-heeled, skintight and most flimsy bright red uniforms graced their perfectly formed forms. At a barked command they stamped to a halt and broke ranks. Assignments had been made and a most attractive blonde with exquisite freckles on her nose marched up to us and gave a very nice salute.

"Sire Diplodocus and sons, I greet you. My name is Deveena De Zoftig, but my friends call me Dee."

"We're your friends!"

"Of course. I am your guide and at your service as long as you are on our wonderful world. May I be most informal and call you Jim, James and Bolivar?"

"You may," the twins chorused, their smiles echoing her white-toothed one.

"Wonderful! Be prepared for the holiday of a lifetime."

"We're prepared," they breathed, and the warm radiance of passion flamed from their skins.

"Then this way if you please. Kindly wave your health certificates in the direction of the doctor there, well done. And now to your luggage, which is awaiting you and being carried by that porterbot. Exit through this gate, thank you. The machine in the gate has X-rayed your wallets and verified your credit cards. You will have a lovely and expensive vacation on our planet."

Such honesty was most refreshing and I was beginning to like Vulkann almost as much as the boys liked Dee. I hated to spoil our fun with business—but that was why we were here.

"We need a luxurious hotel," I said.

"We have thousands."

"We would like one that is close to the Church of the Seekers of the Way where we are meeting some friends."

"You are indeed in luck for also located on Grotsky Square is the Rasumofsky Robotic Rest. A fully automated hostelry without a human employee, that is wide open and wonderful both day and night and never closes."

"Suits our needs," I said. "Lead the way."

"Your rooms are ready and waiting," she said as our taxi stopped in front of the hotel.

"Welcome! Welcome!" Irritatingly cheerful bellboybots chimed as they seized our bags.

"These are for you," Dee said, placing a jeweled flower on each of our shirts. "I will leave you now but I will never forget you. You have but to speak my name into your flower and I will return as quickly as I can. I bid you only to enjoy! Enjoy!"

"We will, we will!" we chorused in return and let ourselves be guided to our rooms. Before we went to work I checked for messages back on Lussuoso. Nothing discovered, no trace of Angelina. I had the gut feeling that we were right to take her advice and follow the trail offplanet.

"Nice," Bolivar said as he spun the cutter against the window and removed a neat disc of glass. The glass cutter clicked back and became a pocketknife as he fixed the camera, that was more than a camera, with its lens projecting through the opening. "Now we can not only photograph them as they come and go, but we can get their voices on the record as well."

"Very good," I said, peeking through the viewfinder. I set the controls and turned it on. "All automatic now."

"Memory?" James asked.

"About ten-thousand hours at a molecular level. More than we are going to need. Now let us get a drink and a meal and some sleep and see what morning will bring."

Morning brought more darkness instead of sunshine since Vulkann had a ten-hour-long day; daylight had come and gone while we slept. The sun was speedily rising again by the time we had finished our breakfast. We looked on unenthusiastically as the servbot cleared away the dishes while the beds made themselves. Since this was an all-robot hotel no notice was taken of our surveillance operations. Across the road the first parishioners were entering the church. None were familiar. By the time the church doors had closed I found myself nibbling my nails: I jumped to my feet.

"I'm going to work out in the gym and have a swim," I announced.

"Be there before you," Bolivar said, hurtling towards the door to his bedroom.

When we entered the pool room and threw aside our towels we were delighted to see that our guide Dee had entered through the other door and had thrown aside her towel as well. Since there is no nudity taboo on Vulkann this was a serious towel-throwing.

"I hope that you are enjoying your visit to our fair world," she said with a broad smile just as lovely as the rest of her.

The answer to that question was obvious. I dived into the

pool and swam a number of enthusiastic laps while the twins indulged in enthusiastic conversation with her, for such is the way of youth. I could see the attraction of this, particularly when I came up for breath and paused to admire the scenery.

We met in the gym and the boys worked up a good lather of sublimation since we were here for work, not dalliance. All this mindless exercise cheered us greatly—and kept our thoughts off of the Seekers of the Way. Refreshed, and with lunch holding breakfast down nicely, we trooped back to our rooms. I fast-reran the recording, then played back some of the conversations. Then amplified the images of the parishioners so I could make prints of their faces. Spread them out on the table so we could look at them.

With mutual feelings of glum depression. It was James who spoke for all of us.

"One thing certain—none of us is going to be able to join up and make any investigations inside that church."

"Not without some radical surgery," Bolivar said with a broad smile; we glowered back.

Everyone who had visited the church so far had been a woman.

"We need help," I said.

"Still in touch with the Special Corps?" James asked.

"There is no escaping them. Though I have not talked to our noble leader, Inskipp, for a long time. Which is all for the best." I glanced at my watch, then hit a few settings and smiled. "Very good news. It is now the middle of the night at Prime Base. I will be forced to wake that dear man up."

His secretary answered first but I knew the code that bypassed its tiny robotic mind. After a number of rings, growing steadily louder since Inskipp was a heavy sleeper, a familiar and angry voice rustled in my ear.

"*If this isn't a major emergency you are dead, whoever you are,*" Inskipp growled.

"Jim diGriz here, good friend. Did I awake you—"

"*I'm issuing an order now to seize all the assets in your bank accounts. Even the ones you think I don't know about!*"

"I need help. Angelina is missing."

"*Details,*" he said, voice calm, threats ended. I told him exactly what had happened. While I was doing this the boys were E-mailing copies of all the files—including Angelina's recorded message. He did not waste time in commiseration and was calling in the troops even as I talked. As head of the Special Corps, the most secret of secret forces that defended the peace and protected the galaxy, his powers were awesome. And he knew how to use them.

"A cruiser is now on the way to Vulkann. Aboard it is a Special Agent who will be using the name Sybil. Up to this moment she has worked directly for me and for no one else. Now she is under your command. I will add that she is the best agent I have ever had."

"Better than me?"

"Everyone is, diGriz, everyone. Report to me when you learn anything." He hung up, and knowing him, was probably already back to sleep.

At flank speed a Special Corps cruiser can outrun—or catch—anything else in space. Time still dragged. I kept busy for some hours as I hacked my way into the local police computer network, a terribly simple job. Once this was done we had no trouble discovering the identities of the church-goers that we had photographed. Nor, after cracking into their totally secret bank records, were we surprised to discover that all of them were filthy rich. The Seekers of the Way, like the followers of the Temple of Eternal Truth, were expected to part with a good few credits if they were to get the blessing of the church and peek in at the joys of the hereafter.

We took turns at the monitor screen and tried not to drink too much when we weren't watching it. I had just returned from doing forty laps in the pool when Bolivar jumped to his feet and shouted "Wow!"

James and I cracked our heads together as we jumped to look at the screen.

"Wow is indeed right," I said. "Even double-wow. Not only is he not of the female persuasion but he looks very familiar."

"Starkey-Fanyimadu?"

"None other."

"He has his right hand in his pocket," Bolivar said.

"So would you," James answered with cold lack of compassion, "if your arm ended at the wrist."

As if in reply the subject lifted his right arm to wave to a parishioner. "Pretty good prosthetic," I said.

"And done pretty fast as well," Bolivar added with more than a trace of suspicion in his voice. "First chance I have I would like to shake hands with that particular villain."

Something caught my attention, a movement of air—a sound perhaps. I looked over my shoulder and saw that the hall door, securely locked and bolted, was now standing open. A woman stepped through and closed it behind her.

"I am Sybil," she said in lush contralto. A tall, tanned redhead, poised and beautiful. Her dress was one of those spun-diamond creations that were so popular, glinting and shining with an albedo like a searchlight. A woman had to have a perfect figure to wear something so outrageous and skintight. She had it.

The twins turned at the sound of her voice—looked at her in appreciative silence. I appreciated that as well, but appreciated her arrival even more.

"I'm Jim diGriz. These are my sons, Bolivar and James. Have you been briefed?"

"Completely."

"Good. What you don't know is that Slakey is here, in that church across the road."

"And he has a new right hand," Bolivar said. "We're glad you're here."

"I'll need to get inside the building as soon as possible. I am sure that you have already found out about the church members while I was on my way here. Which of them have you selected as the best possible contacts?"

"There are three strong possibilities," James said, taking the photos and identification from the stack and handing them to her. "All rich, young, or young-looking after rejuvenation, all very social, attending plenty of parties and receptions, so they will be easy to meet."

"I'll do that now. I'll contact you again after I have become one of the Seekers of the Way."

The door closed behind her and we were all silent for long moments.

"Pretty sure of herself," Bolivar finally said. It was a compliment and not a negative observation. "The best agent he ever had—isn't that what Inskipp said?"

I nodded. "May he be right—just this once."

Apparently he was, because three hours later we saw her walk through the carved marble entrance to the church, arm in arm with Maudi Lesplanes. The first name on the list that we had given her. Almost two hours passed before she emerged from the church. This time we were all staring at the door when it opened and she came in. She looked at us and smiled.

"Would one of you gentlemen mind getting me a drink? Tall, wet and alcoholic if you please."

I stepped aside as the twins rushed the bar. She went to the couch, sat, and signaled me to join her.

"I didn't mean to be brusque earlier, Jim. I was tired and I thought that you would appreciate action before conversation. I'm so sorry about Angelina. I listened to the message that she left for you and I believe, as you do, that she will be found. But not back on Lussuoso. We *will* find her. I promise."

From anyone else these would have been polite words. But Sybil spoke with an authority that rang true. I wanted very much to believe her.

"For you," my son said, holding out a glass.

She took the drink, drank, smiled—and sighed.

"Thank you, Bolivar. I needed that."

"I have another one—if that's not enough."

"Not quite yet, James."

"You're sure you're not mixing them up?" I blurted out.

"Impossible to do, as you well know, Jim. I imagine James has always had that tiny scar on his left earlobe."

I blinked. It was almost impossible to see.

"Since I was four years old. Bolivar bit me."

"Believe that and you'll believe anything."

She smiled at both of them. Then turned to me and was serious again; playtime over.

"The service of the Seekers of the Way seems to be a near replica of the one described in the briefing for the Temple of Eternal Truth. Uplifting organ music, a good bit of incense to mask the smell of tylinyne. As you undoubtedly know that is a mild tranquilizing drug. No lasting effects, but it does relax the subjects, makes suggestion much easier. Not that it was much needed since everyone there was very convinced to begin with. The sermon was most inspiring and very strange to hear from a physicist of Slakey's reputation. Heavily mystical, plenty of guff about the hereafter and the good life and good deeds that pave the road to Heaven. After some more music some of the women spoke with great warmth about their visit to Heaven, after which they donated impressive sums for the furthering of the good works. Sounded very much like the recorded statement of Vivilia VonBrun that Jim made."

"Different church, same scam?" I asked. She nodded.

"If scam is the right word. These people sound absolutely convinced. I'll know more after I've made the trip myself. Inskipp will scream when he sees how much of his funds I have invested to hurry that day."

"When?" Bolivar asked.

"As soon as possible without raising Slakey's suspicions. For the record, he is now called Father Marablis. There is another thing about him that I find particularly interesting. Before leaving I made a point of approaching him to gush over his sermon. He liked that. Nor did he mind when, in the heat of the moment, I seized him by the hand, the right hand, and squeezed it with heartfelt emotion."

I leaned forward intently. As did the twins. We did not have to ask the question. She nodded.

"A warm human hand—not a prosthetic."

"But—" I stammered. "I saw the severed hand. It was positively identified."

"I know. Interesting, isn't it? I look forward to coming events with great anticipation."

The boys stared at her, smitten. Their kind, our kind of person. If anyone could find Angelina she could; I was sure of that now.

Two days—and two very large donations—later she was told to prepare for her visit.

"Do I look all right?" she asked, turning slowly. Women only ask that when they know the answer. She was wearing something black, tight, expensive, with matching hat and even more expensive jewelry. "Are you sure that this can't be detected?" she asked, touching the tiny diamond brooch pinned at her throat.

"Only under a microscope—and you would have to know what to look for," I said. "The center diamond is the lens. I usually wear it as a shirt dress stud. I've added the jeweled setting to make it into a more exotic piece of jewelry so that you can wear it. The diamond lens focuses the image onto a series of nanoformed recording molecules that are carried beneath the lens by Brownian movement, which is energized by body heat so there is no detectable power source. Don't worry about the light level since, like the human eye, it can perceive as little as one photon of light energy. What you see, it will see—and record."

"I've never heard of anything like it before."

"Nor has your boss, Inskipp," James said proudly. "It's one of Dad's inventions."

"However all this turns out you can keep it," I said. "I'll give you the developing and printing module later."

"It's the only one in existence," Bolivar said.

"I—I don't quite know how to thank you." The emotion in her voice was not faked, that was certain. She left quickly.

Moments later we saw her stroll across the street and walk through the door of the church.

CHAPTER 4

A HEAVY TROPICAL RAIN WAS falling, lit by sudden flashes of lightning; thunder rumbled. The Church of the Seekers of the Way was blurred, its outline barely visible through the wet glass. The image from the camera was clear enough, but standing at the window I could see little or nothing. Sybil had been inside the building with Slakey for over an hour. The room was closing in on me.

"I'm going out," I said, pulling on a billed cap with the logo *Cocaine-Cola* spelled out on the front.

"You'll get soaked," Bolivar said.

"It'll look suspicious if you lurk about near the church," James added. I twisted my lip in a sneer.

"Thanks for the solicitude—but your old Dad is not quite senile yet. This cap not only advertises a repulsive drink, it also contains a hydro-repeller field—and I was lurking unseen near churches before you were born."

When they didn't even smile at my strained witticism I knew that they were as uptight as I was. I needed the air.

The hotel lobby was empty—of human life that is. The managerbot bowed and dry-wiped its gloved hands for me. The doormanbot pulled open the door as I approached and drops of rain blew in dotting its metal features.

"A filthy night, sir," it smarmed. "But it will be a sunny day for sure tomorrow, begorra."

"Is that what you are programmed to say whenever it rains?" I snarled.

"Yes, sir, a filthy night, sir, but it will be a sunny day for sure tomorrow, begorra."

My nerves must be going if I was trying to have a conversation with a mindless robot. I went out, bone-dry of course as the electrostatic field repelled the raindrops.

Angelina . . . .

The pain in my chest, my throat, was real. I had been putting all thought of her out of mind—or I wouldn't have been able to function. But she was there at the edge of my consciousness all of the time. I let her in for the moment, relished the memory. Remembering how many times she had saved my life; keeping weapons tucked in with the twins in their baby carriage had been most important more than once. With what joy we had held up banks, relished the excitement—not to mention the money. And the way we saved the universe together, defeating all of those slimy monsters! Memories, memories. We had had our low moments, but at this moment I wanted to be like the inscription on the sundial. And record only the sunny hours. And the fun . . . .

I cut off this train of thought. Feeling sorry would not help—only action could get her back. That was why I was here, the boys as well, and this was the reason why Sybil was possibly risking her life. This was going to work. It had to work.

My walk was not without a purpose; I had seen a cafe just across the square from the Church of the Seekers of the Way. It had a row of tables outside protected by an awning. And a hydro-repeller field as well I realized as I entered; this field and mine flickered with glints of light where they interacted. I touched the brim of my cap and turned mine off, sat at a table with a clear view of the church.

"Welcome, welcome, sir or madam," the table candle said as its wick flickered and lit up.

"Sir, not madam."

"How can we be of service . . . sir not madam?"

The world was full of moronic robots and computers tonight.

"Bring beer. Big, cold."

"Delighted to be of service, sir not madam."

The table vibrated, then a hatch slid back and the beer emerged. I reached for it but could not lift it.

"Two kropotniks, fifty," a colder mechanical voice said. I pushed three coins into the slot and the clamp on the glass was released. "Thank you for the tip," the voice said, keeping my change. I drowned my incipient growl with a swig of beer.

The rain lashed down on the square, thunder rumbled in the distance. An occasional car swished by; the door to the Church of the Seekers of the Way remained closed. The beer was flat. I waited.

Time passed. I finished the first beer and ordered another one.

"Two kropotniks, seventy," the table said.

"Why? The last beer was two fifty."

"That was during the happy hour. Pay."

I fed in the exact amount this time and the glass was released. "Cheapskate," the computer muttered and emitted an electronic raspberry.

The rain finally slackened, stopped, and one of Vulkann's three moons appeared briefly through a gap in the clouds. Then there was flicker of movement across the way and three women emerged from the church. They talked together for a moment before separating. Sybil came towards me and I felt a certain relaxation; at least she was safe. She did not look at me but must have been aware of my presence because she turned and entered the cafe. I took a few minutes to sip my beer. She did not appear to have been followed. I finished my drink, put the glass down and went inside.

She was in one of the rear booths with a cocktail glass before her; she nodded slightly and I went to join her. She took a large swallow, then a second one—and sighed.

"Jim, that was an experience I find difficult to describe. There were three of us and we joined Father Marablis—or Slakey—I'm beginning to be unsure of a lot of things. There were no machines that I could see. He talked to us for a bit then touched his hand to my forehead. Something happened. I can't tell you what. I didn't black out or anything like that. I can only repeat what Vivilia VonBrun said—it was indescribable. But I can clearly remember what happened next. We were walking through a field of very short grass, following Marablis. He stopped and pointed upwards and at the same moment I heard the sound of chimes, most distinctly. He was pointing to a white cloud that drifted towards us. The chimes, the music, was coming from the cloud and when I heard it I felt, well, an elation of some kind. Some sort of spiritual upwelling. Then—and don't laugh—I swear I saw a little flying creature behind the cloud. Just a glimpse."

"A bird?"

"No . . . a tiny pink baby with little wings on its shoulders. Then it was gone and it was over."

"Just like that?"

"I—I just don't know. I remember that Marablis touched my arm, turning me, and I was back in that room in the church again along with the other women. I felt, well just sad, as though I had lost something very precious."

There was little I could say. She had a distant look in her eyes, looking at something I could not see. A tear ran down her cheek and she sniffed, wiped at it and smiled.

"Sorry. I'm not being much help. I know it has to be a con of some kind. I don't believe in day trips to Heaven. But something *did* happen to me. My emotions, they are real."

"I believe you. But there are, well, drugs that can affect the emotions directly."

"I know that. But still . . ." She stood and smoothed down her dress, touched a finger to the brooch. "Instead of listening to me blathering on let's take a look at this recording."

"You've done a great job. Thank you."

The twins had seen us in the street and had the door open as we came down the hall. I heard Sybil telling them about the experience, basically just what she had told me. But she was much more in control of herself now and beginning to get angry at being got to in some way. By the time she had finished her story I had the piece of electronic jewelry clamped into the activation module. The screen lit up with a view of the church moving closer.

The pictures were silent and so were we as we watched her meet the other two women. They talked, then turned to face Slakey when he entered. He was certainly in his Father Marablis mode, brown cassock and unctuous gestures; I was rather glad I couldn't hear what he was saying.

"Up to this point I remember everything," Sybil said. "He is telling us about the joys to come and, see his hand, collecting a few extra checks for the pleasure of our outing. There, that part is done. Here we go."

Slakey must have said something for they all turned and walked after him. The screen went black.

"Is the recorder broken?" Bolivar asked.

"I doubt it." I fast-forwarded the machine and the image reappeared.

"We are back in the room," Sybil said. "Without a record of what I saw. I'm so sorry."

"Don't be." I ran a quick analytical probe. "You did everything that you could. So did the recorder. It worked fine—but there just is no record. I don't know why or how this happened. The electronics appear to have been operating but they, well, just didn't record anything." I scowled at the machine. "And I do not believe in miracles."

"No one's thinking about miracles," James said. "We're thinking technology. Whatever field of force or electronic pervasion created the Heaven trip, well, could it have interfered with the recording?"

"Pretty obviously," I said.

"I have an idea," Bolivar said. "This was a good try—but it just did not work out. Next step. We need a long look around that place. You will remember that there was some kind of machinery that was blown up in the first church. I would like to see if there are any of the same kind of gadgets here . . ."

"No," I said.

"Why not?"

"I don't mean no let's not do it. I mean no you don't do it. Because I do this particular job." I raised my hand to quiet their protests. "I say that not because I am older and wiser, which is true, but because I have had much more experience at this sort of thing. Bolivar, I wouldn't think of making high-profit high-risk investments if you were there to do it for me. After watching that last karate tournament I wouldn't dare face up to your brother in an even fight. It has always been the age of the specialist. Do any of you believe that you can do an unseen breaking and entering and searching job better than I can?" Silence was my only answer. "Thank you," I said—with some warmth. "But you will all have to help. This is the plan."

We had that night and part of the next day to make our preparations. It was going to be a joint effort. The church service for the Seekers of the Way was due to begin at noon. We met for a final rehearsal an hour earlier.

"You first, Sybil," I said.

"I go in with the others. Talk, act naturally and keep my eyes open. If everything goes as it usually does, then I have only one thing to do. I know that the outer door is always locked before the service begins. So when Father Marablis begins his sermon, I squeeze this." She held up a tiny wafer of plastic.

"That is a one-shot communicator," I said. "The battery shorts through the chip, which sends a millisecond-long signal before it burns out. It is undetectable both before and after use. I'll be waiting nearby. As soon as I get the signal I go in through the front door." I held up a modified lockpick. "Sybil took a close look at the lock—which is a make called Bulldog-Bowser. I know it well and it is very easy to open. James, you're next."

"I'll be driving the delivery van, a rental with new identification numbers and fake signs. When Dad goes through the door I drive around and park in front of the church. Bolivar."

"I'm inside the van with passive tracking equipment, magnetometer and heat detectors. I should be able to follow people moving inside. I also have a warning alarm receiver."

I nodded. "Which I can activate in one of four ways in case of emergency. Bite hard on my back tooth, tap one toe quickly two times or—pull off the top button of my shirt."

"That's only three," Sybil said.

"The fourth I have no control over. It will be activated if—my heart stops. Should the alarm go off, the boys break their way in with all guns firing. Any remarks or questions?"

"Stun grenades and blackout gas as well as the guns," James said.

That was it. We had some tall and nonalcoholic drinks and discussed the Vulkann weather. After a time Sybil looked at her watch, stood and went out. We followed.

I waited out of sight around the corner, apparently looking at the gaudy items in a tourist shop window while I patted, one by one, the various lumps in my clothes; weapons, detectors, tools, alarms, that sort of thing. I had no idea of what I would find inside the church so I had visited a number of electronic stores and stacked up on everything I could or might possibly need.

The phone taped behind my ear clicked sharply. I turned about, strolled around the corner and up the two steps to the church door. My left hand on the knob concealed the rapid twisting of the lockpick with my right. It was as fast as turning a key; I do have some experience at this sort of thing. The door opened and I went through without breaking pace. Closed and relocked it behind me.

I was in a dimly lit vestibule with draperies covering the far side. I parted them a hairsbreadth and looked through. Father Slakey-Marablis was behind a high lectern and in full throat, unctuous vapidities washed over the attentive audience below.

". . . doubt shall be taken from you and will be replaced by reassurance. It is written in the Book of Books that the path to salvation leads through the Land of Good Deeds. Good deeds and love must be your guiding stars, the beckoning fingers of the hereafter. A hereafter that lies ahead of you, restful and satisfying, calm and filled with the effervescence that passeth all understanding."

Very good. Not really very good, but really very bad. But good for me. For as long as he burbled on I could penetrate his holy of holies. The staircase was behind the door on the left, as Sybil had told me. She had no idea where it led; that was for me to find out. I went through and closed the door silently behind me, bit down gently on the microlight I held between my teeth. Dusty stairs wound upwards. I climbed them, walking with my feet close to the wall to prevent them from creaking. There was another door at the head of the stairs that opened into a large room, dimly illuminated by a single window.

I was over the main hall and could hear the rumble of the sermon dimly through the floor. I walked silently between the boxes and stacked chairs to a door on the far wall. This was to the rear of the building and should be over the mysterious antechamber that might very well be the entrance to Heaven. This was also roughly the same location as that of the electronic equipment that had been destroyed in the Temple of Eternal Truth. As I opened the door the rumble of the voice on the floor below stopped.

So did I. One foot still raised. Then I relaxed and stepped forward when the organ music began and the women began to sing. A spiral stairway led down. I took it, slowly and silently. Stopped before what I hoped was the last door.

It was stuffy and warm and I was beginning to sweat. From the temperature alone. My pulse rate was normal and my morale high. No more waiting—a time for doing. I turned the light off and pocketed it, then opened the door into darkness and stepped through.

Bright lights came on. Slakey was standing just before me. Smiling.

I had only the briefest of glimpses because at the instant that the lights flared I had dived to one side. Biting down hard with my back teeth.

At least I tried to bite. But as fast as I had been, something else was much faster. I could see and hear—but that was all. My body was flaccid, my eyes open and staring. At the greasy floor because I had landed heavily facedown. My jaw dropped open; I drooled. I felt the panic rising as I realized I could do nothing, could not control a single muscle. But at least I was breathing and my heart was still beating, pounding loud and strong in my ears. A shoe tip appeared in front of my eyes and my vision swirled, settled, staring up at the bright light. Slakey must have rolled me over; I could not feel a thing. His face blotted out the light.

"You can see me, can't you? And hear me as well? My neural neutralizer allows that. I know all about you Jim diGriz. I know everything for I am all-powerful. I know how you invaded this holy place of worship. I know who you came with."

His hands reached down, my head turned. Sybil was lying next to me, sprawled and unmoving. My vision swirled again and Slakey was straightening up. Dressed in full regalia, I saw now. Bright robes with strange symbols covering them, with a high collar, a crown of some kind on his head. He raised his arms and shook his fists on high in a triumphant gesture. Both fists. The right one worked very well indeed and there was no sign of any scar on either wrist when his loose sleeves fell back.

"You are a pitiful mortal and shall be destroyed. You seek enlightenment but you shall not have it. You and this female creature you sent to spy. You wish to see Heaven—then you will go to Heaven. You shall, you shall!"

There was motion, my vision rocked. Stopped. My head was raised and I realized that he had dumped me across Sybil's unresistant body.

"Go, both of you, go. Go to Heaven."

He laughed, choked, laughed even louder.

"Well—not quite Heaven as you shall discover."

Blackout

CHAPTER 5

SOMETHING HAPPENED.

I couldn't remember it, could not begin to describe it. I did not want to think about it. I had far more important things on my mind. Like the fact that I was still paralyzed and lying face-down in red grit of some kind. I couldn't feel it but I could smell it. A rotten, sulfury smell.

Smell! Yes, it certainly was there, and growing stronger and stronger. Which meant something important. After I had been zapped I couldn't smell or feel anything: I could now. Which must mean that the paralysis must be wearing off, because I was vaguely aware of a scratchy pressure on my cheek. I concentrated, struggled hard, harder—then felt my fingertips move ever so slightly.

Recovery did not end quickly, not the way the onset of the paralysis had, but slowly and soon very painfully. Waves of red agony that ran through my reviving body that threatened to block my vision. My eyes were watering, tears ran down my cheeks as I writhed in agony. Slowly, very slowly it died away and I managed to roll over.

Blinking away the tears to stare up at a gray rock ceiling above. There was a low moan and with a great deal of effort I turned my head to see that Sybil was lying on the ground next to me. Her eyes were closed and her body twisted with pain as she moaned again. I knew what she was experiencing. Slowly and exhaustingly, with a great deal of grunting and gasping, I crawled to her, took her hand.

"The pain," I managed to say, "it goes away."

"Jim . . ." Whispered so quietly I could barely hear it.

"None other. You're going to be all right."

This was a pretty pathetic reassurance but was about all that I could think of at the moment. Where were we? What had happened? If this was Heaven it was pretty different from the place that she had described. Sharp volcanic gravel instead of grass; rock instead of sky. Where was the light coming from? And what was the last thing that Slakey had said? Something about not quite being Heaven.

With some effort I managed to sit up and saw the opening in the rock wall: we were in a cleft or a cave of some sort. And beyond the opening was a red sky.

Red? There was a distant deep rumble and I felt the ground beneath me tremble; a cloud of dark smoke roiled across the sky. Clutching to the rock wall I managed to drag myself to my feet and stumble over to Sybil. I helped her sit up with her back to the wall.

She tried to speak, starting coughing instead. Finally squeezed out the words. "Slakey—he was one step ahead of us all the time."

"What do you mean?"

"He was playing with us, and must have known that you were in the building. He cut his sermon short, made some kind of excuse about an unexpected meeting, turned the organ on instead, along with a recording of everyone singing. Asked us all to leave. Everyone except me. He took me aside, said that he had something most important to tell me. I was curious of course, besides the fact that I couldn't think of anything else to do except do as he had asked. Then, as soon as the others were gone, he pointed something at me. I had only the quickest look at something like a silver spiderweb, before I fell down. It was horrible! I couldn't move a muscle, not even my eyes. I was aware of him dragging me into that back room in the darkness—and the worst part was that there wasn't a thing I could do about it. I couldn't move, do anything at all, couldn't warn you that was the worst part. Then the lights were on, and you were there, falling. I remember him talking to you. After that—nothing.

"That's about all that I can remember—until I opened my eyes here."

I patted my side pocket, felt the lump of the communicator, felt a slight touch of hope at the same time. I put it to my ear, turned it on. Nothing. The same went for every other device on my person. All dead. Batteries and power packs drained. I couldn't even open the blade on my Schweitzy Army Knife; it seemed to be welded into a lump. I looked at the small pile of metallic debris and felt the urge to kick it across the cave. I gave in to the urge and did just that. It clattered nicely.

"Just junk now. All dead. Nothing works." I turned and stumbled towards the light.

"Jim, don't leave . . ."

"I'm not going far. I just want to look out, satisfy my curiosity, find out where we are."

Leaning one hand against the rock so I wouldn't trip, I took step after shuffling step until I was at the entrance and staring out. I felt my jaw fall open with shock as I dropped to my knees. For long moments I could only stare. With an effort I turned away, managed to stand again and went back to Sybil. She was sitting up now and very much more in control.

"What's out there, Jim?"

"Certainly not Heaven. The sky is red, not blue, no white clouds and certainly no grass. A geologically unstable area with an active volcano nearby. Plenty of smoke, but at least no lava. And there is a big and swollen sun like no sun—or star—I have ever seen before. It is light red in hue, not white or blue, which explains the russet coloring of the landscape."

"Where are we?"

"Well—" I groped for something intelligent to say. "Well

we know now that we're not on Vulkann," was the best I could come up with. "And . . ."

She noticed my hesitation. "And?"

"I just had a glimpse."

"Some glimpse! You should see your face—you've gone all gray."

I tried to laugh at this, but it came out as a pathetic gurgle. "Yes, I saw someone—or something. For just the shortest instant I could see sort of a figure, going away, fast. Biped, erect." My voice ran down and she looked very concerned. "Sorry. I'm just being stupid. It really moved too fast for me to see any details. But I think, no I'm sure, that it had a tail. And . . . it was bright red."

There was a long silence before she spoke.

"You're right. We're certainly not in Heaven. How is your theology?"

"Not too good—but good enough to know that I should not be thinking what I am thinking. Before you arrived I did a little theological digging in the net about the Heaven concept and all the afterworlds and afterlife, to find out more facts, to get some insight as to what it was all about. I'm afraid that my early religious education was more than neglected. Here is how it goes. There are as many concepts of Heaven as there are different religions. What I did was outline the Heaven as seen by the attendees at the Temple of Eternal Truth and search for comparisons. I found a really interesting assortment of religions with a great variety of names. I narrowed these down to the ones that featured a dichotomy of Heaven and Hell, which are places that are occupied after you die. There is an object called a soul, which you can't see or find or anything like that. It comes from somewhere unspecified. The description was pretty vague at this point. This soul, in some undescribed manner, is supposed to be you. Or the essence of you. Don't look at me like that—I'm not making it up! Anyway, this soul wants to end up in Heaven. There is a mention also of a sort of halfway house called Purgatory. And, I'm sure that you have heard of it, a direct opposite kind of place called Hell."

She looked shocked. "Then you think that . . . perhaps we have ended up in this place called Hell?"

"Well, until a better idea comes along—and I hope it will—that seems to be the conclusion . . . ."

There was a distant rumbling roar, the ground shivered beneath my feet. A sudden weight seemed to press down and I dropped to my knees, put my hands out to break my fall. I was heavy, suddenly very heavy; Sybil was sprawling on the ground again.

Then the strange sensation passed, as quickly as it had come, and I stood again, shakily.

"What—was that?"

"I haven't the slightest idea. I never felt anything like it before. It was like, what? A gravity wave passing over us?"

"There is no such thing as a gravity wave."

"There is now!"

She tried to smile, but shivered instead.

"Don't," I said. "We're someplace strange, and it might very well be a place called Hell. But we appear to be alive—so let us get out of this cave and find out just where in Hell we are!"

She pulled away and straightened up, running her fingers through her hair. And even managed a small smile. "I bet I even look like Hell," she said. "Let's go."

Our little burst of enthusiasm did not last very long. As we walked on, the air grew hotter, uncomfortably hotter. We passed around a spur of rock and found out why. We recoiled from the blast of heat and looked on aghast at the scene before us. Directly ahead ran a wide river of turgid lava. Darkened slag formed on top, cracking and breaking apart as it flowed by to reveal the glowing, turgidly liquid stone below. We retreated. Retracing our steps.

"We'll try the opposite direction," I said, then coughed. Sybil did not answer, just nodded in agreement. Her throat must have been as dry as mine; she would have been just as thirsty. Was there any water in this parched landscape? The answer did not bear thinking about.

Something else did not bear thinking about. Angelina.

Slakey must have sent her someplace just the way he had sent us. To Heaven I hoped. I hoped even harder that it was not to this terrible planet that she had gone.

We retraced our path past the cave mouth from which we had emerged and stumbled on through a landscape of rolling gravel dunes. It was still hot, but not the ovenlike furnace that we had just left.

"A moment," Sybil said, stopping and sitting on a wide boulder. "I'm a little tired." I nodded and sat beside her.

"Not surprising. Whatever that paralysis web was it certainly didn't do us any good. Physically or mentally."

"I feel beat—and depressed. If I knew how to quit I would."

Looking at the despair in her face, hearing the echo of exhaustion in her voice—I grew angry. This fine, strong, attractive agent should not be reduced like this by one man.

"I hate you Slakey!" I shouted. Jumping to my feet and shaking my fist at the sky. A rumble of a distant volcano was not much of an answer. I got even angrier. "You will not get away with this. We are going to get out of this place, yes we are. The air on this planet must have come from someplace, from living green plants. We'll find them—and you cannot stop us!"

"You are wonderful, Jim," Sybil said, standing and smoothing down her wrinkled and filthy dress. "Of course we will go on. And of course we will win."

I nodded angry agreement. Then pointed down the valley. "That way, away from the lava and the volcanoes. It will be a lot better."

And it was. As we walked the air became cooler. After a bit, when the valley widened out, I caught a glimpse of green far ahead. I did not want to mention it at first—but then Sybil saw it as well.

"Green," she said firmly. "Grass or trees or something like that ahead. Or is it just wishful thinking?"

"No way! I can see it as well and it is a very cheering sight indeed. Forward!"

We almost ran as the verdant landscape opened up ahead. It was grass, knee-high, cool and slightly damp as we pushed our way through it. There were clumps of trees farther ahead, then more and more of them, almost a small forest.

"Good old chlorophyll," I exulted. "Bottom of the food chain and from whence all life doth spring. Capturing the sun's energy to manufacture food . . ."

"And water?"

"You better believe it. There has to be water somewhere around here—and we are going to find it—"

"Shhh," she shhhsed. "Do you hear that? A sort of rustling, like dry leaves."

I did hear it, a light crackling sound that was coming towards us from the forest. Then something small came out from under the trees and moved hesitantly into the grass.

"Well, Hello," I said to the tiny reddish-brown form that emerged. It looked up at me with button-black eyes and squealed with fright.

The squeal was echoed by a louder and more angry squeal from the forest. There was a thunder of running hooves and a giant avenging form burst out from under the trees, snorting with massive maternal protectiveness. A good two meters from snuffling nose to twitching tail. Covered all over with protective spines now rigidly erect.

Sybil gasped with horror.

I smiled and cried out, "Sooooy, pig, pig, pig!"

"Jim—what is it?"

"One of the most endearing and lovely creatures in the galaxy, friend of my youth, companion to man. It is a—porcuswine!"

She looked at me as though she thought I was going mad.

"Endearing? Is it going to attack?"

"Not if we don't threaten her swinelet." The tiny creature had lost its fright when its monster dam had appeared and had nosed aside the protecting quills to find some refreshing milk.

I moved slowly, bending over to pick up a windfall branch. Beady and suspicious eyes followed my every movement.

"That's a good girl," I said, stepping forward and making reassuring clucking noises. She quivered a bit but held her ground. Turning her head to follow me as I approached. A drop of saliva formed on a protruding, sharp tusk, then dripped to the ground.

"There, there," I murmured. "Little Jimmy doesn't hurt porcuswine. Little Jimmy *loves* porcuswine."

Reaching down I brushed a handful of quills slowly aside between her ears, reached out and prodded with the end of the branch, then rubbed it strongly through the thick bristles.

Her eyes were half-closed as she burbled contentedly.

"Porcuswine just love to be scratched behind the ears—they can't reach the spot themselves."

"How do you know about these terrible creatures?"

"Terrible? Never! Companions to mankind in his quest to the stars. You should read your galactic history more closely. Read about the strange beasts and deadly creatures that were waiting for the first settlers. Monsters that could eat a cow in a single bite. They learned fear from the faithful porcuswine, let me tell you. An artificial genetic mutation between giant pigs and deadly porcupine. Tusks and hooves to attack, spines to defend. Loyal, faithful and destructive when needs be."

"Good pork chops too?"

"Indeed—but we don't speak about that in their presence. I was raised on a farm and let me tell you, my only friends were our herd of porcuswine. Ahh, here's the boar now!"

I shouted joyous greeting to the immense and deadly form that lumbered out of the forest. He glared at me with red and swiney eyes. Grunted aloud with pleasure as the end of my stick scratched and scratched at his hide. I grunted with the effort—and pleasure as well.

"Where did they come from?" Sybil asked.

"The forest," I said scratching away.

"That's not what I mean. What kind of a place is this with volcanoes, lava flows, gravity waves—and these creatures?"

"A planet that had to have been settled by mankind. We'll find out soon enough. But first let us follow the pigpaths into the forest and find some water. Drink first, cogitate later."

"Agreed," she said leading the way. I followed her and our

newfound porcine friends followed me. Grunting expectantly for more delicious scratching attention. We lost them only when the path led through a clearing surrounded by storoak trees. The boar slammed his tusks into the trunk of one heavy-laden tree and shook it mercilessly. Acorns as big as my head rained down and the little family munched on them happily.

We emerged from the forest into a water meadow that had been stirred up muddily by sharp hooves. It bordered a small lake. The far side was shielded in mist that obscured any details. We left the muddy path and found a shelf of rock that led to the water. Sat at the water's edge and drank cupped handfuls of the clear and cool water until we had drunk our fill.

"Find a few dry sticks, rub them together and it could be pork for dinner," Sybil said, smacking her lips.

"Never! They're friends." My stomach rumbled enticingly. "Well maybe later, much later. And only if we can't find another source of food. I think a little exploring is in order. This is—or was—a settled world. Mankind took the mutated porcuswine and storoak to the stars. There should be farms here."

"I wouldn't even know what one looked like. I was a city girl, or rather a small-town girl. Food was something that you bought in the shop. My mother and father—everyone there—worked at teleconferencing or programming or computing or whatever. No factories, no pollution, that sort of thing was confined to the distant robot construction sites. Our town was just low and ordinary, just a lot of landscaped buildings and green parks. Utterly and totally boring."

I squinted across the lake where the mist appeared to be clearing. I pointed.

"Like that place over there?"

CHAPTER 6

"WHAT PLACE?" SHE ASKED, STANDING and shielding her eyes with her hand. I pointed in silence.

"Seen one, you've seen them all," she muttered, frowning. "They must be factory-produced, stamped out like cereal packages. Fold the thing and glue it and plop it down, hook up the electricity and it starts to work. I couldn't even bear to go to school in Hometown—that is really what it was really called, would you believe it? I graduated first place in my kiddy class, got a scholarship, went away to school and never came back. Knocked around a bit, got involved with police work, liked it. Then I was recruited by the Special Corps and the rest is history."

"Do you want to take a look at this hometown?"

"No, I do not."

"It might be fun—and there should be food there. Unless you want a pork roast so badly that you want to kill a porcuswine with your bare hands?"

"No jokes, please. We'll take a look."

It was not a large lake and the walk was a short one. Sybil, who had started out in good spirits, grew quieter and quieter as we approached the low buildings. She finally stopped.

"No," she said firmly.

"No, what?"

"No it's not a place I really want to visit. They all look exactly alike, I told you, central design, central manufacture. Plug the thing in and watch it go to work. I hated my childhood."

"Didn't we all? But the porcuswine, they were the best part of it. Probably the only part that I remember with any feeling. Now let's go see if we can find a McSwineys and get a sandwich in this bijou townlet."

There was nothing moving in the streets or the buildings ahead. A single road came out of the hamlet and ended abruptly in the grass. There was a billboard sign of some kind beside it, but it was end on and we couldn't read it until we got closer. We walked at an angle as we approached so we could see what it said. Sybil stopped suddenly and clasped her hands so tightly together that her knuckles turned white. Her eyes were closed.

"Read it," she said.

"I did."

"What does it say?"

"Just a coincidence . . ."

Her eyes snapped open and she bit out the words. "Do you believe that? What does it say?"

"It reads, in serifed uppercase red letters on a white foreground, it reads . . ."

" 'Welcome to Hometown.' Are we mad or is this whole planet mad?"

"Neither." I sat down and pulled a blade of grass free, chewed on it. "Something is happening here. Just what we have yet to discover."

"And we are going to discover what by sitting on our chunks and chewing grass."

She was angry now—which was much better than being frightened or depressed. I smiled sweetly and patted the grass beside me. "To action, then. You sit and chew the grass while I scout out the scene. Sit!"

She sat. Because of the force of my personality—or because

she was still tired. I climbed to my feet creakily and wearily and strolled forward into Hometown.

Found out everything I needed to know in a very short time and went back to join her sitting and chewing.

"Strangest thing I have ever seen," I said.

"Jim—don't torture me!"

"Sorry. Didn't mean to—just trying to come to grips with this particular reality. Firstly, the town is empty. No people, dogs, cars, kids. Anything. One of the reasons that it is empty is that everything seems to be in one lump. As though it was made that way. The doorhandles don't turn and the doors themselves appear to be part of the wall. The same with the windows. And you can't look in. Or rather it looks like you're looking in but what is inside is really in the glass of the window. And nothing really seems right or complete. It is more like an idea of Hometown instead of being Hometown itself."

She shook her head. "I have no idea of what you are talking about."

"Don't worry! I'm not so sure myself. I'm just trying to pick my way through a number of very strange occurrences. We arrived here in a sort of a cave. With volcanoes and lava streams and no grass or anything else." I glanced up at the bloated red sun and pointed. "At least the sun is the same. So we went for a walk and found green grass and porcuswine, the porcuswine of my youth."

"And the Hometown of mine. It has to mean something . . ."

"It does!" I jumped to my feet and paced back and forth in a brain-cudgeling pace. "Slakey knew where he was sending us and it wasn't to Heaven he said. So he must have been here before. Not quite Heaven, that's what he said. Maybe he thought he was sending us to Hell. And the spot where we arrived was very Hellish what with the red creature, the volcanoes and lava and everything. Could it have been Hellish because he expected it to be? Because this Hell is his idea of Hell?"

"You lead, Jim—but I just can't follow you."

"I don't blame you, because the idea is too preposterous. We know that someplace named Heaven exists someplace, somewhere. If there is one place there could be others. This is one of the others. With certain unusual properties."

"Like what?"

"Like you see what you expect to see. Let us say this planet or whatever it is was a place that was just a possibility of a place—until Slakey arrived. Then it became the place he was expecting to find. Maybe the red sun got him thinking about Hell. And the more he thought the more Hellish it became. Makes good sense."

"It certainly does not! That's about the most flakey theory I have ever heard."

"You bet it is—and more than that. Absolutely impossible. But we are here, aren't we?"

"Living in another man's Hell?"

"Yes. We did that when we first came here. But we didn't like it and wanted to leave it. I remember thinking that the barren, volcanic world was just about the opposite of the one where I grew up. . . ."

It was my turn to wonder if this whole thing wasn't just institutionalized madness. But Sybil was more practical.

"All right then—let us say that was what happened. We arrived in this Hellish place because Slakey had come here first and everything—what can we say—lived up to his devilish expectations. We didn't like it and you wished very strongly we weren't there but in a place with a better climate. You got very angry about that, which may have helped shaped what we wanted to see. Then we walked on and came to it. We drank, but we were still hungry. Rather I was, so much so I must have thought of my earliest gustatory delights. Which just happened to be in Hometown. Given that all this is true—what do we do next?"

"The only thing that we can do. Go back to Hell."

"Why?"

"Because that is where we came in—and where we must be if we want to get out. Slakey is the only one that knows how to pass between these places. And another thing . . ." My voice was suddenly grim.

"What, Jim? What is it?"

"Just the sobering thought that Angelina may have been sent to this place before we were dispatched. If so, we won't find her in my youth or your youth. She would have to be in Slakey's particular Hell."

"Right," she said, standing and brushing the grass from her dress. "If we are thirsty we can always find our way back here. If we are hungry—"

"Please save that thought for awhile. One step at a time."

"Of course. Shall we go?"

We retraced our steps back through the field and into the forest. A distant, happy grunting cheered me up a good deal. As long as there were porcuswine in existence this galaxy would not be that bad a place. Out of the trees and across the field of grass. That grew sparser and shorter until it disappeared. Volcanic soil again and more than a whiff of sulfur about. The mounds were getting higher as we walked and we labored to climb an even higher one. When we reached the summit we had a clear view of a smoking volcano. It appeared to be the first of very many. And behind it the red sun, which was hovering just above the horizon.

The dunes ended in foothills of cracked and crumbled stone. Red of course. The cleft of a small canyon cut into them and we went that way. A lot easier than climbing another hill. We both heard the scratching sound at the same time; we stopped.

"Wait here," I whispered. "I'll see what it is."

"I go with you, diGriz. We are in this together—all the way."

She was right of course. I nodded and touched my finger to my lips. We went on, as slowly and silently as we could. The scratching grew louder—then stopped. We stopped as well. There was a slurping wet sound from close by, then the scratching started again. We crept forward and looked.

A man was standing on tiptoes, reaching above his head with a shard of rock, scratching at something gray on the cliff face. A piece of it came away and he jammed it into his mouth and began chewing noisily.

This was most interesting. Even more interesting was the fact that he was bright red. His only garment a pair of ancient faded trousers with most of the legs torn off. There was obviously a hole in the seat of these ragged shorts because his red tail emerged from them.

That was when he saw us. Turned in an instant and gaped open a damp mouth with broken black teeth—then hurled the piece of rock in our direction. We ducked as the stone clattered into the stone wall close by. In that instant he was gone, swarming up the sloping cliff face with amazing agility, vanishing over the rim above.

"Red . . ." Sybil said.

"Very red. Did you notice the little red horns on his forehead?"

"Hard to miss. Shall we go see what he was doing?"

"Doing—and eating."

I picked up a sharp fragment of stone and went over to the spot where he had been working. There was a gray and rubbery looking growth protruding from a crevice in the canyon wall. I was taller than our rosy friend and could easily reach it; sliced and chopped at it until a piece fell free.

"What is it?" Sybil asked.

"No idea. Vegetable not animal I imagine. And we did see him chewing it. Want a bite?"

"I wouldn't think of depriving you."

It tasted very gray and slimy, and was very, very chewy. With all the taste and texture of a plastic bag. But it was wet. I swallowed and a piece went down. And stayed down. My stomach rumbled a long complaint.

"Try some," I said. "It's pretty foul but it has water in it and maybe some food value." I tore off a chunk and held it out. Very suspiciously she put it into her mouth. I looked up—jumped and grabbed her and pushed her aside.

A boulder thudded into the spot where we had been standing.

"Angry at losing his dinner," I said. "Let's move out away from the rocks, where we can see what's happening."

We had a quick glimpse of him climbing higher still and finally moving out of sight.

"You stay here," I said. "Keep an eye out for Big Red. I'll get more of this gunge."

The sun did not seem to be appreciably higher in the sky when we had finished our meal. Stomachs full enough, and thirst slaked for the moment, we rested in the shade because the day was growing measurably warmer.

"Not good, but filling," Sybil said, working with her fingernail to dislodge a gristly bit that had lodged between her teeth. When it came free she looked at it disparagingly, then dropped it to the ground. "Any idea what we do next?"

"Put our brains into gear for starters. Since we woke up in this place we have been stumbling from one near-disaster to another. Let's check off what we know."

"Firstly," she said, "we've gone to Slakey's version of Hell. We'll call it that until we learn better. We are in another place—on another planet—or we have gone mad."

"I can't accept that last. We *are* someplace else. We know that machines are involved in this—because they were carefully destroyed in the building on Lussuoso. Angelina was sent someplace from that temple. We were sent someplace from the one on Vulkann. We know that for certain—and we know something even more important. A return trip is possible. You went to Heaven and came back. And we must consider the possibility that Angelina could have come here before us."

"Which means that we need some intelligence—in the military use of the word."

"You bet. Which in turn means we have to find Big Red with the horns and tail and find out all that he knows. About Angelina, about this place, how he—and we—got here. And how we are going to leave . . ."

A sound intruded, a soft, shuffling sound that grew slowly louder. Coming up the canyon floor towards us. Then we could hear the susurration of muttered voices.

"People—," I said as our recently departed devilish friend walked into view. He was followed by a small group of companions, at least twelve of them. Men and women. All bright red. All carrying sharp rocks. I had never seen any of them before—and one glance told me that Angelina was not in this motley crowd. They stopped when they saw us—then started forward when their leader waved them on.

"You can flee, should you wish, but we'll come after you. Run or stay, it makes no difference." He shook the rock at us.

"We are going to kill you. Kill you and eat you.

"Hell is a very hungry place."

CHAPTER 7

I HELD MY HAND UP to them, palm out, the universal sign of peace. Maybe. "Wait," I said. "If you attack us we will be forced to defend ourselves. And we are very dangerous. You will all be hurt, killed if you dare resist us. We are not normal humans but are ruthless killers . . ."

"Dinner!" Red Leader foamed. "Kill!"

I cupped my raised hand, raised the other in defense-offense position, balanced forward on the balls of my feet.

Sybil was at my side, hands held in the same way. "You didn't mean that about killing them—did you?"

"No—but I want them afraid so we can finish this quickly. Now!"

We screamed loudly in unison and attacked. Big Red shrieked and dropped his weapon when I chopped his wrist with the edge of my hand, following through with stiff fingertips into his solar plexus. Went on without stopping and kicked the legs out from under the two people behind him.

I was aware that Sybil had moved to the side to take her antagonists off guard and off balance. Two sharp kidney punches sent two women screaming to the ground.

The stone swung down and I went under it and hit the

wielder on the side of the neck, stepped aside as he fell.

A few more brisk blows and it was all over. The ground was covered with writhing, moaning, red figures. A hand reached out for a rock and I stepped on the wrist. That was the last resistance.

"They are a sorry and feeble lot," Sybil said, dusting of her hands disgustedly.

"No other way to handle it. No broken bones that I can see, and no blood." We picked up the stone weapons and threw them aside. Looked more closely at our battered assailants. They were dressed, if it could be called that, in a tattered and faded collection of clothing fragments. Bits of anatomy, normally concealed, poked out. All of them were bright red with neat little horns and, now flaccid, tails. They drew cravenly aside as I walked between them and picked up their unconscious leader, propped him against the rock wall and waited for him to come around. He groaned and opened his eyes—shrieked and fell over and tried to scrabble away. I straightened him up again.

"Look," I told him. "All the killing and eating was your idea. We were just defending ourselves. Can we call it quits? Just nod your head, that's better. I think we started off on the wrong foot so let's try again. My name is Jim . . ."

There was a thud and a cry of pain from behind me, proof that Sybil was covering my back.

"My name is . . . Cuthbert Podpisy, Professor of Comparative Anatomy, University of Wydawnietwo."

"Please to meet you, Professor. Aren't you a long way from home?"

He rubbed at his sore midriff, looked up at me with bleary red eyes. And sighed.

"I suppose I am. I haven't thought about that very much of late. The hunger and thirst tend to dominate one's consciousness. All we wanted was a bit of protein." He whimpered a bit, feeling very sorry for himself. "The diet is monotonous and not very filling. Lacks many amino acids I am sure. As well as minerals and vitamins."

"The gray stuff you were eating off the rock. That's your diet?"

"The same. It is called colimicon. I don't know what it means. I was told the word when I first came here."

"How did you get here?" Sybil asked, coming over to stand beside me—but not taking her eyes off the battered execution squad.

"I have no idea. I was on term leave, I went to this holiday world. To enjoy myself on the Vulkann beaches. It was all very nice and I had a good tan, not red like this, and I was putting on weight from overeating, destroying my liver with over-drinking, you know. . . . All I can remember is that I went to bed one night—and woke up here."

"How about the others?"

"The ones I have talked to say just about the same thing. The others are mad, they don't talk. It seems that the longer you are here . . . are you going to kill me?"

"Don't be foolish. I've eaten some strange meals in my time but draw the line at professors."

"You say that now, but—"

"I promise, all right? And speaking of professors—have you ever heard of a Professor Justin Slakey?"

"No. Rings no bells. Mine is a small university."

"All right. Now tell me about your red relations here. You said that people arrive here. Do any leave?"

"Only as dinner!" He cackled and drooled a bit around his blackened teeth, not as sane as he had first appeared to be. I changed the subject.

"If you are an anatomy professor perhaps you can explain your interesting skin color. Not to mention your little horns and tail."

He pinched a handful of loose skin at his midriff and blinked at it. "Very interesting," he said in a distant voice. "I used to study the phenomena, take notes, tried to take notes. Not pigmentation at all. I believe the color change to be due to enhanced capillary growth beneath the skin. Ahh, the tail." He groped for his and caressed it. "Might be added bones to the coccyx. Not possible, bone growth though, yes, or cartilage . . ."

I left him mumbling there and waved Sybil to one side where we could keep an eye on the others. Not that they appeared to be any threat. Some were still unconscious while the others sat or lay placidly as though drained of energy. One young man dragged himself to his feet and looked at us with obvious fear. When we did nothing he stumbled away, around the bend in the canyon and out of sight.

"I don't like this at all," Sybil said.

"I never liked it—and I like it even less the longer we stay here. These people aren't natives. They've been brought here. Dumped in this place for some unfathomable reason. At least we know who is responsible. We've got to find our way back—before we end up like these. Am I beginning to turn red yet?"

"No—but you're right. We've got to resist. But what can we do? Is there any point in going back to Hometown—or to your porcuswine?"

"None that I can think of at the moment . . ."

The sky darkened for an instant and we staggered, suddenly heavy. The phenomenon passed as quickly as it had begun. Gravity waves? I didn't let my thoughts dwell on it. What could we possibly do to save ourselves?

"Collect as much of the colimicon as we can carry," I said firmly. "Food and drink will keep us alive, give us a chance to take the next step. . . ." Inspiration failed me, but Sybil was thinking too.

"Go back to the cave where we woke up. We were in such bad shape we didn't search it well. Looking for what—I have no idea."

"But you have a good idea. Whatever brought us here dumped us on that particular spot. It needs a much closer look." I pointed to the sprawled, scarlet figures. "What about this lot?"

"There is nothing we can do for them—not now. Perhaps when we get back, get some answers. Maybe then we can do something. They are alive, so at least they know how to survive. And they did try to kill us."

"Point taken. Let's get moving."

We found some more colimicon and pried rubbery chunks from the rock crevasses. They were difficult to carry until Sybil turned her long skirt into a mini by ripping off a great length of the fabric. "And it's cooler like this," she said as she neatly knotted our food and drink into a bundle. I took it from her and pointed.

"Lead the way."

I did not dare think how long the days here were since the sun appeared to be just as high in the sky as it had been when we first saw it. Perhaps the planet did not rotate on its axis at all and this day was a million years long. We plodded on. Back towards the opening in the rocks where this whole depressing action had begun.

We started up one of the gravel dunes and I stumbled over a largish fragment, fell forward.

Saw the eruption of fragments from the sudden, small pit, heard the missile ricochet away.

"Move!" I shouted. "Someone's shooting at us!"

Sybil was running towards some broken boulders as I did a sideways roll and scrambled to my feet. More shots followed us, but a fast-moving target is hard to hit. I slid, gasping, into the lee of a giant boulder, saw that Sybil had reached shelter as well.

"Where's the sniper?" she called out.

"Top of the slope we were climbing. I had a quick glimpse, just something moving."

"Any particular color?"

"The local favorite."

"Next?"

"Get our breath back. Then spread out and hunt the hunter. Sorry but I dropped our supplies. We'll worry about that later. After we find this redskin. All right with you?"

"Agreed. Whoever it is I want him in front of me rather than behind."

I made the first rush, slanting across the hill then sheltering behind a boulder. A shot hit the rock, sending fragments clattering; another hit the ground. But even as our ambusher was firing Sybil was running just as I had done.

In rushing spurts we slowly made our way up the hill. Our attacker kept shooting; he appeared to have plenty of ammunition.

We were approaching the summit when I saw him. Big, red, running for better cover, a sack over one shoulder, carrying a long-barreled weapon of some kind. I sprinted in his tracks, going fast. I dived again for the shelter of a boulder when he turned and fired. I saw Sybil angle away around the top of the hill while he blasted shot after shot in my direction.

The end came suddenly. I heard him fire in the other direction; he must have seen her. I put my head down and plowed up the slope as fast I could. There he was a few meters away, turning the gun towards me—when a fast-thrown rock caught him in the back. He squealed, jumped—tried to aim.

And I was on him. Twisting the gun away and kicking him hard in the chest. He shrieked again as he fell; the sack dropped from his shoulder, spilling out shiny tubes.

Sybil stumbled up, as exhausted as I was, and looked down at our fallen adversary. He was fat and he was red, with the now normal horns and tail. But he was very familiar. He scrambled backwards, turned to look for a way to escape and I saw his profile.

"It can't be! But he looks like—" Sybil finished the sentence for me.

"It could be Slakey!"

"Or Master Fanyimadu or Father Marablis."

He was that familiar. But of course this could not be. He looked at us with wide eyes, trembling, frightened. Spoke.

"Have we . . . met before?"

"Perhaps," I said, "My name is diGriz. Is that familiar?"

"Not really. Any relation to the Grodzynskis?"

"Not to my knowledge. And your name is . . . ?"

"That's a good question. It might be—Einstein?" He looked hopeful, then stopped smiling when I shook my head *no.*

"Wrong answer. Do Mitchelsen or Morley sound familiar? Epinard?"

"Yes, those names are familiar," Sybil said. "They were all physicists. They're all dead."

"Physics!" He brightened up at that and pointed in the direction of the bloated sun. "Burning continues always. But the nucleus isn't stable, you see. The core, a Fermi sphere. Then the nucleus, lithium not stable . . ."

"Professor . . . ?" I called out.

"Yes? What? But those nuclei simply break up again."

He closed his eyes and swayed slowly back and forth muttering to himself softly all the time.

"He's mad," Sybil said firmly. I nodded agreement.

"Like the others—only more so. But he's saying something about physics. And he did respond when I called him professor."

"There are a lot of professors around."

"Too true." I picked up the gun and turned it in my hands. "And where did he get this? It's in good condition, fires all too well." I tapped a dial on the butt, fully charged, then pointed to the spilled tubes on the ground. "You recognize the weapon?"

"Of course. Linear accelerator gun. The military calls them Gauss rifles."

"Exactly. No moving parts, lots of juice in the nuclear battery—with plenty more steel slugs in these tubes. How did it get here? Do you remember what happened to all that gear that I brought with me, mechanical and electronic? None of it would work. We've seen no other artifacts—until this."

Our demonic friend stopped muttering, saw the gun and jumped to grab it. Sybil put out a foot and he sprawled onto his face. I held the gun up so he could see it.

"Professor—where did you get this?"

"Mine. I gave me the . . . " He looked around bewilderedly. Lay down and closed his eyes and appeared to be asleep.

"Not exactly a bubbling font of information," Sybil said.

"I think this madness is catching—or grows on you the longer you stay here."

"Agreed. So let's go back to the original plan. The cave."

"The cave." I retrieved and shouldered the bag, seized up the gun and ammunition. We looked back as we walked but he never stirred.

"Do you get the feeling that the longer we are in Hell the more questions there are to ask—and the fewer answers?" Sybil nodded glum agreement. Then pointed.

"Isn't that it ahead? The opening in the rocks?"

"Looks like it."

I felt more depressed than I had ever been before in my life. Which says a lot since I have been in some very depressing situations. This search for the cave was a token gesture born of desperation. If there had been any device, any machine—anything at all in the cave—we would have seen it before we left. This was a dead end.

As we approached the cave entrance there was a cracking explosion of sound inside, accompanied by a sudden burst of bright light. Sybil dived aside and I raised the gun, flipped on the power.

Scraping footsteps sounded from inside the cave, something horrible coming towards us. I sighted along the barrel, put steady pressure on the trigger as a man appeared in the entrance.

"Throw that away and come with me—quickly!" my son said.

"Coming, Bolivar!" Sybil shouted as she ran. "We're right behind you!"

CHAPTER 8

I DROPPED THE GUN AND the bag of ammunition, the colimicon, and ran—with Sybil right behind me. Bolivar led the way, stumbled to a halt towards the rear of the cave. He looked around, shuffled his feet. "No, more to the left," he mumbled. "Back, back. Good."

"Fast!" he shouted, raising his arms. "Take my hands!"

We weren't arguing. He seized our hands and, with a powerful muscular contraction, pulled us tight against his chest. I opened my mouth to speak—

It was a completely indescribable sensation. It was like nothing I had ever experienced before, had no relation to heat or pain, cold, emotions, electrocution.

Then it ended; bright light flared and there was a thunderous sound.

"Get down!" someone shouted and Bolivar dragged us after him to the floor of the room. Rapid explosions sounded, gunfire. I had a quick glimpse of a man firing a handweapon, clumsily, for when the gun recoiled he dropped it. From his left hand; his right arm was bandaged. He turned then and ran, followed by other running footsteps.

"James!" Bolivar cried out.

"Fine, fine," a muffled voice answered. He came out from behind the ruins of the burning machine. His face was smeared black and he was brushing glowing embers from his shirt. "Very close. Good thing he wasn't shooting at me. He did a good job on the electronics though."

"Thanks, boys, for getting us back," I said, then coughed raspingly. "My throat hurts like Hell."

There was a hiss of white fumes and the fires were blotted out by the automatic quenchers. An alarm was ringing in the distance.

"Explain later," James said. "Let's get out before anyone else shows up."

I didn't argue. Still numb from the events of the past day. Day? We ran out of the church, it was night, the van was parked at the curb just where we had seen it last—how long ago?

"Into the back," James ordered. He started the engine as the rest of us struggled in through the open rear doors. Barely had time to close them before he kicked in the power. We sprawled and rolled and heard the sound of sirens getting louder—then dying away as the van broadsided around a corner. He slowed after that, drove at what must have been something like normal speed. Turned a few more times and stopped. James spun his driver's seat around to face us and smiled.

"Drinks, anyone?"

Through the windshield a large rotating sign was visible. RODNEY'S ROBOT DRINKING DEN with CHEAPEST AND MOST ALCOHOLIC DRINKS IN TOWN in smaller lettering below. A robotic face appeared at the window. "Welcome to this drunkards' paradise. Orders, please," it grated.

"Four large beers," I told it, then coughed uncontrollably.

"Tell us what happened," Sybil said when I had gasped into silence.

"Sure," Bolivar said. "But first—are you guys all right?" Looking at us intently, relaxing only when we had nodded our heads. "Good, great. You gave us a scare, Dad, when the alarm went off."

"I didn't think that I had time to actuate it."

"You didn't. We only knew something was wrong when your heart stopped. We hit hard then."

"It never stopped!" I said defensively, grabbing at the pulse in my wrist. A nice solid thud-thud.

"That's good to hear. But we didn't know that at the time. We must have broken in just seconds after you went to Hell. Marablis, wearing some kooky outfit, was still working the controls. Bolivar got him with the stunner as he was turning around."

"I dropped him—but you were both gone. That explained the stopped heartbeat. You had been moved, transported, sent—to Hell as we found out. James took care of that. Advanced hypnotism, he's very good."

"Been a bit of a hobby for some years. Marablis was an easy subject. Stress and shock. I eased him under and took control. He told us that he had sent you both to Hell. Bolivar said that he would go after you. I had Marablis work the machine and you know the rest. It was a long five minutes but it worked out fine in the end."

I should have been immune to surprises by this time. I wasn't. "Five minutes! We were in Hell for hours—most of a day at least."

"Different time scales?" Bolivar said. "And I'll tell you something else just as outré. When I was in Hell I was here at the same time, I mean I could see what Bolivar was seeing, hear him speaking."

"And vice versa—"

"Beer," a tinny voice said and Sybil and I leaped forward.

"Four more," Bolivar said as we drained our glasses. He handed us the two remaining full ones.

The cold liquid helped. Gasping with pleasure, my brain got back into gear and I remembered something else. "James! The shooting when we arrived—what happened?"

"Just that. As you were coming back through, this guy burst in waving a gun. I dived for cover while he shot up the machinery. Then he and Marablis ran for it."

"I had a quick look at him," I said. "It couldn't have been, but . . ."

James nodded solemnly. "I could see him very clearly. It was Professor Slakey—with a bandage on the stump of his right wrist."

"Then who, who—?" I said, doing a stunned owl imitation.

"Who was at the controls, you mean? Who sent you to Hell and brought you back? That was also Professor Slakey. Working the controls with his good right hand."

"I have more news," I said. "There is a bright-red, long-tailed and behorned Slakey in Hell."

The silence got longer and longer as we considered the implications, or lack of them, in this information, until Sybil spoke. "James, whistle for the waiter if you please. Order up a bottle of something a bit stronger for the next round."

Nobody argued with that. Everything had happened so fast—and so incomprehensibly—that I had trouble pulling my thoughts together. Then memory struck hard.

"Angelina? Where is she?"

"Not in Hell," James said. "That was the first question I asked Marablis when I put him under. He admitted that much under stress. Fought hard not to answer where she was, almost surfaced from the trance. I put him deep under to bring you two back from Hell. When you were back safe I was going to press him really hard for an answer. But—you know what happened. Sorry . . ."

"No sorry!" I shouted happily. "Angelina is not dead—but has been sent somewhere. Maybe Heaven. We'll find out. Meanwhile, you got us back. Sorry is not the word to use. We'll have to try and work out what happened, what all these puzzles and paradoxes mean. But not right now. There are two things that we must urgently do now. We have to get help. And we've been compromised enough. Slakey knew about Sybil and me when he knocked us out. Now he knows the whole family is after him. He might try and fight back so we have to stay away from the hotel room. And we must contact the Special Corps at once."

"All I need is a phone," Sybil said. "I have a local contact number that will be spliced through directly to Inskipp."

"Perfect. We outline what has happened. Tell him to order a tight guard around that church. No one is to go either in or out. Then tell him to get Professor Coypu here soonest. Anyone who can build a working time machine as well as many other scientific miracles certainly ought to be able to figure out just what is going on with these Hell and Heaven machines. We'll stay out of sight until the professor has arrived—along with the Space Marines. Never forget—we have been to Hell and we came back. We're going to find Angelina and get her back with us the same way."

I suppose that I should have enjoyed the days of forced relaxation at the Vaska Hulja Holiday Heaven, but I had too much to worry about. Always lurking behind all the pleasures of swimming and sunbathing, drinking and eating, was the knowledge that Angelina was still missing. There was some reassurance in the fact that her kidnappers had admitted that she was alive, though not where she was. Small consolation; she was still gone and that could not be denied. A dark memory that would not go away. I knew that the twins shared these feelings, because behind all the horseplay and vying for Sybil's attention was that same memory. I would catch a bleakness of expression when one of them did not know he was being watched.

Nor was it all fun and games. We went to work. The first thing that we had done after checking into this hotel, with false identities, was to list everything we knew, had seen, had experienced. None of it seemed to make sense—yet we knew that it must. We forwarded all of this material to the Special Corps where, hopefully, wiser heads than ours might make sense of it.

They did. Or it did, a wiser head I mean. Our little trip to Hell seemed to have had a scrambling effect on my brain so at times my thoughts would dribble away. I also kept looking in mirrors to see if I was turning red. After awhile I stopped doing this—but I still felt the base of my spine when I was showering to see if I was growing a tail. Disconcerting. This feckless state of affairs ended next morning when I came down early for breakfast and saw a familiar figure at our table.

"Professor Coypu—at last!" I called out in glad greeting. He smiled briefly with his buckteeth popping out between his lips like yellowed gravestones.

"Ahh, Jim, yes. You're looking fit, skin tanned but not red. Any signs of a tail?"

"Thank you, no, I have been keeping track. And you?"

"Fine, fine. On my way here I examined the remains of the destroyed machines at the church and have analyzed all your notes, examined the clothing you wore in Hell, thank you. It all seems fairly straightforward."

"Straightforward! I see nothing but confusion and obfuscation where you . . ."

"See the forest as well as the trees. I can inform you in full confidence that inventing the temporal helix for my time machine was much more difficult." His teeth snapped off a piece of toast and he chewed it with quick rodent-like enthusiasm.

"You wouldn't care to chop some of that metaphorical wood for me—would you?"

"Yes, of course." He patted his lips with his napkin, giving his protruding teeth a surreptitious polish at the same time. "As soon as I discovered that Jiving Justin was involved in this matter, the shape of future things to come became clear . . ."

"Jiving Justin?" I burbled with complete lack of comprehension.

"Yes," he cackled, flashing his teeth at me. "That's what we used to call him at university."

"Who, who?" I was in owl overdrive again.

"Justin Slakey. He used to play the slide trombone in our little jazz quartet. I must admit to being fairly groovy myself on the banjo as well—"

"Professor! The point of it all, please—would you kindly return to it?"

"Of course. Even when I first met him, Slakey was a genius.

Old beyond his years—which considering the state of geriartrics might have been far older than he appeared. He took the theory of galactic strings, which as you undoubtedly know has been around as theory for a long time. No one had ever come close to tackling it until Slakey invented the mathematics to prove their existence. Even the theoretical wormtubes between galaxies were clear to him. He published some papers on these, but never put everything together into a coherent whole. At least, until now, I thought he hadn't completed his theory. It is obvious that he has."

He washed some more nibbled toast down with a quick swig of coffee. I resisted more owl imitations.

"Stop at once!" I suggested. "Start over since I haven't the slightest idea of what you are talking about."

"No reason that you should. The reality of the wormholes between one universe and another can only be described by negative number mathematics. A nonmathematical model would be only a crude approximation—"

"Then crudely approximate for me."

He chewed away, forehead furrowed in thought, unconsciously brushing away a strand of lank hair that floated down in front of his eyes. "Crudely put . . ."

"Yes?"

"*Very* crudely put, our universe is like a badly cooked fried egg. In a pan of equally badly cooked and stringy eggs." Breakfast had obviously inspired this imagery; I had eaten the eggs here before. "The frying pan represents space-time. But it must be an invisible frying pan since it has no dimensions and cannot be measured. Are you with me so far?"

"Yoke and all."

"Good. Entropy will always be the big enemy. Everything is running down, cooling down towards the heat death of the universe. If entropy could be reversed the problem would be easy to solve. But it cannot. But—" This was a big *but* since he raised an exclamatory finger and tapped his teeth. "But although entropy cannot be reversed, the rate of entropic decay can be measured and displayed, only by mathematics of course, and can be proven to proceed at a different rate in different universes. You see the importance of this?"

"No."

"Think! If the rate of entropy in our universe were faster than the rate of entropy in universe X, let us say. Then to a theoretical observer in that universe our universe would appear to be decaying at a great rate. Right?"

"Right."

"Then, it also becomes obvious that if an observer in our universe were to observe universe X, the entropy rate there would appear to be going in the opposite direction, what might be called *reverse* entropy. Though it does not exist it would be observed to exist. Therefore the equation is closed."

He sat back and smiled happily at his conclusions. I hadn't the slightest idea of what he was talking about. I told him that and he frowned.

"I do wish, diGriz, that you had taken a little more mathematics instead of playing hooky from school. To put it even more simply, a phenomenon that is observed to exist *does* exist and can be mathematically described. And what can be described can be affected. What can be affected can be altered. That is the beauty of it. No power source is needed to manipulate the wormholes between the universes, although energy is of course needed to establish the interface. The wormholes themselves are powered by the differences in their entropy rate. Justin Slakey has discovered that and I will be the first man to take my hat off to him."

He lifted an invisible hat from his head, then patted it back into place. I blinked quickly and cudgeled my brain hard, trying to understand just what he was talking about. With great difficulty some sort of order began to emerge from his flights of physical fancy.

"Tell me if I have this right. Different universes exist, right?"

"Yes and no . . ."

"Let's settle for the *yes*—just for a moment. Different universes exist, and if they exist they could be connected by wormholes in space. Then the difference of entropy between these universes might be used to travel through the wormholes from one galaxy to another—and Slakey has invented a machine to do just that. Okay?"

He raised the finger, frowned, shook his head in a very negative no. Thought a bit more, then shrugged. "Okay," he said in a most resigned manner. I hurried on before he changed his mind.

"Hell is a planet in a different universe, with different laws of physics, maybe a different chemistry, where time passes at a different rate. If that is so then Heaven is a different universe connected to ours by wormholes in space and time. There could be more . . ."

"The number of theoretical universes is infinite."

"But with Slakey's machine they can obviously be contacted, over and over again. And what he can do—you can do?"

"Yes and no."

I resisted the temptation to rip out a handful of my hair. "What do you mean yes and no?"

"I mean yes it is theoretically possible. And no, I cannot do it. Not without the mathematical description of the entropy relationships that was recorded in the machine. The one he destroyed."

"There will be other machines."

"Get me one and I'll build you an intergalactic wormhole subway."

"I will do just that," I promised. Not rashly but because I had to do just that to get to Angelina. Which led to the next obvious question. "Who has these machines?"

"Slakey."

"Which Slakey?"

"There is only one Slakey."

"I can't believe that. I saw three at least. One bright red with a tail. Another with no right hand—and a third with a good right hand."

"You saw the same man—only at different times. Just as if you were to take a time machine to visit a baby being born, then went on in time to see the same baby grown—then saw him again as an old man. The mathematics is quite clear. In some manner he has managed to duplicate himself at various times during his existence. He, they, him, are all the same individual, just observed at the same time though he is from various different times. Since they are all the same person they have to share the same thoughts. That's how Slakey no-hand knew that Slakey right-hand was in trouble and came to the rescue. You saw this same phenomenon with your own sons, the twins. Since they are biological twins and divided from the same original egg, they were at one time exactly the same person, or egg. So when they were in different universes they shared the same thoughts. It is all very obvious."

"What's obvious?" Sybil asked as she came into the breakfast room.

"What is obvious," I said, "is that we now know how to get to Heaven and Hell—or wherever else we want to go. The good professor appears to know all about these various universes."

She nodded. "If you know that Professor—do you know how Jim found his porkuswine in Hell?"

"I do. I read your notes concerning that visit and I agree completely with your first conclusions. Hell is obviously a malleable and unformed universe. It must have been geologically active when Slakey first found it. He mistook it for Hell—so it became Hell. You both found his Hell, but also formed a little bit of your remembered worlds there as well."

"Then a question, please?" Sybil asked. "If we did that—why didn't the other people we found there do the same thing?"

"Also obvious," the professor pontificated, always happy with an expectant audience. "They were normal people—not supernormal Special Corps agents. The force of your personalities and your mental strength enabled you to force your memories upon the fabric of that universe, to bend it to your will. Where normal people might run in fear you turn and growl savagely and rend your enemies."

"You make us sound like feral terriers, wild dogs!" I growled savagely,

"You are. Any more questions?"

"Yes. What happens next?" Sybil said.

"I can answer that," I answered. "With Professor Coypu's help we will build a machine to travel to these distant universes. And we will get Angelina back."

"That is wonderful news. But let us not do any of that until after breakfast," she added with womanly practicality. "I'm sure that we will need all our strength to do all of that."

CHAPTER 9

I WAITED UNTIL JAMES AND Bolivar had joined us at the breakfast table, and had eaten their stringy eggs, before I brought them all up to speed.

"Meeting come to order." They all looked intently at me—with the exception of Professor Coypu who was muttering to himself as he scrawled mathematical equations onto a large scratchpad. "The professor will not mind if I simplify drastically what he revealed to me this morning. Heaven and Hell are in different universes and we can get to them. Plus there are other universes we can reach—and Angelina is in one of them. With a little help from us he can build a machine that we can use to get her back. Understood?"

Everyone nodded and smiled. Except for Coypu, who sniffed miffedly. He could apparently do two things at one time because, while still noodling his equations, he spoke.

"Your simplification is utter nonsense. These equations prove . . ."

"That you know what you are doing," I broke in before everything got murky again. "And we know what we are going to do. We are going to find one of the Slakey clones. Unless they used their machine to leave this planet, they must still be here.

I had the Special Corps put the pressure on the local military to seal this planet tight. Like a roach motel they can come in but they can't go out. An intense and thorough search has been going on at this moment . . ."

"Let the Slakeys go," Sybil said.

Silence descended. Even Coypu stopped writing. Sybil smiled sweetly at her stunned audience. "Think latterly," she said. "Think subtly. The trouble with you men is that all the testosterone and other hormones you have whizzing around your systems tend to make your actions very predictable. So try to be a little more devious, just this once. These men you are looking for, Slakey and Company, are just as masculine as the rest of you and will be expecting you to do what you are planning to be doing."

"Then what should we do?" I asked.

"Ease up, allow for loopholes and human error. Let them test the doors until they find one unlocked. When they get out have them followed."

"That won't be easy . . ."

"Yes it will," Coypu said. "I have been considering a new and unique theory about the effects of inter-universe travel," he held up his pages of equations, "that I have now proved to my satisfaction is true. It is called entropic delimitation."

He smiled with scientific satisfaction, so pleased with himself that he tapped happily on his teeth with his fingernails, looked around at our glazed stares.

"I will elucidate. When you were in Hell you observed that certain changes occurred to people there. Skin color became encarmined, new appendages grew, insanity progressed. These equations prove positively that the changes are not physical in the sense that they are made by chemicals in the atmosphere and so forth. No indeed. These changes are caused by entropic delimitation, the basic incompatibility of material taken from one universe to another. Once I had realized this it was simplicity itself to construct an E-meter. A machine that embodies immense possibilities while remaining simple in construction. Here it is."

He dug around in his shirt pocket, took out something small and placed it carefully on the table. We all leaned close.

"It looks like a stone tied to a piece of string," I said.

"It is. When I analyzed your reports and saw the direction in which my researchers were going, I took the precaution of obtaining some Hell-matter. From your discarded clothing, Jim. There were bits of gravel in your pockets, from all that slithering about on the ground I imagine. Now—the proof of the pudding is in the eating."

He picked up the string by the loose end, stood and walked over towards me. Stopped and held this complicated scientific device out so that the stone was suspended just before my nose. I looked at it cross-eyedly.

"Is it moving?" he asked.

"It seems to be swinging towards me."

"It is. You were in Hell long enough for entropic delimitation to affect your body, if ever so slightly." He held the thing out over Sybil's hand and nodded happily. Then walked to the twins, held it in turn behind one head and then the other. He pointed at James.

"You are the brother who operated the machine and did not pass through to Hell."

James could only nod in silence. Coypu admired his invention. "If I can get this strong a response after such a brief transit—just think how Jiving Justin will light up in the dark! As soon as I have manufactured a few thousand meters, simple enough to do, all the restrictions on free movement will be lifted. No attempt will be made to apprehend the miscreants or stop them from leaving—"

"Great!" I cried aloud gustily. "They can run but they cannot hide. Every train, bus, spaceship, scooter, rickshaw, every form of transportation, will have a meter close by. We'll follow them and they will lead us to another of their machines and we will grab it and the good guys will win!"

Of course it didn't happen that easily. Instead of trying to run, Slakey and Slakey had apparently gone to ground. When they didn't walk into any of our traps, the good Professor

Coypu went back to the workbench and improved upon his original model. Which, all things considered, was pretty crude. He built larger ones with amplifying circuits that would work over greater distances. Then military jets quartered the skies over the islands—and had a trace within hours.

"Here," the Special Corps technician said, opening up a large map and tapping his finger on a red-marked site. We all leaned close. "The pilot of the search plane took off, circled for altitude—and all the bells went off."

"That is right in the middle of a city," I said.

"It certainly is. In fact it is the center of the capital of this planet, Hammar City. The first reading we had almost blew the needle off its bearings. And it hasn't moved since we spotted it. But there are two other, weaker traces in the city—and one of them is moving."

"Is it possible—that there could be another machine, which would explain the strong trace? And the other contacts might be a couple of Slakeys?"

"Professor Coypu is of the same opinion. He says if you plan to take any offensive actions you must speak to him first."

"No problem. Where is he?"

"In the nightclub downstairs doing research."

"Research . . . ?" It was mind-boggling time again. "But which club? There are seven in this hotel."

"The Green Lizard. Very ethnic."

I wondered what could be ethnic about lizards; I soon found out. The sound of jungle drums filled the hot, moist air, while the screams of nocturnal animals cut through the semidarkness. I ducked under the low leaves of the trees and almost choked myself on a vine.

"May I be of service, human visitor?" a large green lizard said, smiling fangedly before me. While the head was that of a lizard the green body was human and enthusiastically female. Painted green I realized, this fact was visible even in the dim jungle light. Also visible was the even more interesting fact that paint on skin was all that she was wearing; nothing else. I wondered just what kind of research the professor was doing here.

"Coypu," I said. "I'm joining him. Small man, gray hair, good teeth . . ."

"This way, please, dear human visitor." She led me through the jungle—a fine figure to follow!—to a log table. Coypu sat on a chair stump just as naked, though not as attractive, as my leading lizard. He was sucking at the straw of a tall drink in a section of bamboo while he scribbled equations on a large leaf.

"I'll have whatever he has," I said, then forced my gaze back on the professor when she slithered away.

"Ahh, Jim, sit down."

"I don't want to interrupt your work."

"You're not. I have just finished with all of my research. So that tomorrow I'll be able to finalize my scientific paper titled 'Saurian Substitutions for Reenhancing Subliminal Sexual Inhibitions.' "

"Sounds fascinating."

"Indeed it does. I'm also writing a shorter and more popular version for the Internet called 'Chicklist for Hungry Hunters.' "

"You're onto a winner. What did you want to talk to me about?"

"Plans. We must find a fail-safe way of getting our hands on an intact model of Slakey's universal differentiator. My research cannot proceed until that has been done. Twice now his machines have gone up in flames before they could be examined. Let us try not to let that happen again. I have constructed a device that will make that possible."

"What is it?"

"A temporal inhibitor. An intellectual offspring of my temporal helix. Which you will remember, since you traveled on it, when you traveled back in time and had some interesting adventures while you were busy saving the world. You deserve some credit in this invention as well. You will also remember that when you saved the Special Corps from time attack you met those time travelers from the future, who gave you a machine. It froze everyone around you with a time stasis. Once I knew it could be done the rest was easy."

"You're a great man, Professor."

"I know that. Finish your drink and sally forth. You'll find the temporal inhibitor, or TI for short, on the table in my room. It works just like the one you used before. Turn it on and everything around you freezes in time. Except for you, of course. Go, Jim, go forth with the TI and use it to get the dimensional machine. Leave me now for I have important research to do here and you are a married man."

I went. Picked the lock on his suite and looked at the flashlight on the table. I picked it up and turned it on. Instead of lighting up it hummed industriously. Nothing else appeared to have happened that I could see. I turned it off, dug a coin out of my pocket and threw it into the air, turned on the flashlight. The coin hung in midair, dropped only when I turned the TI off.

"Next stop Hammar City!"

I used the room phone to call the suite where the boys were staying. There was a recorded message for me suggesting that I join them in Waterworld, the most popular nightspot in the hotel. I slipped the TI into my pocket and left, and found the nightspot easily enough, following the sound of wet music and splashing waves. But I hesitated at the entrance, having had more than enough of nightclubs after the Green Lizard. This one was better lit and provided more clean-cut fun. With the lighting effects and almost nul gravity field, the illusion of being underwater was very good. The waitresses had mermaid tails and swam laden trays of drinks and food to the floating tables. The happy customers danced a few feet off the floor, twining themselves sinuously about to the happy beat. I could see Bolivar dancing with Sybil, both enjoying themselves greatly. He didn't seem to mind when James cut in—or was it the other way around? Not that it mattered. They were young and in high spirits and deserved every bit of relaxation they could get. I could take care of getting the machine myself while they danced the night away.

I was picking up some needed devices from my room when the phone pinged and turned itself on. Inskipp glared out of the screen at me.

"What do you think you are doing, diGriz?"

"Just running a little errand. Picking up something for Professor Coypu," I said innocently. A scowl replaced the glare.

"No you're not—at least not alone. I know everything, remember. Including exactly what it is you are getting for Coypu. There have been too many mistakes made of late. Sloppy work. That practice ends now. Captain Grissle of the Space Marines has his squad waiting for you in the lobby at this very moment."

"Thank you, thank you, you are kindness itself. I'll join him right away."

I would of course exit from the back entrance of the hotel and avoid the noxious military presence of the marines. There was a loud hammering on the door.

"While the squad is waiting in the lobby that will be the captain coming for you now. Go."

I seized up the TI and thought of using it on the marine, but the snarl from the phone changed all that.

"I'm watching you, diGriz—no games!"

I muttered a few favorite profanities under my breath as I opened the door. A burly marine with nasty tiny red eyes and a jaw like an anvil was standing outside. He saluted a quivering tense salute. I touched the flashlight-TI to my brow.

"Transportation to the airport is waiting," he shouted. "After you, sir."

It was all very well organized; at least the Special Corps could get this kind of thing right. Marines stamping, guns waving, sirens wailing; the usual. Captain Grissle briefed me on the way, ticking off the points with a raised finger.

"One. The Hammar City police have the area where we are going under close observation. Investigation has shown that the machine you are looking for is in a meeting hall owned by an organization called the Circle of Sanctity. Very exclusive, bigwig politicians and industrialists. Some of the members of this group are being interrogated right now."

"Do you know what this whole operation is about?"

"I do, Agent diGriz. I have been in on this investigation from the very beginning. Point two. Unlike the other churches involved in this investigation, this operation appears to be all male. Instead of looking forward to Heaven, this lot is into money—and power. An industrialist named Baron Krümmung seems to be in charge."

"They get rich, he gets richer."

"That's it."

"Identification?"

"Positive. A bit older, fatter and balder. But he's Slakey, no doubt at all."

Another incarnation. How many of them were there knocking around the galaxy? Depressing thought—there could be any number, armies of the same man, images clicked at different points in time. And all of them sharing the same thoughts and memories. That didn't seem possible—I decided not to even think about it.

"How do you want to handle this operation?" the captain asked.

"Am I in charge?"

"Completely. Orders received from the highest level."

"Inskipp?"

"None other."

"He's getting mellow in his old age."

"I doubt that. We follow your instructions exactly. As long as I and my two sergeants are with you at all times."

CHAPTER 10

THE FLIGHT IN THE BALLISTIC-ORBIT SST did not take very long at all. Plenty of G's at each end, acceleration and deceleration, with free fall in between. I slept when we were weightless, found it to be very relaxing indeed. And I had plenty of sleep to catch up with. Ground transportation, and another marine officer, a lieutenant this time, were waiting for us. There was a lot of snapping of stiff salutes, so dear to the military heart. I waited impatiently until all thumbs were back on seams on trouser legs.

"Tell me, Lieutenant, has anything changed since the last report?"

"Negative, sir. The detectors are keeping track of the two individuals just as before. They have not moved again and we have kept our distance from them. Neither of them is in the vicinity of the machine."

"Do they have any idea they are being tracked?"

"Negative. We have never approached them—never even seen them in fact. Our orders were to keep distant observation until you had secured the machine."

"I'll do that now. Lead the way."

I was keeping this operation as simple as possible since I

didn't want a third goof-up. The front door to the building was already open and secured; more marines were keeping out of sight inside. My armed guard trotted behind me when I trotted, stopped when I stopped.

"Tell me again," I whispered. The lieutenant pointed to high, double doors at the end of the hall.

"That's it, where they meet. It is a conference room, circular, about twenty meters across." He handed me a small metal box with a collection of dials on it. "Your detector, sir."

"Give it to the captain to carry. Is the door unlocked?"

"Don't know, we haven't been near it. But I have the key here."

"Good. Here's what we do. We walk *quietly* up to the door. You put the key into the lock. You try it. If it is locked then you unlock it. As soon as you are sure it is unlocked you give the nod—and pull the door open." I held up the TI. "This is not a flashlight but is a temporal inhibitor. You open the door and I turn it on. Everything in that room will be fixed in time. Nothing there, human or mechanical, will be able to move until I turn it off again. Which I will not do until the machine is secured. Do you all understand?" Their eyes were glazed—and with good reasons. I shrugged.

"You don't have to. Are you all ready?" They nodded enthusiastically. "Then let's do it."

They all saluted again and at least they were quiet about it with no stamping boots this time. Grissle and his two sergeants were breathing on my neck as we crept forward. I readied the TI. The lieutenant put the key in the keyhole, turned it slowly—then pulled hard and the door flew open.

"Zapped!" I shouted as I switched on the TI. It was pitch dark inside and I couldn't see a thing.

"Can you turn on the lights?" I asked. There was no answer. Frozen in time. The lieutenant was strangely off balance and still pulling on the door handle. My glassy-eyed squad were as still as statues. I stepped back a bit and as soon as the field enveloped them they could move.

"We're going in there," I said. "But I can't see a thing—and I don't dare turn this device off to find a light switch. Suggestions?"

"Battle torches," Captain Grissle said, shifting the detector to his left hand and unclicking his torch from his belt. A bright beam flared out, followed by the others.

"Stay close," I said. "Hold hands, hold my arms—or you'll look like him." I pointed to the crouching and immobile lieutenant; they all cuddled together. We shuffled forward slowly like competitors in an eight-legged sack race, towards the far end of the room.

"Reading steady," Grissle said, "and the needle is pointing at that door over there."

The door was open so at least I didn't have to worry about that. Shuffle-shuffle we went, lighting up the interior of the adjoining room.

Revealing the rack of electronics. A duplicate of the last one I had seen—except that this one was intact.

"There!" I pointed. "That's what I want. Cuddle, clutch and shuffle. All right, stop here. Because we have a problem. I will have to turn this TI off if we are going to disconnect this thing." I pointed at a glowing light on the control panel. "We'll have to turn its power supply off as well if we are going to take it away with us. Any suggestions?"

"The sergeants will draw their weapons to protect us," Grissle said. "You and I grab the machine, move it, look for any switches, power lines, whatever. There's nothing else we can do."

I thought about it for a bit and could not think of any alternatives.

"Let's do it. Get your guns out. Shout if you see anything. Or better yet—try to shoot first. I'll turn the time-freezer off and restore the status quo. Ready?"

Grim nods of agreement; the sergeants with guns pointed, the captain taking a firm grip on the machine.

"Here goes . . ."

I touched the switch.

And everything happened at once.

The machine burst into life, lights flickering in quick patterns. With a terrible shriek someone appeared next to me, seized me and pulled me off balance. I grabbed him with my free hand . . . .

We were going. Going someplace, somewhere, the sensations that weren't sensations again. Going.

All I was aware of was my heart thudding louder and louder in an empty silence. Fear? Why not? Back to Hell? Or Heaven . . .

White light, strong, warmer air. And the tinkling, clanking, crash of broken glass.

I was on the ground, sharpness under my back, with a fat and older version of Slakey stumbling away from me. The temporal inhibitor was still in my hand.

"Got you, Slakey," I called out, pointed and pressed the switch.

He ran on, stopped and turned, swaying dizzily, laughing.

"That weapon, whatever it is, won't work here. No imported machine will. You fool, haven't you learned that yet?"

I was learning, but very slowly. And my punctured legs hurt. I put the inoperable TI against the broken crystal on the ground, used it to push against the sharp shards as I stood up. I pulled a sliver of glass from my leg and watched blood stain the fabric.

"We're not in Hell," I said, looking around me. "Is this your Heaven?"

It might very well have been because it was—incredible. I gaped, very much in awe. But not so much that I didn't keep Fat Slakey inside my field of vision. What I saw was like, well, like nothing I had ever seen or imagined before.

A world of transparent beauty, crystalline, exuberant, colored and transparent and rising up around me. Shrubbery of glass, analogs of trees and leaves, transparent and veined, reaching out on all sides.

But not where I was standing I realized. Here it was all broken shards, a circular area of destruction. Broken and fragmented.

"No, not Heaven," Slakey said.

"Where then?"

When he did not answer I took a step towards him and he raised his hands.

"Stop there! No closer. If you stay where you are I'll answer your question. Agreed?"

"For the moment." I was making no promises. But I knew so little that anything that kept him talking would be of help. "If not Heaven—then where are we?"

"Another place. I don't come here often. It is of little or no use. Whimsically I used to call it Silicon Valley. Now—I call it Glass, just Glass."

"You're Professor Slakey. And perhaps you might also be the one who runs the operation we just left—Baron Krümmung."

"If you like." Surly, looking around. I took a tentative step which got his attention. "No!"

"I'm not moving, relax. And tell me what this is all about . . ."

"I tell you nothing."

"Not even about yourself in Hell?"

He slumped when I said that. "A tragic mistake. I won't make that kind of mistake again. I can't leave of course, too long in Hell. Too long. Certain death if I left now."

"The gun? Why the gun?"

"Why? What a stupid question. To live of course, to eat. The colimicon contains little or no nutrition. A slow death that way. A gun to hunt with, a gun for a hunter."

It was a sickening thought, for there was only one other food source in Hell. I was in the company of a madman—and I understood so little of what was happening. But he was talking and I had kept the important question aside, spoke it now as casually as I could.

"That woman on Lussuoso. Where did you send her?"

"That woman?" He laughed, a laugh devoid of humor. "Come now, diGriz, do I look that stupid? Your wife? Your Angelina—and you call her That Woman."

He saw the expression on my face, turned and ran. Down a path of broken crystal through the magic forest. And I was right behind him and gaining.

But he knew where he was going. Running—then stopping, looking down, shuffling sideways. I reached for him. Just as he vanished. Saved by himself, pulled out of this universe.

I was very much alone. Stranded on an alien planet in an alien universe. And not for the first time. I tried to cheer myself up with the thought that I had been in Hell and had come back.

"You'll do it again, Jim. You always win. You're the original good guy and good guys always win."

Thus cheered, I looked around. The crystal forest glinted in the sunlight; nothing moved in the warm silence. The path of broken shards led away from the clearing. Where it went to I had no idea. I walked slowly down the path beneath the glass foliage. It turned and skirted the edge of the cliff now. There was water below, stretching away to the horizon. Off to the left, in the direction the path led, there were some offshore islands. Above me crystalline branches reached out over the water; waves were breaking over the rocks below. There was scud on the water, foam roiling and surging.

I stopped. Slakey was gone and I was very much alone. This was not a very nice thought and I rejected it. It would just be a matter of time, that's all. Captain Grissle and his marines would have the machine disconnected by now and rushed to that dear genius Coypu. Who would analyze and measure and operate the thing to come and find me. I hoped.

What next? Alone in this crystalline universe was very alone indeed. I smiled at the thought and started to laugh. At what? Nothing was funny. I shook my head, suddenly dizzy.

"Oxygen—lots of it," I said aloud to reassure myself.

There was no reason at all that the atmosphere on this alien planet should match the atmospheres of the terraformed and settled planets. Quite the opposite, if anything. Slakey was obviously seeking out and visiting worlds where humans could live and breathe. I held my breath for a bit, then breathed shallowly.

The oxygen high died away and I looked around at the glass forest—with the trampled path through it. The path that now led along the cliff edge. Should I really follow it? I was not used to indecision, so was undecided about it.

But it really was decision time. My trip to Hell had proven that there was a cartographic coordination between leaving and arriving positions when flitting between universes. Sybil and I had arrived in that cave—and gone back from it. So should I go back to the place where I had arrived? Or try to find out more about Glass?

"The answer to that one is obvious, diGriz," I said to myself. I believed in taking advice from someone very intelligent whom I trusted. "Sit on your chunk and wait to be rescued. And quietly die of thirst and/or starvation. Get moving and find out more about this place. For openers—is that ocean fresh water or is it loaded with chemicals? Or is the liquid really water? Go forth and investigate."

I went. Along the glass-sharded path. Happy that the soles of my shoes were made of seringera, an elastic compound that is supposed to be as strong as steel. It had better be.

The crystalline trees were higher along the coast, with meadowlike areas of bluish grass between them. I came around a bend in the path and in the middle of the next meadow was the statue of a glass animal.

Up to this point I had just accepted the presence of crystalline growths. Too much had happened since I arrived here to question the landscape. I did not query their existence; they just were. Maybe natural mineral structures, or perhaps some living creature like coral had secreted them.

Or had all of this been made by some incredible artist? The orange and yellow little creature in the field certainly was a work of art. Glassy fur covered it, each hair separate and clear. The open mouth had two rows of tiny and precisely formed teeth. I looked beneath the tree next to it and jumped back.

An animal, twice as big as I was, stood poised to jump. Unmoving. I relaxed. Admired the knifelike teeth with their serrated edges; giant claws stretched out from each foot. Glass grass crunched underfoot when I walked closer to it. Looked up and admired the artistic construction. The thing's eyes were on a level with mine and were certainly most realistically formed.

Particularly since they were moving ever so slowly to look at me.

These creatures were alive!

I went back and bent over the smaller one, the hunted. Yes one foot was definitely lower, the one on the other side raised a fraction.

I wasn't looking at sculpture or artifacts. I was in a world of slow-moving crystalline life.

"Well why not?" I reassured myself. "You're not mad, Jim, you have just finally used your exquisite powers of observation to observe what should have been obvious from the first."

I tried to remember my chemistry. Glass was neither basically a liquid nor a solid when in a disordered state. And wasn't water glass a liquid? As we are carbon based, so there could be—there certainly were!—life-forms based on silicon. There would surely be some exotic chemical compositions and reactions involved. But all around me was living proof that it could happen.

With the side of my shoe I cleared away enough broken fragments from the path to make a space to sit down. I rested my chin on my arms, braced on my kneecaps, held the position as long as I could.

Yes—the two animals were moving. Slow metabolism and slow life. Entropy obviously moved at a different speed here, at least with these glass creatures. Too bad I couldn't stay and see who won the race. Maybe if I came back in a day or two I would find out. But exploring had better take precedent over sight-seeing; it was hot and I was already beginning to feel thirsty.

The path along the cliff edge was dropping down towards the ocean below, until it eventually ended on a glassy beach. With all the fancy glass this planet sure had great sand. The water—if it were water—was clearer here. It was a tidal sea and the tide was going out. Ahead, in a finger of eroded rock, were sparkling tide pools. I went and bent over the first one—and something scurried into a crack.

It wasn't the only thing living in the pool. Tiny fishlike creatures with trailing appendages flitted away from my shadow. And they didn't look like glass. They were living in the water which maybe wasn't water.

"Try it, Jim, you might like it," I advised myself. I scooped up a handful and sniffed. Smelled like water. Took a drop on my fingertip and touched my tongue to it hesitantly. Water. Slightly tangy but still water. I sipped a bit of it and it went down well with no obvious ill effects.

But that would be enough for now. That tang could be anything—and I wasn't terribly thirsty yet. I would wait and see if there were any bad reactions. I walked on along the beach towards the small islands just offshore. These were little more than sandbars. There were larger ones, also green and farther out, but these were close enough to see in some detail. There was growth of some kind on them. Green, unlike the crystalline forest and plants. Chlorophyll? Why not—anything was possible. Water and possibly food. Things were beginning to look up.

They looked like bushes—and something was moving in them. Not the wind, there was scarcely any to speak of.

Living creatures? Animals of some kind? Edible or intelligent? I would settle for either or both. I strode out knee-deep in the sea towards the closest one. The water was very shallow and I might be able to reach it without swimming.

"Hello!" I called out. "Anyone there? I am a kind and peace-loving stranger from far away and mean you no harm. *Mi vidas vin. Diru min—parolas Esperanto?*"

The figure moved out of the shade, waved and called out.

"About time you showed up."

"Angelina!"

CHAPTER 11

I WAS PARALYZED BY JOY, petrified by pleasure. Standing stock-still, shouting her name aloud. Smiling foolishly while she waved and blew me a kiss.

Then she dived into the water, being far more practical than I was and not just standing there shouting and waving. A half-dozen strong strokes and she rose up out of the water beside me like a goddess from the sea. Damp and solid with her clothing dripping wet and in my arms. Laughing aloud with pleasure, kissing me with an excess of loving enthusiasm.

Forced to stop from lack of breath, still holding to each other, not wanting to be separated.

"You feel all right—feel great," I finally said. "You are all right, aren't you?"

"Couldn't be better, particularly now with you here. Bolivar and James—?"

"They're the same. We've all been working hard to find you. I won't lie to you and say we weren't worried. I'm sure that you can well imagine our feelings."

"I certainly can! But you got here so fast. It hasn't been much time at all. How long have I been away? It can't be more than two, maybe three days at the most. The days are so short here that it is hard to tell."

We started back to the beach. I shook my head. "You were here only a few days—from your point of view. I'm glad of that because that means that you didn't have much of a chance to really get worried. But we are beginning to find out that time seems to move at a different rate in each different universe. Different entropy rate, that's what Professor Coypu says."

"I don't understand—different rates? And different universes?"

"That is what this whole thing appears to be about. Slakey has found a way of moving between these universes. So while only a few days went by here for you—it has been well over a month that has gone by since you vanished. I'll tell you in great detail what fascinating things have gone on during that time, but first, please, what happened to you?"

She was no longer smiling. "I made a mistake, Jim, and I'm so sorry that I got everyone all worried and involved. I thought I could do this on my own. I really thought that the Heaven thing that the other girls believed in was all some kind of crooked scam. And I know all about crooks—and scams. Master Fanyimadu seemed such a greasy slimeball I never thought he would react like he did—or that he would be helped by his twin brother . . ."

"Wait, my love—please start again, and from the beginning I beg of you. Sit beside me in the sand, that's right, arms entwined. Big kiss or two, right. Now from the very beginning if you will. All I know about what happened is that message you left for me in my computer."

"I was pretty cocky when I recorded it. Rowena and all the other girls were so excited about seeing Heaven that, I, well, wanted to see for myself. It took a good deal of convincing—as well as a lot of money—to set up the trip. I didn't want go unarmed so I had my gun, a grenade or two, the normal items. I planned to take a look at Heaven—then find out what kind of con job Fanyimadu was playing. But it never got that far. We met him at the temple and he gave us a theological pep talk, then told us that it was time to go. He took us by the hands and Rowena and I were following him when there was some kind of movement, some kind of thing happening, I can't describe it."

"Neither can I. It's the going through or over or to a different universe."

"Then you'll know what I mean. But it ended suddenly and we were still in the temple when this stranger appeared, looked just like Fanyimadu, and was shouting some kind of warning and pointing at me. Well, you understand, I just worked by reflex then—"

"Reflex involved a certain amount of gunfire, some explosions, a little self-defense?"

"Of course, you know how it is. Rowena was screaming and fainting, I was knocked down, but I still did plenty of damage you will be happy to hear. Then, I don't know how it happened, we were here in this crystal world, the three of us. The two men and me. They ignored me; one of them seemed to be hurt and the other was bandaging him. I was just diving towards them when they were gone. Just like that. Bang. When I found myself alone I, well, just looked around."

"Was anyone else here?"

"No one that I could see. It was lonely of course, and I missed you, and it was sort of frightening and depressing at first. But that was easy enough to ignore once I started exploring. There was really nothing else that I could do. I followed that broken-glass path to the ocean—isn't this the most incredible place you have ever been! I drank the ocean water and it seemed all right. There is a kind of grass and some shrubs on the little islands. They bear tiny orange fruity things too—but they are poison. I found that out the hard way . . ."

"But—you're all right?"

"I am now. I was getting hungry so I sniffed the fruit, it seemed all right. That was when I took one little bite and was very sick for a very long time. So I just stayed there on the island and took it easy until I felt a little better. I was thinking about seeing what was on the bigger islands as soon as I had the strength. There is the ocean of water here, but no food. I was beginning to get a little worried—and that's when I heard you calling. Now tell me what is happening, what it all means."

A little worried! Any woman other than my Angelina would be a basket case left alone like this. I kissed her passionately which was very good.

"Things have been very busy since you vanished. The boys helped me, but we couldn't get the job done alone. So we called in the Special Corps and Inskipp sent in the troops. As well as Professor Coypu and an agent named Sybil who penetrated another fake church with still another Slakey. He seems to have multiplied himself over and over again. We had a plan to find the machine he uses but Sybil and I were caught before we even got started. We ended up in a place called Hell. It's Coypu's theory that each of these places is in a different universe. Heaven is one, and Hell and this Glass are others. Then we set up a plan and I managed to get into another one of Slakey's front operations, trying to lay my hands on one of the machines for the Professor to examine. It didn't quite work out as planned—which is how I ended up here."

"You have been busy. Now tell me more about this Hell place and your companion, what was her name? Sybil?"

I recognized that tone of voice and told her in greater detail about my visit to Hell. Sybil had only a brief mention and I think that I came out of it pretty well, certainly Hell had not been the time or the place for romance of any kind.

"Good," she finally said. "And the last time you saw the boys they were enjoying themselves with this female agent. How old is she—about their age, you think?"

There were daggers behind her words and I walked ever so carefully. Yes, would you believe it, exactly the same age as the boys. Mutual interests, nice to see. But it was even nicer to be with her here. Which led to some enthusiastic cuddling and no more talk of Sybil.

"Enough," she said finally, standing and brushing the sand off her clothes. "With James and Bolivar in good health and enjoying themselves, Inskipp in charge of the investigation and

Coypu busy inventing his brains out, we have no need to worry about any of them."

"Correct—we worry about ourselves. Only we don't worry. One can die of thirst in three days, but we have an ocean full of water so that's not going to happen."

"Yes—but you can also die of starvation in a month. And I'm beginning to get hungry." She pointed out at the larger islands. "There could be food out there. Why don't we take a look? I have had plenty of time to think about the situation here and I was going to do just that. Did you notice how all the crystal life-forms stay away from the shore?"

I hadn't—but I did now. "I'll bet you know why."

"I do. I made a simple experiment. Whatever the living crystals are, they are not glass. They dissolve in water. Not right at first, it takes awhile. Then they get sort of soft and swell up, and eventually melt completely."

"What happens when it rains?"

"It never does. Look—no clouds."

"And the water doesn't bother the other kinds of life here? I saw things swimming around in a rock pool."

"Some of the green growths extend roots or something into the water. Meaning they are a water-based life-form like we are . . ."

"And might very well be edible," I said with growing enthusiasm. "While we can't eat the glass creatures, we might find something we can nosh on the islands."

"My thinking exactly."

I rubbed my jaw and looked over at the sandy beach on the nearest island, no more than two hundred meters away. Beyond the beach there were green growths of some kind, much bigger than the shrubs that covered the small island that Angelina had explored.

"But we also have to think about leaving Glass," I said. "We should go back to that spot where I appeared. So Coypu can find us when he gets his machine working."

"He can only get it working after he invents it and builds it," she said with great practicality. "I suggest that we leave a message there telling him where we are. Then do a little exploring. If we are going to be here any length of time we are going to need food."

"My genius," I said, kissing her enthusiastically. "Rest and save your strength. I'll trot back and do just that."

While I trotted, then slowed down as the oxygen got me giggling, I considered a vital problem—how was I going to leave a message? By the time I reached the clearing I had the problem solved. My wallet was still in my pocket and was filled with unusable money and valueless credit cards. With my current name on each one.

In the clearing I used my shoes to kick and scrape clear a circle in the sand. In the middle of it I placed the wallet. Then, picking up the pieces of glass, with great delicacy using a fragment of shirttail, I constructed an arrow of colored fragments that pointed back down the path. With other pieces I spelled out the single word ISLANDS.

"Very artistic, Jim," I said, stepping back to admire my handiwork. "Very artistic indeed. When our rescuers arrive they will figure that out instantly."

I stepped over my announcement and went back to join Angelina. It was growing dark and she was sound asleep. It was warm and the sand was soft—and it had been a busy day. I sat beside her and must have fallen asleep as well, for the next I knew it was daylight and she was lightly patting my shoulder.

"Rise and shine, sleeping beauty badly in need of a shave. Rise and drink your fill from the ocean, then let's swim over and see if we can find some breakfast."

"Let me show you something," I said, removing the cloth bundle from my pocket. "Used my shirttail. Wrapped another piece of shirt around it to make a handle."

"You are so practical, my darling," she said, taking up the glass dagger and admiring it, then handing it back. "But won't it dissolve when you go into the water?"

"Not if I hold it over my head and swim with one arm."

"My husband, the athlete. Shall we go?"

It took her only a few strokes to reach the first, smaller island, where she waited patiently while I thrashed over to join her. When we started across to the other side she stopped and pointed.

"There," she said, "under that thing that looks like a cross between a sick octopus and a dead cactus. Those are the shrubs I told you about. The ones with the orange fruit. Pure poison."

"Let's see if we can find something better on that larger island."

It was a tiring swim for me but I did it without getting a drop of water on the blade. I emerged from the water panting and puffing and looked around.

"There may be other berries or fruits or such that aren't too obnoxious," I said. "That looks like a path over there."

"If there is a path—then something made it. And that something could be dangerous."

"Remember my trusty knife," I said, unwrapping it and brandishing it happily.

"In that case you may lead the way."

The path really was a path, trodden flat and turning and twisting through the strange growths. There were analogs of trees, shrubs and bushes, even a green groundcover halfway between grass and moss. But nothing was in any way familiar. Or looked in any way edible. It was Angelina who saw a possibility first.

"There," she said, parting the fronds of a feathery growth. "Those bluish bumps on the trunk."

The bumps had a nasty resemblance to blue carbuncles. I bent and prodded one with my fingernail; a thin skin split and blue juice oozed out.

"Possibly edible?" Angelina asked.

"Possibly," I said with deep suspicion. "And there is only one way to find out. It's my turn to be guinea pig."

I reached out gingerly and poked my finger into the juice. Brought it to my nose and sniffed.

"Yukk!" I said. "Even if it is edible it will come up even faster than it went down. Press on."

I wiped my finger in the soil until it was filthy but cleansed of the juice, then started warily down the path again. It wound around the larger growths but always continued in the same direction. Uphill and away from the shore.

"Wait," Angelina said. "Do you hear anything?"

I stopped and cocked an ear, then nodded. "A sort of booming sound, coming from up ahead."

"Jungle drums. Perhaps the natives are restless."

"We'll soon find out."

I tried to sound more cheerful than I felt. Stranded on an alien planet in an alien universe. No food to eat, unknown dangers to face. Most depressing. But at least I had Angelina again and that was incredibly cheering. I grabbed the mood swing as it went up and tried to hold onto the good feeling. I still walked slowly and silently with the knife probing out before me.

The booming was louder and the beat most irregular, slowing then quickening in an unpredictable manner. Well why not? We couldn't expect a big-band sound here. Now the larger growths were thinning out and I could see what appeared to be a clearing beyond the bole of the last, much larger, one. The path turned there and appeared to go on, skirting the clearing and not crossing it.

"Very suspicious," Angelina said. "Whatever creature made this path it appears that it didn't want to cross that clearing."

"It might be shy—or nocturnal or something like that."

"There also might be something in the clearing that it didn't want to get near. And that's where the sound is coming from."

We stopped behind the big, bulging growth that appeared to be covered with thick green hair; then cautiously looked out.

"Wow!" Angelina gasped.

Wow indeed. In the very center of the clearing was a single grayish, lumpy thing like a great pile of slumped mud. A long growth emerged from its summit and hung down almost to the ground. Growing on this, like fruit on a branch, were glistening red spheres.

"Fruit maybe," I said. "Possibly edible."

"Possibly dangerous," she said. "I don't like the way that

thing is out there alone—and the way the path circles around it."

I did not like it either. "Two choices then. We follow the path and stay away from the thing. Or we get closer and find out more about it."

"Knowing you, Jim diGriz, your mind is already made up. But I'm going with you."

"A deal—as long as you stay behind me."

When we stepped into the clearing the drumming sound stopped. It knew we were there. In a moment the sound started again, faster and not as loud as before. This continued as I walked slowly in its direction. Stopped and looked at it closely and shook my head. Indeed, I thought, it sure is ugly.

A wet orifice opened in the center of the bloated form and a deep and rasping voice spoke.

"*It . . . sure is ugly,*" it said.

CHAPTER 12

"IT CAN TALK!" ANGELINA SAID.

"Not only talk—but it can read minds too. That is just what I was thinking before it spoke."

"*I wonder if it can read my mind too . . .*" the thing said hoarsely.

Angelina stepped back. "That is what *I* was thinking. I don't like this thing, not at all. Let's get out of here."

"In a moment. I would still like to find out what those globes are."

I did find out—far faster than I really wanted to. With incredible speed the branch-like growth whipped towards me. Before I could jump back it wrapped around my neck and pulled me forward.

"Grrkk . . ." was all I could say as I sawed at the thing with the glass knife. Yellow ichor dripped from the wound; the thing was incredibly tough to cut and I was still being pulled forward.

"Hack it off!" Angelina shouted, seizing me around the waist and pulling back as hard as she could. It helped a bit, but I was still being pulled towards the opening that had emitted the voice.

It had stopped speaking now as the opening gaped wider and wider, moist and filled with sharp, dark ridges.

I sawed and choked. I couldn't see very well. I kept on sawing.

The opening was just in front of my face when I cut the last fibrous strand and fell backwards.

I was vaguely aware of Angelina dragging me along the ground away from the thing which was now booming out loudly and hoarsely.

"I wonder if . . . it sure . . . read my ugly . . ."

I sat up and rubbed my sore throat. "That was . . . too close."

"How do you feel?"

"Bruised—but all right." I looked down and realized that the knife and my right hand were covered with the thick and sticky liquid. And I was still clutching the severed end of the stalk, with a red globe attached to it, in my other hand.

"Let's go back to the ocean," I said, as hoarsely as our opponent who was still talking, feeding back a mixture of our thoughts to us. "I want to wash off this gunk—and see what this red thing is."

"I'll carry it," Angelina said. "Move—before this monster pulls itself out of the ground and comes after us."

She meant it as a jest, but I did walk that much faster. Back to the shore where I scrubbed and cleaned off the congealing liquid. Angelina was beside me dunking the globe into the water.

"Let me have the knife," she said. "It's my turn to try the local cuisine."

"The knife is getting soft."

"I'll be quick."

Before I could stop her she had sliced the thing open to reveal wet and even redder tissue inside. It looked uncomfortably like flesh. She cut off a sliver and sniffed it.

"Doesn't smell too bad."

"Don't!" I said, but I was too late. She had popped it into her mouth, chewed quickly—and swallowed it.

"Not too bad," she said. "Tastes sort of like a cross between seafood and candy."

"You shouldn't have done that . . ."

"Why not? Someone had to. And as I said—it was my turn to do the testing. And I still feel fine."

"Well, at least we know why the path went around the clearing, Ouch!" I had touched my sore neck. "We stay on the path from now on. You were right about that. That thing, it's like an angler fish."

"A what?"

"A fish that lives at pelagic depths in the ocean. It has sort of a fishing-pole organ growing out of the top of its head that dangles in front of its mouth—hence the name. It has a lump at the end that glows in the dark and attracts other fish. They snap at it—and get eaten."

"But why the mind-reading stunt?"

I sighed and shrugged. "Anyone's guess. It must work well on the local life forms—what are you doing?"

She had cut off another piece of the red globe and was chewing on it.

"Eating, of course. I still feel fine, and I am more than a little hungry."

I watched the shadows move and tried to estimate how much time had elapsed. Angelina looked at my face, then reached out and patted my hand.

"Poor Jim. You look so worried. I'm fine, but still hungry."

"Let me try some before you eat any more of it. Maybe it is a sex-specific poison."

"What a charming thought," she said and scowled fiercely.

"Sorry, shouldn't say things like that. This place must be getting me down." I cut, chewed and swallowed. "Not bad. But after we finish this fruit I'm not going back for a second try at that thing."

"Agreed. And you have noticed that it is getting dark again?"

"I have. I suggest we doze here until dawn and then press on along the path. Second the motion?"

"Absolutely."

When the sun woke us we were alive and well and hungry. We divided up the fruit and ate it all. Washed off the juice, yawned and stretched and looked at the path.

"Can I have the knife today?" Angelina asked. "So I can break trail."

"Gone," I said, pointing to a damp knife-shaped spot in the sand.

"I'll see if I can find a rock that will do."

She found one shaped not unlike a hand ax, traditional tool of mankind. I looked for another one, then put a few more rocks in my pockets. Angelina led the way since she was as strong and fit as I was, possibly with better reflexes. And I was not about to start discussing the equality of the sexes with her at any time.

With our stomachs full, our bodies rested, we made good time. And followed the path around the clearing. I stopped just long enough to throw a rock at the creature there; I had carried it all the way from the beach just for this moment. It thudded nicely and the tentacle thrashed violently.

"I wish . . . I had a power saw . . ." the thing said.

"Did you think that?" I asked.

"You better believe it."

We struggled up the last and steepest part of the path to the ridge at the top. And stopped.

"Quite a change," Angelina said.

All the green growth ended sharply. As though a line had been drawn along the summit. A bowl in the hills stretched out ahead of us. Completely devoid of life. Sand and rock and nothing more; an empty, barren desert.

"You said that it never rains on this planet?" I asked.

"Never."

"If it did that would also be a sloppy end for the glass lifeforms. It also means that the carbon and chlorophyll life can't get too far from the ocean. I'll bet they dip their roots into it or get dew from the air. So up here—no water, so no life."

"But the path goes on," she said, pointing.

"Interesting. So I guess that we do too."

We followed it as it twisted and turned between boulders as big as houses, on to a central flat desert of sand.

"What on earth is *that?"* Angelina asked. I could not think of an answer.

In the sand was a small pyramid apparently made of rock. It was seamless—but hollow. That was obvious because the top was broken off and we could see inside. It was empty. But what was most interesting was the slightly larger pyramid close by. Also with an opening in the top. And the next and the next. Stretching out in a straight line across the desert. Each one with an opening in the top, each larger than the one before.

"An alien enigma," I said brightly; Angelina just sniffed, not considering this worth an answer. We left the path and walked along the line of pyramids. There were over thirty of them, the final one taller than we were.

"The last one," Angelina said, pointing. "The top. It comes to a point—and it is solid. Any explanations?"

For a rare moment I was silent.

"Shall I tell you what is happening?" she said.

"Speak, I beg of you."

"This has obviously been constructed by a silicon life form. It digests sand and excretes rock, thus building a pyramid around itself. When it grows too big for the pyramid it cracks out, moves along and builds another one."

"Highly interesting," I said, dazed by her logic. "But how did it get to build the first one in the first place—and how does it build a pyramid from the inside?"

"You can't expect me to know everything," she said, with impeccable logic. "Let's get back to the path."

"Let's not quite yet," I said pointing. "Isn't that something following the path and moving towards us?"

"Some things not a thing."

"You're right. Any reason we shouldn't stay out of sight until we see what they are?"

She nodded and we stepped into the shadow of the largest pyramid where we might see and possibly not be seen. Angelina cocked her head, then pressed her ear to the side of the pyramid. "Listen," she said. "Isn't there a kind of crunching sound coming from inside?"

"Please, not now. Possibly later. One alien mystery at a time if you don't mind."

The marching file of creatures was surely mystery enough. There were eleven of them and they were roughly man-size. But the resemblance ended right there. A fringe of legs or tentacles or something twitched quickly against the ground and carried each creature along. These moving parts supported a solid trunk the color and texture of tree bark—it could be a tree trunk for all we knew. A single stalk, very much like the one on the creature that had tried to eat me, emerged from the top of the trunk with what looked like a bulbous eye at the end. The eyes bobbed and looked about, apparently not seeing us pyramid-lurking in the shadow.

They shuffled by in silence, stirring up a quickly settling cloud of dust, climbed over the rim and vanished down the ridge on the other side.

"Now will you listen to the pyramid?" Angelina asked.

"Yes, of course, sure." I listened and perhaps I did hear a distant crunching. "I can hear something . . ."

"They're coming back," she said.

And so they were. Whether it was the same bunch or a different lot it was of course impossible to tell. Different ones, surely, because in the brief time they had been out of sight they had changed completely. The ribbed trunks had become globe-shaped and transparent, expanded from within so the ribbing now formed irregular stripes on the surface.

"They're filled with water," Angelina said, and I nodded dumb agreement.

"Possibly, possibly," I muttered.

"They march out of the desert and fill with water from a spring or from the ocean. Then march back with it. Why?"

"There is only way to find out—follow them."

Perhaps it was not wise. Possibly dangerous. But there were too many curious and unsolvable puzzles on this planet. We both had the desire to see if we might possibly solve at least one of these. When they were out of sight we followed them down the path.

Nor did we have far to go. The path led to a row of large boulders and vanished between two of them.

"Suspicious," I said. "Those rocks have been placed there."

"It could be a natural formation."

"It could, but the problem is the same. Do we stay out—or go in to investigate. And you will recall what happened the last time I got nosy . . ."

"Behind you!"

I took one look and jumped aside. Another string of water-carriers was approaching—and they were almost upon us. We stood by the path tense and ready to fight.

And while they were aware of us, our presence was completely ignored. The string shuffled on by in silence, each eye focusing on us in turn as they passed.

"They don't seem too interested in us," I said.

"Well I'm interested in them. Let's go."

We did. Slipping between the large boulders, then following the path between a second row to walk inside a circular, rock-girt area. Where we stopped—and did our best not to gape and bulge our eyes as though we had a joint IQ about that of body temperature.

It was so alien that it was hard to make out just what was happening here. One thing at least was certain—we knew where the water was going. The creatures we had been following wandered through a green labyrinth spraying water and shrinking their bodies at the same time. When this was finished, one walked away from the growth, then another and another. They milled about in a little group until, with sudden decision—or obeying some unseen signal—a line formed and they shuffled through the exit and were gone.

We walked closer to the confused growth, stopped when we saw movement under the broad, leaflike structures. In the semi-darkness, spiderlike creatures were climbing about, apparently tending the growth. Fragments of green fell down to the ground where other creatures cleaned them up. Another dropped down on the end of a cord or tentacle clutching something red.

"Very much like that fruit you got your neck squeezed for," Angelina said.

"Could be, could be—and look where it's going."

A tall opening in the rock led to some kind of cavern beyond. I bent to try and look inside when there was a light pulling at my leg, a feathery touch.

"What is that?" Angelina asked.

As always on this world there was no easy answer. It was like a soft bundle of sticks, or a complex insect made of twigs. Whatever it was it was plucking at my trouser leg. Then it stopped and shuffled towards the cave. Stopped and waited. Then returned and rustled the fabric once again.

"It's trying to communicate," I said. "I think it wants me to follow it. Well—why not?"

"No arguments. We've come this far."

When we started forward it scurried ahead. Stopped and waited, then moved ahead again. Sunshine filtered through the mouth of the cave, more than enough to see the sprouting creature that sprawled inside.

That was the only way to describe it. It was covered with complex structures that were apparently growing from its green hide. Some I recognized; there was the top half of a water carrier. Another was a bristle of growths bundled together like our guide. And there were others that were totally incomprehensible. Then one of the working creatures hurried by with a red globe which it dropped into an opening in the thing's side.

"It's looking at us," Angelina said, pointing. A group of whip-like tentacles, each ending in a bulging eye, had turned towards us.

"Hello," I said.

"Hello," it boomed out in return.

CHAPTER 13

"TALKING—OR MIMICKING?" ANGELINA SAID.

"Talking—talking—talking."

Which wasn't much of an answer. The eye-stalks still swayed in our direction—as did another organ or mushrooming growth that started to form under the eyes. It began as a swelling, then opened up into a sort of trumpet-shaped flower. This moved back and forth as though searching for something, then turned and pointed directly at me. I stepped back—

Color, sound, movement, terror.

Pain and red sounds, sharp memories.

A scream . . . a shout . . .

Then it ended and I realized that the person shouting was me. Hands on my arms, I blinked my eyes clear, saw that Angelina was holding on to me.

"What happened?" she asked.

"I . . . don't know. What did you see?"

"You closed your eyes and, well, just dropped to the ground. Then you just sort of scrunched up, shouting and twisting. It only lasted a moment."

"That thing," I said, my breathing rough. "It was in my brain, trying to communicate or something. Big and strong—"

"Did it try to hurt you?"

"Not at all, quite the opposite. There was curiosity there but I had no sensation of threat or menace. Whatever it wanted it, well, didn't find. It just pulled out. Perhaps I'm not in its intellectual league."

While I was talking the flower growth closed and disappeared. Next to it the water-carrier that had been growing larger stopped and began a sort of twisting motion. Then, with a plopping sound, it pulled free of the surface. Jumped to the ground and hurried away.

"It's the queen thing," Angelina said. "Growing parts of the colony."

"Or maybe it is the colony."

After that one attempt to communicate the creature never tried again. The eyes were withdrawn as though it had lost all interest. But it knew we were there because one of the leg creatures came hurrying into the cave with two of the red fruit we had seen growing outside. It plopped one into an opening in the giant creature's hide—then dropped the other one in front of us before rushing outside again.

"Thanks, Queenie," I said. "Very kind of you. Is it chow time? Looks like the one we ate before—and our friend here just ate one. Shall we give it a try?" I squatted down to look more closely at it. I prodded it with my finger and it split open. I licked the juice from my hand. "Tastes very much like the other one we had to fight for."

"Why not? If that murderous thing in the clearing is offering tempting goodies I suppose they must be edible. Give me a piece, if you please."

We finished it between us. Then, feeling very much ignored, we went back out of the cave into the alien garden.

"What about another one?" I asked.

"You're on."

None of the scurrying creatures came near us—nor took any notice when I reached up high and plucked another red fruit. We sat comfortably against the rock wall and ate it. It was very pulpy and liquid, food and drink at the same time.

"Now what?" Angelina asked, licking the last drop of juice from her fingers.

"A good question. And I suggest that we sleep on it."

"One of us at a time though. I still don't trust this queen-of-the-hive creature."

"Then we'll get out of here, find a secluded spot away from the path. We can always come back when we get hungry."

Angelina yawned gracefully. "You are on, husband mine. It certainly has been a long day."

We did this for two of the short days and nights. Sleeping, then going back for more fruit, mulling over our options, very limited indeed, and trying to figure out just what we should do next. With great effort at cogitation, we managed to never reach any important conclusions. Then we would sleep and start the whole process over again. On the third daylet Angelina came up with an observation that finally forced us to make a decision. She had been on this exotic world longer than I had—and had gone much longer without a decent meal.

"You are losing weight, Jim. And so am I." Which was true, but I just did not want to mention it to her. "The fruit is filling all right—but do you notice how quickly you get hungry again after eating?"

"I have been thinking about it, wondering really."

"Stop wondering. Water is water, hydrogen and oxygen. Since we don't get thirsty we must have been getting enough to drink from the fruit. But the food is a different matter. Who knows what kind of elements and molecules make up this fruit. I don't think we are ingesting any nourishment at all. If we stay here and keep on eating this stuff—we are just going to curl up and die of starvation in the end."

I sighed unhappily. "I'm forced to agree. The idea was tickling at my brain but I thought I was being stupid. It's been sort of fun here in a completely alien way. Back to Glass land?"

"Nothing else to do. And you have strange tastes if you think our stay here was fun. I say back to civilization and some good food and a hot bath. Let's head for that clearing where we arrived. We'll see if anyone has found your message yet."

I waved as we left. "Bye. Thanks for the hospitality." Of course there was no response. We went down the hill, skirted the killer angler, and swam back to the mainland.

"Onward—to the glass forest," I said, trying to be as cheerful as I could. "Coypu will have the machine analyzed by now and will quickly build one of his own. Which he will then use to track us down and rescue us. We'll be settling down to a steak dinner before you know it."

After three more of the local days had gone by I wanted to eat those words—since there was nothing else to eat on this world of Glass. My wallet was just where I had left it, my glass arrow and message undisturbed. I ground the crystal fragments to smithereens, growling darkly.

After that—it was just waiting. The crystal glade in the forest remained empty. No one came, nothing happened at all. We stayed there, making only the briefest of forays back to the ocean to drink. Time dragged by so sluggishly that we felt we were making about the same progress as the crystalline carnivore. It was catching up on its fleeing prey, but so slowly, slowly. Another night fell and was followed by another sunny day. And another. I took a second notch in my belt and tried to ignore the growing thinness of Angelina's face. By the fifth day I began to worry.

"There must be something else we can do," I complained.

"I don't see what. You're the one who told me that all we had to do was wait. You must be patient."

"I'm not!"

"You never were. But you must make the effort or you will worry yourself into an ulcer."

"I would rather drink myself into an ulcer!" The thought of strong spirits and cold beer got my spittle flowing. I spat into the forest and watched a stem of grass dissolve. Good thing it never rained here.

I awoke with the sun on the morning of our sixth day of waiting, watching its green-striped disk shining through the multicolored foliage. It was no longer exciting to look at, nor did I wonder anymore what made the stripes. Angelina was pale and drawn, moaning under her breath as she slept. I didn't want to wake her; sleep was our only escape from hunger. And the endless waiting. I walked down the path a bit and looked out over the ocean. The waves surged turgidly against the cliffs; nothing else moved. Depression struggled onto the back of depression. I sighed mightily and went back to the clearing.

When Angelina did wake up we talked a bit. I was thirsty but she wasn't, so I walked down to the beach to drink. There was nothing that we could carry water in. Therefore we took turns drinking so that someone would always be in the clearing. Waiting.

The walk was tiring—but it had to be done. I drank my fill, then a little more. Filling the stomach helped for awhile with the hunger. The walk back, uphill part of the way, was particularly exhausting. And I had to walk slowly or I would have an oxygen jag.

"Home is the drinker, home from the sea!" I called out. A feeble attempt at humor. "Hello!"

Maybe she was asleep again. I shut up but walked faster.

Stopped. Frozen.

The cleared area was empty.

"Angelina!"

This was the blackest of blackest moments that I had ever experienced. If Coypu had his machine working—he could have saved her. That had to be it. Coypu had done this, not Slakey. Could that be it? But Coypu was an unknown. If the marines had grabbed a machine, and if it were intact, and if Coypu had built a machine. . . . An awful lot of ifs. But Slakey had plenty of machines and knew that we were here. He could have returned and seized Angelina and left me here to starve quietly. Was it Slakey who got here first and grabbed her off this world?

"Who did this? Where are you?"

I shouted aloud, brimming over with frustration and anger. And fear. It must be Coypu. It had to be him.

I hoped.

But if it had been him why had he taken just Angelina and

left me here? There should have been a message, at least a message. I frantically kicked about among the broken crystal. No note, no traces of anything.

For a very, very long time nothing happened. I was giggling with fear. Too much oxygen. Slow down, Jim, take it easy. I sat in the cleared area where we slept and breathed more slowly. With one last snicker the laughter died. Depression took over.

The days on Glass were short—but this was the longest one I had ever lived through. It was growing dark and I must have nodded off with my head slumped on my chest. Fear, worry, hunger, everything. Too much, far more than too much.

"Dad—over here!" Bolivar said. I blinked my eyelids, still half asleep, dreaming.

"Are you all right? We have to move fast."

No dream! I set a new record for the broken glass sprint. Slammed into him and almost knocked him from his feet. We were falling—

—backward into a brightly lit hotel room, onto a soft, carpeted floor. I just lay there, looking up at Professor Coypu seated before a great mass of breadboarded electronics.

And Angelina smiling down on me.

"I hope they gave you something nice to eat," I said, inanely, still not believing that it was all over and she was all right. She knelt and took my hands in hers.

"Sorry it took so long. The professor says that he has trouble aligning the machine."

"Calibration errors, cumulative, entropy slippage," Coypu said. "Gets better each time though."

"Something to eat, Dad," Bolivar said, helping me to my feet and handing me a giant roast meat sandwich. Saliva sported as I growled and tore off an immense bite, chewed; paradisical. I took the proffered beer bottle by the neck and drank and drank until the back of my nose hurt from the cold.

"Here, sit at the table," Angelina said, pulling out a chair. "And don't eat so fast or you'll make yourself sick—"

"Warfle?" I said.

"—and don't talk with your mouth full. Eat slowly, that's better, while I tell you what happened. It was Bolivar who came for me. No time to wait, he said. The alignment was difficult—just seconds. I held back but he grabbed me and that was that. It took so long to get through to you again, I knew what you were feeling. But it is all all right now. We are all together this time. The end of worrying."

"The beginning of a lot of big worrying for some of us," Inskipp snarled in his friendly and ingratiating way as he walked into the room. He dropped into a chair and glared menacingly. "All right for you people to relax and cheer each other up with stories of your strange adventures. You forget that the rest of us are weighed down with responsibilities. Since this whole mess began we have been behind the eight ball, stuck in the mud, up the creek paddleless and getting nowhere as fast as a turgid turtle."

Instead of pointing out the tangled syntax of his mixed metaphor I reached for another sandwich. Priorities exist. He chuntered on.

"We have been tottering from calamity to calamity, our hand forced at every turn. Not one of the Slakeys has been apprehended. As soon as we close in on one of them another pops up and whips him away. All of our efforts so far have been spent in getting you out of trouble, diGriz. And the costs keep growing. I imagine it was your smart idea to rent this entire hotel, the Vaska Hulja Holiday Heaven, as center of this operation. Do you know how many millions of credits it has cost so far?"

"More than the gross annual income of a rich planet—I hope!" I belched rotundly. "Sorry. Ate too fast. Another beer? Thanks, James. And every credit well spent, Inskipp, you old skinflint. Rockets have roared, Space Marines have exercised furiously, news broadcasters have been working overtime, the galaxy is an exciting place and zillions of happy citizens have been entertained delightfully. You should bless me as a galactic asset instead of whining about your overdraft. Nothing but good has come out of this operation."

He turned bright red and bulged his eyes, opened his mouth. But Angelina spoke first.

"You are both right and wrong, Jim. It looks like Slakey has been put out of business. The search is still on, but it has been a long time since the detectors found any trace of him—on any civilized planet that we have contacted. The search is now spreading to every recorded world, as our great leader, H. P. Inskipp has kindly pointed out."

She smiled but Inskipp was immune to the kind word and the gentle touch. "I'm going to pull the plug and cut our losses," he said. I was suddenly very angry.

"No you are not, you monetarial moron! All of the civilized planets pay large sums to keep the Special Corps in business—and they never ask you for any kind of accounting. We are now faced with one of the biggest threats that mankind has ever faced—and you want to cut and run."

"What threat? What can one man do that can threaten a thousand worlds?"

"Think!" I said, grabbing up another beer to hold down the sandwiches. "Professor Justin Slakey may have started out as a top scientist and a genius. But this popping back and forth between universes has not only addled his mutual brains but in some way has multiplied his numbers. Do you want these madmen to go on multiplying and causing more and more trouble? We know he has sent people to Hell to provide lunch for his insane personification there. At the very least Slakey is a mass-murderer. Who will go on committing murder and who knows what other forms of insane evil until he is stopped. And more than that . . ."

I really had their attention now. All eyes were on me, all mouths mute as I raised the bottle and drank in dramatic silence. Then raised a hortatory finger.

"Much *much* more than that. Look at all the lengths he went to, all the churches and organizations he created. All the masses of money he has collected. And why did he do all this? For the money, that's obvious. The sums involved are staggering. So ask yourself—what does he want the money for?

"What are his plans?

"Anyone who thinks they are for the mutual benefit of mankind may leave the room. All who stay will have the pleasure of hearing how we can find Slakey and stop him.

"Now—would you like to know how that can be done?"

CHAPTER 14

"OF COURSE WE WANT TO hear your plan, darling." Angelina said, then leaned over and kissed my cheek. "My husband the genius."

Facetious or not it was heartwarming. Bolivar and James were giving me cheerful thumbs-up signs, Sybil did the same and even Coypu was nodding in reluctant agreement. The only glum one was Inskipp, still counting his mounting debts. I rapped on the table with my beer bottle.

"I hereby declare this meeting of the Galactic Salvation League to be open. Who is taking the minutes?"

"My recorder is running," Sybil said, sitting down and putting it on the table before her. "Welcome home, Jim diGriz. You had us all very worried."

"I had myself very worried. What Slakey did to you and me in Hell—or to Angelina and me on Glass—is reason enough to pursue him to the edges of the galaxy and put him out of business. But we have more reason to go after all the hims other than simple vindictiveness."

Inskipp sneered lightly. "And just what is that?"

"I never thought that you would ask. I notice that while I

was away you managed to lose track of him completely. Is that correct?"

"Loosely speaking, why possibly, yes."

"Speaking very tightly I would say that now is the time for a plan that cannot miss. Professor—how goes your universe machine?"

"Very well, thank you. The little matter of calibration will soon be licked."

"I'm cheered to hear that. How many universes do you have access to?"

He clattered his fingernails against his teeth, forehead furrowed in thought. "Theoretically of course the number is infinite. Perhaps we even create these universes when we enter them, as you suggested when you came back from Hell. But, as of this moment, we have investigated or entered a little over forty-one."

"Is one of them Heaven?"

"No—but we are still looking. While the machine we captured has settings for different destinations I have no way of identifying them without activation and entry."

"What about Hell?"

"We very definitely can go to Hell. You will remember that your son James hypnotized a Slakey and made him send Bolivar there to find you."

"Well that's it, then." I sat back and sighed with satisfaction. "I could do with just a bit more to eat, if the sandwiches aren't all gone."

"Stop toying with us, Jim diGriz, or you'll get more than a sandwich in your gob!" Angelina suggested.

"Sorry, my love. I don't mean to make light of the situation. But it has been pretty grim of late and I was indulging myself."

"You're forgiven. What's so important about Hell?"

"Slakey is there. In his red, fat, insane, well-armed condition. Don't you think that if the other Slakeys could get him out of there—that they would? But they don't. Probably because it would certainly kill him, that's what Slakey on Glass told me. So we launch a little expedition to find him. And talk to him. An expedition in force because what one Slakey knows they all know. They won't kill him—that would be too much like committing suicide. But they will have no compunction about polishing the rest of us off when we try to talk to him. But if we get there fast, maybe use a bit of hypnotism on him, ask a question or two, right, James?"

"A piece of cake, Dad."

"We will then ask him to answer two incredibly important questions. Where is Heaven—and what is the overall plan? It is imperative that we find out what the snakey Slakeys want all the money for."

"Do it," Inskipp said, a man who always makes his mind up quickly. "What are you going to need for this job?"

It was a good plan, and a tight one. As soon as Slakey found out what we were up to he would react. Violently. And he was well ahead of us technically. Coypu still had not found a means of getting any operable machines into another universe. But Slakey in Hell had a working gauss rifle. I just hoped that there wasn't any more universally transportable weaponry in Slakey's hands.

Our advantage would have to be speed of attack. And numbers.

But our primary hit team had to be small so it could move fast. I would go because the whole thing was my idea. Then James had to be with me since he had to hypnotize the old red devil. And Angelina of course, she would not let me go alone. And of course Bolivar, who naturally would not permit a family outing without being present himself. We would go in fast and hit hard.

But our flank would be protected by two hundred very mean and obnoxious Combat Marines. They would be armed only with their hands and feet and combative know-how. Which should be enough. They would be guided by Sybil, who certainly knew her away around Hell. Also, I had caught a number of dark looks from Angelina whenever she saw me talking to the female agent. Which meant that life would be a lot smoother if Sybil led the troopers.

My old companion, Marine Captain Grissle, would be in charge of the troops and I received a message that he urgently wanted to see me. I sent for him.

"No guns?" he asked as he stamped through the door. "A marine is not a marine without a weapon."

"Unarmed combat, they're supposed to know all about that kind of thing."

"They do. But they would do better with a grenade or two."

"They would fuse into lumps and would not go off. I couldn't even open the blades on my pocketknife in Glass."

"Bayonets?"

"They will get stuck in their scabbards. And don't say leave the scabbards behind. I do not relish the thought of two hundred marines popping through into Hell and falling all over each other with naked bayonets in their hands. But, yes, I have thought about it and think that something can be done. We will all be carrying weapons."

"What?"

"I will work out the details and you will see just before we leave. Dismissed."

It took a few days to make all the preparations, which gave us a useful breathing period. Angelina had had a chance to put some weight back on, four good meals a day helped, and we were all raring to go. Coypu had been fiddling with his equations and his circuits and had built a superior model of his dimensional doorway.

"Basically its just a matter of power," he explained. "Slakey had to conceal his machines, keep them small and out of sight. We have no such restrictions."

The new machine was most impressive. At great expense he had tapped directly into the planetwide and international electrical grid. A large, red, insulated cable, over a meter in diameter, led into the main ballroom of the hotel, now converted into an electronic jungle. In the middle of the dance floor was a full-sized garage door mounted in a frame. I admired it—from the front only of course. Since it had no back. That is if you walked around it you couldn't see it or it wasn't there or something. But it looked sound and solid from the front.

"Take a peek and see what we have got," Coypu said, making some adjustments on his operating console. I turned the garage-door handle and opened the door a crack—then slammed it when the air began to whistle through.

"All black—with stars. And lower pressure. That's not Hell."

"But I'm very close, that's the adjoining one. Try it now."

A red sun burned down from the red sky. I sneezed when a whiff of hydrogen sulfide drifted out. "That's it," I said closing the door again. "Shall I call in the troops?"

"I'm ready when you are."

They were all waiting expectantly for the signal. Sybil and Angelina were the first to get there. Moments later the tramp of marching feet heralded the arrival of the marines. They stamped in, marched in position, faced front and thundered to a halt.

"Great," I said. "Stand them at ease and be prepared for issue of weapons."

"Weapons!" Captain Grissle's great jaw cracked into a unaccustomed smile.

"There!" I said as James and Bolivar drove in with the laden freight wagons. I opened one of the boxes and pulled out a bloated red form and waved it on high.

"A *salami* . . ." Grissle gasped.

"Very observant," I said. "A both deadly and edible weapon. Issue them to your men."

"You're not playing the fool again, are you?" Angelina said as she and Sybil looked on dubiously.

"Never, my love. This is a very serious decision and one that was worked out with impeccable logic. Instead of fighting with the inhabitants of Hell, we feed them. If they have been resorting to cannibalism, a redolent salami will make Hell a paradise for them. However, since most of them are a little insane we must expect trouble. Then, in any emergency, you will discover that a ten-kilo salami can wreak fearful damage. And if we overstay our leave we can always eat them ourselves."

The marines were issued one salami each. "And no nibbling," I warned. Sybil and the twins took theirs, but the look in Angelina's eyes warned me not to even wave one in her direction. I took mine and held it aloft.

"Are we ready, Professor?"

"Locked on."

"Then here we go!" I shouted, throwing open the garage door to Hell and pointing my salami. "Attack!"

It was a lovely sight. With their salamis at slope arms and in perfect step, the marines charged straight into Hell behind Sybil. My family followed.

As instructed, the marines had spread out in a long skirmish line. Sybil waved her salami and indicated the direction for them to take. Away from the lava lake and towards the foothills.

"This is a terrible place," Angelina said. The ground trembled as flame and smoke shot from a distant volcano.

"We'll get out as fast as we can. But it has to be done."

"Some trouble over there," Bolivar said. One of the marines had been ambushed by two of the locals who had leaped out of hiding and tackled him. He swung his salami with trained skill and bowled them both over. This broke the salami in two which must have released a deliciously garlicky smell that brought instant attention from the sprawled men. They scrambled in the sand, the marine forgotten, seized up their booty and fled.

"Well done," Angelina said, lifting her face and giving me a quick kiss on the cheek.

"Man down!" the captain shouted. "Take cover."

"Let's go," I shouted and led the rush.

Everything went according to plan; red Slakey would be easier to capture with so many marines involved in stalking him. It would be faster too.

Two of the marines carried their wounded comrade by.

"Flesh wound," one of them called out.

"Back through the door, the hotel doctor is waiting," I called after them.

We slowed to a walk, panting and perspiring. By the time we reached the scene the marines had done their job and Slakey had been captured and disarmed. He was being held fast by two of the largest marines. Bolivar and James grabbed the prisoner while the marines fanned out in a wide circular formation around us.

"We meet again, Professor Slakey," I said. He foamed a little and writhed in the twins' unbreakable grip but did not speak. I grabbed his arm so James could do his hypnotizing. Which, unhappily, did not seem to be working.

"I can't get his attention, sorry," James said. "I've never worked with anyone in this insane state before."

"Let me try," I said, breaking off a great chunk of salami and holding it close to the prisoner's nose. He stopped struggling and gaped; his nostrils twitched. Then he snapped at it and his teeth clacked together when I jerked it back. I handed the redolent salami to James.

"You've got his attention now."

"You're hungry," James said, "hungry and sleepy. Bite, eat, chew, that's it. Swallow, good man. Want more, nod, that's it."

"Quiet!" a dark-suited Professor Slakey said, running up the hill towards us. An attacking marine swung a powerful salami and felled him. He rolled down the hill and vanished from sight.

It was a good thing we had brought so many marines. One Slakey after another appeared—until at one point there were twelve attacking at the same time. The important thing was that they were all unarmed; apparently they had made only the single gun for Hell and we had caught them unprepared. Try as they might they never made it through the perimeter of muscular guardians. One of the Slakeys appeared almost on top of us, reaching for the now silent devilish form, but Angelina caught him and twisted and hurled him back down the hill.

Then the attack was over as swiftly as it had begun. Our prisoner was now sitting on the ground happily chewing his rations.

"They've stopped," I called out. "But stay alert—it could be a ruse—be ready for anything."

"They won't be back," James said around a chewy mouthful. "What one knows they all know. So they all know now that the prisoner let me down on the Slakey motivation for this entire thing. His brain is so addled that he had no idea of what I was talking about or what all that money is needed for. But he remembers Heaven, clearly, knows its importance. Once I had the information, the code sequence, the other Slakeys stopped the attack."

"You've memorized it?"

"Better than that." He held up the remaining half of his salami. "I scratched it on this with my fingernail."

CHAPTER 15

I WORKED OUT IN THE hotel's health club every day. The first day I was exhausted after an hour, the aftereffects of starvation on Glass saw to that. But the trainer sweated with me full time; weights, bike, hydrotherapy, 2G sprints and all the rest. It wasn't too long before I was able to put in a five-hour day and I was feeling fit and perky. My morale was also cheered on by the fact that I had put all of my lost weight back on as muscle. The layer of fat on my love handles, product of all dissolute and boozing living on Lussuoso no doubt, was gone. I jogged and I swam and realized I could no longer put off the moment of truth. Because I was sure that Angelina would not like it.

"I don't like it," she said very affirmatively. "No."

"My love—light of my life," I said clutching her hands in mine. The bar was empty and only the robot bartender was observing this digital act of passion. With a lithe twist she slipped her hands free, picked up her glass and sipped. I tried logic.

"If you look at the question from all sides you will see that this is the only possible answer."

"I can think of a lot more possibilities."

"But none that will work. We need to know what is happening in Heaven. The more people that go bumbling around there, the more chance there is of someone being spotted. One person must go in alone. One super-agent of superlative talent and experience, a lone wolf, he who slinks by night, lithe, handsome, unbeatable—the galaxy's best agent. And I can give you a hint about his name. Some call him 'Stalowy Szczur,' others 'Ratinox,' and even 'Rustimuna Stalrato'—"

"You?"

"How nice of you to say so! Now that you have spoken the truth aloud—can you think of anyone who is better qualified?"

She frowned and sipped her drink in silence, with perhaps the slightest gurgle from her straw when the last drop vanished. Stirred to life by this sound, the barbot whistled its wheels along the rails behind the bar and juddered to a stop. It spoke in a deep and sensual voice. "Does madam require a refill of her delicious drink, a Pink Rocket-popsy?"

"Why not?" A metal tentacle snaked out, curled around the stem of the glass and zipped it away out of sight. A door in the thing's chest opened and a new chilled glass appeared, brimming with drink.

"And for Sire? Drinkey?"

I was in training and not ready to get smashed to the eyeballs on booze. "Diet-whiskey with a slice of fruit."

"I can't argue with that," she finally said. "You are the best agent that Inskipp has. You know it and I can't deny it. Mostly because you are not an effete trainee new to the job, or a do-gooder officer of the law. Instead, you are basically a bent and twisted crook with a lifetime of experience in crime."

"You make it sound so good."

"I should know. But that still doesn't mean you go to Heaven alone. I'll go with you."

"No, you will not. You will keep the homefires burning, guard my back and . . ."

"One more word of that male chauvinist pig dreck and I will claw your eyes out."

When she used that tone of voice she meant it. I leaned back when I saw her fingers arch.

"I apologize, I'm sorry, I didn't mean it. Misplaced attempt at levity. I grovel at your feet," I said, dropping to the floor and doing a nice grovel and writhe.

She had to laugh and the air was cleared and I took her hands in mine again. "I have to go, and I have to go alone."

She sighed. "I know that, although I hate to admit it. But you will take care of yourself?"

"A promise—that I will keep."

"When do you leave?"

"I'll find out this afternoon. Our dear friend Coypu thinks he has finally licked the communication problem between us and the next universe."

"I thought he said that it was impossible."

"That was on a bad day. Today is a good one."

"I'll go with you."

The professor had tidied up all the breadboarded devices and looping wires that had made up his machine. Everything had now been integrated into a hulking black console that was all readouts and twinkling lights, tesla coils and glowing screen. Only the giant electrical cable was the same.

"Ah, James," he said when we came in, turned and rattled through a file drawer. "I have something for you."

He proudly produced a featureless flat black disk with a hole in the middle, dusted it off and passed it over.

"A music recording?" I asked, puzzled.

"You must not act like you have the intelligence level of plant life," he miffed. "What you are holding is a singularly remarkable invention. It is solid-state, has no moving parts, and even the electrons are pseudo-electrons, so they move at zero speed. It is impossible to detect it or affect it in any way. I've tried it in a number of universes and it works fine."

"What does it do?"

"When activated it signals the mother machine here. Which reaches out and brings you back. Simple."

"It certainly is. But how do I activate it?"

"Even simpler. It detects brain waves. You think at it and it takes you home."

I stared at the disk with admiration. What a wonder. I

spun it on my finger. All I had to do was to think *"Take me home . . ."*

Then I was across the room and slammed up tight against the machine, my hand held to its surface by the disk, my finger through the hole feeling as though it had been amputated.

"Can't . . . breathe . . ." I choked out.

Coypu hit a switch and I dropped to the floor. "A few little adjustments will take care of that."

I stood up, rubbing my sore ribs, still clutching the disk as I pulled my swollen finger out of the hole.

"Very impressive, " Angelina said. "Thank you, Professor. I'll have less to worry about now. When does he leave?"

"Whenever he wants to." He threw another switch and bolts of lightning coruscated deep inside the machine and the tesla coil snapped out loud sparks. "But there are a few other factors that must be considered before he departs. I managed to poke the tip of a universal analyzer through into Heaven. Some very interesting results. See." A screen lit up filled with rolling numbers and wiggling graphs.

"See what?" I said. "Makes no sense to me."

Coypu snorted with disgust and sneered with superiority. In that order. Then tapped the screen of the spectral gas analyzer. "It is obvious."

"Only to a genius like you, Professor. Explain, please."

I was sorry I asked. He explained at great and boring length. Gravity, air pressure, oxygen tension, speed of light, all that was okay. But there was too much more of electron spin, chaos dispersion, water quality, sewage disposal, fractal fracture and such. When he got on to analysis of atmospheric components I stopped him.

"What was that you said about some kind of gas?"

He pointed to the analysis bar on the screen. "This. A compound I have never seen before, so it has no name. I call it nitox-cubed. Because it acts somewhat like nitrous oxide."

"Laughing gas?"

"Correct. But with the pleasure factor cubed. So everyone goes around half-stoned. Then, if they leave Heaven, they get withdrawal symptoms, as is noted in the interviews in the record."

"I don't like that," Angelina said. "Could be habit-forming and Jim has enough bad habits right now. Can you do anything about it?"

"Of course." He held up a vial of purple liquid. "This will cancel the effects, an antidote. Roll up your sleeve, diGriz."

He filled a subdermal injector and gave my arm a spritz, blasting the antidote through my skin and right into my bloodstream.

"This is the only precaution you need take. Are you ready to go now?" He pressed a button and power surged through the machine.

"No rush!" I said, suddenly feeling rushed. "I need a good meal and a night's sleep first. We'll do it tomorrow morning, nice and early, at the crack of dawn. I will be off to Heaven."

We went out on the town that night, savoring the pleasures of this holiday world for the first time. Angelina and I held hands while Sybil had each of the lads by the arm and it was a great evening. The sound and light display was something else again, with an aurora borealis in the sky above and a two-thousand-piece orchestra in the pit below. Food, the best. Drink, better. Except for me; with morning getting ever closer I stuck to the diet-whiskey.

At dawn, leaving Angelina smiling in her sleep, I tiptoed out of the bedroom and headed for my appointment with destiny.

"You're late," Coypu said belligerently. "Getting cold feet?"

"Kindly knock off the pep talk, Prof. I'm ready whenever you are."

"Do you have the interuniversal activator?"

"Sealed inside my bootheel. We shall not be parted."

"Good luck, then." He threw more switches and the machine buzzed ominously. "The door is unlocked."

I opened the garage door and peeked. It looked good. I threw it wide and stepped through.

Nice. A warm yellow sun shone in the blue sky above, very different from the bloated red one in Hell. A small white cloud floated by at shoulder height. I poked it with my finger and it bounced away, giving off a pleasant chiming sound.

The landscape was most serene, low rolling hills covered with short grass. A grove of trees nearby shaded what looked like a paved road. I walked over and poked it with my toe. It was indeed a road, paved with soft cobblestones. It wound out of sight among the trees to the right. To the left it curled up a valley into the hills. Which way should I go?

There was a distant rumble like thunder from the direction of the hills. Curiosity, as always, won. I went that way. Curiosity paid off pretty quickly when I saw the road junction ahead with pointing-finger signs. I approached them with great interest.

"Three ways to go," I said, peering up at the boards. "I have apparently come from the direction of RUBBISH DUMP—which does not sound too exciting so I shall not retrace my steps. But, problems, problems, how do I choose between VALHALLA and PARADISE?"

Paradise sounded Paradisical, and brought to mind that fine planet named Paraiso Aqui. Which indeed did become Paradise Here after I had been elected president. I had dim memories of Valhalla from my religious research, something to do with snow, axes and horned helmets. Paradise sounded much better.

Then I noticed the piece of paper that had been nailed to the pole supporting the signs. It read PARADISE CLOSED FOR REPAIRS. Which, as you might imagine, made my decision much easier.

The road wound up into the hills and through a small valley. It ended at what appeared to be a high and crudely constructed wall. Large tree trunks, still covered with bark, were set into the ground. There was a metal door waiting invitingly, set into the wood. It was a false invitation. It had a handle that would not turn. I pushed against the metal, which resisted strongly. I was about to try my luck in Paradise when I noticed the sign above the door.

SERVICE ENTRANCE it read. Which implied strongly that there had to be another entrance. Which I would have to find. There was a path trampled in the grass and I followed it along the wall until it turned a corner.

"Now that's more like it," I said with sincere admiration.

No service entrance this! What looked like solid gold pillars held up a jewel covered pediment above a massive golden door. The precious stones glowed with inner light. There was the sudden blast of unseen horns, followed by loud and heroic music. Marching to its very enthusiastic beat I approached the entrance with great interest. When I came closer I saw that the jewels spelled out a message that I was unable to read. Probably because it was in some unknown language made up of strangely shaped letters that looked very much like crossed sticks. Not only strangely shaped but in an unknown alphabet, unknown that is at least to me. Above the jewels was an immense golden ax crossed with a golden hammer.

"Looks great, doesn't it?" a voice said.

I jumped, turned, landed ready for action. The music had covered the sound of his approach. But there appeared to be no threat from the newcomer. He was middle-aged and plump, wearing an expensive business suit and a white lace shirt with a blood-red necktie, and was smiling in the most friendly manner.

"You here same as me? Take a look at Valhalla."

"Sure am," I said, relaxing. And taking note that woven into his tie with gold thread was the same crossed axe and hammer that hung above the entrance. "Valhalla here we come . . ."

"Not yet!" he said quickly, raising his hand. "A look, sure, that's what I'm after. A quick look to see what the afterlife holds. Not quite ready for the real thing quite yet—"

His voice was drowned out by a blasting blare of horns and a tremendous drumroll as the golden door slowly swung open. As the music died away a woman's voice bid us welcome.

"I bid you welcome. Enter, good followers of the League of the Longboat and Life Friends of Freya. Enter and behold that which one day will be yours for eternity. As long as you pay your loyal tithe. Here is Valhalla! The mead-hall at rainbow's end. Come forward—and don't trip over the snake."

Some snake! It must have been a yard thick and vanished out of sight in both directions. It writhed slowly as we stepped over it.

"Uroboros!" my companion said. "Goes right around the world."

"Be quick," our invisible guide called out, "for you do not have much time. I shall part the veil, but can do this only briefly. Only by special dispensation of the gods is this possible. Thor always smiles upon warriors of the League of the Longboat, and Loki is away in Hel right now, so Thor, in his generosity, permits your presence for a quick peek at that which is yet to come. So look, breathe deep and enjoy for someday, one day, this will be yours . . . ."

The interior was veiled in darkness which slowly lightened. I stepped forward for a closer look and slammed my nose into an invisible barrier. It went down to the ground, stretched higher than I could reach. My companion rapped it with his knuckles.

"The Wall of Eternity," he said. "Glad it's there. You have to be dead to pass it."

"Thanks. I'll pass on passing. Zowie!"

The exclamation was pulled out of me by the bizarre scene that was suddenly revealed on the other side of the barrier. A fire roared in a massive stone fireplace and some entire giant beast was being cooked over it. At long wooden tables lots of big men with long blond hair and beards were really living it up. There was plenty of mad drinking and eating. Great mugs of drink were slopped onto the wooden tables, to be seized up and guzzled down. With one hand, because in the other hand most of the men held steaming meaty bones or the legs of very large birds. Their voices could be dimly heard like distant echoes, shouting and swearing. Some were singing. Great blond waitresses with mighty thews and even mightier busts were passing out the food and drink. An occasional shrill cry cut through the roar of masculine voices as buttocks were clutched; occasionally there was a thud as quick female action slammed a mug into a groper's head. Yet the large ladies laughed and tweaked many a Viking beard with more than a hint of orgies to come. In fact, dimly on a table in the distance, a meaty couple appeared to be doing just that, giggling in distant laughter. Which died away as darkness descended again.

"Isn't that something!" my companion said, eyes staring with admiration.

"Not for a vegetarian," I muttered, but not loud enough to spoil his fun. "I wonder if we belong to the same church?" I asked smarmily.

There was no answer—because he was no longer there. Opportunity missed; I should have been prying information out of him instead of goggling the joys of Valhalla. I went outside, but he really had gone back to wherever he had come from. Behind me the door slammed shut and the glowing jewels stopped glowing.

The show was over—and what had I found out?

"A lot," I reassured myself. "But this is surely not the Heaven as Vivilia VonBrun described it. Valhalla looks like a man's idea of a night out with the boys going on forever. Which means there must be more than one heaven in Heaven. Perhaps she saw the other one, Paradise. Which means I should take a look at it—even if it is closed."

Prodded by this stern logic I retraced my steps to the signboards, turned and followed the path to Paradise. It twisted its way through a thick stand of trees and brush.

Then I stopped as I heard the rumble of a vehicle's engine ahead. Putting caution before boldness I dropped to the ground and crawled forward through the bushes.

Parted the last one and looked out.

CHAPTER 16

WHAT I WAS LOOKING AT was, or so it appeared, a normal building site that you would find on any planet. Beyond it were some low, temple-like buildings around a decorative lake. Just near me there was the framework of a half-constructed building, very much like the others. Earthmovers were landscaping around it, riggers swinging a steel beam into place. They were human too, not robots, for I heard one of them shout "*Bonega—veldu gin nun.*" Civilized Esperanto speakers talking about welding the structure. It was all so commonplace that I wondered what it was doing in this paradisical corner of Heaven.

Once I get the curiosity itch, I have to scratch. I stayed under the protective bush and watched the action. I wished, not for the first time, that Coypu could find a way for machines to be taken between the universes. I would dearly love to have had a telescope with me to watch the goings-on. And to take a much closer look at each of the working men on the site. If Slakey was one of them I would have to rethink any plans to investigate fuller on the site.

He didn't seem to be working here. All the builders I could see were lean and young. Though there was one older man in a hard hat, a foreman of some kind. Fairly fat—but he bore no resemblance to any of the Slakeys I had seen.

After a good time had passed I realized that it was pretty boring just lurking here in the shrubbery: I suppressed a yawn. I either had to do something positive or get out of there and do some research in the rubbish dump. But before I could make my mind up it was made up for me.

Older-and-Fatter looked at his watch—then blew loudly on his whistle. Everyone downed tools and turned off engines. At first I thought they were quitting for the day, until the roache coache came trundling up. Familiar from a thousand building sites and factory entrances around the galaxy. Filled with frozen food and armed with microwave. Selection of choice, porcuswine cutlets or deep-fried crustacean limbs, buttons pressed, steaming meal delivered.

The laborers lined up, shouting guttural oaths at one another and producing loud badinage as workers across the galaxy are wont to do, and received their meals as they were extruded from the delivery slots. Some sat down on the beams and boxes that littered the site. Happily a few of them decided to make a picnic out of the meal and strolled up the slope to sprawl on a patch of grass near me. Not near enough to hear what they were saying though, but close enough to start ideas curdling about in my brain. The fat foreman was one of the picnickers, tucking into a steaming and meaty rib that was big enough to have come from a brontosaurus.

I waited a bit, then rose and strolled towards them, whistling as I went.

"Lovely day, isn't it?" I said ingratiatingly. And was greeted by a sullen silence and surly scowls.

"Work going well?"

"Who the hell are you?" the foreman said, throwing his rib away and hauling himself to his feet.

"I'm an accountant. Work for the boss."

"For Slakey?"

"I call him Mr. Justin Slakey since he pays the bills. And you would be . . . ?"

"Grusher. I'm the gaffer here."

"My pleasure. Are you the one who reported the shortage in the cement supplies?"

"I reported nothing. What's this all about?" He was now eyeing me suspiciously—as were all of them.

"A minor matter . . ."

"Look bowb, who do you think you are just walking up here and asking questions? I worked for Slakey for years. I hire the roughnecks, chippies, brickies, the whole lot. I order building materials, build what he asks me to build like adding to this fun park here. He never asks questions—just pays the bills I send him. It's a cash deal."

"I don't like this guy," one of the workers growled. A particularly obnoxious one with bulging biceps. "You said there would be no trouble when we signed on, Grusher. Secret location for business reasons. Knocked us out before we came here. Good money and good hours and everything in cash."

"You from the tax people?" another equally ugly worker asked.

"He's the tax man," Bulging Biceps said as he pulled the spud wrench from the loop in his belt.

"Make him welcome," Grusher said, smiling coldly, as they moved in a circle about me. "He's interested in cement—well, we're pouring concrete today. Let's give him a closer look—from down inside."

I jumped aside so that the wrench whistled by me, then ducked under a wild punch. I'm good at self-defense—but not this good. Nine, ten to one and all fit and obnoxious. And closing in.

"You're right!" I shouted. "And you're all under arrest for tax invasion. Now go quietly . . ."

They roared in anger and hurled their muscled forms forward.

"Take me home!" I thought. *"Now!"*

I crashed into the metal panel on the machine, hung there spread-eagled.

"Professor . . . cut the power . . ."

"Sorry," Coypu said, "I knew I forgot something. Meant to make those adjustments before you came back."

He touched a button and I slumped to the floor. There was an open bottle of beer on his console; I stumbled over and drained it.

"What have you discovered?"

"Very little. My heavenly tour was just beginning. There is a suburb of Heaven named Valhalla with a pretty rough crowd and not my idea of heaven. Then there is Paradise, which is still being built. I better keep on looking. So I just popped back for a beer and to let you know what was going on. A little trouble there, nothing to mention. If Angelina should ask about me say that everything is going fine. Now—can you send me back, but not quite to the same spot if you don't mind?"

"Not a problem since I have calibrated the spherical locator during your absence. Would a kilometer laterally do?"

"Fine." I opened the garage door a crack, saw only blue sky and green grass. "This will be great. See you later."

I stepped through and felt the sun warm on my back. A light breeze was blowing and wafting some small clouds in my direction, drifting slowly above my head.

There were more of them appearing, some even drifting against the wind which was ominous. One of them floated by in the other direction. It tinkled—and more. Was that laughter coming from it? It drifted along and I drifted after it. Along a path of sorts that had been trodden in the grass. Then, far ahead, I saw a white structure of some kind that topped a distant hill. Another puffy cloud drifted after the first one, chiming pleasantly as well. Follow the path, that seemed obvious. It was made of yellow bricks that were resiliently soft. A cloud of birds was swirling about above the road ahead. At least I thought that they were birds. I quickly changed my mind about this when I got closer. They were pink and round, with little white wings that were surely too small to support them. They began to look very familiar.

When I had done my religious research about Heaven—and Hell—I had been most taken by the illustrations. It soon became clear that all of the religions of history, while being pretty divisive for the most part, had on the other hand provided plenty of artistic inspiration. Poems and songs, books and paintings, architecture, as well as some strange and interesting sculpture. Somewhere in all those data banks I had seen these pink pirouetters.

They circled ever closer until I stopped and bulged my eyes at them.

They were little, fat, pink babies hovering on hazy wings. All of them had golden curls of hair on their heads and were of indeterminate sex. I say this because they all had what appeared to be wispy lengths of silky cloth about their loins. They fluttered closer until they were circling above my head like a cloud of gnats; I strongly resisted the impulse to leap up and get one by the leg for a closer look. They circled and smiled and laughed aloud with a sound like tiny tinkling bells.

Then they pointed and stirred with excitement for coming towards us was another flock of the same little creatures. The new lot appeared to be carrying guns of some kind; I looked for cover.

"Shame, Jim," I said when they had fluttered closer. "You've got a nasty and suspicious mind." They weren't carrying guns but instead were armed with tiny golden harps. They strummed as they flew, swooping into a circling formation with the first lot. I sat down on the yellow brick road to watch. And discovered that the road was warm as well as soft.

After an arpeggio of plaintive pluckings, the entire airborne swarm burst into song. It was nice enough, though a little high-pitched for my liking, and sung in an unfamiliar language.

"*Die entführung aus dem Serail!*" one chirrupy lot sang as they swooped away. But another bunch had already fluttered into position to have a go of their own.

"Per queste tue manine,
In quale eccessi, mi tradei,
un bacio de mano . . . ."

This was followed by a song in Esperanto. I could understand it, although I wasn't quite sure what it was about.

> *"Profunde li elfosis min*
> *Bele li masonis min,*
> *Alte li konstruis min.*
> *Sed Bil-Auld estas foririnta . . . ."*

And so forth. The singing was not bad, at first, but a little too tinkling and twittery for my tastes. They could have done with a couple of good bassos to back them up.

It all finally ended on a high-piercing note that made my teeth hurt. They swirled upward and away.

"Great," I called after them. Then an afterthought. "Is there a good bar or cantina nearby?" Only the sound of high-pitched laughter sounded from above. "Thanks a lot," I muttered sourly. Stood and scuffed down the road trying to ignore my growing thirst. The white building on the hill appeared no closer and the sun was hot on my shoulders. But a turn in the road held out some promise of succor. A little plaid tent of some kind was set up beside the road. Gilt chairs with ornate arms were arrayed on the grass before it. A woman in a white dress sat on one of the chairs sipping from a golden mug.

She smiled broadly at me as I approached. A rather fixed smile that did not change—nor did her eyes move to follow me. More frosted mugs were on a table in the tent. I took up one, sniffed and tasted it; cold sweet and definitely alcoholic.

"Not bad," I said in my most friendly manner. She did not turn her head or reply. I went and sat in the chair next to hers. A very attractive woman, firm of breast and fair of brow. I was glad that Angelina wasn't here, for the moment at least. I leaned forward.

"Do you come here often?" I asked, all conversational originality. But at least it did get her attention. She turned her head slowly and fixed her dark and lovely eyes upon me, opened moist red lips.

"Is it time to go already?" she husked richly, put her glass down, rose and left.

"Well, Jim—you do have a way with women," I mused and drank my drink. Then blinked quickly as she stepped onto the yellow brick road and vanished. It was quite abrupt and soundless. I walked over and looked but there was no trace of a trapdoor or device of any kind.

"Slakey!" I said, spun about, but I was alone. "Was she here on one of your day tours, a quick look at Heaven then back to the checkbook?" I remembered what Coypu had said about the narcotic gas in the air here; she had really looked stoned, on that and the drink maybe. I put mine down without finishing it.

Refreshed enough, I went on. A twist in the road led through a flowered ravine and I saw that the building on the hill was now closer and clearer. Gracious white marble columns supported a gilded roof. As I came close I saw that stone steps led up from the road. I stopped as they began to move.

"A Heaven-sized escalator," I said, eyeing them with glum suspicion. "You have been observed Jim—or have actuated some concealed switch."

There seemed to be no point in retreating. My presence was known—and after all I was here to investigate. So I did. Stepping gingerly onto the steps that carried me gracefully up to my destination.

A large single room filled the interior of the building, with blue sky visible between the columns that framed it. A shining marble floor, dust and blemish free, stretched to the throne at the far end. A man sat there, old and plump with white hair, occasionally strumming a chord on the harp he held. If nothing else, Heaven was surely big on harps. A golden halo floated above his head.

As I walked closer, the noble head turned towards me, the halo bobbing and moving with it. He nodded and the lips turned up in a smile.

"Welcome to Heaven, James Bolivar diGriz," he said.

The voice was rich and warm, the profile familiar.

"Professor Slakey, I presume?"

CHAPTER 17

I WAS SORELY TEMPTED TO think *get me out of here and take me home* but restrained myself. I had a foolproof means of escape, or so Coypu had reassured me, and my escape from the building site had proved him right, so I should hang around for a bit. I wasn't being threatened, at least not yet, and this was supposed to be a reconnaissance mission.

"No hard feelings?" I asked.

"Should there be?"

"You tell me. The last time we met, or I met with a number of your incarnations, mayhem and murder seemed to be the name of the game."

"Of course. Hell." He nodded. "I wasn't there but of course I was aware of what was happening. That was very good salami—you must give me the name of your supplier."

This conversation was getting a little surrealistic, but I decided to press on. This was the first time I had talked to Slakey without some kind of instant violence in the offing.

"Where is Heaven?" I asked.

"All around you. Isn't it enjoyable?"

"Is this the Heaven the seriously religious hope to go to when they die?"

"Pleasant, isn't it? Did you enjoy the cherubs?" He smiled benignly. I decided to be a little more direct.

"Why are you here in Heaven?"

"The same reason you are."

"Let's get down to facts. You are a crook with a number of cons. A murderer as well, since you shipped all those people off to Hell. And you have been giving suckers daytrips to Heaven. To a variety of Heavens." He pursed his lips and nodded as though in thought.

"If you say so, dear boy. I want no dissension in Heaven."

"What is the purpose of all this? What are you doing with all the money you bamboozle out of people?"

This time the cold look in his eye was pure Slakey. "You are getting tiresome, Jim. And boring. And a bit of a nuisance—don't you think so?"

Now that he mentioned it I realized that I wasn't exactly being the life of the party. "I'm sorry, Professor. I'm not usually like this."

"Apology accepted, of course. It's so nice here in Heaven that we shouldn't quarrel. There—why don't you sit down there and rest?"

There was a chair beside me that hadn't been there an instant before. A good thing too since he was right, I really was tired. Very, very tired. I dropped into it. Slakey nodded again.

"Time to get comfortable, Jim. Take off your boots, stretch your toes . . ."

What a good idea—or was it? What was wrong with it? I couldn't quite remember. Meanwhile I was taking off one boot, then the other, and tossing them aside.

Slakey smiled toothily and snapped his fingers and my lassitude vanished. The boot heel! *Get me out of here!* I blasted the thought out so loudly that it rattled around inside my skull.

The boots were gone and nothing had happened. Or rather something not too nice happened, because when I jumped to my feet and turned to run I fell flat on my face. Staring at the golden bracelet around my ankle. Attached to a length of gilt chain that vanished into the ground.

"Good trick," I said sternly, although it came out a little squeakily. I climbed to my feet and sat down again in the chair.

"Not really. You are a stupid little man and very easy to outthink. Didn't you realize that your undetectable device would be detected? An interuniversal activator indeed! I sneer at it. My science is so far ahead of yours that I hesitate to describe the difference. Not only my science but my intellect. More child's play to outwit you. First I used hypnotic gas to make you amenable, then it was only a matter of simple suggestion to control a simple mind. You were happy to turn over your boots to me. Along with your life, you must realize. I am the master of science, of life and death, time and entropy!"

Also one brick short of a load, one nut short of a nutcake, I thought grimly. It was not going to be easy to get out of this one.

"You are indeed," I said with all sincerity. "But you are also a man of mystery as well. With all your talents why are you going to all the trouble setting up your con games?"

He chose not to answer; insane or not he kept his secrets. And he was beginning to lose his temper.

"Wispy, time-shortened man—do you know how old I am?"

"No, but I'm sure that you will tell me. Not that I really care."

I turned away and yawned and watched out of the corner of my eye as his face turned purple.

"You have strained my patience, diGriz. You must show respect and, yes, awe for someone like me—who is over eight thousand years old!"

"Amazing!" I said. "I wouldn't pick you as a year over seven thousand . . ."

"Enough!" he raged, leaping to his feet. "I am tired of you. Therefore I now condemn you to Purgatory. Bring him."

This last command was directed at a hulking, man-shaped robot that came clanking up the stairs. It was dented and scarred, red with rust and coated with black dust. One electronic eye glowed balefully; the other had been torn out of its socket. It stamped towards me and I quailed back, so great was the thing's insensate menace. It hissed and bent, reached out and with its sharp-bladed fingers it cut the chain that secured me . I jumped away—but it caught me in midair with clutching hands the size of shovels. Grabbed me and crushed me to its metal chest, its grip unbreakable and painful. Fat and white-haired Slakey grunted with the effort as he pulled himself to his feet and waddled away, my captor clomping after him. Down the stairs we went and out onto the yellow brick road.

Slakey stamped his foot and there was a slathering, liquid sound as the road lifted up like a great yellow tongue. A dark pit was revealed from which rose a dreadful stench.

"The doomed enter Purgatory," he intoned. "None return. Go."

My captive robot, still clutching me, leaned forward. More and more.

Until we dropped face-first down into the pit.

There have been a number of times in my adventurous life when I have strongly wished I was elsewhere. This was definitely one of them. My past life did not flash before me, but the jagged stone walls certainly did. They were lit by a ruddy glow from below that we were rapidly approaching at what must be terminal velocity.

Was this the way it was going to end? Not with a whimper, but with a resounding crash when my metallic captor hit the ground. Which was rushing towards us far too fast. A bleak, black landscape lit by sporadic gouts of flame. I wriggled ineffectively in the robot's iron grasp.

Then we juddered and slowed and I almost slipped out of the thing's embrace as deceleration hit it. But it just clamped harder on my chest until I couldn't breathe.

With a resounding clang we hit the ground and I crashed down as the thing let go of me. Before I could get my breath back it had me by the arm and was dragging me along. I had very little choice; I went. Limping because the stony ground was exceedingly hard on my stockinged feet. I wished that I was back in Heaven with my boots.

What I could see of the surroundings was far from inspiring. A miasma hung in the air that not only stank but irritated my air passages as well. I coughed and, as though in ghastly echo, there was the sound of heavy coughing from up ahead. We went around a mound of crushed rock and I saw the cause.

Stretching out and vanishing into the distance, barely revealed by the ruddy light, were long, low, almost table-like structures of some kind. Standing along both sides were bent figures with their arms extended. They were doing something, just what I could not say. As we passed close to one of the structures there was a rumbling sound and from the mouth of an apparatus there fell a mass of some dark powdered substance. A wisp of it came my way and I coughed again for this was the source of the stench and irritation.

It was difficult to see clearly what was going on since my metallic captor neither slowed nor stumbled, just dragged me forward steadily. Yet, since the scene repeated itself over and over, I began to see what was happening. I couldn't understand it—but I could observe it.

The dust was flowing, or being carried, slowly down the length of the table-like constructions. The laborers, they were all women I could see now, ran their fingers over the surface. That was all they did, slowly and repetitiously, never looking up, never stopping. One of them picked up something, I could not tell what it was, and dropped it into a container at her side. I dragged by.

By far the worst part was there total lack of interest or attention to anything other than their work. I would have certainly looked up if a giant, decrepit robot dragged someone by me. They did not.

We passed more and more of them. All engaged in the same mysterious task, silently and continuously. This went on for a very long time. There were hundreds, possibly thousands, of laboring women. Then we were past the last ones and I was being hauled off into the semidarkness.

"I say, good robot guide, where are you taking me?" It

plodded on. I pried at its clamped fingers. "Cease!" I shouted. "This is the voice of your master, your human master. Stop now you animated junkyard."

It neither slowed nor paid me any heed, dragging me along like a dead beast. I walked again, stumbling, which was somewhat better than being dragged. To a metal door set into the rock face. It opened the door and pulled me through. I heard it clang shut behind us although I could see nothing in the darkness. It started up an unseen stairway, apparently seeing all right with its single operating eye. I fell and banged my shins, fell again and again until I grew used to the stairs. I was reeling with exhaustion by the time it stopped again and opened another door. Seized me up and threw me through it.

Behind me the door clanged shut even before I hit the ground. Reality twisted, the sensation of passing from one universe to another. There was sudden light and I banged down hard onto a stone floor.

Cold light lit the even colder scene; my teeth began chattering. I was in a metal-walled room with a barred door set in the far wall. Snow and frigid air blew in between the bars.

Had I been hauled down to Purgatory, then tossed through the machine, just to be allowed to freeze to death? It didn't make sense. There certainly must be lots of easier and less complicated ways of disposing of me. My blue and bare toes, protruding from the ruins of my socks, kicked against something. I looked down at the heaped clothing, thick boots, gloves. This was a message that I was happy to receive.

My fingers were trembling as I pulled on the heavy socks and trousers, then kicked into the boots. They didn't fit that well—but they kept out the cold. Everything I put on was a depressing shade of ash gray which did not disturb me in the slightest. The clothing was warm and not too uncomfortable. I wound a scarf around my neck, popped on a seedy fur hat, then wriggled my fingers into the thick gloves.

Right on cue the barred door swung open and more snow blew in. I ignored it and turned around to see if there was any way of getting out the same way I had come in.

"I am called Buboe," a menacingly deep voice said. I sighed and turned to look at my newest tormentor.

Dressed like me. Almost of a height, but he was heavier and wider. In his hands he held a flexible metal rod that I looked at very suspiciously. Particularly when he waggled it in my direction.

"This is Buboe's bioclast. Bioclast hurts lot. It kills too. You do what Buboe say, you live. Don't do it, you hurt and die. This is hurt."

He flicked the thing at me. I jumped aside so that the tip barely grazed me.

This was a new kind of pain. It felt like my flesh had been sliced to the bone and boiling acid then poured into the wound. I could only stand, holding my wounded arm and waiting for the pain to pass. It did, eventually, and it was hard to believe that both clothing and arm were still intact. Buboe waggled the bioclast at me and I shivered away.

"Learn fast, live. No learn, die."

His linguistic abilities were not of the best but he had an unassailable and thoroughly convincing argument. And at least he could talk; I could only nod agreement not trusting myself to speak yet.

"Work," he said, pointing his weapon at the open door. I stumbled through it into blue-lit daylight, a desolate, snow-whipped frigid hell. Large machines were moving around me, but until my eyes stopped tearing at the sudden cold I could not see what they were doing.

I soon found out. This was an opencast mine, a great sunken pit of broken stone and heaped gravel. The black layers were being torn open by hulking machines; the rubble they heaped up was then carried away by many-wheeled devices. At first I thought that the machines were workrobots. Then I saw that each vehicle had a rider or an operator. The machines did the digging and carrying under the men's guidance.

"You go up," Buboe said, rapping on an immobile machine. The sight of his thin rod sent me scurrying up the handholds on its side. I wriggled into the bucket seat, looked out through the scarred and chipped window before me, wondered what to do next. A loudspeaker above my head scratched to life.

"Detection. Unknown individual. Identify yourself."

"Who are you?" I asked, looking around for an operator, but I was alone. It was my steel chariot that was speaking to me.

"I am Model Ninety-one surface debrider and masculator. Give identity."

"Why?" I asked angrily, having never enjoyed conversations with machines.

"Give identity," was all it would say.

"My name is none of your business," I said sulkily—then regretted the words the instant I had spoken them.

"State work experience with this Model Ninety-one, None-ofyourbusiness."

"I will give the orders. Now hear this . . ."

"State work experience with this Model Ninety-one, None-ofyourbusiness."

There was no way to win this argument. "None."

"Orientation instructions begin."

They did, and they went on for far too long in far too stupid detail, geared to the thought processes of a retarded two-year-old. I listened just long enough to find out how the thing operated, then looked around for some way out of this dilemma. Knowing that it was not going to be easy.

". . . now power is on, Noneofyourbusiness. Work begins."

It surely did. There were levers by each knee, along with the two pedals, controlled direction and speed. A single, knobbed control moved the hydraulically powered arm that projected forward from right below the cab. This was first pressed against the rock surface and the trigger pulled. Fragments of rock blasted out in all directions—including towards the cab, which explained the thickness and scars on the forward-facing window. When enough rock had been broken free I touched the glowing red button that signaled for the bucketbil. This trundled over on its two rows of heavy wheels and backed into position below. I worked the controls for the loading arms which stuck out just below my face.

The first time I dumped a load I I waved to the driver of the bucketbil. His grim expression never changed, but he was considerate enough to raise a thick middle finger to me. I loaded and he left.

Light was fading from the sky. Night approached and work would cease for the day. A nice thought, but not a very accurate one. Worklights came on above, the headlights of my Model 91 illuminated the falling snowflakes and the rock face: the work continued.

An indeterminate, but long, time later there was a warbling sound from the cab's loudspeaker and the machine's power was switched off. I saw the driver of the nearest stopped Model 91 climbing wearily down from his machine. I did the same, and just as wearily. There was another heavily dressed man waiting on the ground, who climbed up the machine as soon as I got down. He said nothing to me—nor did I have anything to say to him in return. I shuffled after the other shuffling man. Through a door in the canyon wall. Into a large and warm hall filled with men and redolent with the strong pong of B.O. My new home.

It was worse than any army camp or work camp that I had ever been in. There was an overlay of despair that could not be avoided. These men were condemned and bereft of any spark of will. Or hope.

The only note of interest came after I had found an empty bunk to dump my heavy outer clothing, then followed the others to the eating tables. I was looking at the appalling food on my battered tray when a large hand seized my shoulder painfully.

"I eat your kreno," said the overweight and obnoxious individual who was attached to the hand. Another hand of the same size reached for the purple steaming lump on my tray. I lowered the tray to the table, waited until the kreno was well-clutched—then grabbed the wrist.

This was the only decent thing that had happened to me since I had left for Heaven this morning. Or a week ago. Or something.

Since he was very big, obviously obnoxious and undoubtedly strong, I played no fancy games. As his thick head went by I cracked him across the bridge of the nose with the side of my hand. He squealed in pain so I generously gave him peace by punching his neck in the right place with stiffened fingertips. He kept on going to the floor and did not move. I picked up my tray and took the kreno from his limp fingers. Looked around at the other diners.

"Any of you lot want to try for my kreno?" I asked.

The few who had bothered to look up from their food quickly lowered their eyes. The man at my feet began to snore. The only other sound was the slurp and crunch of masticating food.

"It's really nice to meet you guys," I said to the tops of heads. Sat down and ate hungrily.

Forcing myself not to think about where I was and what I was going to do.

Or what the unforeseeable future might be like.

CHAPTER 18

A GREAT NUMBER OF STRENUOUS days passed, not to say nights, in endless, brainless toil. The food was disgusting but kept the body's furnace stoked. My kreno-clutching friend, whose name I had soon discovered was Lasche, was the barrack's bully. He stayed out of my way, though he glared at me from behind the pair of black-and-blue eyes I had given him, then found other, more vulnerable men to pick on.

The routine could not have been simpler—or more mind-destroyingly boring. There were two shifts, one worked while the other slept, and there were no days off. The day started when the lights came on and Buboe appeared to stir the laggards along with his bioclast. As we filed out of the barracks the other shift stumbled in. It was the hot-bed system with one worker getting out of bed just before the other one crawled into it. Since the rough blankets were never changed or cleaned this made for an unusual miasma in the sleeping quarters. That was the way the day began; it ended when the lights went out.

In between working and sleeping, sleeping and working, we ate the repulsive meals that had been prepared in the robot kitchen. There was very little talking among the inmates, undoubtedly because there was absolutely nothing to talk about.

The only change in this routine was when I operated a bucketbil rather than a Model 91. This was even more distasteful and boring since it involved only driving away with a full load, dumping it and coming back empty.

I had a spurt of interest when I went to dump my first load, trundling along in the wake of another filled machine. Our destination proved to be nothing more exciting than a giant metal hopper set into the ground. There was no indication at all where the crushed rock was going. Or why. Was there a cave or a conveyor underground? I didn't think so. I had come to this planet courtesy of Slakey's universe machine. The chances were that crushed rock was going somewhere the same way. I thought about this for a bit, but soon forgot to think about it under the pressure of work and fatigue.

It must have been the fatigue that put me off guard. I had concerned myself with Lasche for the first few days as his shiners turned from black to green and other interesting colors. He seemed to have forgotten about me as well.

But he hadn't. I was wiping up the cold remains of the evening meal when I noticed the expression on the face of the man across the table from me. He was looking up over my shoulder and I saw his eyes widen. It was reflex that made me jump aside—and just blind luck that my skull wasn't crushed. The rock that Lasche was wielding struck my shoulder a numbing blow, knocking me off the bench. I roared with pain and rolled aside, stumbled to my feet and stood dizzily with my back to the wall. I made a fist with my left hand, but my right arm was numb and powerless. I shuffled along the wall until I had a clear space before me. Lasche followed me, lifting the rock menacingly.

"Now you're gonna be dead," he said. I felt no desire to join in the conversation. I watched his beady and nasty little eyes, waiting for him to attack.

He did—but fell forward as the man at the table behind him stuck out his foot and tripped him. I made the most of it, bringing my knee up to meet his face as he went down. He screamed hoarsely and dropped the rock. I grabbed it up with my good hand, ready to slam it into his skull.

"If you kill him, or maim him so he can't work, Buboe will kill you," the man said. He of the tripping toe. I dropped the rock and satisfied myself with a quick kick in the thug's ribs and a punch in his neural ganglion that would keep him quiet for some time.

"Thanks," I said. "I owe you one."

He was thin and wiry, with black hair and even blacker grease on his hands. I kneaded my sore right arm with my hand as it tingled back to life.

"My name is Berkk," he said.

"Jim."

"Can you operate an arcwelder?"

"I'm an expert."

"I thought you might be. I have been watching you since you came here. You know how to take care of yourself. Let's go see Buboe."

Our brutal keeper had a room of his own, absolute luxury in this place. And a heating coil as well. When we found him he was stirring an unappealing orange mass in a battered pot. But it smelled all right and would surely be better than the slop we were fed.

"What you want?" He scowled at us. Probably found the effort to speak coherently a tiring one.

"I need help putting that Model Ninety-one back together. The one that fell off the rockface."

"Why help?"

"Because I say so, that's why. It's a two man job. Jim here can work a welder."

He stopped stirring and looked at us suspiciously, his bulging red eyes moving from Berkk's face to mine. It took some time; obviously coherent thought was as alien to him as articulate speech. In the end he grunted and went back to stirring his meal. Berkk turned to leave and I followed him out.

"Would you care to translate?" I asked.

"You'll work with me in the repair shop for awhile."

"All that from a grunt?"

"Sure. If he had said no that would have ended it."

"I want to thank you . . ."

"Don't. It's heavy and dirty work. Let's go."

He lifted a grease-stained finger to rub his nose—and it touched his pursed lips for a second.

He wanted silence, he got silence. There was more here than met the eye—and I felt the first spurt of hope since I had arrived in this terrible place.

We went down the corridor beyond Buboe's lair to a large, locked door. Berkk obviously didn't have the key, because he sat down with his back to the wall. I joined him and we waited some time in silence until Buboe finally appeared, still chewing some last gristly bit of his meal. He unlocked the door, let us in sealed it again behind us.

"Let's get started," Berkk said. "I hope you meant it about the arcwelder."

"I can work that and every kind of machine tool, repair printed circuits, anything. If it's broken I can fix it."

"We'll find out."

The wrecked Model 91 had its side stove in, in addition to a broken axle. I cut out the crumpled area while Berkk levered a steel plate onto a dolly and rolled it over. We used a chain hoist to lift it. Without any robots to help it was hard work.

"We can talk here," he said as he hammered the plate into position. "I've been watching you. You don't act as stupid as the muscular morons here."

"Nor do you."

He smiled wryly. "Would you believe it—I volunteered. Everyone else here got drunk or hit in the head or something. Then woke up in this place. Not me, no. I answered an ad in the net for an experienced machinist. Incredible salary. Looked really great. I went to this lab, met a Professor Slakey. Blackout—and I woke up here."

"Where is here?"

"I haven't the slightest idea. Do you know?"

"Some. I know Slakey and I know that you can get here from Heaven. No, don't look at me like that, let me explain. I was thrown into a room and ended up in a different one. In a different universe I am sure. The same thing must have happened to you when you came here."

While we repaired the machine I filled him in on Slakey's operations. It all must have sounded really far out, but he had no choice other than to believe it. When the repairs were done we took a break and he produced a jar filled with a very ominous-looking liquid.

"I got some raw krenoj from the kitchen, I go there to keep the machines running. Took scrapings from some of the vegetables and managed to isolate a decent strain of yeast. Fermented the krenoj, terrible! Alcoholic all right but undrinkable. But, some plastic tubing—"

"The worm! Heat source, evaporated, cooled and condensed, distilled and now waiting our attention." I swirled the liquid happily in the flask.

"Be warned. There's alcohol in there all right. But the taste—"

"Let me be the judge," I said rashly. Raised and drank, lowered the flask and retched dryly. "I think . . ." I gasped, and my voice was so harsh my words were almost indistinguishable. "I think that that—is the foulest thing I have ever drunk in—a lifetime of drinking foul beverages."

"Thank you. Now if you will pass it over."

It did not get any better with more drinking. But at least the ethyl alcohol began to take effect, which possibly made the entire exercise worthwhile.

"I can put some of the pieces together," he said, then wiped his finger across the coating on his teeth that the drink had deposited. "We had a guy here once, very briefly, with a big mouth. Said that he had helped repair the rollers in a pulverizing mill someplace. He thought that they were grinding up our rock."

"Did he say why?"

"No—and he was gone next day. He talked too much.

That's why we have to be careful. I don't know who or what is listening—"

"I know who. Slakey in one of his manifestations. He has this rock dug out here, then it is sent somewhere. Then it is ground up, then sent to the women who sort it and take something out of it."

"What?"

"I don't know what—except that it is terribly expensive. In money and in human lives."

"I'm sure of it. And we won't find the answer here. I want out of this place and I need help."

What music to my ears! I seized his hand and pummeled him on the back with joy. "You have a plan?"

"An idea. I don't think we can get out the way we came in. Through that barred room." I nodded agreement.

"That is undoubtedly a dimensional doorway operated by Slakey himself. But what other way is there to go? I have looked carefully and could not see any way to climb out of this valley. And even if we did—where would we go? This might be a barren planet at the end of the universe."

"I agree completely. Which leaves only the other way. Think for yourself—"

"Of course. The broken rock goes into the pit. We go with it and are crushed to death, right?"

"Wrong. I have been working on this for a long, long time. But I needed someone to help me—"

"I'm your man," I said. Slightly blurrily.

"Back to work," he said, climbing swayingly to his feet. "Gotta finish repairs first."

Work had a sobering effect and no more was said that day. An electric bell summoned Buboe who opened the large locked door that opened to the outside. I shivered and stamped my feet while Berkk drove the Model 91 out and parked it there. The door was sealed again and Buboe unlocked the other door that led us back to our quarters. And searched us ruthlessly before letting us out.

There was a backlog of repairs needed on the machines and we had plenty to do. Slowly. I would be back as a driver as soon as the job was complete. And Berkk never spoke again about his plan. I did not want to ask, figuring that it was his idea and he would know when the time was right. Life was work and sleep, work and sleep—with loathsome meals ingested briefly between. Berkk remained silent until the day when we were finishing the job of replacing a wheel on a bucketbil. We lay side by side beneath the thing, one holding, one hammering.

"This is the last repair you are going to do," he said. "Buboe says he is shorthanded and wants you back on the digging. I've been putting this off but we can't put it off anymore. You ready to go?" he asked. I did not ask where.

"Yes. When?"

"Now." He turned to look at me and I saw that his face was suddenly grim. "Have you ever killed a man?" he asked.

"Why? Is it important?"

"Very. If we are to go, then Buboe will have to be disarmed, maybe killed. I'm not much of a fighter—"

"I am. I'll take care of him. And hopefully not kill him. Then what?"

"Then these. We must get them into this bucketbil and out of here without being seen."

He kicked a tarpaulin aside, let the worklight play over them for an instant, then covered them again.

They were two frames made of rebar. They were shaped like coffins and were the same size as coffins. The finger-thick lengths of reinforcing bar were closely placed and crossed at right angles, then had been welded into place to form the cages. One side of each cage was hinged so it could be opened. Open this and crawl in. Close and turn the latch. Then—what he planned was obvious.

"Is this the only way?" I asked.

"Do you know of another?"

"It's suicide."

"It's certain death here if we don't try."

"We go into the hopper with the crushed rock, then through to—somewhere."

I took a deep breath, then let it out in a long, slow sigh.

"Let's do it," I finally said. "The quicker the better because I don't want to have time to think about it, or estimate our chances to get out alive instead of being pulverized."

CHAPTER 19

THIS WAS THE LAST BUCKETBIL in need of repair. We stretched the work out as long as we dared. Knowing that when it went back to work—so would I. In the rockpit. Before that happened we had to make our break together. One man could not do it alone.

All our preparations for escape had been made long since. It was just the idea of getting crushed along with the rest of the rocks that had been holding us back. I ran the file over the protruding bolthead. Stepped back to admire my work—then threw the tool onto the ground.

"Let's do it—and quick."

Berkk hesitated a moment, then nodded grim agreement. I dug into the scrap pile and found the cosh that I had made. I pulled its strap onto my wrist and slipped the thing up my sleeve. It was just a plastic tube filled with ball bearings but would surely do the job.

Berkk looked at me and I gave him what I hoped was a reassuring smile and a thumbs-up. He wheeled about and stabbed the button that would summon our keeper.

Who was very slow about arriving. Undoubtedly involved in some other sordid task. Minutes slipped by and I saw the beads of perspiration form on Berkk's forehead—even though the workshop was chill.

"Press it again," I said. "Maybe he didn't hear it the first time."

Again. And a third time. I slammed the cosh against my palm, testing it. Behind me the door rattled open and I just had time to get it back up my sleeve again as Buboe appeared.

"What you ring so much for?"

"Finished," Berkk said, slapping the metal flank of the bucketbil.

"Take out," Buboe said, turning his key in the lock. Cold wind blew in and he turned to glare at me. "You out of here. Go work." He continued to stare at me, his back to the bucketbil, slapping the bioclast against his trouser leg.

"Sure, whatever you say." I smiled insincerely instead of screaming.

This was not going right. He was supposed to be looking at Berkk so I could work my will upon him without getting a bioclast blast at full power. Behind him I could see Berkk climbing up the ladder and dropping into the control seat. The motor hammered and burst into life. And our captor still stared at me. And stepped forward.

"Out, go," he commanded. Lifting the bioclast towards me.

The bucketbil's engine idled roughly and died.

"Something's very wrong here," Berkk called out, staring down in horror.

We stayed that way as long seconds ticked by. The bioclast waving before me, the brute's eyes fixed on mine, Berkk clutching the steering wheel not knowing what else to do.

Luckily our thuggish warder's brain was incapable of entertaining two thoughts at one time. When the meaning of Berkk's words finally penetrated, he turned around.

"What happen?"

"This," I said, released from frightened paralysis, taking a single step forward. The cosh dropped into my hand, I swung—

—and he dropped heavily to the ground. I raised the cosh

again but he lay, unmoving. Not stirring even when I pried the weapon from his grip.

"Let's do it!" I shouted, pulling the tarpaulin from off our horde.

Berkk lifted the first rebar cage and heaved it up into the bucket. I used the prepared lengths of wire to bind the unconscious man, ankles and wrists, then wired his legs and arms one to the other. He could untwist the wire when he came around, but it would take time. While we, hopefully, would be long gone. I tied the gag into his mouth and dragged him back just as Berkk was heaving up the second cage. I pulled the tarp over the bound man and straightened up. Berkk had the big outer door partly open, held it that way as I clambered up the side of the machine and dropped into the bucket.

"Anyone out there?" I asked as he got into the driver's seat.

"No machines, no one in sight." He started the engine again and I could see his hands trembling.

"Slowly now, take your time. A deep breath, that's it. Now—go! And don't forget that you have to close the door once we're outside!"

The way he had revved the engine told me that he had forgotten the next step, driven now by panic and not intelligence. But having been reminded, he now did just as we had planned. Drove out through the door and stopped. Kicked the thing out of gear and locked the brakes. Climbed slowly to the ground and closed the workshop door. "Locked," he said as he climbed back up again.

As we drove into the darkness, I pulled myself up so I could look over the lip of the bucket. Lights and trundling machines were working in the open pit ahead.

"Did you . . . did you kill him?" Berkk asked.

"Far from it. Skull like rock. He'll have a headache—"

"And we'll be gone. There's a bucketbil dumping right now."

"Only one?"

"Yes."

"Go slower, take the long way. Don't get there until it's gone."

We slowed and rumbled on; I ducked back down as headlights washed over us. Moments later we stopped. The engine died but the headlights stayed on, illuminating the black bulk of the hopper.

"Let's go!" he shouted and jumped to the ground.

I realized I was still holding the bioclast. I threw it far out into the hopper and it vanished from sight. Then I heaved the first cage up and over the side onto the ground, bent and dragged up the other one. It followed the first and I went right after it.

We had planned this, step by step. And as long as we kept moving we did not have to think about what the last and final step was going to be. Berkk had clambered up onto the wide lip of the hopper, turned and reached down and grabbed the first cage when I pushed it up to him. Then the other. Only when I had climbed up beside him did I see that he was shaking from head to toe.

"Can't—do it!" He gasped, sat down and put his arms over his head. Beyond him I saw the sudden flare of approaching headlights.

"Too late to go back!" I shouted as I scrabbled at the steel frame and pulled the door open. "Get in!"

"No . . . ," He pulled back. I balled a fist and hit him on the jaw. Not enough to knock him unconscious—I hoped!—but enough to addle his thoughts.

It worked. I hauled his limp body into the cage and was closing the sealing hasp when he began screaming and tearing at me through the bars.

"Keep your hands inside!" I shouted as I kicked the cage off the ledge. It rattled down into the hopper and vanished from sight.

Now—could I do that to myself?

"Good enough for him, Jim. It better be good enough for you,"

Easy enough to say; harder to do. I opened the hinged side

and looked down into the cage. It was like looking into a rebar coffin.

I don't know how long I stood like that, unable to move, unable to commit myself to the destiny I had so easily tipped my partner into.

Headlights washed over me. "Bowb!" I grimaced between grated teeth. Dropped down, crawled in, locked the gate. Took a very deep breath.

Reached through the bars to grab the edge. Pulled myself over.

Dropped into darkness.

As we go through life we should learn from experience. Some of us never do. I have done a number of foolhardy and very dangerous things in my lifetime. One would think that I would have learned by experience. I never have. I cursed loudly as my cage banged and clattered down the wall, held tight to the inside handles.

The banging stopped and I was in free fall. I clung tight, bent my knees and braced my feet against the bars—and waited for the inevitable impact. There was the twisting interuniversely feeling and a red glow appeared suddenly below, grew brighter. I was falling into a furnace!

Panic possessed me. My heart began to beat like a triphammer and I knew this was the end. A mound of blackness suddenly slammed into the cage with almost deadly impact.

There would have been no *almost* with that *deadly* if the broken rock had not heaped itself into a conical pile.

Pain burst hard upon my body as the cage hit the piled rock at an angle, bounced and slithered down. More pain in my side as a rock point stabbed in between the bars. Clattering and banging, sliding, finally thudding to a stop.

I had to move, but I couldn't. The next load of rock would fall on top of me, crushing and entombing me. If I didn't get out now I never would.

With trembling fingers I pulled at the lock bar of the door. It would not move, had been bent inwards by the impact. Panic helped. I grabbed it with both hands, pulled and twisted with all my strength. Heard the roar of falling stone above me.

Pulled it free. Threw the door open and crawled out. Clambered across the broken surface as lumps of rock rolled by around me. One bounced off my leg, felling me. I crawled on. Until I noticed that the boulders were now moving out from under me, carrying me forward. There was just enough ruddy light to see that a wide, moving belt was carrying the rock—and me—to an unknown destination. Not a good one I was sure. Stumbling and falling I made my way to the edge, dropped off it onto the solid ground.

"Berkk!" I shouted. Where was he?

He was not being carried off with the crushed rock that I could see. But perhaps he had landed and bounced in a different direction, had gone down the pyramid of broken stone at a different place?

I was staggering, not walking. My leg still numb, a sharp pain in my side when I moved. Falling and climbing to my feet again and going on.

When I fell next time I grabbed a bar instead of stone to lever myself to my feet.

Bar?

I pulled and tore at the rocks over the half-buried cage until I uncovered his face. Still and pale. Dead? I had no time to stop and find out because the rocks around the cage were churning and beginning to move. I hurled lumps of stone aside until I uncovered the gate that I had closed such a very long time ago. By pure chance it was on top. If it had not been he would have gone on to certain death because I did not have the strength to turn it over.

In fact, I hadn't even the strength to pull him out once I had grabbed the gate open.

I had my hands under his shoulders, pulling. Nothing happened. He was too heavy, too tightly wedged. I exerted all my strength once again—and he still didn't move. I had to let go or we would both be in the rock crusher.

Then I felt him stir.

"Berkk, you miserable bastard!" I screamed into his ear. "Push with your feet. Try. Or you have had it. Push!"

In the end he did. I kept pulling as he pushed against the imprisoning bars—until he tumbled out of the cage and fell on top of me. After that we crawled, on all fours, because that was all we were able to do. Across the lacerating rock surface until we were free of it. Went on until we had stumbled over the last of the boulders. Collapsed onto the ground.

Under the reddish glow his blood looked black—and there was a lot of it on his pale, filthy face. His clothing was torn, his skin cut and abraded. But he was alive. We both were.

"Do I look as bad as you do—?" I asked, my voice grating and rough with dust, ending in a coughing fit.

"Worse," was all he managed to say.

I looked up at the pyramid of rock down which we had tumbled, as high as a mountain it seemed. By all rights we should have been dead.

But it was done. We were out.

"Let us not do that again," I said with some feeling.

"We won't have to. Because—we did it! We're away from the mine and we're never going back."

CHAPTER 20

I GENTLY TOUCHED MY RIBS and yelped. "Sore, maybe broken—but there is nothing we can do about it now. And you?"

Berkk had climbed slowly to his feet and was hobbling painfully. "The same, I guess. I hurt from all that banging about. I panicked, didn't I?"

"It can happen to anyone."

"It didn't happen to you. You got me into the cage and into the pit—and got yourself into it as well."

"Let's say that I have had more experience at this kind of thing—so don't let it bother you. Most important is what do we do next?"

"Whatever you say we should do. You saved my life and I owe you—"

"But you saved mine when you tripped the thug who was trying to brain me. So we are even. Right?"

"Right. But you still decide what we should do now. Maybe I made the rebar cages, but it was you who made the plan work. What's next?"

I looked around. "Find out where we are, and try to do it without being seen. I have had more than enough excitement for one day."

We walked beside the moving belt, trying to look ahead into the red-lit darkness. A distant rumbling grew louder as we went. We passed one of the glowing pits that provided the feeble illumination and I looked into it. It was filled with a liquid, maybe water, and the glow was coming from the bottom. I dropped in a piece of rock. It splashed nicely then slowly vanished from sight as it went under. Another mystery, but not one of any great importance at the moment.

"Lights ahead," Berkk said, and so there were. White for a change—and they were on our side of the rumbling, moving belt.

"Wrong side," I said. "I would prefer to be in the dark when investigating. Think you can climb over this thing?"

"Lead the way."

It was easy enough once we had clambered, slowly and painfully, up onto the belt, since it wasn't moving very fast. We slipped and stumbled over the broken stone, jumped painfully down on the other side. Walked alongside it as we came closer to the lights, the rumbling getting louder all the time. We bent over as we walked, hiding in the shadows. Trying not to stumble over the bits of rock that had fallen from the belt. Reached the end of the belt and looked out.

It was about what I had expected. Seen one rock crusher you have seen them all. The belt ended and the crushed rock fell from the end into a wide hopper. Below this a series of paired metal rollers, each set above the other, crushed the rock into ever-smaller pieces. Undoubtedly ending up as the fine dust that I had seen dumped onto the sorting tables. The rollers were set into a steel frame that vanished out of sight into an immense pit below. Spotlights were set into the pit walls to illuminate the scene. We bent over, then crawled the last bit and peered over the edge. Berkk pointed.

"Steps. Looks like they go all the way to the bottom."

I nodded agreement, leaning out so I could see. "Landings at various levels to service the machine. And what looks like a control area at the very bottom."

"See anyone?"

"No—but we are still going to be very careful. I'll take a look down the stairs—"

"No way! You move, I move. We're in this together."

He was correct, of course. There was no point in splitting up at this time.

"All right—but I go first. Stay behind and cover my back. Ready?"

"No," he admitted with a rueful grin. "And I doubt if I ever will be. But it's not going to get any better. So I guess that I'm as ready as I am ever going to be."

He was learning fast. I moved over against the wall and started down. When I reached the first landing I waved him after me, then stayed in the shadows of a great discarded and cracked roller. When he had joined me I pointed at the thick dust on the stairs. "Notice anything?" I shouted over the clattering roar of the rock crushers.

"Yes—the only footprints are ours."

"And the dust is centimeters thick. No one has been on these stairs in a very long time. But they could be waiting for us down below. Careful as we go."

The noise grew with each level we dropped, until it reached an almost brain-destroying volume. Still no one in sight—nor footsteps in the dust. I went faster now, driven on by the noise. Slower when I was just above the floor of the pit with the grouped instrumentation and controls. I waved Berkk to my side and pointed; he nodded agreement. There was no way that we could hear anything other than the eternal roar. But we could see where the dust had been disturbed, scuffed and covered with footprints in front of the controls. On the far side a jumbled trail of prints led beside a thick pipe that vanished into the wall.

Beside the pipe there was a sturdy metal door set into the same wall.

I pointed at the door and punched my fist into the air in a victorious gesture.

Now—out of the pit—before my brain was curdled. I let the cosh, still secured in place by its strap, slip into my hand. I crouched before the door and touched the big locking wheel that was set into it, then pointed to Berkk. He clutched it in both hands, exerted his strength. Muscles stood out in his neck with the strain.

Nothing happened. I pulled at his arm and when he looked around I made gestures of turning the wheel in the opposite direction, clockwise.

This worked fine. It turned and the door opened a fraction when I put my weight against it. Massive and heavy. I pushed it open enough to look through the crack into a small, metal-walled room. Empty as far as I could see—with another door set into the far wall. We pushed it wide and went in, closed and sealed it behind us. As we did the sound was cut to a distant rumbling.

"It's like an airlock," Berkk said. I could barely hear because of the ringing in my ears.

"More like a soundlock."

There was still a rumbling sound. From overhead. I looked up at the thick pipe that passed through the room; the rumbling was coming from it.

"Try the other door?" Berkk asked.

"In a moment—when the jackhammer in my head goes away."

The room was featureless. Nothing on the walls, just a light in the ceiling next to the pipe. And a track of dirty footprints leading from one door to the other. Ending in a floor mat. I kicked my boots clean on it.

"There must be something a little more civilized on the other side. Keeping their floor clean—"

I shut up as the wheel on the door in front of me began to turn.

"Behind the door!" I whispered as I plastered myself against the wall.

I could take care of one man all right. If there were more than one we were in trouble.

It opened wider. I crouched and raised my weapon. A metal foot and a metal leg appeared. I lowered the cosh as the robot stepped in. It ignored us completely as it turned and sealed the door through which it had entered. I leaned forward and read the identification plate on the back of its shining skull.

"It's a compbot-707. Wonderful! It's little more than a meter reader with legs. Have you ever used one?"

Berkk nodded happily. "I ran a string of fifteen of them once, in an assembly plant that I managed. After they have been programmed they can do only what's in their memory. The thing has no idea that we are even here."

We watched as it sealed the door, went over to the other door and opened it. We covered our ears as the sound blasted in, then died away as the door swung shut.

"Now let's see what's on the other side," I said as I spun the inner wheel and opened the door a crack. A hall with no one in sight. I opened it wide, stepped through.

"Going to leave me here?" He sounded worried.

"Not for long. But we have to find out what we're getting into. Let me take a quick look."

What I got into was a long, well-lit corridor with the rumbling pipe running the length of it, just below the ceiling. Doors opened off it, and there was another door at the far end—which might very well open at any time. I hurried to the first door I had seen, tried the handle, found it unlocked. Took a breath, readied the cosh—then opened it.

A storeroom, shelves and boxes—and perfect for our needs. I hurried back to Berkk.

"Let's get out of here. There's a storeroom we can get into."

With this last door closed behind me I slid down and sat on the floor. Berkk did the same.

"What do we do next?" he asked eagerly, as though I knew all the answers. I wished I did.

"Rest. And plan. No, no plan. We can't do anything until we find where in hell—or Heaven—we are." I shut up because I was getting light-headed. All the banging, crushing, crawling, bleeding, clotting had not done me any good. "You rest," I said, clambering painfully to my feet. "I'm going to check out the other doors and find out what I can. Be right back."

The first three rooms I looked into were spectacularly uninteresting. Cases of ball-bearing races, computer boards, miles of wire. Nothing that we could use, eat, or drink. But I hit the jackpot on the fourth, hurried back to get Berkk.

"All of the doors along the hallway open into storerooms—but I found one that is not only filled with bogey wheels but also has a medical emergency box. So not only can we clean up and get some dressings on—but some good person put a bottle of medicinal brandy in with the rest of the gear."

We drank the drinking medicine before we went on to antiseptics and bandages. Considering what we had been through we had gotten off lightly. Cleansed and purified—and half-sloshed—I thought of the future.

"Rest, sleep if you can," I said. "I'm going to take a reccy."

"What's that? Is it a pill?"

"No, you civilian, it's a military term left over from my army career. Short for reconnoiter. I'll try not to take any chances and will be back as soon as I can. One person can do this far better than two, so don't argue."

He didn't. "Good luck," he said.

"I don't believe in it. I make my own luck," I bragged. To lift his morale—or my own. I left.

The door at the end of the corridor opened into a very large open-plan room. The thick pipe carried on across to the center of the room where it made a bend and vanished down through the floor. I didn't like this room. I kept my eye to the crack for a long time. There were workbenches in there, with chairs before them. And chairs meant people. Instrument consoles glittered with lights and in the distance there was the sound of running motors. If it was empty for now—how long would it stay empty?

The waiting didn't help because nothing stirred, no one came. Muttering darkly I finally opened the door wide and slipped through. Slinked along between the workbenches, trying to look over my shoulder and in every direction at the same time. Through swinging doors and into an even bigger and brightly lit room. Still no one—though I found this hard to believe. I crept on, wondering how long my luck was going to hold out. I passed a door with a round window set into it, looked in carefully before going by. And swallowed.

A food and drink dispenser—it could be nothing else.

I was through it, the door closed behind me, and punching the button for drink. Caffeine-aide—exactly what I wanted, needed.

Paradisical . . . I drained two cups in a row before I slowed down. Triggered the controls that slipped a frozen catwich and a dogburger into the microwave while I sipped. I glanced out occasionally, but my heart wasn't in it. Food and drink first, more reccy later. I felt a slight twinge of sympathy for Berkk, but food washed it away. He was sleeping and resting and I would bring some of this back for him, or take him to it.

Stomach rounded, swishing inside as I walked, I decided to see what was around just one more bend before I returned.

Around the bend was something new. A stairwell leading down between rough concrete walls. And I remembered that the pipe with its contents of ground rock had gone down through the floor. Which meant its destination might be down here. Should I look? Why not? My stomach was full, caffeine was coursing through my blood—and I was very, very curious.

I went down the steps into a wide corridor that stretched away in both directions. There was a thick tubular thing hanging in the middle of it, running in both directions as well. It was made of polished metal and was much bigger than the ground-rock pipe we had been following. The corridor walls were even rougher, with rock shapes under the plastering. It had been drilled and dug out of the solid rock. Heavy electrical cables hung in festoons and electronic gear was mounted on the metal tube. I could make no sense of it. I walked along it a bit and realized that tunnel and pipe were both curved. A steady, long curve that remained the same. I walked on and the curve, the radius, never changed. If it stayed like this it would eventually form an immense circle and I would be back where I started. A circular tunnel with a circular pipe in the middle of it. It seemed familiar and—

There was the sound of footsteps coming towards me along the tunnel. Time to leave—but they stopped.

Leave, Jim, leave, while you are still in one piece!

Any sensible person would have beaten a hasty and silent retreat and saved curiosity for another day. I have always thought of myself as a sensible person.

Then why was I easing off my heavy working boots and stuffing them into my jacket? For what sane reason was I tip-toeing forward, trying to see around the curve.

I stopped, one foot raised, frozen.

My curiosity was satisfied in a rather large way.

There, just meters away, was Professor Justin Slakey peering through a window into the large tube's interior.

CHAPTER 21

I DREW BACK INSTANTLY. SURELY he could hear the bass drum of my heartbeat echoing loudly in that quiet corridor. Had he seen me? I waited one second, two—and there was no sound of pursuing footsteps.

I started back as silently as I had come—just as the following footsteps sounded behind me. All I could do was run. Trying to stay ahead of the plodding sound. If he went a bit faster, or if I went slower, he would be far enough around the curve in the tunnel to see me. Or if I made a sound. Or—there were too many ors.

There were the stairs ahead of me, where I had come down. Should I try to climb them? No, they went straight up and weren't curved like the tunnel. I would still be climbing them when he came to their base. Onward ever onward. I passed them. Solid concrete steps leading up out of the tunnel. With a dark recess under them.

I took the chance, jumped and pressed myself against the wall under the steps. Tried to slow down my breathing, which sounded in my ears like a porcuswine in heat. Slakey's footsteps came closer. Was he passing by the stairs? If he did he would discover me. And no matter how fast I attacked and rendered him unconscious, he would have seen me and every other Slakey would know at the same time that I was here.

That would be the end.

Slap, slap, the sound of his footsteps came closer. Sounded different, closer—then dying away. He *was* going up the stairs.

When the last clack-clack had dimmed and vanished I let myself slump down to sit against the wall. And put my shoes back on.

Jim, I said silently to myself, *I do hope you enjoyed your little reccy. You were that close to ending the whole thing.*

Then I waited, a good long time. I waited far longer than I thought necessary, then I waited some more. By the time I did move my bottom was numb from the hard floor. Creaking, I stealthily climbed the steps. I twisted my head about so much that I quickly got an even sorer neck. Back through the large lab and out the door. Unseen as far as I could tell. Down the corridor and into the storeroom.

Jumped back in fright at the horrible growling sound.

Relaxed and closed the door behind me as Berkk emitted another gargling snore. My toe lightly planted in his ribs brought him around.

"Snoring on duty is punishable by death," I said.

He nodded glum agreement. "Sorry. Meant to stay awake. Thought I could. Didn't. What did you find?"

"Food and drink for openers. That got your attention, didn't it? Look at you—up on your feet, nostrils flaring, snoring forgotten. After I lead you to it I'll tell you what else I found."

We didn't linger in the food hall. In and out and back as fast as we could in case Slakey had a touch of appetite.

"It could have ended in disaster just as easily," I said, licking a last crumb from my fingers. "Maybe it was that luck you wished me. If so—thanks."

"Don't mention it. We're alive, full of food and drink, safe for a moment—and we even know our way around a bit. And we are out of the rock works at last. A good beginning!"

"Indeed." I ticked the points off on my fingers. "It is a rocky road that we have taken—but we're still on the move. First, we got away from the rock-digging works along with a lot more rocks. Second, we find that our rock is being ground to dust in an underground rock-grinding mill." I touched another finger. "Third, after the rock is ground it is moved through a pipe to the place where we are now hiding. And we are still underground. The circular tunnel I found at the foot of the stairs has been dug, drilled and plastered with great effort. And fitted out with some pretty complex machines. For what reason I do not know. Can you think of anything it might be used for?"

"Not a clue. But what I do know is that we are still not out of the woods. Or the tunnels."

"Quite right. We can rest a bit, eat a bit—but that is not going to solve our problem. Sooner or later we are going to have to move on. It stands to reason that the ground-up rock is going someplace for some important reason. Slakey has gone to an awful lot of trouble and expense to get it this far. I'm willing to bet that it eventually ends up in that place with the tables and the women I told you about."

"Yes. Where you were just before you came through to the rock works."

I thought about that hard. "I went from the tables to the stairs that led up to the room that opens into the rock works. But you went from a different planet right to the room." He nodded agreement. "Which means that the interuniversal transmitter leads from that room. But—" My head was beginning to ache but I pressed on. "But I entered the table place by falling down a hole in Heaven . . ."

Sudden realization sizzled and burned in my brain and I leapt to my feet with the strength of it. "Think about it. We both went through the transmitter to the room that opens on the frozen planet where the opencast mine is. Then we dropped into the pit with the crushed rock. We undoubtedly went through another transmitter. To Heaven! Maybe we are underground on Heaven right now—and the entire complicated operation is completed here."

He had a glazed look and was not following me.

"Think!" I ordered. "If we are in Heaven—then we are at the heart of the Slakey operation. Everything begins here and ends here. Whatever he has been up to, whatever he is spending all those billions of credits on is right around us." I stabbed a finger upwards. "There, on the surface, is Heaven. And Professor Coypu of the Special Corps knows how to get there!"

"Great. But what good is that going to do us now?"

I slumped back to the floor, deeply depressed. "None, really. We're still in deep doodoo and still trying to find a way out."

He looked worried. "Are we? If what you figured out is correct then all we have to do is go on. Follow the ground rock to this place with the tables that you talked about. You came in there—so there might still be a way out. We just follow the rock dust."

"It's not that simple."

"Why not?"

Why not indeed? We couldn't go back—so we had to press on. It was the only chance we had.

"You're right—we'll go on in the same direction."

"Now?"

I thought about that for a bit. "Slakey is awake and wandering around. But he might not be alone. And there is always a chance someone will come into this storeroom. It's taking a chance whatever we do."

"Aren't you tired?"

I thought about it, then shook my head. "In fact I'm jumping with caffeine. Not in the least tired. So let's get moving."

We did. Scurrying like mice through the rooms ahead. More mysterious machinery—and a hopeful sign. Berkk pointed and I nodded agreement. A thick pipe had emerged from some complicated apparatus and was rumbling on nicely overhead. Through a large opening in the wall and into a room beyond. Not really a room, more of a cavern carved from solid rock. It was dimly lit by feeble lights, the concrete floor pitted and dusty. But the pipe was still there, no longer suspended from the ceiling but running along the floor now.

"It's still rumbling," Berkk said, putting his hand against it. "Vibrating. Something is surely going through it."

Which was fine. The only thing wrong was that the pipe went straight ahead and vanished into the roughly carved wall. A very solid-looking rock wall with no openings in it.

"No door," Berkk said.

"There *has* to be a door!"

"Why?" he asked with repulsively simple logic.

Why indeed? Just because we had been able to follow the pipe this far didn't mean it was always going to be easy.

"Think!" I said, thinking very hard. "That black rock was dug up with great labor. Dumped down here where, with even more labor, it was ground to dust. In those rooms or in the tunnel back there something was done to that dust, it was processed somehow, something added or subtracted or who knows what. Then the stuff keeps moving on to . . . where?"

"To the place you told me about, with the robot and the women and everything. There has to be some way of getting there, though it doesn't have be anywhere near the pipe."

"You're right, of course, good man. We look and we find. But which way first?"

"Left," he said with positive assurance. "When I was a Boy Sprout we always started to march—"

"With your left foot. So we go left."

We did. With no results whatsoever. The lights behind us grew dim and distant. We moved in almost complete blackness, feeling our way along the rough stone wall. Which resulted in nothing more than sore fingertips. We came to a corner, then an endless time later to another one. Then as dim lights appeared we saw that there, right ahead of us, was the pipe again. We had worked our way around three sides of the rock chamber to the place where we had come in.

"Maybe we should have gone right," Berkk said brightly. This did not deserve an answer.

Back to where the pipe ended. But we turned right this time and went on into the darkness, Berkk first, running abraded fingertips along the stone.

"Ouch!" he said.

"Why ouch?"

"Because I cracked my knuckles on what feels like a door frame."

We traced the outline with our hands and it not only felt like a door frame but it was one. With a very familiar wheel in the middle of it. It was not easy to turn, but between us we managed to get it moving a bit; metal squealed and grated inside.

"Long time . . . between openings," I grunted. "Keep it going."

With a final squawk of protest the locking bolt was free and the door swung away. We looked into a small room, feebly lit by green glowing plates on the wall. This was more than enough light for our darkness-adjusted eyes to see another door on the far wall. With a handle.

"And a combination lock!" Berkk said, reaching out.

"Stop!" I said, slapping his hand away. "Let me look at it before we try anything."

I blinked at the thing, trying to make out the details in the feeble light, moved my head from side to side.

"I can just about make out the numbers," I said. "It is an antique drum lock that was old when I was young. I know this lock."

"Can you open it?"

"Very possibly. Possibly not since there are no tumblers to drop that I could listen for. But—there is one long chance. To lock this lock it must be turned from the last number that is set in when you open it. Many people forget to do that."

I did not add that most people did not forget most of the time. The thought was too depressing. And we couldn't go back. I needed some luck again—a very lot was riding on this. My fingers were damp and I rubbed them on my shirt. Reached out and grabbed the handle and pulled.

The door didn't budge.

But the handle rattled a bit in my hand. Did it turn? I tried.

And it did. The lock had not been locked after all.

I pulled the door open a bit and put my eye to the crack.

CHAPTER 22

"WHAT DO YOU SEE?" BERKK WHISPERED.

"Nothing. Dark."

And very quiet. I opened the door all the way and enough light filtered through from the glowing plates to reveal a rough floor littered with debris. A bent sign on the wall spelled out, in glowing letters:

PLEASE LEAVE THIS PLACE AS YOU FOUND IT

They must have found it pretty awful if was like this now. Broken lengths of plastic littered the floor, as well as empty, half-crushed containers. And it stank.

"Yukk," Berkk said. "Something is rotten in here."

"No, not in here. In this entire place, that's the smell I told you about, that came from the dust or sand. I'm back where I started. In Heaven."

"Doesn't smell like Heaven."

"That is because Heaven is up there on the surface. I was grabbed there by that robot with a built-in gravchute. We dropped into a pit and ended up here. Heaven is above."

"It usually is."

"On the planet's surface, you idiot. The planet is named Heaven."

"Great. But how do we get up there?"

"That is a very good question. For which, at this moment, I do not have an answer. So let us start by getting out of this place first. Is that a chink of light over there? Close the door partway—enough. Yes, stay here while I take a look."

I stumbled and kicked my way through the junk to a vertical crack of some kind with a reddish light shining through it. My fingers pulled at the edges, apparently the gap between two thin metal plates. I pressed my eyes close and looked out. A barren landscape with glowing red pits in the ground, some with bursts of flame rising from them. And that smell, blowing in stronger. I was back in the same place in the underworld where I had arrived.

"Berkk."

"Yes?"

"Feel around in the junk and see if you can find something thin to pry with. This wall, or whatever it is, is made of sheet metal plates—and not too well joined."

The first shard of hard plastic bent, then snapped. We tried again with a length of angled metal and managed to make a bigger opening. It was wide enough to get our fingers through, to pull and curse as the sharp edges cut into our flesh.

"Heave now, together," I said. And we did. Something screeched and broke free, leaving a gap big enough for us to push through.

Out of one prison and into another. I kept such defeatist thoughts to myself and looked around. Dark shapes.

"Buildings," I said. "I didn't see them when I was brought here that first time. Not that I had much of a chance to see anything while I was dragged along."

"Shall we take a look?"

"Any choice?"

There was no answer to that one. In the red-shot semidarkness it was hard to see very far. The landscape was open with no place to hide. But no one moved, there was nothing in sight.

"Let's go."

When were closer we could see that they were buildings, with dark openings cut into their sides. They looked like windows and doors without glass or covering. There were more of the glowing plates inside shedding some light; we approached cautiously. No sound, no one in sight. Looking through the empty rectangle of a window I could see rows of what could only be beds or bunks.

"The women," I whispered, pointing. "They can't work all the time—and some of the bunks are occupied."

"Like us digging rock, two shifts maybe, so work goes on right around the clock."

We skirted around the silent building—and there they were—stretching out of sight in red-lit darkness. The tables. The women bent over them. The sudden rustle of sound, accompanied by the foul odor, as another mass of the finely ground rock was released.

"I want to talk to them," I said. "They will certainly know more than we do about this place. They came here from somewhere—so if there is a way in there must be a way out."

I started up and Berkk held my arm. "Not alone. I'm coming with you."

We ran together to the nearest table, dropped down in its shadows by the legs of one of the workers. If she knew we were there she gave no sign.

"*Ni estas amikoj,*" I said. "*Parolas Esperanto?*"

At first she did not answer or respond. Just kept her arms swinging in slow motion over the moving surface of the table. Then she stopped but did not look down.

"Yes. Who are you—what are you doing here?"

"Friends. What can you tell us about this place?"

"There is nothing to tell. We work. Finding that which must be found. When we find enough, that *thing* knows about it. It always knows. Then it comes and takes what we have found and then we can eat and sleep. Then we work again. That is all there is."

As her voice died away her hands began their slow sweeping motions again.

"What *thing?"* I asked. "What makes you work?"

She lifted her arm, then turned and slowly pointed across the table. "That thing, over there."

I raised my head up just high enough to look—dropped down instantly and fearfully pulled Berkk after me into deeper shadow.

"Her *thing* is my robot. The one I told you about, that brought me here. It's the devil in this particular corner of hell."

"What do we do?" There was fear in his voice as well—for good reason.

"I tell you what we don't do—we don't let it see us. We'll be dead, or at the very best back with the rocks and our obnoxious keeper, Buboe."

We pressed as hard as we could against the dusty flank of the table. Hoping that we were concealed by the shadows as the robot appeared farther down the line of structures.

A woman was with it, head down, shuffling slowly along. They walked towards the building we had so recently left. Passed so close that the smears of rust were clearly visible on the robot's flank. That single glowing eye. As they entered one of the doorways I scrambled to my feet.

"Let's go—as far away from that robot as we can get!"

Berkk needed no urging, was in fact well ahead of me in what was possibly a life-or-death race.

No heads turned in our direction as we ran by; the women's arms kept sweeping, brushing.

"Something up ahead there, lights of some kind. Maybe buildings," Berkk said.

I took a look behind us and put on a panic burst of speed, enough to pass him.

"It's seen us. It's coming after us!"

When I dared to look again it was closer, running faster than us, steel legs pumping like pistons. We couldn't win—

I turned my head back just in time to see one of the women leave her position at the table, just a silhouetted figure against the distant lights. She turned and was stepping out in front of me. I tried to go around her but she put her arms out to grab me. A sudden twist and I was thrown breathless to the ground.

An instant later Berkk fell on top of me. And the robot was almost there!

The woman arrived first. Throwing her body forward so that she landed on top of both of us, her face almost pressing against mine.

"It's about time you showed up," Angelina said.

CHAPTER 23

DARKNESS VANISHED AND I BLINKED against the sudden glare of bright lights. I could feel Berkk writhing under me—while directly before my eyes was the most beautiful sight in all of the known, and unknown, galaxy.

Angelina's black-smeared, smiling face. I lifted my head and kissed the tip of her nose.

"Errgle . . ." Berkk errgled, trying to wriggle out from under our weight. I moved a bit so he could get free, still clutching harder to Angelina's warm, firm body. We kissed enthusiastically and it was more of heaven than the Heaven we had just left would ever be.

"When you are through with that you might report what you found," Coypu said. I would recognize that voice anywhere. We separated reluctantly and stood up. Still holding hands.

Behind Coypu was a very familiar laboratory.

"We're in Special Corps Prime Base!" I said.

"Obviously. We moved the entire operation back here when you failed to return from Heaven. Slakey is very dangerous people. Soon after we got here there were a number of attempts to penetrate our defenses. They have all failed and the shields are stronger than ever."

"You would like a drink?" Angelina said, whistling over the robar. "Two double Venerian Vodka Coolers."

"After you, my darling. And another for my friend, Berkk, here."

He still sat on the floor, looking around and gaping. His fingers clutched the glass the robar gave him and we all glugged enthusiastically.

"Now, tell me, Professor," I said, holding out my glass for a refill. "What was Angelina doing in that terrible place—and how did she get us back?"

Before he could answer the door burst open and Bolivar—or was it James?—burst in followed by his brother. With Sybil a short pace behind.

"Dad!"

There were enthusiastic embraces all around, and some more drinks from the robar so we could toast our successful return. As we lowered our glasses Berkk dropped his. When he bent over to pick it up he just kept going, falling heavily to the floor, unconscious. I grabbed his wrist—almost no pulse at all.

"Medic!" I shouted as I rolled him onto his back and opened his mouth to make sure that his air passages were clear. But as I did this I was pushed not-too-gently aside by the medbot that had dropped out of the ceiling. It put a manipulator into Berkk's mouth to secure his tongue. At the same time it pressed an analyzer against his skin, took a blood sample, extruded a pillow under his head, did a fast body scan, covered him with a blanket and had already radioed for a doctor who burst through the door scant instants later.

"Stand clear," he ordered as the medbot slid an expanding metal web under Berkk's body, popped wheels out of the ends and carefully drove off with him. "The surgeon is standing by," the doctor said. "There appears to be a small blood clot on the patient's brain, undoubtedly caused by a blow to the skull. Prognosis good." He hurried after the medbot while Sybil hurried after him.

"I'll see what happens and report back," she said. She left with Bolivar and James right behind her. The three were inseparable now. Which might lead to problems that I did not wish to consider at this moment.

This put a bit of a damper on the party and we sipped glumly at our drinks. Before we finished them—modern medicine sure works fast—Coypu's phone rang and he grabbed it up. Listened, nodded, then smiled.

"Thank you, Sybil," he said and hung up. "Operation successful, out of danger, no permanent brain damage. He'll stay in narcsleep until the treatment is finished."

We cheered at that. "Thank you, Professor," I said. "With this last emergency out of the way we can now relax and listen. While you tell us how my Angelina managed to drag me out of the hell in Heaven and how she got there in the first place. After which we will try to figure out what all the strange happenings that have been going on really mean. Professor."

"We will take the explanation one step a time, if you don't mind. To go back to the beginning. When you did not return after a good deal of time had passed I activated your undetectable interuniversal activator and the boot returned. Without you. Since you were not wearing the boot I reached the inescapable conclusion that my machine had been detected. Therefore I had to improve its undetectability. I did this rather quickly because I was feeling very, very rushed."

"I held a gun to the back of his head with my finger trembling on the trigger," Angelina said, smiling sweetly. "I was going after you and intended to bring you back—with a better machine than the duff one he had supplied you with."

"It was an early model," Coypu muttered defensively. "I improved the design greatly then constructed three devices of varying degrees of undetectability."

"I carried the first hidden in the lining of my purse," Angelina said. "The second was under the skin on my arm, here." She rubbed at the long white scar, easily visible under the dusty smears, and scowled. "I will have to get this unsightly thing removed."

"That is not the only thing that is going to be removed," I grated through tight-clamped teeth. "I'm going to kill that particular Slakey for that botched bit of surgery."

"Not if I get there first, darling. He of course very quickly found the one in my purse, and then he detected this one, with great difficulty I must say. He was so pleased with himself that he never considered that there might be a third."

"Where is it?" I asked.

"Where Slakey obviously could not find it," Coypu said, happily rattling his fingers on his foreteeth. "I knew that there was no way to detect the pseudo-electrons, so it must have been the pseudo-electron paths in the solid state circuitry that he found. So I impressed my neural network on Angelina's neural network where it would be concealed by her neural activity."

"You mean that you built your machine right into her nervous system?"

"Exactly so. Since my pseudo electrons move at pseudo speed, there would be no interference with the electrical function of her synapses. The circuitry ended directly in her brain."

"So when I thought *go,* we all went," she said, throwing her empty glass towards the robar, which plucked it out of the air with a flip of a tentacle. "Now I am going to wash off this mud and stench and I suggest, Jim diGriz, that you do the same."

"I will—after I ask you a single question . . ."

"It can wait." Then she was gone. I whistled up another drink.

"Tell me all that happened," Coypu said.

"You let her go after Slakey alone!" I accused. "With all the massed strength of the Corps to hand."

"And a gun to my head. Do you think that there was any way to stop her?"

"No—but you could at least have tried."

"I did. What happened?"

I slumped in a chair, sipped my drink, and told him the entire repulsive story. My descent into Purgatory from Heaven and the women at the sorting tables there. Then being tossed through Slakey's machine to the living hell of the mining world.

He popped his eyes a bit when I told him about our escape in the rebar cages. Narrowed his eyes into pensive slits when he heard about the laboratory and the mysterious circular tunnel.

"And that was that. My dearest Angelina was there and whisked us back here and you know the rest."

"Well, well, well!" Coypu said when I had finished, jumping to his feet with excitement and pacing back and forth.

"Now we know what he is doing and how he is doing it—we just don't know what he is doing it for."

"Perhaps you know, Professor, but some of us are still in the dark."

"It's all so obvious." He stopped pacing and raised a didactic finger. "Heaven is the seat of all of his activities, we can be sure of that now. It matters not in the slightest where the mineral is mined. Because it was brought to Heaven after you and the male slaves extracted it from the ground. Dropped through an interuniversal field to end up in Heaven where it is ground finely and bombarded in a cyclotron—"

"A what?"

"A cyclotron, that is the machine that you saw in the tunnel. Your description was quite apt, even if in your ignorance you did not know what you were looking at. It is an ancient and rather clumsy bit of research apparatus that is not used much anymore. It is basically a very large, circular tube that has all the air inside evacuated. Then ions are pumped in and whirled around and around through the tube, held in orbit away from the tube walls by electromagnets. After building up tremendous speeds the ions smash into a metallic target."

"Why?"

"My good friend, how did you manage to obtain an education without studying basic science in school? Any first-year student would remember the simple fact that if you bombard platinum with neon ions you obtain element a hundred and four, called unnilquadium. It follows, obviously, that if you hit lead isotopes with a beam of chromium you will obtain unnilsextium."

"What is that?"

"A transuranic element. In the Stone Age of physics there were believed to be only ninety-eight elements, the heaviest of which was uranium. As new ones were discovered they were named, we think, after household gods. Curium after the god of medicine who cures disease, that sort of thing. Anyway, after the discovery of mendelevium, nobelium and such, the elements were numbered in an ancient and lost language. One hundred and four is unnilquadium, one hundred and five unnilquintium and so forth. Slakey has created a new element, much further up the atomic number table I am sure. It is obviously generated in very small quantities and comes out of the cyclotron still mixed with the original ore. Machines cannot detect it or they would have been used for this onerous task. But obviously women, and not men, can find it. Angelina will tell us more about that . . ."

"About what?" she asked. Making a glorious entrance in a green space jumper that went beautifully with her now red-gold hair.

"What were you and the other women looking for in the grit?" I asked.

"I have no idea."

"But exactly what were you doing?"

"An interesting phenomenon. All the bits of sand and gravel looked exactly alike. But some of the grains, when you touched them they felt—slow? No, that's not right, perhaps the other grains felt faster. It's almost impossible to describe. But once felt never forgotten."

"Entropy," Coypu said firmly. "That's Slakey's special field of research. I am certain now that he is producing particles with different entropy."

"Why?"

"That is what we will have to find out."

"How?" I asked. Puzzled, bothered and bewildered.

"You will find a way, you always do," Angelina said, patting me on the arm. Her smile turned to a frown when she looked at her filthy fingertips. "Go burn those clothes," she ordered. "Then wash until your skin glows, then wash some more."

I went willingly, well aware now of the stench, itch and scratch of my battered body. In the guest suite a burst of flame in the bathroom burner incinerated my clothing. I punched for antiseptics as well as soap in the bath, sank with a sigh under the warm water with a weary *whew*. . . .

Woke up drowning as my nose slipped beneath the surface. Hawked and spat out water; I must have fallen asleep. My body was giving me a message that I was happy to receive. Dried and dusted I went on all fours into the bedroom, crawled dizzily into bed and knew nothing more.

Angelina and I were having a relaxed drink before dinner. The twins and Sybil were off somewhere, while the professor was busy in his laboratory. We had a few moments alone.

"Any particular way you would like me to kill Slakey in Heaven?" I asked.

"Messy and painful. Though he wasn't really that awful to me. But he was an irritating fat old git. Cackling with joy when the surgicalbot cut out the implant. Painless really, just messy. He couldn't have cared less after that. I was just another woman for his slave labor at the tables. That terrible one-eyed robot grabbed me—now *that* is one piece of rusty iron I intend to dispatch personally—and took me off to the sorting place. One of the other women let me touch a grain she had found and that was that. Unlike those other poor creatures I knew that I could leave at any time, so it wasn't too awful. I also knew that you would be making a breakout from somewhere somehow as soon as you could, so I didn't mind waiting. I worked along with the others until I saw you and your friend running away from the robot. That was when I decided that it would be better if we all came back here."

Better! Not a word of complaint about what she had gone through to rescue me. My angel, my Angelina! Words could not express my gratitude, but some fervid kisses did get the message across. We separated when Coypu arrived. I ordered him his favorite Crocktail while Angelina went out to do whatever women do when their hair is mussed.

"A question, if you please, Professor."

"What?" He sipped and smacked his lips happily.

"How are you doing with that little difficulty you had—about not being able to send machines through between the universes? You will recall that when we went to Hell the only weapons that worked were salamis."

"I do recall it—and that is why I instantly tackled the problem. It is solved. An energy cage protects any object you wish from the effects of transition. You have an idea?"

"I certainly do. You will remember that my son James hypnotized that old devil Slakey in Hell."

"Unhappily, unsuccessfully. He was too insane to be questioned easily. And there wasn't enough time to do more."

"What if you had him or any other of the Slakeys here?"

"No problem at all then. We have highly skilled psychologists who work with computerized probes that can track thought processes down through all the levels of the brain. Mental blocks can be removed, traumas healed, memories accessed. But we don't have him here or any of the others. And the one in Hell. We know that he has been there too long. He will die if he is moved out."

"I know—and I'm not suggesting that. Now run your mind back to the adventurous past. You must recall the time war when the Special Corps was almost destroyed?"

"*Was* destroyed!" He shivered and sipped. "You restored us to reality when you won the war. Shan't forget that."

"Anything to help a friend. But what I am interested in now is the time fixator. The machine you built when reality was getting weaker and people were popping out of existence. You told me that as long as a person remembered who he was he was safe from the effects of the time attack. So you put together the machine that records the memories of an individual and feeds them back every three milliseconds."

"Of course I remember the time fixator—since I invented it. We have plenty in stock now. Why?"

"Patience. Then you will also remember that I took *your* memories with me. Then, when I had to move back through time again, I let your memories take over my body to build a time helix, the time-traveling machine that is also your invention."

His eyes opened wide as his speedy thoughts leaped to the conclusion that I was slowly building towards. He smiled broadly, finished his drink, jumped to his feet, rushed over and seized my hand and pumped it enthusiastically.

"Brilliantly done! An idea that is as good, almost, as one I might have thought up. We take the time fixator to Hell—"

"Plug Slakey into it and take a recording. Then leave him there in the flesh—but bring back all of his memories!"

Angelina had returned and heard this last. "If you are off on one more interuniversal trip you are not going alone this time."

Said without anger but with an unshakeable firmness. I opened my mouth to protest. Closed it and nodded.

"Of course. We're going back to Hell. Wear your lightest clothes."

"But no salamis this time."

"Quite right. That was an emergency measure—that succeeded I must remind you—that won't be needed now. We'll take the marines again, but well-armored and armed this time. To defend us while we make a memory recording of the Slakey in red."

"No troops," she said. "They would only get in the way. It will be just you and I in a fast armored scout tank. A lightning attack, find the old devil. Then I fight off anyone who gets in the way while you plug his brain into the memory fixator. After that it will be home in time for lunch. Tomorrow?"

"Why not? They want me in the hospital today. Some therapy for my bruises and cuts, and a broken rib or two that they are going to put right. Tomorrow morning will be fine."

It was. The body scan showed that two of my ribs were cracked. But microwindow surgery soon took care of them. The incision was so small that all that was needed was a local anesthetic. Since I am always very interested when someone fiddles around with my insides, I insisted upon having a hologram monitor, just like the surgeon's, so I could watch what was happening in glorious color 3D. The flexible needle snaked in through my skin and on into the bone of the rib itself. Once in place nanotechnology devices poured out of the tip of the needle, a submicroscopic crowd of molecular machines that grabbed the broken bone ends with their manipulators, then held tight onto each other. Micromotors whirred and the broken ends were neatly pulled together. Wonderful. The little machines would remain in place as new bone grew over them. I went right from the operating table to the laboratory where the interuniversal transporter and Angelina were waiting.

"I'm ready whenever you are," she said. She certainly was. Tastefully garbed in a black uniform, all metal studs and grenade clips, black boots—and a heavy weapon holstered on each hip.

"Very fetching," I said, slipping on the backpack that held the time fixator. "How was the test drive in your steel steed?"

"Very nice indeed," she said, patting the armor plate on the scout tank. "Fast, tough, with impressive fire power. More than enough weaponry to cover you in Hell. How was the bone operation?"

"Fast and efficient and I'm all mended and raring to go. Shall we?"

"In a moment. Before we leave I want to impress on Professor Coypu a few important facts. Like the fact that we are not setting up housekeeping in Hell and want to be returned here soonest."

"Exactly."

Coypu strolled over from his control console looking decidedly miffed. "There will be no problems with the operation of the interuniversal activator this time, I can assure you of that."

"That's what you told me when you sent me to Heaven and I almost died with my boots off."

"Improvements have been made since then. Your vehicle has one activator built into the hull while you once again have one in your bootheel. And if worse comes to worse just clutch Angelina tightly—"

"Always a pleasant thought!"

"—and she will bring you both back."

"I feel relieved," I said, feeling relieved as I climbed into the scout tank and slammed the hatch. Angelina revved the engines and I gave Coypu the thumbs-up. His image scowled back at me from the communicator screen.

"You can turn the engine off," he said. "We have a small problem."

"How small?"

"Well . . . perhaps I should say big. I can't seem to find Hell."

"What do you mean you can't find it?"

"Just that. It appears to be gone."

CHAPTER 24

ANGELINA CUT THE POWER, I opened the hatch, and, quivering gently from *actio interruptus,* we slammed over to interrogate Professor Coypu who was laboring anxiously away at the controls.

"Why did you say *not there . . . ?*" Angelina asked angrily.

"I said that because it isn't. Where the hell has Hell gone?"

"It is a little difficult to lose an entire universe?"

"I didn't exactly lose it. It's just not where it should be."

"Sounds the same as losing it," I said.

He gave me a surly scowl before turning back to his button pushing and switch throwing. Apparently with no good results. "I cannot access Hell with the former setting. I have checked it a number of times. There appears to be no universe at all there."

"Destroyed?" Angelina asked.

"Since that takes a great number of billions of years I doubt it very much."

"Is Heaven still there?" I asked.

"Of course." He made some rapid adjustments and pressed a button. Widened his eyes and gasped. Groped behind him for his chair and dropped into it. "Not possible," he muttered to himself.

"Are you all right, Professor?" Angelina asked, but he didn't hear her. His fingers were flashing across the keyboard now and the screen was filled with rapidly flowing mathematical equations.

"Leave him to it," I said. "If anyone can find out what happened it's him. We're just in the way now."

We went to the lounge area and I snapped my fingers for the barbot. Angelina scowled.

"Little early to hit the booze, isn't it?"

"No booze, just a simple glass of beer to slake my thirst. Join me?"

"Not at this time of day."

I sipped and thought. "We have to go back to the very beginning of events. Forget the other universes for the moment. When this entire thing started, when you disappeared from Lussuoso, I had Bolivar and James do a thorough sweep of all the planets, to see if there were any other operations run by a Slakey under a different cover. We didn't find another Temple of Eternal Truth, but we did uncover the same kind of operation under a different name. We went to Vulkann and located the fake church. Went in there—and you know what happened after that."

"From Glass to Hell to Heaven and back here. Where we are stuck since the good professor can't find any of them any more."

"We don't have to wait for him." I grabbed for the phone. "The search we instigated may have uncovered other Slakey operations on other planets. Let's see what the boys found out."

I heard the splash of water and shrieks of joy in the background when Bolivar, or James, answered the phone.

"Can I interrupt your jollities?" I asked.

"Just a day at the beach, Dad. What's up?"

"I'll tell you when you get here. But first, do you remember if there were any other Slakey operations uncovered by the original search, when we were on Lussuoso?"

"We dropped everything and got out of there so fast—I just don't know. But I do know that the computer was still running the search program when we left. We'll get onto it. See you there as soon as we have the records."

Professor Coypu was still hammering out equations, Angelina had a cup of tea, and I was thinking of another beer when the boys arrived.

"News?" I asked.

"Good!" they said in unison.

I flipped through the printouts, then passed them to Angelina.

"Very good indeed," I said. "A few remote possibles, a couple of maybe probables."

"And one dead certain," Angelina said. "The Sorority of the Bleating Lamb. A women-only congregation, and rich women at that."

"Did you note the name of the planet where this operation is now taking place?"

"I certainly did—Cliaand of all places. You boys are too young to remember the planet, in fact you were in your baby carriage at the time. There were certain difficulties on Cliaand, but your father and I sorted them out. We'll tell you about it when we have the time. The important thing is that now it is a museum world."

"A museum of what?"

"Warfare, militarism, fascism, jingoism and all that sort of old nonsense. It was a very poor planet when we saw it last, but that must have changed by now. Tourist money, no doubt. Shall we go see?"

A heartfelt groan caught our attention. Professor Coypu was in the pits of despair. "No good," he groaned again. "No reason to it. Nothing makes sense. Gone. Heaven and Hell. All gone."

He looked so glum that Angelina went over and patted his arm.

"There, there, it is going to be all right. While you were sweating away at your equations—we have located what we are sure is another Slakey religious operation. We must now plan, very carefully, how this matter should be handled. I don't think we can afford to make any more mistakes."

There was a serious nodding of heads on all sides.

"Can we use the TI, temporal inhibitor again?" I asked.

"I don't see why not," Coypu said, coming up for air, his depression forgotten at the thought of action. "You told me that it did not work in the Glass universe. Did you leave it there?"

"Threw it into the ocean—it was just a worthless lump of metal. And I remember! Slakey said something like whatever my weapon was, it wouldn't work. So he does not know that we used the TI when we went to that church to grab his machine."

"In that case there is no reason why we cannot use the TI along with the time fixator."

"We'll do it! Hit hard without warning, during one of the services when we know that Slakey will be there. Freeze them all in time with the TI, walk in and put the TF on Slakey's head and make a copy of everything there. Can that be done, Professor?"

"Of course. Both machines operate on basically the same principle. They can be connected by an interlock switch. It will turn off the TI just as it turns on the TF, and will reverse the process a millisecond later."

I was rubbing my hands together in happy anticipation. "Freeze them solid, stroll in and pump his memories dry, walk out—and when we are well clear turn off the TI back in church. The Slakey service and operation will then go on as usual since he will have no idea that we have copied his mind. But we will need a bigger machine, something that will stop them and keep them frozen in a time stasis, everyone in the building. With a much bigger neutralization field than last time, which only protected a few operators. We will have to open doors to get inside the building."

For Professor Coypu all things scientific were like unto child's play. "I envisage no problems. There will be a large TI that will produce a field exactly the shape and size of the building you wish to enter. Time will stop and no one will be able to move in or out. Except you. Your TII, temporal inhibitor inhibitor, will cover you alone."

"Not alone," Angelina said. "Not ever again. It makes good sense to have aid and backup. Shall we do it?"

We were looking forward to a small family-sized operation, but Inskipp, who had spies and electronic snoopers everywhere, complained as soon as he heard about how the operation was planned. I obeyed his royal command and appeared at his office.

"Sincerely, do we really need more than four people?" I asked.

"Sincerely, the number of operators involved in this operation is not the point. It's your nepotism at work that bothers me. This is a Special Corps operation and it is going to be run by Special Corps rules. Not by familial felicity."

"How can there be rules for use of a temporal inhibitor to be used to get a time fixator into a church? Show me where it says that in the rules!"

"When I say *rules* I mean *my* rules. You are going to take another special agent with you so I will know just what is going on."

"Who?"

"Sybil. I am sending her ahead to survey the target."

"Agreed. Then all systems are go?"

"Go." He pointed at the door and I was gone.

The machines were manufactured and tested, but it was almost a week before our interplanetary travel in a warpdrive cruiser was completed. We left the military at the orbital station and went planetside in a shuttle along with a number of cruise ship passengers. Like them we were holiday makers in holiday clothes, with nothing in our luggage except a few souvenirs; our weapons and equipment were going down in a diplomatic pouch.

"For old times' sake I have booked us all into the most luxurious hotel in town—the Zlato-Zlato."

"Why is that name familiar?" Angelina asked. "Isn't that the same hotel where we stayed, where that horrible gray man tried to kill you?"

"The same—and you saved my life."

"Memories," she said, smiling warmly. "Memories. . . ."

When we reached the hotel the manager himself was there to greet us. Tall and handsome, a touch of gray at the temples, bowing and smiling.

"Welcome to Cliaand, General and Mrs. James diGriz and sons. Doubly welcome on your return visit."

"Is that you, Ostrov? Still here?"

"Of course, General. I own the hotel now."

"Any assassins booked in?"

"Not this time. May I show you to your suite?"

There was a fine sitting room, glass-walled on one side with a spectacular view of the surrounding countryside. But James and Bolivar cried aloud with pleasure at a spectacular view of their own.

"Sybil!" they said while she smiled warm greetings.

"Target survey completed?" I asked, hating to intrude business into all this pleasure.

"All here," she said, handing me a briefcase. "There will be a solemn assembly of the Sorority of the Bleating Lamb tomorrow morning at eleven."

"We shall be there—if our equipment arrives on time."

"Already arrived. The large trunk over there with the skull and crossbones patterns on it."

Angelina had a lovely time passing out the weapons while I unpacked the time fixator, which very cunningly had a casing constructed to resemble a Cliaand burglar alarm. It would stick to the outside wall of the assembly hall of the Sorority of the Bleating Lamb where it would attract no notice. Nor could it be dislodged once activated since it would be frozen in time along with the building. I popped out the holoscreen and fed in the building's dimensions and shape from Sybil's complete and efficient report.

"Done," I said happily. I clipped the metal case of the TII, the temporal inhibitor inhibitor, to my belt and actuated it. Nothing happened until I pressed the red button on the case that turned on the TI. Silence fell. But nothing else did. My family and Sybil were frozen, immobile in time. I turned it off; sound and movement returned. All the machines were in working order, all systems go.

There was celebration this night, dining and drinking and dancing, but early to bed. Next morning, a few minutes after eleven, my merry band was strolling down Glupost Avenue, admiring the scenery—but admiring Angelina even more where she stood on the corner waving to us. The wire from her earphone led to the musicman that she was wearing, which was really an eavesdropper amplifier.

"That stained-glass window up there," she said, pointing unobtrusively, "is in their assembly hall. Slakey's vile voice is vibrating the glass and I can hear him far too clearly. He is in the middle of some porcuswine-wash pontificating."

"Time," I said, and we joined arms and strolled happily across the street, dodging the pedcabs and goatmobiles. The rest of us went on while Bolivar stepped into the alleyway beside the building and pressed his beach bag against the wall. The beach bag cover stripped away and a handsome burglar alarm hung in its place. No one on the street had noticed. He rejoined us as we approached the front door.

"This is it, guys," I said. "Showtime."

I turned on the TII, then the TI. Nothing happened. Nothing happened that anyone could see that is. But the building and its contents were frozen now in time. Would remain that way—for an hour or a year—until I turned the machine off. The people inside would feel nothing, know nothing. Though they might be puzzled by the fact that their watches all seemed to be reading the same wrong time.

"James, the door if you please."

The field of my TII interacted with the field of the TI and released the front door from time stasis. James pulled it open, closed it behind us, and we marched into the building. Once the door was closed not even an atom bomb would be able to open it. Such power I possessed!

"The big double doors ahead," Sybil said.

"The ones with the blue baa-baas on them?" She nodded.

"Despicable taste," Angelina said and her arm holster whipped her gun out and back in microseconds. She was looking for trouble and I hoped she didn't find it.

The boys each took a handle—and pulled when I nodded. There, directly ahead of us and staring at us was Slakey.

Reflex whipped out six guns, Angelina had one in each hand, which were slowly replaced.

Like his frozen audience, Slakey was pinned into an instant of time. Mouth open in full smarmy flight, fixed beads of perspiration on his brow. Not a pretty sight.

We walked around his audience and up the steps to his pulpit. "Are you ready my love?" I asked Angelina.

"Never readier."

She reached out and placed the contact disk of the temporal inhibitor against the side of his head, just above his ear. She nodded and I touched the button.

Nothing that we could observe happened. But for that brief millisecond the TII field had been turned off and the machine had sucked a copy of Slakey's memory, his intelligence, his every thought into its electronic recesses.

"The readout reads full!" Angelina said.

"Slakey, you devil from Heaven and Hell," I exulted. "I have you now!"

CHAPTER 25

I WORRIED AT A FINGERNAIL with my incisors, waiting for something to go wrong. Slakey had been one step ahead of us every time so far—and not one of our operations against him had ever succeeded to any measurable degree. We had avoided disaster only through heroic efforts and last-minute leaps. It did not seem possible that on this occasion everything had worked according to plan. I had both hands around the TF; I kept it with me at all times. Now it sat on my lap as the shuttle eased into Special Corps Prime Base. I looked at the needle, as I had hundreds, thousands of times before, and it was up against the red post that read *full.*

Full of Professor Justin Slakey? It had better be.

It was an expectant crowd that assembled in the laboratory. Even Berkk was there, fully recovered from the brain operation and now enjoying some much deserved R and R. The talking died away and a hushed silence prevailed when I presented, almost ceremoniously, the TF to an expectant Professor Coypu.

"Is he in there?" I asked.

"I don't see why not." He tapped the dial. "Reads full. We'll see. But of course there remains the major problem. How do we get Slakey out of this TF? I can't feed him into another machine—there would still be no way to access him. I need a human host. You will remember what that is like, Jim, when you used my brain and memories to build a time machine."

"I let you take over my own gray matter. It was not nice. And you left me a note saying it was the hardest thing you ever did, to switch the TF off after you had built the temporal helix. To literally commit suicide."

"Exactly. We need a volunteer to be plugged into this TF so that a madman can control his brain and body. And Slakey will not want to leave once he is there. Not too tempting a prospect. So—with those facts in mind, who will volunteer?"

This got a very impressive silent silence as everyone present thought hard about it. I realized that I had better volunteer again, better me than my wife or sons. But as I opened my mouth Berkk spoke up.

"Professor, I think you have your man. I owe you people an awful lot, owe Jim who got me out of the rock works, owe Angelina who got us out of that hell in Heaven. I was dying down there with the others. I owe my life to you both and I don't want to see you or your sons, or Sybil, letting this nut-case near their gray matter. Just one question, Professor Coypu. Are you sure you can get him out—and get me back in when it is all over?"

Coypu nodded furiously. "Can be done, no doubt, just blast him out with a neural charge if I have to."

"Wonderful—what will happen to the *me* in there if you do that?"

"Interesting thought. A neural blast cleans everything out and sets the synapses back to neutral. But—not to worry. We'll make a recording of you in a different TF. This technique works quite well, as Jim will tell you. So whatever happens with Slakey, in the end we will get yourself back inside yourself."

"All right." He rose to his feet slowly, his face very pale under the dark scars. "Do it quickly before I have a chance to change my mind."

Quickly really was very quick with Coypu. He must have been holding a psycho blaster in his lap because there was a loud humming and Berkk folded. Angelina and I were there to catch him before he hit the floor.

A padded operating table rolled out of the massed machinery and we placed him gently on it. Coypu got to work. He took an empty TF from the shelf and plugged it into the back of Berkk's head. Worked the controls and nodded happily. "There. This very brave young man can now go back on the shelf. If Slakey causes trouble I will then zap him out of the neurons and get Berkk back with this. Now—to work."

He seized up the Slakey TF and placed it onto the workbench, then slipped a multiganged plug into the TF's socket. He ran an electronic check of the contents before reeling out the contact and connecting it to Berkk's head.

"Wait," I said. He stopped. "How about securing Berkk's body in place so he doesn't hurt himself—or us."

"I will have him securely under electronic control—"

"Slakey has *never* been under control in the past. So let us be sure and take no chances now."

Coypu threw a few switches and padded clamps hummed out from below the table. I locked them securely into place on ankles and wrists. Found a large belt and secured that around his waist and nodded to Coypu. He put the final connection into place, then threw some more switches as he swung a microphone down in front of his mouth.

"You are asleep. Very much asleep. But you can hear me. Hear my words. You will not wake up. But you will hear me. Can you hear me?"

The speaker rustled a bit and there was a sound like a sigh. Then the words, almost inaudible:

"I can hear you."

"That's very good." He turned up the amplification a bit. "Now, tell me—who are you?"

I don't know why they are called pregnant silences, perhaps because they are pregnant with possibilities. This one had all kinds of possibilities. The loudspeaker rustled again.

"My name is . . . Justin Slakey . . ."

Who can blame us for shouting with joy. We had done it!

Not quite. Berkk, or his body, was writhing and fighting against the bonds. He bit his lips until they bled. Then his eyes opened.

"What are you doing to me? Are you trying to kill me? I'll kill you first . . ."

The writhing stopped and he dropped back heavily as Coypu let him have it with his handy psycho blaster.

It was not going to be easy. Even with James helping, a far more skilled hypnotist than Coypu, it was impossible to exercise any control over Slakey. Just about the time they would hypnotize one Slakey another would take over. And all the subsequent thrashing about wasn't doing Berkk's body much good, what with fighting against the restraints, chewing on his lips and so forth.

"Time for some professional help," Coypu said. "Dr. Mastigophora is on his way. He is the leading clinical psychosemanticist in the Corps."

"Super-shrink?" I asked.

"Absolutely."

Dr. Mastigophora was lean to the point of emaciation, all sinew and leather, carrying an instrument case and sporting a great growth of gray hair. "I assume that is the patient?" he said, pointing a long and knobby finger.

"It is," Coypu said. Mastigophora glared around at his audience.

"Everyone out of here," he ordered as he opened his instrument case. "With the single exception of Professor Coypu."

"There is a physical problem with the patient," I explained. "We don't want him to hurt the body, which is only on loan."

"Up to your mind-swapping tricks again, hey Coypu? One of these days you will go too far—" He looked at me and scowled. "I said out and I mean out. All of you."

As he said this he sprang forward and seized my wrist and applied a very good armlock. Of course I let him do it since I don't beat up on doctors. He was strong and good enough—I hoped—to handle Berkk's body in an emergency. I left with the others as soon as he let go.

A number of hours passed and we were beginning to yawn and head for bed when the communicator buzzed. Angelina and I were wanted in the lab.

Coypu and Mastigophora were slouched deep in their chairs trying to outmatch each other in looking depressed.

"Impossible," Mastigophora moaned. "No control, can't erect blocks, can't access, terrible. It's the multiple personality thing, you see. My colleague has explained that Professor Slakey has in some unspecified manner multiplied his body, or bodies. His brain or brains or personality is in constant communica tion or something like that. It sounds like absolute porcuswine-wash. But I have seen it in action. I can do nothing."

"Nothing," Coypu echoed hollowly.

"Nothing?" I shouted. "There has to be something!"

"Nothing . . ." they intoned together.

"There is something," Angelina said, ever the practical one. "Forget Slakey and get back to looking into the guts of your interuniversal machine. Surely there has to be some way to get it working again."

Coypu shook his head looking, if possible, even gloomier. "While Dr. Mastigophora was brain-draining I tackled the problem again. I even stopped all the other projects that were running in the Special Corps Prime Base Central Computer. In case you didn't know it, the SCPBCC is the largest, fastest and most powerful computer ever built in the entire history of mankind." He turned on the visiscreen and pointed. "Do you see that satellite out there? Almost a third the size of this entire station. That's not a satellite—that's the computer. I had it working flat out on this problem and this problem alone. I used the equivalent of about one billion years of computer time."

"And?"

"It has tackled this question from every point of view in every way. And the conclusion was the same every time. It is impossible to alter the access frequencies in the interuniversal commutator."

"But it happened?" I said.

"Obviously."

"Nothing is obvious to me!" I was very tired and my temper was shredding and all this gloom and doom was beginning to be very irritating. I jumped to my feet, walked over to the shiny steel control console, looked at its blinking lights and tracing graphs. And kicked it. I hurt my toe but at least I had the pleasure of seeing one of the needles on a meter jump a bit. I started to bring my foot back for another kick. And froze.

Stood there on one leg for long seconds while my brain raced around in circles.

"He has just had an idea," Angelina said, her voice seemingly coming from a great distance. "Whenever he freezes up like that it means he has thought of something, had an inspiration of some kind. In a moment he will tell us—"

"I'll tell you now!" I shouted, jumping about to face them and neatly clicking my heels in the air as I did. "Your computer is absolutely right, Professor, and you should have more respect for its conclusions. Those universes will always be in the same place. As soon as we realize that, why the answer becomes obvious. We must look for the real reason why you cannot access those universes. Do you know what that is?"

I had them now, professorial jaws gaping, heads shaking, Angelina nodding proudly, waiting for my explanation.

"Sabotage," I said, and pointed at the control console. "Someone has changed the settings on the controls."

"But I set them myself," Coypu said. "And I have checked the original calculations and conclusions over and over again."

"Then they must have been changed too."

"Impossible!"

"That's the right word for it. When all the possibilities have been tried—then it is time to look to the impossible."

"My first notes, I think that I still have them," he said, stumbling across the room and tearing open a drawer. It fell to the floor and spilled out pens, paper clips, bits of paper, cigar butts and empty soup cans, all the things we leave in desk drawers. He scrabbled among the debris and pulled out a crumpled piece of paper, smoothed it and held it up.

"Here. My own writing, my first calculations, the beginnings of determining the locations and settings. This could not be changed." He stamped over to the controls, flickered his fingers across the console keys, pointed a victorious finger at the equation on the screen. "There you see—the same as this."

He looked at the paper, then at the screen, then back to the paper until it looked like he was watching an invisible Ping-Pong match.

"Different . . ." he said hoarsely. I must admit that my smile was a bit smug and I did enjoy it when Angelina gave me a loving hug and a kiss.

"My husband the genius," she whispered.

While Coypu hammered away at the computer, Dr. Mastigophora went to look at his patient.

"How is he?" I asked.

"Unconscious. We had to use the psycho blaster on him, paralyze his entire body as well as the brain. Nothing else seems to work."

"There it is! Hell!" Coypu shouted and we turned to look at his screen which showed a loathsome red landscape under a redder and even more loathsome sun.

"Hell," he said. "And Heaven. They are all there still. It was the calculations, the primary equations. Changed, just slightly, just enough to make the later calculations vary farther and farther from the correct figures. But—how did it happen? Who has done this?"

"I told you—a saboteur. There is a spy in our midst." I said, very firmly.

"Impossible! There are no spies in the Special Corps. Certainly none here in Prime Base. Impossible."

"Very possible. I have been thinking about it in great detail and, unhappy as I am to say this, I can identify the spy."

I had them now. Even Angelina was leaning forward, waiting for further revelation. I smiled serenely, buffed my fingers on my shirt, turned and pointed.

"There's your spy."

They all turned to look.

"The spy is none other than my good companion from the rock mine—Berkk."

CHAPTER 26

"HOW CAN YOU SAY THAT, Jim!" Angelina said. "He saved your life."

"He did—and I saved his."

"He was a prisoner like you. He wouldn't spy for Slakey."

"He was. And he did."

Coypu got into the disbelieving act. "Impossible. You told me, he's a simple mechanic. It would take a mathematician of incredible skill to alter those equations so subtly that I would never notice the changes."

I raised my hands to silence the growing protest.

"Dear friends—why don't we put this to the empirical test. Let's ask him."

In a matter of seconds the professor had pumped a massive electronic charge into Berkk's brain and drained it out of his heel. Leaving the brain empty of all intelligence. The captive Slakey was now just random fizzling electrons, which was fine; there were certainly enough other manifestations of him around. Then Coypu seized up the other fully charged TF that was full of Berkk and plugged it back to his body. A switch was thrown and, hopefully, Berkk was back home again. Dr. Mastigophora filled a hypodermic with psycho blaster antidote and shot it into Berkk's arm. He stirred and moaned and his eyes fluttered open.

"Why am I strapped down?"

I recognized his voice. Slakey was gone and Berkk was home again.

"Free him if you please, Professor." The clamps jumped open and I went to remove the restraining belt.

"Ouch," Berkk said, touching his bruised lips. "It was Slakey, wasn't it? He did this to me." He sat up and groaned. "Was it worth it? Did you get what you needed?"

"Not quite," I said. "But before we go into that—I would like to ask you one simple question."

"What's that?"

"Why did you sabotage Professor Coypu's interuniversal transporter?"

"Why . . . why do you think I would do a thing like that?"

"You tell me, Berkk."

He looked around at us, not smiling, with a very trapped-animal look. This suddenly changed. He looked up blankly; and a horrified expression transformed his face. "No!" he shouted hoarsely. "Don't do that—you can't . . ."

Then he dropped his face into his hands and wept unashamedly. No one spoke, not knowing what was happening. Finally he looked up, dragged his sleeve across his wet eyes.

"Gone," he said. "Back to the rock quarrying. Back to that hell in Heaven."

"Would you be kind enough to explain?" I asked.

"Me, I, you know. Me twice. He, I mean me, is back in the quarry. Grabbed by that foul one-eyed robot."

Sudden realization struck. "Did Slakey duplicate you the way he duplicates himself?"

"Yes."

"Then all is clear," I said smugly.

"Not to a lot of us, diGriz," Angelina said, all patience gone. "Spell it out so we peasants can understand. And quickly."

"Sorry, my love. But the explanation is a simple one. When Slakey had me thrown into the rock works he must have been worried about my presence in Heaven, and even more concerned about what Coypu or the Special Corps would do next. So he enlisted Berkk here to watch me. Doubled him and must have done horrible things to one of him to make the other be his spy."

"Chains," Berkk moaned. "Torture. Electric shock. I had to do what he told me because I felt everything that he was doing to the other me. Chained to the wall in Slakey's lab."

"And of course because you knew everything that you and I were doing, the other you also knew everything that we were doing and reported it to Slakey?"

"All the time. Slakey had me build those rebar cages so we could escape. He knew just what we were doing at the very moment we were doing it."

"But escaping in those cages was very dangerous!"

"What did he care? If we died it wouldn't have bothered him in the slightest. But once we had landed on the rock pile safely, he cleared out the cyclotron building so we could get through it. When we reached the unnildecnovum sorting tables he sent the robot after us to see what would happen, if we had any way of escaping. We did."

"You spying rat," Angelina said, and I saw her fingers arching into claws. "A viper in our bosom. We save your life and all you can do is sabotage the professor's machine."

"I had no choice," Ron moaned. "The me with Slakey told him everything. Slakey was ready to kill that me at any time if I didn't do what he ordered. When I woke up after the operation you had all gone away. I came here and this laboratory was empty—the professor was sleeping. That was Slakey's perfect chance to do the sabotage. I did exactly what he told me to do. Changed the equations and the settings and everything."

"Did he also order you to volunteer to have his brain pumped into your head?"

"That was my idea, I really meant I was volunteering—he also ordered me to do it, knowing you would get nothing out of it. And it would add to my credibility. I had no choice . . ."

"Forget it," I said. "It's all in the past and we can get through to the other universes again since the professor has undone your damage. Your spying days for Slakey are over, so now you can spy for us. You could very well be the key to putting paid to all the Slakeys. Help us and maybe we will be able to save the other you."

"Could you really?"

"We can but try. Now—the first question. What is going on with all the rock mining and crushing and sorting? We still have no idea of what Slakey's operation is all about. You used the word 'unnildecnovum.' What is it?"

"I have no idea. But since the other me was with Slakey all of the time I could see and hear everything that he did. He used the word in reference to the sorting tables, just once."

"It must be the substance we were looking for," Angelina said. "But what is it used for?"

"I don't know. But I do know it is the most important thing for Slakey. Nothing else really matters. And I think I know where it goes. Slakey kept me chained to the machine, the one like the professor's there, so I could tell him everything that was happening. But I could also see everything that he was doing. There were sometimes up to three of him present at one time. They didn't talk because, after all, they were all the same person. But one time he had that robot on the screen and he said something like 'Take the unnildecnovum there.' That was all."

"That's enough," Professor Coypu said, throwing some switches and pointing at the screen. Blue skies and floating white clouds. "Heaven. That's where it is all happening. He could have his mine on any one of a thousand planets, but what he mines ends up in Heaven for processing—"

"Just a moment if you please, Professor," I said. "What was that remark about any one of a thousand planets?"

"The substance he is mining. Very common."

"You know what it is?"

"Of course. Your clothing and Angelina's were coated with it. It is called coal. A crystalline form of carbon. It can be found on a great number of planets. He has it mined and ground to a fine powder. It is then bombarded in the cyclotron where a certain small proportion is changed to unnildecnovum, which is then sorted out by the women. Its very name reveals its identity. Unnildecnovum, one hundred and nineteen in the periodic table. A new element with unknown qualities. Entropy is involved, that is all we can be sure of. The women can detect that, so they can sort the unnildecnovum from the coal dust. This is then collected by that shoddy robot and taken—some place for some reason."

"Find the place—and we find the reason," I said triumphantly. "It *has* to be in Heaven, that is one thing we can be sure of."

"I'll take care of that," Inskipp said as he marched in. He had undoubtedly been monitoring everything that was happening in the lab and had picked the right moment to take over. "The Space Marines are on their way here. Gunships, tanks, flame throwers, field guns . . ."

"No way, José," I said with a great deal of feeling. "You can't hijack my operation at this late date. Nor do we need all the troops and armaments. We keep this small. Remember—we have only one man to fight. Even if he has a number of manifestations. Him—and his rickety robot which Angelina has promised to take care of in a suitably destructive manner. We have put together a good fighting team and we all go in together. If Professor Coypu can give us defenses against Slakey's weapons."

"Already done," Coypu said with unseemly self-satisfaction. "I have analyzed the atmosphere of Heaven. I know that he uses energy weapons and has an hypnotic gas, in addition to the addictive gases already present in the atmosphere."

He pressed a button and what appeared to be a transparent space suit popped out on the end of an extending arm. He pointed out its attributes.

"It is made of transparent seringera. A substance that is almost indestructible, unpierceable, a barrier to force fields and impervious to gases. Under the outer surface there is a nanomolecular structure that responds in a microsecond to a sudden impact such as a bullet. These molecules lock together and become stronger than the strongest steel, stopping the projectile before it has penetrated less than a millimeter. This small powerpack on the back, here, recycles and reconstitutes the gases and water in your breath so the suit may be sealed and worn for up to one hundred hours. It also powers a built-in gravchute that can be used for levitating if needs be. I will demonstrate."

He tore off his shoes, stripped off shirt and sarong, to reveal the fact that he wore purple undershorts with little mauve robots embroidered on them, trimmed with gold. He seized the transparent suit and wriggled into it, pulled the bubble helmet down to seal it. His voice rasped from the external speaker.

"There is no blade sharp enough to cut it." He opened a box of equipment and seized up a knife, plunged it into his chest. It bounced off. As did the other weapons he attacked himself with. Powering up the gravchute, he bounced off the ceiling, still firing his deadly devices. Soon the air was filled with noxious gases, whizzing missiles that threatened the rest of us, if not him. Coughing and gasping, we fled the chamber and did not return until the demonstration was over and the aircon turned up high.

"Wonderful, Professor," I said dabbing my eyes with the corner of my handkerchief. "We pull on your fancy suits and go to Heaven. When I say *we* I of course mean me and my family, along with Berkk and Sybil. The professor monitors our movements and our leader, Inskipp, stands ready to send any reinforcements that we might need. Any questions?"

"Sounds just insane enough to succeed," Angelina said. "How soon do we get our playsuits, Professor?"

"They'll be ready by morning."

"Fine." She smiled at us all. "We can have a little party tonight to celebrate our coming victory, the rout of Slakey, and the reunification of Berkk with himself. All right?"

A chorus of agreement was her answer. The robar hurried over to open the cocktail hour, and even Inskipp condescended this once to sipping a small dry sherry.

"I am very interested in this unnildecnovum," he said licking a trace of wine from his lips. "This madman has organized numerous religions to raise money to imprison slaves to mine coal to convert it to unnildecnovum—why? It must have some very unusual properties or why should he go to all this effort? I am very curious about what can be done with it. Or what it does to other things, or whatever. And I am going to find out. Go forth, Jim, and succeed. And bring me back a sample and an explanation."

"Good as done," I said and raised my glass.

We all drank to that.

CHAPTER 27

WE ALL WORE SWIMMING OUTFITS under the transparent suits. Angelina and Sybil looked quite fetching. I quickly averted my eyes from one, blew a kiss to the other.

"Equipment check," I said, drawing my gun and holding it up. "One paralysis pistol, fully charged. A container of sleep-gas grenades, another of smoke. Combat knife with silver toothpick. Manacles for securing prisoners, truth drug injector for making them talk."

"Plus a diamond-blade power saw for cutting up a certain robot," Angelina said, holding up the lethal looking object.

"All in order, all accounted for. Just one thing more." I picked up a backpack that had a medical red cross on a white background printed on it. "For emergencies. Are you on the circuit, all-powerful Inskipp?"

"I am," his voice rattled in my ear. "I have countless deadly standbys standing by in case you need help."

"Wonderful! Professor Coypu, if you please—unlock the door."

He threw the switch and the red light above the steel door, studded with boltheads and massive rivets, turned to green. I grabbed the handle and turned it, threw the door wide and we strode into Heaven.

"What's with the clouds?" I asked, pushing my finger into one floating by; it tinkled merrily.

"*A life-form indigenous to this planet,*" Coypu's voice said in my ear. "*It has crystalline guts, which explains the tinkling sound, and it floats because it generates methane. Be careful with sparks because they could blow up.*"

Not only could, but did. In a blast of flame that washed over me. I blinked at the glare but felt nothing. Apparently Slakey had us under observation and had opened fire. Other clouds were now floating our way, but were shot down before they could get close. They blew up nicely. When the last cloud of smoke had drifted away I pointed across the neatly cut greensward.

"There, that's the way we go. Valhalla is a con and just for show and Paradise is still being rebuilt. Nor do we wish to visit the rubbish dump. The bit of Heaven I found Slakey in is off in that direction. All we have to do is follow the yellow brick road."

Angelina looked around as we walked. "This would be a very pleasant planet if it weren't for Slakey."

"We are here to do something about that."

"We will. Do I hear music?"

"Are those birds up ahead?" Sybil asked.

"Not quite," I said, recognizing the fluttering creatures. "I looked them up in a volume called *Everything You Wanted to Know About Religion But Were Afraid to Ask.* They are legendary creatures called cherubim or cherubs. Asexual apparently, and great harp players, not to mention choristers."

The flying cloud came closer, plucked strings tinkling and falsettos singing. Another swarm appeared, singing lustily despite the fact they had no lungs, being just heads with wings sprouting from behind their ears. This was pretty strange and I was beginning to have certain suspicions.

"Are these creatures native to this planet?" Angelina asked.

"I have no idea—but I would dearly love to find out."

They flew lower, circling and chorusing high-pitchedly just above our heads. I bent my knees—and sprang. Grabbing one by the leg before it could float away. It kept on singing, blue eyes staring upwards. I squeezed it, touched the wings, tried to lift the ribbons around its loins. So that was it. I twisted with both hands and tore its head off.

"Jim—you monster!" Angelina cried.

"Not really." I pulled the head away and wires came out of its neck. It kept on singing and fluttering its butterfly wings. I released it and it floated away still singing from its dangling head.

"Null-G robots filled with recorded music. Slakey must have built them to add verisimilitude to the landscape for conning his suckers."

The road curved through a glen filled with flowering shrubs. As we approached something burst out of the bushes and galloped towards us.

"That's mine!" Angelina cried out happily as she ran towards it. A stained and scratched robot with one good eye. I hurried after her, not to spoil her fun but to stand by in case of accidents.

There were none. It was all done quite deliberately. When it swung its mighty hand, tipped with razor-sharp fingers, at her she swung her power saw up even faster. The hand clanked down on the road leaving the robot with a metal stump. Two stumps an instant later.

It tried to kick her. There was another clang and it tried to hop away on its remaining leg. Then, limbless, it rolled along the ground.

"You are not nice to people," she said, saw ready. "You are just insensate metal so you do not feel what I am doing to you. You do only as you are instructed. It is your master who is next."

The head rolled over close to my feet. I looked down and smiled as the light in its single eye faded and died.

"One down," I said as I kicked it aside. "Now we follow this road to its master's lair. And please stay alert, gang. Slakey knows that we are coming and will throw everything at us that he can."

Sudden memory flashed and I jumped. Shouting.

"Off the road!"

A little too late. The slurping sounded and the road rolled out from under our feet disclosing the chasm beneath.

"Gravchutes!" I ordered, turning mine on. Our descent into the pit stopped just before we hit the jagged stalagmites and sharp blades that projected up from the pit floor below. We zoomed up and out to safety and our advance continued. Beside the road.

"There it is," I said, pointing to the white temple on the hill ahead. "That's where I met a fat old Slakey playing God in this unheavenly Heaven. I wonder if he'll be there now?"

We were about to find out, approaching the marble steps with caution. They were not moving this time, no celestial escalator for us. We strode up resolutely until we could see the throne. And Slakey sitting on it. Scowling ferociously.

"You are not welcome here," he said, shaking his head. His fat jowls jiggled and the golden halo bounced with the movement.

"Don't be inhospitable, Professor," I said. "Answer a few questions and we'll be on our way."

"*This* is my answer," he snarled as he reached back and seized his halo—and hurled it at me. It exploded as it struck my suit, knocking me down with the impact. I climbed back to my feet and saw Slakey, throne and all, vanish into the floor.

As he went down—so did the ceiling. The supporting pillars must have been pistons as well. Before we could escape out of the way the entire thing, stone ceiling, roof and lintels and all, crushed us like beetles.

Or it would have crushed us like beetles if we hadn't been wearing our battle suits. As the weight of stone struck the nanomolecules in the fabric locked and the suits became as rigid as steel.

Steel coffins. "Can anyone move?" I shouted. My only answer was grunts and groans. Was this the end? Crushed under a power-operated temple in Heaven. Waiting for our air to run out. One hundred hours—and then asphyxiation.

"No . . . way!" I muttered angrily. My hands were at my sides. All the pressure was on my chest which stayed as hard as nanosteel. But there was no weight on my hand and I could wiggle my fingers. Move them, feeling along my belt in the darkness. Plucking out a percussion grenade by feel. Pushing it into the rubble of broken stone, as far out as I could reach. Taking as deep a breath as I could. Triggering it.

Flame and a great explosion of sound. Smoke and dust of course—that settled and blew away to disclose a crater in the stone. With sunlight filtering in.

A few more grenades did the job. I stumbled to my feet, staggering as another explosion rocked the ruin of the temple, and Angelina emerged from the cloud of smoke. We embraced, then blasted free the others.

"Could we please not do that again," Sybil said, more than a little shaken by the experience.

"An act of desperation on his part," I told her. "Trying to pick us off before we closed in on them. It didn't work—and now we take the fight to them."

"How?" Angelina asked, ever practical.

"This way," I said, leading them back down the steps. "That first pit we fell into in the road was just that. A pitfall pit for killing people. But this pit leads to the underworld where his entire operation is taking place."

As I said that, I flipped another grenade towards the place on the road where I and the robot had dropped through. It blew up nicely and opened a hole into the deep chasm below.

"I'll lead since I've been this way before."

We powered up our gravchutes and leaped into the jagged opening. Floated down slowly instead of dropping as I had the first time. The jagged stone walls moved past at a leisurely pace, lit by the ruddy glow from below. Then the bleak, black landscape with its sporadic gouts of flame came into view. The table-like structures were still there, barely revealed by the ruddy light. But there was a difference—the women were gone.

We soon discovered why. They were all grouped together before the buildings. My troops landed and spread out, weapons ready.

"Don't shoot!" Angelina called out. "Those women, they're the victims, the workers here."

As we warily came closer we could hear a low moaning, and the familiar coughing. It was pretty obvious why. They were tied together, ten or twenty in a bunch, bound with ropes.

"Safety is here!" I called out. "We've come to free you."

"Oh no you're not," Slakey said in chorus. Behind each group of women was a Slakey with a gun. They all spoke at the same time because of course they were all the same person.

"Leave or we kill them," he/they chorused as each of them raised his gun and aimed it at the captive victims.

It was stalemate.

"You can't get away with this," I said, playing for time, wondering what I could do to save them.

"Yes I can," the massed voices said. "I will count to three. If you have not gone by then, one in every group will die. You will have killed them. Then another and another. One . . . two . . ."

"Stop," I called out. "We're going."

But we didn't—the women did. The coughing and moaning was replaced by silence and a whooshing sound as they popped out of existence. I had a moment of dreadful fear that they were gone, dead—until I saw the shocked expression on every Slakey's face.

Professor Coypu—of course! He had been watching and had snatched them out of Heaven to the safety of Prime Base.

I raised my gun and shot the nearest Slakey, ran towards his inert body. Everyone else was shooting now and a blast of fire rocked me back. I stumbled, ran on, grabbed for the Slakey I had shot.

Grabbed empty air as he vanished. The firing was dying down, stopped, as the Slakeys disappeared one by one. Angelina reholstered her gun and came over to me, patted my arm. "I saw that you killed one. Congratulations."

"Premature. I used my paralysis pistol since I wanted to talk to him."

"What next?"

"A very good question. There is no point in going to the coal mines right now because that's just the place that supplies the raw ingredient. The same goes for the cyclotron chamber because we know that the unnildecnovum is made there, but brought here for separation from the coal dust."

"Then we find where it is taken."

"Of course—and it can't be far." I turned to Berkk. "You heard Slakey order the now extinct robot to bring it somewhere?"

"That's right."

I turned and pointed past the rows of empty tables. "That way, it has to be that way. The opposite direction from the cyclotron. Let's go look."

We went. Warily. Knowing that we were getting close to the end of our quest and that Slakey would not like this in any way. He didn't.

"Take cover!" I shouted as I dived. I had only a quick glimpse of the weapon as it floated into position in front of us, a large field gun of some kind.

It fired and the shell exploded close by. The ground rose and slammed into me; chunks of shrapnel and shattered rock rained down. This was not good at all—even Coypu's battle suits could not protect a body from a direct hit. It fired again—then vanished.

"*Got it,*" Coypu's voice spoke in my radio earpiece. "*A remote controlled siege gun. I dropped it into a volcano in Hell from a great height. Are there any more?*"

"Not that I can see. But—thanks for the quick action."

We advanced, past the spot where the gun had appeared, and on towards a solid metal fortress-like structure. I didn't like the look of it—liked it even less when ports flipped open and rapid-firing weapons appeared. Firing rapidly.

"Professor Coypu!" I shouted as slugs struck all around us, and into us, knocking us down and rolling us over.

The professor rose to the occasion. An armored gun carrier appeared between us and the building, firing even as it thudded to the ground. The weapon traversed and the weapon positions were obliterated one by one. With the defense silenced the gun traversed once more and blew away the front entrance to the building. A hatch opened as I passed the machine and Captain Grissle of the Space Marines poked his head out.

"I'll cover you when you go in. Just shout and point."

"Right—and thanks." I pumped my right fist in the air, then pointed forward. "Charge!"

We did. Right up to the front of the building, beside the gaping hole where the door used to be.

"Grissle—can you hear me?"

"Loud and clear."

"Put a couple of rounds in there before we go in."

"No problem."

A couple proved to be more than a hundred; he must have had plenty of ammo. Flame and smoke exploded inside the building. Sounding farther and farther away as the interior was demolished. The firing stopped. Then a last large-caliber shell whistled by—the resultant explosion was so distant it sounded like a mere crump.

"Holed through to the other side."

"Cease fire then—we're going in."

Whatever defenses and traps that would have been awaiting us were gone now. Flame and destruction had blasted any obstruction aside. We felt our way through the debris in the darkness. Which began to lift as the smoke cleared. Light poured in from a ragged opening in the wall ahead. Weapons at the ready, we crept forward, looked out.

"Now isn't that nice?" Angelina said. "It looks like we have finally reached the end of the trail."

CHAPTER 28

WE WERE LOOKING OUT ON the pleasant valley of Heaven. Blue sky above, green grass below. A gentle breeze stirred the leaves on the ornamental trees and brought sweet perfumes to our noses. Set into the valley floor were white marquees, small buildings with tiled roofs half concealed by flower-filled gardens. Paths twined through the landscape, past fountains and statuary. All of this surrounded the most unusual object I had seen in my unusual life. A matte-black sphere at least ten meters high. Smooth and unmarked in any way; a giant eight ball without the eight, a Brobdingnagian bowling ball without finger holes. We stood and gaped.

"Can't you feel it," Angelina said, holding out her hand towards the enigmatic object. "That sensation, indescribable—but that's what we looked for in the coal dust."

As soon as she said this I became distantly aware of what she meant, knew why the sensation could not be described. A weight that was no weight, an experience unfelt, a movement that stayed still. Women could detect small quantities—but there was enough in the sphere before us for mere men to feel.

"Unnildecnovum," I said. "That's where it all has been going, that's what Slakey has been doing with it. A few particles of unnildecnovum at a time to make that thing. It must have taken an awful lot of years."

"Why is he doing it?" Angelina asked.

"I don't know—but I think that we are going to find out very soon. Look."

A round, fat figure that could only be the Slakey from the temple waddled out of one of the tents and made his way to a conference table surrounded by chairs, dropped into the largest chair. He sat staring at the ground for long seconds before looking up. He looked angrily in our direction—then made a single wave of his hand to signal us forward.

"It's a trap," Angelina said.

"Possibly—but I think not. This is his grail, whatever it is, that he has been working so energetically to build, fighting so hard to defend. The battle is over. So let's go down and see what he has to say."

Warily, spread out with our weapons ready, we walked down the valley. It was peaceful and serene and undoubtedly very dangerous. I felt better when I approached Slakey, closer and closer. I was too near to him now for the other Slakeys to use heavy weapons. I sat down in the chair nearest to him, swung my backpack off so that it rested on my lap. Leaned back comfortably and smiled. Slakey scowled.

"Draw up some chairs, guys, and listen," I said, "this is going to be interesting."

"How I wish I could kill you, diGriz. That was my primary mistake. If I had killed you the first time I saw you none of this would have happened."

"We all make mistakes, Slakey. You have made a lot of them. It's the end now and you know it."

His face blazed with suppressed fury. I could hear his teeth grating together. It was very nice to look at and my smile broadened.

"I knew that we would get you in the end," I said, "So I made certain precautions. This is for you."

I took the backpack off my lap and set it on the table between us. This was totally unexpected; he looked at it with bewilderment, at the square white cross on the red background.

"Are you mad? First aid . . . medicine?"

"Sorry," I said. "This will make it much clearer." I leaned over and peeled off the cross.

Underneath was a glaring red radiation symbol. And a notice spelled out in red letters:

TEN-MEGATON ATOMIC BOMB
HANDLE WITH CARE
KEEP AWAY FROM CHILDREN

"Just a small precaution. I armed it when I put it down. It has nothing to do with me now, although it is tempting to look at the switch. You see, Professor Coypu has another ignition switch and is watching us closely at the present time. Keep that in mind at all times."

"You can't—"

"Oh, but I did. I am very serious about this. Just one more thing before we draw this matter to its close. Professor Coypu, now is the time."

I had arranged it all with him, beaten down his reluctance and convinced him that it was the only course possible. Slakey had to be stopped and this was the only way that it could be done. I smiled with relief when Angelina and the twins, Sybil and Berkk, all vanished.

"Safe back in Main Station." I looked up and waved. "Sorry, Angelina, but I had to do this my way. If you were here I would not have had the guts to go through with it. Now I can. If something should go wrong—and I don't think it will—remember . . . that I have always loved you."

I jumped to my feet and patted the bomb. "Enough emotion. I shall put love aside for the moment and get involved in some solid hatred. And, oh, how I hate you you multibodied monster. And I have you at last. There is no escape. It's just you and I now, Slakey. End of the line."

"I want to make an arrangement with you, diGriz—"

"No deals. Just unconditional surrender. And don't make

me angry or I might lose my temper and just press the button and settle you once and for all."

"But wait until you hear my offer. It is an irresistible one. You see—I am going to offer you eternal life. Wouldn't you like that?"

He was right. It *was* a very attractive offer. But this nutcake was a fruitcake and I couldn't believe anything that he said.

"Tell me about it, Professor Slakey. Convince me and perhaps I will consider it."

"Entropy," he said sinking automatically into professorial didactic lecture mode. "That is my field of expertise, as you know. But you do not know how far I have advanced my knowledge, or to what lengths my research has gone. In the beginning was the theory. I did a mathematical analysis of the transuranic elements. I found that as the atomic numbers became higher the rate of entropy slowed. By very little, but the reaction was there. When I extended the equations they revealed that the maximum reverse entropy would be at element one hundred and nineteen. And the equation was correct! When the cyclotron produced the first speck of unnildecnovum I could feel it. And the more concentrated the mass the greater the effect." He hauled himself to his feet. "Come, I will show you."

"Mind if I bring this?" I asked, pointing at the bomb. He hissed with anger.

"Eternity is about to be revealed to you—and still you jest . . ." He got his temper under control at last, turned and walked towards the black sphere of unnildecnovum. Someone moved out of sight in one of the white buildings that we passed and I knew that the other Slakeys were present and watching. Closer and closer to the featureless sphere we walked until we stood next to it, with the bulge of blackness blocking out the sky above.

"Touch it," Slakey whispered. Leaning out and pressing his hand flat against it. I hesitated, then did the same.

Indescribable but incredibly exciting. This was a sensation I could learn to live with.

"Follow me," he said, walking around the sphere, running

his hand along it as he went. I followed, doing the same. There was a short flight of white steps ahead, the top resting against the sphere. He touched a button beside the steps and a great plug of unnildecnovum swung out above us, leaving an opening in the sphere's exterior. We climbed the steps and went inside.

The sphere was hollow and the wall was at least a meter thick. And the indescribable sensation was even more indescribable. Slakey pointed at the row of black coffin-like structures in the center of the sphere. We approached them and looked into the first. A thin Slakey was lying inside, eyes closed, scarcely breathing. His right arm lay across his chest and I recognized him now. His hand was missing.

Not quite. I leaned over and looked and saw that a tiny pink hand was growing out of the stump.

"Life everlasting!" Slakey shouted. Drops of spittle flew. "I rest here and rejuvenate. If I am wounded, my body repairs itself. And I grow younger here. Surrounded by the unnildecnovum, entropy is reversed. Instead of getting older, tireder, senescent—I grow younger, energeticer, youthfuler. And the more unnildecnovum I add to the sphere the faster reverse entropy moves. So you see what I am offering you? Eternity. Join me and live forever! One of these entropy shells could be yours."

That is the kind of offer that is very hard to refuse. Who could possibly say no to the offer of immortality?

I could for one. Not because I wanted to but because I had to. If I joined him I would be no better than him. I must admit I quavered. But I thought of Angelina waiting for me and summoned up all the strength that I could. It was impossible to move. Almost impossible. I turned, very slowly I must admit, and walked—even more slowly—towards the light of day.

This was not for me, not alone. But it was oh so tempting! Maybe I could do it if I took Angelina with me. But then we would of course have to bring the boys too. And naturally Professor Coypu would like the idea—as would our boss Inskipp. It would get to be mighty crowded inside the sphere.

If it was hard to walk away, it was even incredibly harder

to get out of the thing. I don't know how long I stood in the exit. I couldn't force myself to step forward and leave. It took every iota of willpower I possessed to just shift my weight, to lean forward, off balance. I fell, automatically did a shoulder roll down the stairs and out onto the grass. I lay unmoving for quite a time. Finally sighed and climbed to my feet. Slakey was standing at the entrance above.

"I must say that you make a very good offer, Professor."

"I do. And you will of course accept."

"Let's go sit by the bomb and discuss it."

I didn't really care about the bomb; I just wanted to be as far away from the lure of eternity as I could get.

"Let's talk offers," I said patting the bomb. He nodded stiffly. "I am saying no to your offer. Thanks a lot but no thanks."

"Inconceivable!" he spluttered.

"For you—but not for me. Thousands must have died because of you and your obsessive desire to hold onto your single miserable life. If I could snuff it out at this moment I would. In all of its multiple aspects. I wish I had the guts to trigger this bomb—but I value my own life too much. I have a lot to live for—and I look forward to living a long and happy and rejuvenated life. Now we come to you."

I leaned over the bomb and pointed a judicial finger in his face. "Here is what you will do. You will mine no more coal. The miners will be restored to their loved ones. The two Berkks will be reunited. Buboe will be turned over to the shrinks. The cyclotron will cycle no more. The women of the tables will work no more. They will get a good wash and return to their homes and their loved ones as well. This operation is closed down."

"I won't be—"

"Oh yes you will. The reconstruction of Paradise will stop and the building crews will be paid off. The mead will be swilled no more in Valhalla. You have no choice. You will also close down all your religious operations on every one of the planets and all of your personas will return here. When you are assembled in all your strength you will remain here. Forever."

"You cannot do that!" he screamed.

"It has just been done."

"How can I trust you?"

"You have no other choice."

"You will set off the bomb."

"Only if you force us to. You see that is our mutual guarantee. We can never be sure that one of you is still not out there, ready to start this whole monstrous process again. The bomb is our guarantee that you won't do that. And we can't detonate it if we think that one of you *is* still out there. It is a paradox, a problem with no solution. A beginning with no end—like your reverse entropy. So you sit and think about it, talk to yourself about it. Remember that this is the last, first and only offer that you are going to get."

I rose wearily and stretched.

"Get me out of here, Professor Coypu. It has been a very very long day."

CHAPTER 29

"THERE MUST BE FIFTY SLAKEYS at least," Angelina said, curling her lips in disgust. "All of them equally repulsive. Press the button, Professor, and set off the bomb. We will all sleep better at night."

The three of us sat staring into the permanent screen set up to monitor Slakey. Coypu looked very unhappy as he shook his head no.

"Too risky. All he needs is one of him out there on one of the thousands of planets in the millions of universes to get the whole process moving again."

"We'll monitor, watch, be on our guard . . ."

"I wish we could set off the bomb," I said with deep sorrow. "His death could never make up for the death and destruction he has caused—but it would sure help. But the professor is right. He may be mad but he's not stupid. If he did this all again he would not use the fake-religion ploy. He would do it in a more undetectable manner. Find another planet with a decent climate and resources of coal and set up another operation there. He would proceed slowly and carefully and untraceably—after all, he has all eternity to do it in. Ahh—there they go!"

A flicker of motion beside the unnildecnovum sphere showed where the Space Marines were springing into action. They had practiced the operation countless times in order to speed it up and perfect it. They got the time down to three seconds and that was all it took now. Two large marines slammed the heavy hydrogen bomb against the sphere, where it stuck. Captain Grissle hit the activating switch and then they all vanished as quickly as they had appeared. A viewscreen beside the professor lit up and Berkk's image appeared.

"In the green, Professor. Monitoring apparatus engaged and auto switch operating."

"Thank you, very good."

"Over and out."

His image twinkled and vanished and Coypu sighed with relief. "A good technician, Berkk. I'm glad he decided to accept a position with the Corps. Both of him. He helped me design the auto switch so that it is completely fail-safe."

"Am I missing something?" Angelina asked.

"Last night. I couldn't sleep and you were doing fine. I came here and found a very red-eyed Professor Coypu staring at the screen, worrying at the same worry that was worrying me. A what-if."

"Which what-if?"

"What if a Slakey is still out there somewhere. What if he builds a big enough interuniversal transporter to grab and transport that unnildecnovum sphere to another universe? The Slakeys would get away and start the whole deadly cycle over again. Between us we worked out a solution. We got a hydrogen bomb from stock, fixed it up with a molebind, a molecular binder that makes it part of the sphere."

"And," Coypu said, "it contains a detector. If the sphere does go somewhere it gets there as a mushroom cloud. If that thing goes away the bomb goes off."

"But if he doesn't try to move the sphere, why then he is still very much alive in his multiple bodies?" Angelina asked with irresistible female logic. "What do we do to get rid of this possibly eternal threat?"

The professor and I sighed a duet of sighs.

"We have experts working on other possibilities," I said. "We have prepared our dilemma as an abstract problem that will be presented on all of the tests given in every philosophy department in every university in the galaxy. Someone, somewhere, may come up with the answer. Meanwhile—all we can do is watch."

"Forever? Some legacy for our grandchildren. And theirs until the nth generation."

It was all too depressing to think of and I changed the subject.

"At least we have done something for Slakey's victims. The women from Purgatory, the ones who didn't need hospitalization that is, have all gone to the planets of their choice. With lifetime pensions—mostly paid for by the seizure of Slakey's various properties. The same thing has been done for the miners—with the exception of one. Buboe is on the way to a hospital for the criminally insane, to see if he might be cured."

"What about those poor creatures in Hell?" Angelina asked. "Can't anything be done for them?"

"A lot. Since they can't leave Hell we will have to do the best we can for them there. Interstellar charities have already put up temporary—and air-conditioned—buildings for them. Volunteers are giving them medical treatment, meals, outdoor barbecues, booze, counseling, that sort of thing. Since they can never leave Hell, permanent provision must be made for them. They should be self-supporting soon."

Angelina's eyebrows rose at that. "Self-supporting—in Hell?"

"There is no accounting for taste," I said. "A firm named Holidays in Hell has already been formed and the first tourists are happily on their way. They photograph the natives—for a fee. Grill steaks on the lava, shudder when the gravity waves grab them. Generally have a frightening but safe time."

"Outrageous! I hope that old red devil Slakey shoots and eats them."

"Alas, that is not possible now. Before we got there the locals grew tired of being shot at and, well, sort of had him for dinner."

"Wonderful! They can cook up all the rest of the Slakeys as far as I'm concerned. That would be a good solution. Which reminds me. A question or two, Professor, something that has been bothering me for a long time. Why so many Slakeys—and how did he do it?"

As usual, Coypu had all the answers. "The answer to your first question is obvious. Who else could he trust? He wanted to keep eternal life for himself. So he went into partnership with himselves to set up the operation. As to how he duplicated himself, I discovered that by accident. You will remember that we obtained the frequency settings from one of their machines for many other universes. That is how I found you on Glass and brought you back. When I have had the time I have been investigating some of the other universes. Some of them are rather nasty. To keep under budget and not lose too many machines I constructed an armor-plated recorder that I sent through to measure temperature, gravity density, air pressure and contents, the usual things. I was greatly surprised when it returned from Gemelli, which I named this universe for obvious reasons, with a replica of itself. A little bit of research showed me that all of the radiation frequencies are doubled there. So matter from our universe is doubled as well when it returns here. Interesting phenomenon. So every time Slakey needed reinforcements he popped in and out of Gemelli. You know that you are the second person to ask me that question today."

"Who was the other?"

"Me." Sybil said, walking in through the door and smiling happily. "Mr. and Mrs. diGriz—I would very much like to call you Mom and Dad. I can conceal it no longer. I am madly in love with your son and wish to marry him."

"Which one?" Angelina asked.

"Both of them," Sybil said walking in through the door again. The same words were spoken by both Sybils at the same time.

I looked from one to the other and for the first time in my life was at a loss for words. Angelina wasn't.

"You have duplicated yourself. You are now two Sybils."

"Of course. I had no choice," she said with impeccable female logic. "I was in love with your sons, and love can always find a way."

"Have you broken the good news to them yet?"

"Not yet," the Sybils said in unison. "But I know they love me, women can tell, just as much as I love them. But they are both too noble, honest, brave and irreverent to ask for my hand because it would mean the other one losing out. That problem has now been solved."

"Indeed it has," Angelina said firmly, with the instant decision women make in matters of the heart. "And what do you say, Jim?"

"I say it is up to the boys to decide."

She nodded agreement.

"They should be here soon," the doubled voice said. "I sent a message before I came."

James and Bolivar came in at that moment and did the best double act of double-takes I had ever seen in my life. Before they could speak each Sybil stepped forward and seized a twin and kissed him with passion. The response, I could tell, was equally passionate.

"I love you," Sybil breathed. "From the bottom of my heart, with all the depth of my being. Do you love me?"

That, as you might very well realize, was that. Angelina and I, smiling happily, joined hands and turned our backs on the embracing couples, sat and began to discuss their wedding plans.

It would be the grandest social occasion the Special Corps Prime Base had ever seen.

I snapped my fingers at the robar, which produced a chilled bottle of sparkling wine, opened it dexterously with its two right hands, poured and passed us brimming glasses. We clinked and drank.

"A toast," I said, "Can you think of one?"

"Of course. To the future newlyweds. And may their lives be filled with happiness."

"Like ours," I said.

"Of course."

We kissed and drank the toast. Over Angelina's shoulder I could see the screen with the image of that monstrous black sphere.

I turned my back on it, not wanting to spoil this memorable day. Still, I couldn't stop thinking about it. Neither could Angelina.

"Do we have enough money in the bank to buy a cyclotron?" she asked.

I nodded. "We could even afford a coal mine as well. Why do you ask?"

"I was just thinking. What a wonderful and unusual wedding present we could give the newlyweds . . ."

A DEVILISHLY GOOD PIECE OF ADVICE

JIM DIGRIZ HAS A SWOLLEN ego these days, ever since he discovered that his annals have been published in a great number of countries and languages. In addition to the American and English editions his adventures have been read in all of the Western European countries, as well as in Japan and China. Since glasnost he has penetrated Russia, Poland, and Estonia. A total of fifteen countries. And very soon now we will see the first publication of *Rustimuna Ŝtalrato Naskiĝas*. That's *The Rat Is Born* in Esperanto.

Esperanto? There's that word again. We know that Jim speaks it like a native. As does almost everyone else he meets. But does it exist in the present?

It certainly does. It is a growing, living language with millions of speakers right around the world. It is easy to learn and fun to use—and a lot more practical than Klingon. There are many books, magazines, and even newspapers published in Esperanto.

So be the first on your block to enjoy the excitement and fun. Put your name and address on a postcard and send it to this address:

Esperanto
PO Box 1129
El Cerrito, CA 94530

Tell them the Rat sent you. You will never regret it!

—Harry Harrison